A writer since high school, **Terry Brooks** published his first novel, *The Sword of Shannara*, in 1977. It became the first work of fiction ever to appear on *The New York Times* Trade Paperback bestseller list, where it remained for more than five months. He has published numerous bestselling novels since.

A practising attorney for many years, Terry Brooks now writes full time and lives with his wife, Judine, in the Pacific Northwest and Hawaii.

Find out more about Terry Brooks and other Orbit authors by registering for the free monthly newsletter at www.orbitbooks.co.uk

By Terry Brooks

TERRY BROOKS

ANGEL FIRE EAST

Book Three of THE WORD AND THE VOID

www.orbitbooks.co.uk

ORBIT

First published by Ballantine Books,
a division of Random House, Inc. 1999
First published in Great Britain by Orbit 1999
First published in paperback by Orbit 2000
This edition published in 2006 by Orbit

A CIP catalogue record for this book
is available from the British Library.

ISBN-13: 978-1-84149-546-0
ISBN-10: 1-84149-546-8

Printed and bound in Great Britain by
Mackays of Chatham plc, Chatham, Kent

Orbit
An imprint of
Little, Brown Book Group
Brettenham House
Lancaster Place
London WC2E 7EN

A member of the Hachette Livre Group of Companies

www.littlebrown.co.uk

TO MY FATHER, DEAN BROOKS

Who made sacrifices as an aspiring writer then so that
I could be a published writer now.

ANGEL FIRE EAST

PROLOGUE

He stands at the edge of a barren and ravaged orchard looking up from the base of a gentle rise to where the man hangs from a wooden cross. Iron spikes have been hammered through the man's hands and feet, and his wrists and ankles have been lashed tightly in place so he will not tear free. Slash wounds crisscross his broken body, and he bleeds from a deep puncture in his side. His head droops in the shadow of his long, lank hair, and the rise and fall of his chest as he breathes is shallow and weak.

Behind him, serving as a poignant backdrop to the travesty of his dying, stands the fire-blackened shell of a tiny, burned-out country church. The cross from which the man hangs has been stripped from the sanctuary, torn free from the metal brackets that secured it to the wall behind the altar, and set into the earth. Patches of polished oak glisten faintly in the gray daylight, attesting to the importance it was once accorded in the worshipping of God.

Somewhere in the distance, back where the little town that once supported this church lies, screams rise up against the unmistakable sounds of butchery.

John Ross stands motionless for the longest time, pondering the implications of the horrific scene before him. There is nothing he can do for the man on the cross. He is not a doctor; he does not possess medical skills. His magic can heal and sustain only himself and no other. He is a Knight of the Word, but he is a failure, too. He lives out his days alone in a future he could not prevent. What he looks upon is not unusual in the postapocalyptic horror of civilization's demise, but is sadly familiar and disturbingly mundane.

He can take the man down, he decides finally, even if he cannot save him. By his presence, Ross can give the man a small measure of peace and comfort.

Beneath a wintry sky that belies the summer season, he strides up the rise to the man on the cross. The man does not lift his head or stir in any way that would indicate he knows Ross is present. Beneath a sheen of sweat and blood, his lean, muscular body is marked with old wounds and scars. He has endured hardships and abuse somewhere in his past, and it seems unfair that he should end his days in still more pain and desolation.

Ross slows as he nears, his eyes drifting across the blackened facade of the church and the trees surrounding it. Eyes glimmer in the shadows, revealing the presence of feeders. They hover at the fringes of his vision and in the concealment of sunless corners, waiting to assuage their hunger. They do not wait for Ross. They wait for the man on the cross. They wait for him to die, so they can taste his passing from life into death—the most exquisite, fulfilling, and rare of the human emotions they crave.

Ross stares at them until the light dims in their lantern eyes and they slip back into darkness to bide their time.

A shattered length of wood catches the Knight's attention, and his eyes shift to the foot of the cross. The remains of a polished black staff lie before him—a staff like the one he carries in his hands. A shock goes through him. He stares closely, unable to believe what he has discovered. There must be a mistake, he thinks. There must be another explanation.

But there is neither. Like himself, the man on the cross is a Knight of the Word.

He moves quickly now, striding forward to help, to lower the cross, to remove the spikes, to free the man who hangs helplessly before him.

But the man senses him now and in a ragged, whispery voice says, Don't touch me.

Ross stops instantly, the force of the other's words and the surprise of his consciousness bringing him to a halt.

They have poisoned me, the other says.

Ross draws a long, slow breath and exhales in weary recognition: Those who have crucified this Knight of the Word have coated him in a poison conjured of demon magic. He is without hope.

Ross steps back, looking up at the Knight on the cross, at the slow, shallow rise and fall of his breast, at the rivulets of blood leaking from his wounds, at the shadow of his face, still concealed within the curtain of his long hair.

They caught me when I did not have my magic to protect me, the stricken Knight says softly. I had expended it all on an effort to escape them earlier. I could not replenish it quickly enough. Sensing I was weak, they gave chase. They hunted me down. Demons and once-men, a small army hunting pockets of resistance beyond the protection of the city fortresses. They found me hiding in the town below. They dragged me here and hung me on this cross to die. Now they kill all those who tried to help me.

Ross finds his attention drawn once more to the shrieks that come from the town. They are beginning to fade, to drain away into a deep, ominous silence.

I have not done well in my efforts to save mankind, the Knight whispers. He gasps and chokes on the dryness in his throat. Blood bubbles to his lips and runs down his chin to his chest.

Nor have any of us, Ross says.

There were chances. There were times when we might have made a difference.

Ross sighs. We did with them what we could.

A bird's soft warble wafts through the trees. Black smoke curls skyward from the direction of the town, rife with the scent of human carnage.

Perhaps you were sent to me.

Ross turns from the smoke to look again at the man on the cross, not understanding.

Perhaps the Word sent you to me. A final chance at redemption.

No one sent me, Ross thinks, but does not speak the words.

You will wake in the present and go on. I will die here. You will have a chance to make a difference still. I will not.

No one sent me, Ross says quickly now, suddenly uneasy.

But the other is not listening. In late fall, three days after Thanksgiving, once long ago, when I was on the Oregon coast, I captured a gypsy morph.

His words wheeze from his mouth, coated in the sounds of his dying. But as he speaks, his voice seems to gain intensity.

It is my greatest regret, that I found it, so rare, so precious, made it my own, and could not solve the mystery of its magic. The chance of a lifetime, and I let it slip away.

The man on the cross goes silent then, gasping slowly for breath, fighting to stay alive just a few moments longer, broken and shattered within and without, left in his final moments to contemplate the failures he perceives are his. Eyes reappear in the shadows of the burned-out church and blighted orchard, the feeders beginning to gather in anticipation. Ross can scorch the earth with their gnarled bodies, can strew their cunning eyes like leaves in the wind, but it will all be pointless. The feeders are a part of life, of the natural order of things, and you might as well decide there is no place for humans either, for it is the humans who draw the feeders and sustain them.

The Knight of the Word who hangs from the cross is speaking again, telling him of the gypsy morph, of how and when and where it will be found, of the chance Ross might have of finding it again. He is giving Ross the details, preparing him for the hunt, thinking to give another the precious opportunity that he has lost. But he is giving Ross the chance to fail as well, and it is on that alone his listener settles in black contemplation.

Do this for me if you can, the man whispers, his voice beginning to fail him completely, drying up with the draining away of his life, turning parched and sandy in his throat. Do it for yourself.

Ross feels the implications of the stricken Knight's charge razor through him. If he undertakes so grave and important a mission, if he embraces so difficult a cause, it may be his own undoing.

Yet, how can he do otherwise?

Promise me.

The words are thin and weak and empty of life. Ross stares in silence at the man.

Promise me ...

John Ross awoke with sunshine streaming down on his face and the sound of children's voices ringing in his ears. The air was hot and sticky, and the smell of fresh turned earth and new leaves rose on a sudden breeze. He blinked and sat up. He was hitch-hiking west through Pennsylvania, and he had stopped at a park outside Allentown to rest, then fallen asleep beneath the canopy of an old hardwood. He had thought only to doze for a few minutes, but he hadn't slept well in days, and the lack of sleep had finally caught up to him.

He gazed around slowly to regain his bearings. The park

was large and thickly wooded, and he had chosen a spot well back from the roads and playgrounds to rest. He was alone. He looked down at his backpack and duffel bag, then at the polished black staff in his hands. His throat was dry and his head ached. A spot deep in his chest burned with the fury of hot coals.

His dream shimmered in a haze of sunlight just before his eyes, images from a private hell.

He was a Knight of the Word, living one life in the present and another in the future, one while awake and another while asleep, one in which he was given a chance to change the world and another in which he must live forever with the consequences of his failure to do so. He had accepted the charge almost twenty-five years ago and had lived with it ever since. He had spent almost the whole of his adult life engaged in a war that had begun with the inception of life and would not end until its demise. There were no boundaries to the battlefield on which he fought—neither of space nor of time. There could be no final resolution.

But the magic of a gypsy morph could provide leverage of a sort that could change everything.

He reached in his backpack and brought forth a battered water bottle. Removing the cap, he drank deeply from its lukewarm contents, finding momentary relief for the dryness in his throat and mouth. He had trouble fitting the cap in place again. The dream had shaken him. His dreams did so often, for they were of a world in which madness ruled and horror was commonplace. There was hope in the present of his waking, but none in the future of his sleep.

Still, this dream was different.

He climbed to his feet, strapped the backpack in place, picked up the duffel bag, and walked back through the park toward the two-lane blacktop that wound west toward Pittsburgh. As always, the events of his dream would occur soon in his present, giving him a chance to affect them in a positive way. It was June. The gypsy morph would be born three days after Thanksgiving. If he was present and if he was quick enough, he would be able to capture it.

Then he would have roughly thirty days to change the course of history.

That challenge would have shaken any man, but it was not the challenge of the gypsy morph that haunted Ross as he walked from the park to begin his journey west. It was his memory of the man on the cross in his dream, the fallen Knight of the Word. It was the man's face as it had lifted from the shadow of his long hair in the final moments of his life.

For the face of the man hanging on the cross had been his own.

SUNDAY,

DECEMBER 21

CHAPTER 1

Nest Freemark had just finished dressing for church when she heard the knock at the front door. She paused in the middle of applying her mascara at the bathroom mirror and glanced over her shoulder, thinking she might have been mistaken, that she wasn't expecting anyone and it was early on a Sunday morning for visitors to come around without calling first.

She went back to applying her makeup. A few minutes later the knock came again.

She grimaced, then glanced quickly at her watch for confirmation. Sure enough. Eight forty-five. She put down her mascara, straightened her dress, and checked her appearance in the mirror. She was tall, a shade under five-ten, lean, and fit, with a distance runner's long legs, narrow hips, and small waist. She had seemed gangly and bony all through her early teens, except when she ran, but she had finally grown into her body. At twenty-nine, she moved with an easy, fluid model's grace that belied the strength and endurance she had acquired and maintained through years of rigorous training.

She studied herself in the mirror with the same frank, open stare she gave everyone. Her green eyes were wide-set beneath arched brows in her round, smooth Charlie Brown face. Her cinnamon hair was cut short and curled tightly about her head, framing her small, even features. People told her all the time she was pretty, but she never quite believed them. Her friends had known her all her life and were inclined to be generous in their assessments. Strangers were just being polite.

Still, she told herself with more than a trace of irony, fluffing her hair into place, you never know when Prince Charming will come calling. Best to be ready so you don't lose out.

She left the mirror and the bathroom and walked through her bedroom to the hall beyond. She had been up since five-thirty, running on the mostly empty roads that stretched from Sinnissippi Park east to Moonlight Bay. Winter had set in several weeks before with the first serious snowfall, but the snow had melted during a warm spot a week ago, and there had been no further accumulation. Patches of sooty white still lay in the darker, shadowy parts of the woods and in the culverts and ditches where the snowplows had pushed them, but the blacktop of the country roads was dry and clear. She did five miles, then showered, fixed herself breakfast, ate, and dressed. She was due in church to help in the nursery at nine-thirty, and whoever it was who had come calling would have to be quick.

She passed the aged black-and-white tintypes and photographs of the women of her family, their faces severe and spare in the plain wooden picture frames, backdropped by the dark webbing of trunks and limbs of the park trees. Gwendolyn Wills, Carolyn Glynn, and Opal Anders. Her grandmother's picture was there, too. Nest had added it after Gran's death. She had chosen an early picture, one in which Evelyn Freemark appeared youthful and raw and wild, hair all tousled, eyes filled with excitement and promise. That was the way Nest liked to remember Gran. It spoke to the strengths and weaknesses that had defined Gran's life.

Nest scanned the group as she went down the hallway, admiring the resolve in their eyes. The Freemark women, she liked to call them. All had entered into the service of the Word, partnering themselves with Pick to help the sylvan keep in balance the strong, core magic that existed in the park. All had been born with magic of their own, though not all had managed it well. She thought briefly of the dark secrets her grandmother had kept, of the deceptions she herself had employed in the workings of her own magic, and of the price she had paid for doing so.

Her mother's picture was missing from the group. Caitlin Anne Freemark had been too fragile for the magic's demands. She had died young, just after Nest was born, a victim of her demon lover's treachery. Nest kept her pictures on a table in the living room where it was always sunlit and cheerful.

The knock came a third time just as she reached the door and opened it. The tiny silver bells that encircled the bough wreath that hung beneath the peephole tinkled softly with the movement. She had not done much with Christmas decorations—no tree, no lights, no tinsel, only fresh greens, a scattering of brightly colored bows, and a few wall hangings that had belonged to Gran. This year Christmas would be celebrated mostly in her heart.

The chill, dry winter air was sharp and bracing as she unlatched the storm door, pushed it away, and stepped out onto the porch.

The old man who stood waiting was dressed all in black. He was wearing what in other times would have been called a frock coat, which was double-breasted with wide lapels and hung to his knees. A flat-brimmed black hat sat firmly in place over wisps of white hair that stuck out from underneath as if trying to escape. His face was seamed and browned by the wind and sun, and his eyes were a watery gray as they blinked at her. When he smiled, as he was doing, his whole face seemed to join in, creasing cheerfully from forehead to chin. He was taller than Nest by several inches, and he stooped as if to make up for the disparity.

She was reminded suddenly of an old-time preacher, the kind that appeared in southern gothics and ghost stories, railing against godlessness and mankind's paucity of moral resolve.

'Good morning,' he said, his voice gravelly and deep. He dipped his head slightly, reaching up to touch the brim of his odd hat.

'Good morning,' she replied.

'Miss Freemark, my name is Findo Gask,' he announced. 'I am a minister of the faith and a bearer of the holy word.'

As if to emphasize the point, he held up a black, leather-bound tome from which dangled a silken bookmark.

She nodded, waiting. Somehow he knew her name, although she had no memory of meeting him before.

'It is a fine, grand morning to be out and about, so I won't keep you,' he said, smiling reassuringly. 'I see you are on your way to church. I wouldn't want to stand in the way of a young lady and her time of worship. Take what comfort you can in the moment, I say. Ours is a restless, dissatisfied world, full of uncertainties and calamities and impending disasters, and we would do well to be mindful of the fact that small steps and little cautions are always prudent.'

It wasn't so much the words themselves, but the way in which he spoke them that aroused a vague uneasiness in Nest. He made it sound more like an admonition than the reassurance it was intended to be.

'What can I do for you, Mr. Gask?' she asked, anxious for him to get to the point.

His head cocked slightly to one side. 'I'm looking for a man,' he said. 'His name is John Ross.'

Nest started visibly, unable to hide her reaction. John Ross. She hadn't seen or communicated with him for more than ten years. She hadn't even heard his name spoken by anyone but Pick.

'John Ross,' she repeated flatly. Her uneasiness heightened.

The old man smiled. 'Has he contacted you recently, Miss Freemark? Has he phoned or written you of late?'

She shook her head no. 'Why would he do that, Mr. Gask?'

The smile broadened, as if to underline the silliness of such a question. The watery gray eyes peered over her shoulder speculatively. 'Is he here already, Miss Freemark?'

A hint of irritation crept into her voice. 'Who are you, Mr. Gask? Why are you interested in John Ross?'

'I already told you who I am, Miss Freemark. I am a minister of the faith. As for my interest in Mr. Ross, he has something that belongs to me.'

She stared at him. Something wasn't right about this. The air about her warmed noticeably, changed color and taste and texture. She felt a roiling inside, where Wraith lay dormant and dangerously ready, the protector chained to her soul.

'Perhaps we could talk inside?' Findo Gask suggested.

He moved as if to enter her home, a subtle shift of weight from one foot to the other, and she found herself tempted simply to step aside and let him pass. But she held her ground, the uneasiness becoming a tingling in the pit of her stomach. She forced herself to look carefully at him, to meet his eyes directly.

The tingling changed abruptly to a wave of nausea.

She took a deep, steadying breath and exhaled. She was in the presence of a demon.

'I know what you are,' she said quietly.

The smile stayed in place, but any trace of warmth disappeared. 'And I know what you are, Miss Freemark,' Findo Gask replied smoothly. 'Now, is Mr. Ross inside or isn't he?'

Nest felt the chill of the winter air for the first time and shivered in spite of herself. A demon coming to her home with such bold intent was unnerving. 'If he was, I wouldn't tell you. Why don't you get off my porch, Mr. Gask?'

Findo Gask shifted once more, a kind of settling in that indicated he had no intention of moving until he was ready. She felt Wraith stir awake inside, sensing her danger.

'Let me just say a few things to you, Miss Freemark, and then I'll go,' Findo Gask said, a bored sigh escaping his lips. 'We are not so different, you and I. When I said I know what you are, I meant it. You are your father's daughter, and we know what he was, don't we? Perhaps you don't care much for the reality of your parentage, but truth will out, Miss Freemark. You are what you are, so there isn't much point in pretending otherwise, though you work very hard at doing so, don't you?'

Nest flushed with anger, but Findo Gask waved her off. 'I also said I was a minister of the faith. You assumed I meant your faith naturally, but you were mistaken. I am a servant of the Void, and it is the Void's faith I embrace. You would pretend it is an evil, wicked faith. But that is a highly subjective conclusion. Your faith and mine, like you and I, are not so different. Both are codifications of the higher power we seek to comprehend and, to the extent we are able, manipulate. Both can be curative or destructive. Both have their supporters and their detractors, and each seeks dominance over the other. The struggle between them has been going on for eons; it won't end today or tomorrow or the day after or anytime soon.'

He stepped forward, kindly face set in a condescending smile that did nothing to hide the threat behind it. 'But one day it will end, and the Word will be destroyed. It will happen, Miss Freemark, because the magic of the Void has always been the stronger of the two. Always. The frailties and weaknesses of mankind are insurmountable. The misguided belief that the human condition is worth salvaging is patently ridiculous. Look at the way the world functions,

Miss Freemark. Human frailties and weaknesses abound.
Moral corruption here, venal desires there. Greed, envy, sloth,
and all the rest at every turn. The followers of the Word rail
against them endlessly and futilely. The Void embraces them,
and turns a weakness into a strength. Pacifism and meek
acceptance? Charity and goodwill? Kindness and virtue?
Rubbish!'

'Mr. Gask—'

'No, no, hear me out, young lady. A little of that famous
courtesy, please.' He cut short her protestation with a sharp
hiss. 'I don't tell you this to frighten you. I don't tell it to you
to persuade you of my cause. I could care less what you feel
or think about me. I tell it to you to demonstrate the depth
of my conviction and my commitment. I am not easily
deterred. I want you to understand that my interest in Mr.
Ross is of paramount importance. Think of me as a tidal
wave and yourself as a sand castle on a beach. Nothing can
save you from me if you stand in my way. It would be best
for you to let me move you aside. There is no reason for you
not to let me do so. None at all. You have nothing vested in
this matter. You have nothing to gain by intervening and
everything to lose.'

He paused then, lifting the leather-bound book and
pressing it almost reverently against his chest. 'These are the
names of those who have opposed me, Miss Freemark. The
names of the dead. I like to keep track of them, to think
back on who they were. I have been alive a very long time,
and I shall still be alive long after you are gone.'

He lowered the book and put a finger to his lips. 'This is
what I want you to do. You will have no trouble under-

standing my request, because I will put it to you in familiar terms. In the terms of your own faith. I want you to deny John Ross. I want you to cast him out of your heart and mind and soul as you would a cancer. I want you to shun him as a leper. Do this for yourself, Miss Freemark, not for me. I will have him anyway, in the end. I do not need to claim you as well.'

Nest was buffeted by so many emotions she could no longer distinguish them. She had kept quiet during the whole of his noxious, execrable presentation, fighting to keep herself and an increasingly agitated Wraith under control. She didn't think Findo Gask knew of Wraith, and she did not want him to discover Wraith was there unless that became unavoidable. She needed to know more of what was going on first, because she wasn't for a moment thinking of acceding to a single demand he had made.

'John Ross isn't here,' she managed, gripping the storm-door frame so tightly with one hand her knuckles turned white.

'I accept that, Miss Freemark,' Findo Gask said with a slight dip of his flat-brimmed hat. 'But he will be.'

'What makes you so sure?'

She could see in his eyes that he believed he had won her over, that she was trying to find a way to cooperate with him. 'Call it a hunch. I have been following his progress for a time, and I think I know him pretty well. He will come. When he does, or even if he tries to make contact another way, don't do anything to help him.'

'What does he have that you want?' she pressed, curious now.

The demon shrugged. 'A magic, Miss Freemark. A magic he would attempt to use against me, I'm afraid.'

She nodded slowly. 'But that you will attempt to use against him, instead?'

Findo Gask stepped back, reaching up to touch the brim of his hat. 'I have taken up enough of your time. Your Sunday worship awaits. I'll look forward to your call.'

'Mr. Gask,' she called to him as he started down the porch steps toward the walk. He turned back to her, squinting against the bright December sunlight. 'My grandfather kept a shotgun in his bedroom closet for duck hunting. When my father tried to come back into this house fifteen years ago, my grandmother used that shotgun to prevent him from doing so. I still have that shotgun. If you ever step foot on my property again, I will use it on you. I will blow away your miserable disguise and leave you naked in your demon form for however long it takes you to put yourself back together and all the while be hoping to God you won't be able to do so!'

Findo Gask stared at her speechless, and then his face underwent such a terrible transformation that she thought he might come at her. Instead he turned away, strode up the walk to the roadway without looking back, and disappeared.

Nest Freemark waited until he was out of sight, then walked back inside and slammed the door so hard the jolt knocked the pictures of the Freemark women askew.

CHAPTER 2

On the drive to church, Nest considered the prospect of another encounter with John Ross.

As usual, her feelings about him were mixed. For as little time as she had spent with him, maybe seven days all told over a span of fifteen years, he had made an extraordinary impact on her life. Much of who and what she was could be traced directly to their strange, sad relationship.

He had come to her for the first time when she was still a girl, just turned fourteen and beginning to discover that she wasn't at all who she thought she was. The secrets of her family were unraveling around her, and Ross had pulled on the ends of the tangle until Nest had almost strangled in the resulting knots. But her assessment wasn't really fair. Ross had done what was necessary in giving her the truth. Had he not, she would probably be dead. Or worse. Her father had killed her mother and grandmother, and tried to kill her grandfather. He had done so to get to her, to claim her, to subvert her, to turn her to the life he had embraced himself long ago. Findo Gask had been right about him. Her father was a demon, a monster capable of great evil. Ross had helped Nest put an end to him. Ross had given her back her life, and with it a chance to discover who she was meant to be.

Of course, he would just as quickly have taken her life had she been turned to the demon's cause, which was a good part of the reason for her mixed feelings about him. That, and the fact that at one time she believed Ross to be her father. It seemed strange, thinking back on it. She had rejoiced in the prospect of John Ross as her father. She found him tender and caring; she thought she probably loved him. She was still a girl, and she had never known her father. She had made up a life for her father; she had invented a place for him in her own. It seemed to her John Ross had come to fill that place.

Gran warned her, of course. In her own way, without saying as much, she indicated over and over that her father was not somebody Nest would want to know. But it seemed as if Gran's cautions were selfish and misplaced. Nest believed John Ross was a good man. When she learned that he was not her father and the demon was, she was crushed. When she learned that he had come to save her if he could but to put an end to her otherwise, the knowledge almost broke her heart.

Most of her anger and dismay had abated by the time she encountered him again five years later in Seattle, where he was the victim and she the rescuer. Ross was the one in danger of being claimed, and if Nest had not been able to save him, he would have been.

Ten years had passed since then, and she hadn't seen or heard from him.

She shook her head, watching the houses of Hopewell, Illinois, drift past as she drove her new Taurus slowly along Lincoln Highway toward downtown. The day was bright and sunny, the skies clear and blue and depthless. Another storm was predicted for Tuesday, but at the moment it was hard to imagine.

She cracked a window to let in some fresh air, listening to the sound of the tires crunch over a residue of road dirt and cinders. As she drove past the post office, the Petersons pulled up to the mail drop. Her neighbors for the whole of her life, the Petersons had been there when Gran was still young. But they were growing old, and she worried about them. She reminded herself to stop by later and take them some cookies.

She turned off Fourth Street down Second Avenue and drove past the First Congregational Church to find a parking space in the adjoining bank lot. She climbed out of the car, triggered the door locks, and walked back toward the church.

Josie Jackson was coming up the sidewalk from her bake shop and restaurant across Third, so Nest waited for her. Bright and chipper and full of life, Josie was one of those women who never seemed to age. Even at forty-eight, she was still youthful and vivacious, waving and smiling like a young girl as she came up, tousled blond hair flouncing about her pretty face. She still had that smile, too. No one ever forgot Josie Jackson's smile.

Nest wondered if John Ross still remembered.

'Good morning, Nest,' Josie said, falling into step with the younger woman, matching her long stride easily. 'I hear we've got baby duty together this morning.'

Nest smiled. 'Yes. Experience counts, and you've got a whole lot more than me. How many are we expecting?'

'Oh, gosh, somewhere in the low teens, if you count the three- and four-year-olds.' Josie shrugged. 'Alice Wilton will be there to help out, and her niece, what's-her-name Anna.'

'Royce-Anna.'

'Royce-Anna Colson.' Josie grimaced. 'What the heck kind of name is that?'

Nest laughed. 'One we wouldn't give our own children.'

They mounted the steps of the church and pushed through the heavy oak doors into the cool dark of the narthex. Nest wondered if Josie ever thought about John Ross. There had been something between them once, back when he had first come to Hopewell and Nest was still a girl. For months after he disappeared, she asked Nest about him. But it had been years now since she had even mentioned his name.

It would be strange, Nest thought, if he was to return to Hopewell after all this time. Findo Gask had seemed sure he would, and despite her doubts about anything a demon would tell her, she was inclined to think from the effort he had expended to convince her that maybe it would happen.

That was an unsettling prospect. An appearance by John Ross, especially with a demon already looking for him, meant trouble. It almost certainly foreshadowed a fresh upheaval in her life, something she didn't need, since she was just getting used to her life the way it was.

What would bring him back to her after so long?

Unable to find an answer, she walked with Josie down the

empty, shadowed hallway, stained glass and burnished wood wrapping her in a cocoon of silence.

She spent the next two hours working in the nursery, having a good time with the babies and Josie, doing something that kept her from thinking too much about things she would just as soon forget. She concentrated instead on diaper changing, bottle feeding, telling stories, and playing games, and left the world outside her bright, cheery room of crayon pictures and colored posters to get on by itself as best it could.

Once or twice, she thought about Paul. It was impossible for her to be around babies and not think about Paul, but she had found a way to block the pain by taking refuge in the possibility that she was not meant to have children of her own but to be a mother to the children of others. It was heartbreaking to think that way, but it was the best she could do. Her legacy of magic from the Freemark women would not allow her to think otherwise.

Josie helped pass the time with wry jokes and colorful stories of people they both knew, and mostly Nest found herself thinking she was pretty lucky.

When the service was over, a fellowship was held in the reception room just off the sanctuary. After returning her small charges to their proper parents, Nest joined the congregation in sipping coffee and punch, eating cookies and cake, and exchanging pleasantries and gossip. She wandered from group to group, saying hello, asking after old people and children come home for the holidays, wishing Christmas cheer to all.

'What's the world coming to, young lady?' an indignant Blanche Stern asked when she paused to greet a gaggle of elderly church widows standing by the narthex entry. She peered at Nest through her bifocals. 'This is your generation's responsibility, these children who do such awful things! It makes me weep!'

Nest had no idea what she was talking about.

'It's that boy shooting those teachers yesterday at an outing in Pennsylvania,' Addie Hull explained, pursing her thin lips and nodding solemnly for emphasis. 'It was all over the papers this morning. Only thirteen years old.'

'Takes down his father's shotgun, rides off to school on his bike, and lets them have it in front of two dozen other students!' Winnie Ricedorf snapped in her no-nonsense teacher's voice.

'I haven't read the papers yet,' Nest explained. 'Sounds awful. Why did he do it?'

'He didn't like the grades they were giving him for his work in some advanced study program,' Blanche continued, her face tightening. She sighed. 'Goodness sakes alive, he was a scholar of some promise, they say, and he threw it all away on a bad grade.'

'Off to his Saturday Challenge Class,' Winnie said, 'armed with a shotgun and a heart full of hate. What's that tell you about today's children, Nest?'

'Remember that boy down in Tennessee last year?' Addie Hull asked suddenly. Her thin hands crooked around her coffee cup more tightly. 'Took some sort of automatic rifle to school and ambushed some young people during a lunch break? Killed three of them and wounded half a dozen more.

Said he was tired of being picked on. Well, I'm tired of being picked on, too, but I don't go hunting down the garbage collectors and the postal delivery man and the IRS examiner who keeps asking for those Goodwill receipts!'

'That IRS man they caught dressing in women's clothes earlier this month, good heavens!' Winnie Ricedorf huffed, and took a sip of her coffee.

'His wife didn't mind, as I recall,' Blanche Stern advised primly, giving Nest a wink. 'She liked to dress up as a man.'

Nest excused herself and moved on. Similar topics of conversation could be found almost everywhere, save where clusters of out-of-season golfers looking forward to a few weeks in Florida replayed their favorite holes and wrestled with the rest of the sports problems of the world while the teenagers next to them spoke movie and rap and computer talk. She drifted from group to group, able to fit in anywhere because she really belonged nowhere at all. She could talk the talk and pretend she was a part of things, but she would never be anything but an outsider. She was accepted because she had been born in Hopewell and was a part of its history. But her legacy of magic and her knowledge of Pick's world and the larger life she led set her apart as surely as if she had just stepped off the bus from New York City.

She sipped at her coffee and looked off at the blue winter sky through the high windows that lined the west wall. What was she doing with herself anyway?

'Wish you were out there running?' a friendly voice asked.

She turned to find Larry Spence standing next to her. She gave him a perfunctory smile. 'Something like that.'

'You could still do it, girl. You could still get back into training, be ready in time for St. Petersburg.'

The Olympics in four years, he was saying. 'My competitive days are over, Larry. Been there, done that.'

He was just trying to make conversation, but it felt like he was trying to make time as well, and that annoyed her. He was a big, good-looking man in his mid-thirties, athletic and charming, the divorced father of two. He worked as a deputy sheriff with the county and moonlighted nights as a bouncer at a dance club. His family were all from Hopewell and the little farm towns surrounding. She had known him only a short while and not well, but somewhere along the line he had decided he wanted to change the nature of their relationship. He had asked her out repeatedly, and she had politely, but firmly, declined. That should have been the end of it, but somehow it wasn't.

'You were the best, girl,' he said, putting on his serious-guy mask. He always called her 'girl.' Like it was some sort of compliment, an endearment intended to make her feel special. It made her want to smack him.

'How are the kids?' she asked.

'Good. Growing like weeds.' He edged closer. 'Miss having their mother with them, though. Like there was ever anything about her for them to miss.'

Marcy Spence had not been what anyone could call dependable even before she had children, and having children hadn't improved her. She was a party girl with a party girl's tastes. After numerous flings with just about anyone inclined to show her a good time, and a number of screaming knock-down-drag-outs with her husband, the marriage was over.

Marcy was on the road and out of Hopewell even before the papers were filed, husband and kids be damned. She was twenty-four when she left. 'Babies raising babies,' Nest had heard the old ladies tut-tut.

'Got any plans for Christmas?' Larry asked her suddenly. His brow furrowed. 'You know, it would be good for the kids to have a woman around for the present opening and all.'

Nest nodded, straight-faced. 'Sort of a stand-in mother.'

Larry paused. 'Well, yeah, sort of, I guess. But I'd like it if you were there, too.'

She gave him a pointed look. 'Larry, we barely know each other.'

'Not my fault,' he said.

'Also, I've met your children exactly once. They probably don't even know who I am.'

'Sure, they do. They know.'

She shook her head. 'The timing's not right,' she said diplomatically. 'In any case, I have my own plans.'

'Hey, just thought I'd ask.' He shrugged, trying to downplay the importance of the request. 'No big deal.'

It was, of course, as any teenage girl, let alone a woman of Nest's age, could see in a heartbeat. But Larry Spence had already demonstrated with Marcy that he was far from wise in the ways of women. In any case, he was in way over his head with Nest. He had no idea what he was letting himself in for by pursuing her, and she was not about to encourage him by spending Christmas at his home with his children. In this instance ignorance was bliss. Let him tie up with someone normal; he would be far better off.

She caught sight of Robert Heppler across the room. 'Larry, I see someone I need to talk to. Thank you for the invitation.'

She hurried past him before he could respond, anxious to forestall any other misguided offers he might be inclined to make. Larry was a nice guy, but she had no interest in him at all. Why he couldn't see that was a mystery to her, but it was the sort of mystery commonplace in relationships between men and women.

She came up to Robert with a grin. 'Hey,' she said.

'Hey, there you are,' he replied, grinning back.

She reached out and gave him a hug and a kiss on the cheek. Still rail thin and towheaded, still looking very much like a mischievous little boy, Robert might have been mistaken by those who hadn't seen him in a while for the same smart-ass kid he had been all through school. But Robert had grown up when no one was looking. Right out of graduate school, he had married a small, strong-minded young woman named Amy Pruitt, and Amy had set him straight. Forthright, no-nonsense, and practical to a fault, she loved Robert so much she was willing to take him on as a project. Robert spent most of his life with his head somewhere else, developing codes, languages, programs, and systems for computers. Always convinced of his own brilliance and impossibly impatient with the perceived shortcomings of others, he had gotten as far as he had mostly on grades and the high expectations of his professors that one day they could point to him with pride in cataloging their academic accomplishments. But the real world has an entirely different grading system, and Amy was quick to recognize that Robert was ill equipped to succeed in the absence of a serious attitude adjustment.

She performed the surgery with flawless precision. Nest could hardly believe the difference in Robert between the time he met Amy and the time he married her, scarcely ten months later. Robert seemed totally unaware of the transformation she had wrought, believing he was just the same as he had always been. But after getting to know her a little better, Nest was quick to realize that Amy was the best thing that could have happened to her old friend.

Now they had one child, a boy of two who was clinging to Robert's leg playfully, and another on the way. Robert had a family and a life. He was a real person at last.

'Hey there, Kyle,' she said, bending down to ruffle the boy's blond hair. 'We missed you downstairs today.'

'Was 'n churtch,' the little boy mumbled, then blew her a kiss.

'I kept him with me,' Robert admitted, shrugging. 'I wanted some companionship. Amy stayed home. Not feeling so good this morning when she woke. This pregnancy has been a little rough.'

'Is everything okay?'

'Yeah, sure. You know Amy. Tough as nails. But she's being careful. She's a little over six months. Kind of a touchy time.'

'You'll let me know if I can do anything?'

Robert laughed. 'I'll let you know if *I* can do anything. With my parents and my sister and her husband hovering over her twenty-four hours a day, I can't get close enough to find out!'

He glanced over at Larry Spence, who was watching

surreptitiously from behind his coffee cup. 'I see you can still draw bees like honey. Or maybe *horseflies* would be a better choice of word.'

She arched one eyebrow. 'I see you still haven't lost your rapierlike wit, Robert.'

He shrugged. 'I'm just being protective. He reminds me a little of that guy who kept coming on to you the summer before we entered high school, the one I would have decked if you hadn't hypnotized him into falling over his own feet. What was his name, anyway? Bobby something?'

'Danny Abbott,' she said quietly.

'Yeah. That was a summer, wasn't it? I was in trouble all the time. Of course, you were the one playing around with magic.'

He meant it as a joke, but it was closer to the truth than he realized. Nest forced a smile.

'You remember that business on the Fourth with John Ross and those fireworks exploding all over the place?' he pressed. 'I was chasing after you through the park, and I fell down or something, hit my head. I can still remember the way you looked at me. You said afterward you used magic.' He paused, suddenly thoughtful. 'You know, I never did understand what really happened.'

Nest reached down abruptly, snatched up a squealing Kyle, and thrust him at his father. 'Here, Kyle, you explain it to him,' she urged.

'Splane,' Kyle repeated, giggling.

Robert took his son into his arms, jiggling him gently. 'Don't forget the Christmas party Tuesday night,' he said to Nest, kissing Kyle's fat cheeks. 'You got the invitation, didn't you?'

She nodded. 'Sure. I'll be there.'

'Good. My parents are sure to find a way to blame me, if you aren't.'

'Serve you right,' she said, moving away. 'See you later, Robert. Bye, Kyle.' She wiggled her fingers at the boy, who hid his face in his father's shoulder.

'Hey, don't scare him like that!' Robert threw after her.

She put her coffee cup on a tray near the kitchen door, ready to leave. Larry Spence was still watching her, but she tried not to notice. *Life in a small town is filled with moments of trying not to notice,* she thought wearily.

She was just departing the reception room to retrieve her coat from the narthex when a tall, angular young woman with wild red hair and acrylic green eyes came up to her.

'Are you Nest Freemark?' the young woman asked, eyes wide and staring like a cat's. Actually, on closer inspection, she seemed more a girl barely out of her teens than a woman. Nest nodded. 'I'm Penny,' the other announced.

She stuck out her hand, and Nest took it in her own. Penny's grip was strong and sure. 'I just wanted you to know how much I admire you. I've followed your career, like, ever since the Melbourne Olympics. I was just a little girl, but you were such a great inspiration to me! I wanted to be a runner, but I didn't grow up with strong enough lungs or something. So I became an actress. Can you tell?' She giggled. 'Anyway, I thought you should know there's someone who still remembers you. You know, from back when you were famous.' She giggled some more. 'Hey, it was nice meeting you. You'll be seeing me around, I expect. Bye-bye.'

She was gone before Nest could reply, disappearing into

the crowd gathered by the coffee urn. *Someone who remembers you from back when you were famous?* Nest grimaced. What a strange remark! She had never seen the young woman before and had no idea who she was. She didn't even look like anyone Nest knew, so it was impossible to match her up to a Hopewell family.

Must be someone new in town, she thought, still staring after the young woman. *Things around here change so quickly,* she thought, mimicking Alice in Wonderland.

Speaking of which, there was Larry Spence, moving in her direction with a decidedly hopeful look in his eye. She turned as if remembering something and hurried out the door.

CHAPTER 3

Findo Gask stood across the street from the First Congregational Church, just in front of the Hopewell Gazette, waiting patiently for Penny's return. He was an incongruous figure standing there in his frock coat and flat-brimmed hat, his tall, stooped figure silhouetted against the white stone of the newspaper building by the bright winter sunlight. With his black book held in front of him like a shield, he might have been a modern-day prophet come to pronounce judgment on an unsuspecting populace.

The truth, however, was a good deal scarier.

Even as demons went, Findo Gask was very old. He was centuries old, and this was unusual. For the most part, demons had a tendency to self-destruct or fall prey to their own peculiar excesses rather early in their careers. In completing their transformations, demons shed their human trappings, reducing themselves to hard, winged husks, so that when stripped of their disguises they looked not unlike bats.

But as hard as they worked to shed their human skins,

they remained surprisingly dependent on their origins. To disguise themselves, they were forced to resume looking like the creatures they had been. To satisfy their desperate need to escape their past, they were forced to prey upon the creatures they pretended to be. And to survive in their new forms, they were forced to struggle constantly against a small, but intransigent truth—they hungered endlessly and helplessly for contact with the creatures they despised.

As a direct result, they were torn by the dichotomy of their existence. In their efforts to give vent to their schizophrenic personalities, they descended swiftly into madness and bestiality. Their control over themselves collapsed, their sanity fragmented, and they disintegrated like wheels spinning so fast and so hard they succumbed to the heat of their own friction.

Findo Gask had avoided this end because he was not driven by emotion. He was not hungry for power or personal gratification. Revenge did not interest him. Validation of his existence was never a cause he was tempted to pursue. No, he was simply curious. Curiosity provided a limitless supply of inspiration for Findo Gask. He was smart and inventive and able. As a man, he might have uncovered secrets and solved riddles. He might have accomplished great things through research. But a man lived a finite number of years and was hampered by rules Findo Gask did not necessarily accept. A demon, he was quick to see, could do so much more. If he was willing to let go of the part of him that was human, a part he considered of no particular consequence or purpose in any case, he could explore and discover and dissect forever.

Moreover, he realized early on, humans made great sub-
jects for his studies. They fit with his needs and his wants
perfectly. All that was required was that he separate himself.

He had done so with surprising ease. It was difficult to
recall the details now. He had been alive for so long, a demon
for so many centuries, that he no longer remembered anything of his human history. Even the century of his
transformation had been forgotten. He was the oldest of
his kind perhaps, though it didn't matter to him if he was
because he took no satisfaction from it. The Void was his
master, but his master was a vague, substanceless presence
who pretty much left him alone to do what he wished,
appearing only now and then as a brief presence—a whisper,
a shadow, a dream of something remembered.

Other demons envied him. Some hated him openly. He
had what they wanted and did not know how to get. He was
older and wiser and stronger and more immune to the trappings of humanness that still tore at them like razors. His
insights into humans were deeper. His assimilation of both
demon and human worlds was more complete. He under-
took the challenges that interested him and gave himself
over to the studies that intrigued him.

Except that every once in a while the Void reminded him
there was a price for everything and choice was not always an
option, no matter who he was . . .

He watched Penny emerge from the church, red hair
uncoiling from her head like a mass of severed electrical
wires, gawky form working its way along the sidewalk and
across the street, a poorly made marionette, jerked and
tugged by invisible strings. He smiled indulgently, watching

her progress. Outwardly, she was a mess, but one couldn't always judge a book by its cover. Inside, she was twisted and corrosive and lethal. Penny Dreadful. She'd heard that the name applied to the dime-store crime novels of an earlier century. That's me, she'd said with a wicked grin, and took the name as her own.

She came up to Findo Gask with a skipping motion, putting on her little-girl facade, coquettish and sly. 'Greetings, Gramps,' she gushed, circling him once, then throwing her arms around him with such abandon that two elderly ladies passing on the other side of the street paused to have a look.

Gently, patiently, he disengaged himself from her grasp. He understood her excesses, which were greater than those of most demons. Unlike himself, she had no interest in staying alive. Penny Dreadful was intent on self-destructing, was enamored of the idea in fact, ensnared by her own special blend of madness and looking to write her finish in a particularly spectacular manner. Gask considered her a live hand grenade, but he was hopeful she would last long enough to be of some use to him in this matter.

'Did you do as I asked?' he inquired, arching one eyebrow in what might have been misinterpreted as a conciliatory gesture.

Penny, missing nothing, played dumb anyway. 'Sure. Hey, you know something, Gramps?' She called him that all the time, emphasizing their age difference in a continuing, if futile, effort to annoy him. 'That girl isn't anything special, you know? Nest Freemark. She isn't anything at all. I could snuff her out just like that.'

She snapped her fingers lightly, grinning at him.

He took her by the arm without a word and guided her down the sidewalk to the car. 'Get in,' he ordered, not bothering even to look at her.

She did, snickering and casting small glances in his direction, a clever little girl playing to an indulgent grandfather. Findo Gask felt like rolling his eyes. Or perhaps hers.

When they were seated inside, relatively secluded from passersby, he took a long moment to study her before speaking. 'Who did you find?'

She sighed at his unwillingness to play along with her latest game. She shrugged. 'Some dork named Larry Spence. He's a deputy sheriff, got some clout in the department 'cause he's been there ten years or so. He was happy to tell me all about himself, little me, all wide-eyed and impressed. He's got it real bad for Tracy Track Shoes. Like, totally. Do anything if he thought it would help her. He's perfect, for what you seem to want.'

She arched her eyebrows and met his gaze for the first time. 'Which is what exactly, Gramps? Why are we wasting our time on this creepo?'

'Watch the church door,' he said, ignoring her questions. 'When you see him come out, tell me.'

She held his gaze only a moment, then huffed disdainfully, slouched behind the steering wheel, and did as he asked. She was pretty good at that, for all the back talk she liked to give him. He let her get away with it precisely because back talk never went any further than talk with Penny. With Twitch, it was another matter, of course.

They sat silently in the warmth of the Sunday morning

sunshine as midday came and went. The congregation was filing out in steadily increasing numbers, bundled in their coats, heading home for the noontime meal.

'Wish he'd hurry it up,' Penny groused.

'Let me give you some advice,' Findo Gask said quietly. 'Grandfatherly advice, if you prefer. Don't underestimate Nest Freemark. She's tougher than you think.'

She glanced at him with a sneer, about to say something in rebuttal, but he shook his head at her and pointed back toward the church.

A few moments later, Larry Spence emerged, a small girl hanging off one hand, a boy only slightly older hanging off the other. Penny identified him, and Findo Gask told her to start the car. When Spence pulled out of the parking lot with his children, Findo Gask told Penny to follow. It was annoying having to issue all these instructions, but he couldn't rely on any of them to do what was necessary on their own. Three demons, each one more difficult to manage than the others, each a paradox even in demon terms. He had recruited them after Salt Lake City, realizing that in Ross he was up against someone who might prove his undoing. After all, by then he knew the Void's wishes, and he understood there was not going to be any margin for error.

He sighed wearily and looked out the window at the passing houses as Penny followed Larry Spence and his children down First Avenue toward the north end of town. He had been in Hopewell for almost a week, waiting patiently for Ross to show, knowing Ross would come, sensing it instinctively, the way he always did. It was an advantage he enjoyed over other demons, although he did not understand exactly why he had this power. Perhaps his instincts were sharper simply because he had lived so long and survived so much. Perhaps it was because he was a seeker of answers and more attuned to the possibilities of human behavior than others of his kind. Whatever the case, he would succeed where they would not. Demons would be hunting Ross all over the United States, peeking in every closet and looking under every bed. But he was the one who had found Ross the last time, and he would be the one to find him this time, too.

His hands moved lovingly over the worn leather cover of his Book of Names. He called it that, a simple designation for his record of the humans he had dispatched in one way or another over the centuries. He didn't bother with times or dates or places when he recorded their passing. The details didn't interest him. What he cared about was collecting lives and making them his own. What interested him was the nature of their dying, what they gave up, how they struggled, what they made him feel as they took their last breath. Something in their dying could be possessed, he discovered early on. Something of them could be claimed. It was a tribute to his continuing interest in collecting the names that he could always remember who they belonged to. Common memories were pale and insubstantial. But a memory of death was strong and lasting, and he kept each one, many hundreds in all, carefully catalogued and stored away.

He sighed. When he quit being interested in seeing them die, he supposed, he would quit collecting their names.

'He's home, Gramps,' Penny advised, cutting into his reverie.

He shifted his eyes to the front, watching as Larry Spence turned his car into a driveway leading to a small bungalow on Second Avenue, just off LeFevre Road.

'Drive past a couple of blocks and then turn around and come back,' he instructed.

Penny took the car up Second for a short distance, then turned into someone's drive, backed out, and came down the street from the other direction. Just before they reached Spence's house, she pulled the car over to the curb and parked. Switching off the ignition, she looked over. 'Now what, Grampa Gask?'

'Come with me,' he said.

Larry Spence was already inside the house with his kids, and Gask and Penny heard the ticking of his still-warm engine as they walked up the drive. The house seemed small and spare from the outside, shorn by winter's coming of the softening foliage of the bushes and trees surrounding it, its faded, peeling paint and splintered trim left bare and revealed. Findo Gask reflected on the pathetic lives of humans as he knocked on the front door, but only for a moment.

Larry Spence appeared almost immediately. He was still wearing his church clothes, but his tie was loosened and he had a dish towel in his hand. He pushed open the storm door and looked at them questioningly.

'Mr. Spence?' Findo Gask asked politely, his voice friendly but businesslike. Spence nodded. 'Mr. Larry Spence?'

'What do you want?' Spence replied warily.

Findo Gask produced a leather identification holder and flipped it open. 'Special Agent George Robinson, Mr. Spence. I'm with the FBI. Can you spare a moment?'

The other's confidence turned to uncertainty as he studied the identity card in its plastic slipcase. 'Something wrong?'

Now Gask gave him a reassuring smile. 'Nothing that involves you directly, Mr. Spence. But we need to talk with you about someone you know. This is my assistant, Penny. May we come inside?'

Larry Spence's big, athletic frame shifted in the doorway, and he brushed back his dark hair with spread fingers. 'Well, the kids are here, Mr. Robinson,' he replied uncertainly.

Findo Gask nodded. 'I wouldn't come to you on a Sunday, Mr. Spence, if it wasn't important. I wouldn't come to your home if I could handle the matter in your office.' He paused meaningfully. 'This won't take long. Penny can play with the children.'

Spence hesitated a moment longer, his brow furrowed, then nodded. 'All right. Come on in.'

They entered a small hallway that led to a tiny, cramped living room strewn with toys and magazines and pieces of the Sunday *Chicago Tribune*. Evidently Larry Spence hadn't done his housework before going off to church. The little boy appeared at the end of a hallway leading farther back into the house and looked at them questioningly.

'It's okay, Billy,' Spence said quickly, sounding less than certain that it was.

'Mr. Spence, perhaps Billy would like to show Penny his room,' Findo Gask suggested, smiling anew. 'Penny has a brother just about his age.'

'Sure, that would be fine.' Spence jumped on the suggestion. 'What do you say, Billy?'

'Hey, little man.' Penny came forward to greet the boy. 'You got any cool stuff to show me?'

She guided him back down the hallway, talking at him a mile a minute, Billy staring up at her like a deer caught in the headlights. Findo Gask hoped she would behave herself.

'Why don't we sit down, Mr. Spence,' he suggested.

He didn't bother removing his coat. He didn't bother putting down the book. Larry Spence wasn't seeing either one. He wasn't even seeing Findo Gask the way he appeared. Gask had clouded his vision the moment he opened the door, leaving him only vaguely aware of what the man he was talking to looked like. The trick wouldn't work with someone like Nest Freemark, but Larry Spence was a different matter. Already beset by doubts and confusion, he would probably stay that way until Findo Gask was done with him.

They moved over to a pair of worn easy chairs and seated themselves. Sunlight filtered, sharp-edged, through cracks in the drawn blinds, and Matchbox cars lay overturned on the carpet like miniature accidents.

'Mr. Spence, as a law enforcement officer yourself, you are undoubtedly familiar with the work we do,' Findo Gask opened the conversation. 'I'm here in Hopewell because of my work, and I need your help. But I don't want anyone else to know about this, not even your superiors. Usually, we try to work openly with the local law enforcement agencies, but in this case that isn't possible. At least, not yet. That's why I've come to your house rather than approach you at your office. No one but you even knows we are here.'

He paused. 'I understand you are acquainted with a young woman named Nest Freemark.'

Larry Spence looked startled. 'Nest? Sure, but I don't think she would ever—'

'Please, Mr. Spence, don't jump to conclusions,' Gask interrupted smoothly, cutting him short. 'Just let me finish. The bureau's interest in Miss Freemark is only peripheral in this matter. Our real interest is in a man named John Ross.'

Spence was still holding the dish towel, twisting the fabric between his big hands nervously. He saw what he was doing and set the towel aside. He cleared his throat. 'I never heard of anyone named John Ross.'

Findo Gask nodded. 'I didn't think you had. But Nest Freemark knows him quite well. Their friendship was formed some years ago when she was still a little girl and highly impressionable. He was an older man, good looking in a rugged sort of way, and very attentive toward her. He was a friend of her dead mother, and Nest was eager to make the connection with him for that reason if for no other. I suspect that she had quite a crush on him. She formed a strong attachment to him in any case, and she still thinks of him as her close friend.'

Gask chose his words carefully, working on the assumption that Larry Spence already felt possessive about Nest and would not welcome the idea of a rival, particularly one to whom she was attracted.

'John Ross is not the man Miss Freemark thinks he is, Mr. Spence,' he continued earnestly. 'He is a very dangerous criminal. She believes him to be her knight in shining armor, the man she knew fifteen years ago, the handsome, older man who paid so much attention to a young, insecure girl. She has deceived herself, and she will not be quick to change her thinking.'

He was laying it on a bit thick, but when dealing with a man as enamored of a woman as Larry Spence was of Nest Freemark, he could get away with it.

'What's he done?' Spence demanded, stiffening in his seat, ready to charge out and do battle with his duplicitous, unsavory rival. Gask smiled inwardly.

'I'd prefer not to discuss that aspect of the case with you, Mr. Spence.' *Let him use his imagination,* Gask thought. 'What should be of concern to you, as it is to us, is not so much what he's done elsewhere, but what he may do once he comes here.'

'He's coming to Hopewell?' Spence swallowed. 'So you think he'll look up Nest?'

Gask nodded, pleased that the deputy was doing all the work for him. 'There is every reason to believe he will try to contact her. When he does, he will ask her to keep his presence a secret. He will lay low for the duration of his visit. He will not show himself readily. That's where you come in.'

Larry Spence leaned forward, his hands knotted. 'What do you want me to do?'

Findo Gask wished everything in life were this easy. 'Miss Freemark is your friend. She knows of your interest in her, and she will not be suspicious if you find an excuse to visit her. Do so. Do so at least once every day. Get inside her house any way you can and look around. You may not see Ross, but you may see some sign of his presence. If you do, don't do anything foolish. Just call this number immediately.'

Gask drew out a white business card and handed it to Larry Spence. It bore his fake identity and rank and a local number to which an answer phone would respond.

'I don't have to tell you how grateful the bureau is for your cooperation, Mr. Spence,' Gask announced, rising to his feet. 'I won't take up any more of your time today, but I'll stay in touch.'

He shook the deputy's hand, leaving a final imprint of his presence so that the other would not be quick to forget what he had been told. 'Penny!' he called down the hallway.

Penny Dreadful emerged on cue, smiling demurely, trying to hide the hungry look in her eyes. She was like this every time she got around children. Gask took her by the arm and steered her out the front door, nodding in the direction of Larry Spence as they departed.

'I was just starting to have fun,' she pouted. 'I had some of my toys out, and I was showing him how to cut things. I took off one of my fingers with a razor.' She giggled and held up the severed digit, then stuck it back in place, ligaments and flesh knitting seamlessly.

'Penny, Penny, Penny,' he sighed wearily.

'Don't get your underwear in a bundle, Gramps. I made sure he won't remember any of it until tonight, after he's asleep, when he'll wake up screaming. Deputy daddy will think it's just a bad dream.'

They climbed back into the car, clicking their seat belts into place. Findo Gask wondered how much longer he was going to be able to keep her in line. It was bad enough with Twitch, but to have Penny pushing the envelope as well was a bit much. He rolled down the window and breathed in the winter air. The temperature had risen to almost forty, and the day felt warm and crisp against his skin. Odd, he thought, that he could still feel things like that, even in a body that wasn't his.

He thought for a moment about the enormity of the struggle between the Word and the Void. It had been going on since the dawn of time, a hard-fought, bitter struggle for control of the human race. Sometimes one gained the upper hand, sometimes the other. But the Void always gained a little more ground in these exchanges because the Word relied on the strengths of humans to keep in balance the magic that held the world together and the Void relied on their weaknesses to knock it askew. It was a foregone conclusion as to which would ultimately prevail. The weaknesses of humans would always erode their strengths. There might be more humans than demons, but numbers alone were insufficient to win this battle.

And while it was true that demons were prone to self-destruct, humans were likely to get there much quicker.

'Home, Penny,' he instructed, realizing she was waiting for him to tell her what to do.

She pulled out into the street, swerving suddenly toward a cat that just barely managed to get out of the way. 'I was listening to you in there,' she declared suddenly.

He nodded. 'Good for you.'

'So what's the point of having this dork hang around Miss Olympic Big Bore to find out if this Ross guy is staying with her?'

'What's the matter, Penny? Don't you believe in cooperating with your local law enforcement officers?'

She was staring at the road intently. 'Like that matters to you, Gramps. We could find out easy enough if Ross is out there without help from Deputy Dawg. I don't get it.'

He stretched his lanky frame and shrugged. 'You don't have to get it, Penny. You just have to do what you're told.'

She pouted in silence a moment, then said, 'He'll just get in the way, Gramps. You'll see.'

Findo Gask smiled. *Right you are, Penny*, he thought. *That's just exactly what he'll do. I'm counting on it.*

CHAPTER 4

D riving home from church, Nest Freemark brooded some more about John Ross. It was a futile exercise, one that darkened her mood considerably more than she intended. Ross was a flashpoint for all the things about her life that troubled her. Even though he wasn't directly responsible for any of them, he was the common link. By the time she parked the car in her driveway and climbed out, she was ready to get back in again and start driving to some other time zone.

She went inside resignedly, knowing there was nothing she could do to stop him from coming to see her if that's what he intended to do, nothing she could do to prevent yet another upheaval in her life. She changed into jeans and a sweatshirt and pulled on heavy walking shoes, then went into the kitchen to fix herself some lunch. She sat alone at the worn, wooden table she had shared with Gran for so many years, wondering what advice the old lady would give her about John Ross. She could just imagine. Gran had been a no-nonsense sort, the kind who took life's challenges as they came and dealt with them as best she could. She hadn't been the sort to fantasize about possibilities and what-ifs. It was a lesson that hadn't been lost on her granddaughter.

Polishing off a glass of milk and a sandwich of leftover chicken, she pulled on her winter parka and walked out the back door. Tomorrow was the winter solstice, and the days had shortened to barely more than eight hours. Already the sun was dropping westward, marking the passing of the early afternoon. By four-thirty, it would be dark. Even so, the air felt warm this winter day, and she left her parka open, striding across her backyard toward the hedgerow and the park. Her old sandbox and tire swing were gone, crumbled with age and lack of use years ago. The trees and bushes were a tangle of bare, skeletal limbs, webbing across the blue sky, casting odd shadows on the wintry gray-green grass. It was a time of sleep, of the old year and its seasons passing into the new, of waiting patiently for rebirth. Nest Freemark wondered if her own life was keeping pace or just standing still.

She pushed through a gap in the bare branches of the hedge and crossed the service road that ran behind her house. Sinnissippi Park stretched away before her, barren and empty in the winter light. The crossbar at the entrance was down. Residents living in the houses that crowded up against its edges walked their dogs and themselves and played with their kids in the snow when there was snow to be played in, but there was no one about at the moment. In the evenings, weather permitting, the park opened from six to ten at night for tobogganing on the park slide and ice skating on the bayou.

If the temperature dropped and the forecast for snow proved out, both would be open by tomorrow night.

She hiked deliberately toward the cliffs, passing through a familiar stand of spruce clustered just beyond the backstop of the nearest baseball diamond, and Pick dropped from its branches onto her shoulder.

'You took your sweet time getting out here!' he snapped irritably, settling himself in place against the down folds of her collar.

'Church ran a little long,' she replied, refusing to be baited. Pick was always either irritable or coming up on it, so she was used to his abrupt pronouncements and sometimes scathing rebukes. 'You probably got a lot done without me anyway.'

'That's not the point!' he snapped. 'When you make a commitment—'

'—you stick to it,' she finished, having heard this chestnut at least a thousand times. 'But I can't ignore the rest of my life, either.'

Pick muttered something unintelligible and squirmed restlessly. A hundred and sixty-five years old, he was a sylvan, a forest creature composed of sticks and moss, conceived by magic, and born in a pod. In every woods and forest in the world, sylvans worked to balance the magic that was centered there so that all living things could coexist in the way the Word had intended. It was not an easy job and not without its disappointments; many species had been lost through natural evolution or the depredations of humans. Even woods and forests were destroyed, taking with them all the creatures who lived there, including the sylvans who tended them. Erosion of the forest magic over the passing of the centuries had been slow, but steady, and Pick declared often and ominously that time was running out.

'The park looks pretty good,' she offered, banishing such thoughts from her mind, trying to put a positive spin on things for the duration of her afternoon.

Pick was having none of it. 'Appearances are deceiving. There's trouble brewing.'

'Trouble of what sort?'

'Ha! You haven't even noticed, have you?'

'Why don't you just tell me?'

They crossed the entry road and walked up toward the turnaround at the west end that overlooked the Rock River from the edge of the bluffs. Beyond the chain-link fence marking the park's farthest point lay Riverside Cemetery. She had not been out to the graves of her mother or grandparents in more than a week, and she felt a pang of guilt at her oversight.

'The feeders have been out,' Pick advised with a grunt, 'skulking about the park in more numbers than I've seen in a long time.'

'How many?'

'Lots. Too many to count. Something's got them stirred up, and I don't know what it is.'

Shadowy creatures that lurked on the edges of people's lives, feeders lapped up the energy given off by expenditure of emotions. The darker and stronger the emotions, the greater the number of feeders who gathered to feast. Parasitic beings who responded to their instincts, they did not judge and they did not make choices. Most humans never saw them, except when death came violently and unexpectedly, and they were the last image to register before the lights went out for good. Only those like Nest, who were born with magic themselves, knew there were feeders out there.

Pick gave her a sharp look, his pinched wooden face all wizened and rough, his gnarled limbs drawn up about his crooked body so that he took on the look of a bird's nest. His strange, flat eyes locked on her. 'You know something about this, don't you?'

She nodded. 'Maybe.'

She told him about Findo Gask and the possibility that John Ross was returning to Hopewell. 'A demon's presence would account for all the feeders, I expect,' she finished.

They walked up through the playground equipment and picnic tables that occupied the wooded area situated across the road from the Indian mounds and the bluffs. When they reached the turnaround, she slowed, suddenly aware that Pick hadn't spoken a word since she had told him about Findo Gask and John Ross. He hadn't even told her what work he wanted her to do that day in the park.

'What do you think?' she asked, trying to draw him out.

He sat motionless on her shoulder, silent and remote. She crossed the road to the edge of the bluffs and moved out to where she could see the frozen expanse of the Rock River. Even with the warmer temperatures of the past few days, the bayou that lay between the near shore and the raised levy on which the railroad tracks had been laid remained frozen. Beyond, where the wider channel opened south on its way to the Mississippi, the Rock was patchy with ice, the swifter movement of the water keeping the river from freezing over completely. That would change when January arrived.

'Another demon,' Pick said softly. 'You'd think one in a lifetime would be enough.'

She nodded wordlessly, eyes scanning the tangle of tree trunks and limbs immediately below, searching for movement in the lengthening shadows. The feeders, if they were out yet, would be there, watching.

'Some sylvans go through their entire lives and never encounter a demon.' Pick's voice was soft and contemplative. 'Hundreds of years, and not a one.'

'It's my fault,' she said.

'Not hardly!'

'It is,' she insisted. 'It began with my father.'

'Which was your grandmother's mistake!' he snapped.

She glanced down at him, all fiery-eyed and defensive of her, and she gave him a smile. 'Where would I be without you, Pick?'

'Somewhere else, I expect.'

She sighed. Over the past fifteen years she had attempted to move away from the park. To leave the park was unthinkable for Pick; the park was his home and his charge. For the sylvan, nothing else existed. It was different for her, of course, but Pick didn't see it that way. Pick saw things in black-and-white terms. Even an inherited obligation—in this case, an obligation passed down through six generations of Freemark women to help care for the park—wasn't to be ignored, no matter what. She belonged here, working with him, keeping the magic in balance and looking after the park. But this was all Pick knew. It was all he had done for more than one hundred fifty years. Nest didn't have one hundred fifty years, and she wasn't so sure that tending the magic and looking after the park was what she wanted to spend the rest of her life doing.

She looked off across the Rock River, at the hazy midafternoon twilight beginning to steal out of the east as the shortened winter day slipped westward. 'What do you want to do today, Pick?' she asked quietly.

He shrugged. 'Too late to do much, I expect.' He did not say it in a gruff way; he simply sounded resigned. 'Let's just have a look around, see if anything needs doing, and we can see to it tomorrow.' He sniffed and straightened. 'If you think you can spare the time, of course.'

'Of course,' she echoed.

They left the bluffs and walked down the road from the turnaround to where it split, one branch doubling back under a bridge to descend to the base of the bluffs and what she thought of as the feeder caves, the other continuing on along the high ground to the east end of the park, where the bulk of the woods and picnic areas were located. They followed the latter route, working their way along the fringes of the trees, taking note of how everything was doing, not finding much that didn't appear as it should. The park was in good shape, even if Pick wasn't willing to acknowledge as much. Winter had put her to sleep in good order, and the magic, dormant and restful in the long, slow passing of the season, was in perfect balance.

The world of Sinnissippi Park is at peace, Nest thought to herself, glancing off across the open flats of the ball diamonds and playgrounds and through the skeletal trees and rolling stretches of woodland. Why couldn't her world be the same?

But she knew the answer to that question. She had known it for a long time. The answer was Wraith.

Three years earlier, she had been acclaimed as the greatest American long-distance runner of all time. She had already competed in one Olympics and had won a pair of gold medals and set two world records. She had won thirty-two consecutive races since. She owned a combined eight world titles in the three and five thousand. She was competing in her second Olympics, and she had won the three by such a wide margin that a double in the five seemed almost a given.

She remembered that last race vividly. She had watched the video a thousand times. She could replay it in her own mind from memory, every moment, frame by frame.

Looking off into the trees, she did so now.

She breaks smoothly from the start line, content to stay with the pack for several laps, for this longer distance places a higher premium on patience and endurance than on speed. There are eight lead changes in the first two thousand meters, and then her competitors begin boxing her in. Working in shifts, the Ukrainians, the Ethiopians, a Moroccan, and a Spaniard pin her against the inside of the track. She has gone undefeated in the three- and five-thousand-meter events for four years. You don't do that, no matter how well liked or respected you are, and not make enemies. In any case, she has never been all that close to the other athletes. She trains with her college coach or alone. She stays by herself when she travels to events. She keeps apart because of the nature of her life. She is careful not to get too close to anyone. Her legacy of magic has made her wary.

With fifteen hundred meters to go, she is locked in the middle of a pack of runners and unable to break free.

At the thousand-meter mark, a scuffle for position ensues, and she is pushed hard, loses her balance, and tumbles from the track.

She comes back to her feet almost as quickly as she has gone down and regains the track. Furious at being trapped, jostled, and knocked sprawling, she gives chase, unaware that she is bleeding profusely from a spike wound on her ankle. Zoning into that place where she sometimes goes when she runs, where there is only the sound of her breathing and beat of her heart, she catches and passes the pack. She doesn't just draw up on them gradually; she runs them down. There is something raw and primal working inside her as she cranks up her speed a notch at a time. The edges of her vision turn red and fuzzy, her breathing burns in her throat like fire, and the pumping of her arms and legs threatens to tear her body apart.

She is running with such determination and with so little regard for herself that she fails to realize that something is wrong.

Then she hears the gasps of the Ethiopians as she passes them in the three and four positions and sees the look of horror on the face of the Spaniard when she catches her two hundred meters from the finish.

A tiger-striped face surges in the air before her, faintly visible in the shimmer of heat and dust. Wraith is emerging from her body. He is breaking free, coming out of her, unbidden and out of control. Wraith, formed of her father's demon magic and bequeathed to her as a child. Wraith, created as her protector, but become a presence that threatens in ways she can barely tolerate. Wraith, who lives inside her now, a magic she cannot rid herself of and therefore must work constantly to conceal.

It happens all at once. Emerging initially as a faint image that clings to her in a shimmer of light, he begins to take recognizable shape. Only those who are close can see what is happening, and even they are unsure. But their uncertainty is only momentary. If he comes out of her all the way, there will be no more doubt. If he breaks free entirely, he may attack the other runners.

She fights to regain control of him, desperate to do so, unable to understand why he would appear when she has not summoned him and is not threatened with harm.

Powering down the straightaway, her body wracked by pain and fatigue and by her struggle to rein in the ghost wolf, she catches the Moroccan at fifty meters. The Moroccan's intense, frightened eyes momentarily lock on her as she powers past. Nest's teeth are bared and Wraith surges in and out of her skin in a flurry of small, quick movements, his terrifying visage flickering in the bright sunlight like an iridescent mirage. The Moroccan swerves from both in terror, and Nest is alone in the lead.

She crosses the finish line first, the winner of the gold medal by ten meters. She knows it is the end of her career, even before the questions on how she could have recovered from her fall and gone on to win turn to rumors on the use of performance-enhancing drugs. Her control over Wraith, always tenuous at best, has eroded further, and she does not understand why. His presence is bearable when she can rely on keeping him in check. But if he can appear anytime she loses control of her emotions, it marks the end of her competitive running days as surely as sunset does the coming of night.

'I'm getting old,' Pick said suddenly, kicking at her shoulder in what she supposed was frustration.

'You've always been old,' she reminded him. 'You were old when I was born. You've already lived twice as long as most humans.'

He glared at her, but said nothing.

She watched clouds fill the edges of the western sky beyond the scraggly tops of the bare hardwoods, rolling out of the plains. The expected storm was on its way. She could feel a drop in the temperature, a bite in the wind that gusted out of the shadows. She pulled the parka tight against her body and zipped it up.

'Hard freeze coming in,' Pick said from his perch on her shoulder. 'Let's give it up for today.'

She turned and began the long walk home. Dead leaves rustled in dry clusters against the bare ground and the trunks of trees. She kicked at pieces of deadwood, her thoughts moody and unsettled, fragments of the race and its aftermath still playing out in her mind.

It had taken months to put an end to the newspaper reports, even after she had taken a voluntary drug test in an effort to end the speculation. Everyone wanted to know why she would quit competitive running when she was at the peak of her career, when she was so young, after she had won so often. She had given interviews freely on the subject for months, and finally she had just given up. She couldn't explain it to them, of course. She couldn't begin to make them understand. She couldn't tell them about the magic or Wraith. She could only say she was tired of running and wanted to do something else. She could only repeat herself, over and over and over again.

Only a month ago, she had received a phone call from an editor at the sports magazine Paul worked for. The editor told her the magazine wanted to do a story on her. She reminded him she didn't give interviews anymore.

'Change your policy, Nest,' he pressed. 'Next summer is the Olympics. People want to know if you'll come out of retirement and run again. You're the greatest long-distance runner in your country's history—you can't pretend that doesn't mean something. How about it?'

'No, thanks.'

'Why? Does it have anything to do with your quitting competitive running after your race in the five thousand in the last Olympics? Does it have anything to do with the rumors of drug use? There was a lot of speculation about what happened—'

She'd hung up on him abruptly. He hadn't called back.

In truth, quitting was the hardest thing she had ever done. She loved the competition. She loved how being the best made her feel. She couldn't deny giving it up took something away from her, that it hollowed her out. She still trained, because she couldn't imagine life without the sort of discipline and order that training demanded. She stayed fit and strong, and every so often she would sneak back into the city and have herself timed by her old coach. She did it out of pride and a need to know she was still worth something.

Her life had been a mixed bag since. She lived comfortably enough on money she had saved from endorsements and appearance fees, earning a little extra now and then by writing articles for the running magazines. The writing didn't pay her much, but it gave her something to do. Something besides helping Pick with the park. Something besides charity and church work. Something besides sitting around remembering her marriage to Paul and how it had fallen apart.

She crossed out of the ravine that divided the bulk of the park from the deep woods and climbed the slope toward the toboggan slide and the pavilion. From out of the distance came the piercing wail of a freight-train whistle followed by the slow, thunderous buildup of engines and wheels. She

paused to look south, seeing the long freight drive out of the
west toward Chicago, stark and lonely against the empty
expanse of the winter landscape.

She waited until it passed, then continued on. Oddly
enough, Pick hadn't said a word in complaint. Perhaps he
sensed her sadness. Perhaps he was wrestling with concerns
of his own. She let him be, striding across the open ball diamonds toward the service road and the hedgerow that
marked the boundary between the park and her backyard.
Pick left her somewhere along the way. Lost in thought, she
didn't see him go. She just looked down and he wasn't there.

As she crossed the yard Hawkeye skittered along the rear
of the house, stalking something Nest couldn't see. A big,
orange stray who had adopted her, he was the sort of cat
who put up with you if you fed him and expected you to
stay out of his way the rest of the time. She liked having a
mouser about, but Hawkeye made her nervous. His name
came from the way he looked at her, which she caught him
doing all the time. It was a sort of sideways stare, full of
trickery and cool appraisal. Pick said he was just trying to
figure out how to turn her into dinner.

As she came up beside the garage, she saw a young woman
and a little girl sitting on her back steps. The little girl was
bundled in an old, shabby red parka with the hood drawn
up. Her face was bent toward a rag doll she held protectively
in her lap. The woman was barely out of her teens, if that,
short and slender with long, tangled dark hair spilling down
over her shoulders. She wore a leather biker's jacket over a
miniskirt and high boots. No gloves, no hat, no scarf.

Her head came up at Nest's approach, and she climbed to

her feet watchfully. The pale afternoon light glinted dully off the silver rings that pierced her ears, nose, and one eyebrow. The deep blue markings of a tattoo darkened the back of one hand where it folded into the other to ward off the cold.

Nest came up to her slowly, thinking, *I know this girl.*

Then, for just a moment, something of the child she remembered from fifteen years ago surfaced in the young woman's face.

'Ben Ben?' Nest asked in disbelief.

A smile appeared. 'Guess what, Nest? I've come home.'

Sure enough, it was Bennett Scott.

CHAPTER 5

The demon who called himself Findo Gask climbed out of the passenger seat of the car and let Penny Dreadful pull ahead into the narrow garage. He stretched, smoothed down the wrinkles in his frock coat, and glanced around at his new neighborhood. The homes were large, faded mansions that had seen better days. The neighborhood had been one of Hopewell's finest, once upon a time, when only the well-to-do and wellborn lived there. Most of the homes sat on a minimum of two acres of rolling lawn and enjoyed the benefits of swimming pools, tennis courts, ornamental gardens, and gazebos. Lavish parties were held under the stars as fine brandies and ports were sipped and imported cigars smoked and live music played until dawn.

All that was before Midwest Continental Steel began expanding its plant west out of the city just below the back property lines, forming a wall of corrugated iron, scrap metal shriek, and molten fire between itself and the river. When that happened, the well-to-do and wellborn migrated to less offensive, more secluded sections of the city, and property values began to plummet. For a time, upper-middle-class families raised their children in these old homes, happy to find a neighborhood that exuded a sense of prestige and provided real space. But such families lasted only a short decade or so, when it became clear to all that the cost of upkeep and the proximity of the mill far outweighed any benefits.

After that, most of the homes were converted to apartments and town houses, save for a few where the original owners, now in their late seventies or eighties, had made the decision to hang on till the end. But even the conversions to multifamily dwellings had mixed results. Because the homes were old, they lacked reasonable heating, cooling, plumbing, and wiring, and even with modifications and improvements they were still dated, cavernous, and vaguely spooky. Besides, nothing could be done about the obvious presence of MidCon Steel, sitting right outside the back door at the end of the yard, and most people who might have considered renting at the rates sought wanted someplace with at least a modicum of tranquillity and ambiance.

Soon, rents dropped to a level that attracted transients and what was commonly referred to in the community as trailer trash. Renters came and went with the regularity of midseason TV shows. The banks and mortgage companies sold what they could of their inventory and put off any repairs or improvements that weren't absolutely necessary. The neighborhood continued its steady decline toward rock bottom, and eventually those renting were pretty much the kind of people who got through life by preying on each other.

Findo Gask had learned all this from the real estate lady at ERA with whom he had inspected his present home two days earlier. It was an old Victorian, four bedrooms, three baths, living room, dining room, study, powder room, basement recreation room, two screened porches, a swimming pool that had been converted to a pathetic Japanese rock garden, and a spacious lawn that ran down to a tall line of spruce trees that effectively screened away the sights, if not the smells and sounds, of MidCon and was the best feature of the property. The house was painted lavender and blueberry, and there were flower boxes set at all the windows on the lower floor.

The real estate lady had insisted it was a real bargain.

He smiled now, thinking of her. She had been quite anxious to sell him the place, poor woman. What she didn't realize was that he wasn't even considering renting, let alone buying. It took him a few, ugly moments to convince her of this. When he was done, she was so frightened she could barely manage to draw up the necessary papers, but at least she had given up on the sales pitch. By the time she recovered her wits enough to realize what she had done, he would be long gone.

Findo Gask left Penny to her own devices and walked up the drive to the front of the house. Leather-bound book held in both hands, he stood surveying the old building, wondering at its endurance. It was sagging and splintering and cracking at every corner and seam. He thought that if he took a deep breath and exhaled sharply enough, it would simply collapse.

He shook his head. It was just another crumbling, pathetic edifice in a crumbling, pathetic world.

He walked up the steps and through the front door. The hallway was dark and cool, and the house silent. It was always like that when Penny was out. The other two never made any noise. He wouldn't have known Twitch was even there if he hadn't listened closely for the television, which Twitch watched incessantly when he wasn't hanging around bars, looking for someone to traumatize.

Findo Gask frowned. At least with Twitch, there was the television to home in on when you wanted to know if he was around. With the other . . .

Where could it be, anyway?

He glanced into the living and dining rooms out of habit, then started upstairs. He climbed slowly and deliberately, letting each step take his full weight, making certain the creaking of the old boards preceded him. Best not to appear too unexpectedly. Some demons didn't like that, and this one was among them. You could never be certain of its reaction if you caught it by surprise.

Findo Gask searched through all the bedrooms, bathrooms, closets, nooks, and crannies. It would be up here rather than in the basement with Twitch, because it didn't like Twitch and it didn't like lights or television. Mostly, it liked being alone in silent, dark places where it could disappear entirely.

Gask looked around, perplexed. *Come out, come out, wherever you are.*

Findo Gask didn't like Twitch either. Or lights or television or Penny or anything about this house and the time he spent in it. He endured all of it solely because he was intrigued by the prospect of adding John Ross to his book.

And perhaps, he thought suddenly, *of adding Nest Freemark as well.* He nodded to himself. *Yes, perhaps.*

A small noise caught his attention—a scrape, no more. Gask peered up at the ceiling. The attic, of course. He walked down the hall to the concealed stairway, opened the door, and began to climb. The ceiling light was out, so the only illumination came from sunlight that seeped through a pair of dirt-encrusted dormer windows set at either end of the chamber. Gask reached the top of the stairs and stopped. Everything was wrapped in shadows, inky and forbidding, layer upon layer. The air smelled of dust and old wood, and he could hear the sound of his own breathing in the silence.

'Are you up here?' he asked quietly.

The ur'droch brushed against him before he even realized it was close enough to do so, and then it was gone again, melting back into the shadows. Its touch made him shudder in spite of himself. He wished it would talk once in a while, but it never said a word or uttered a sound. It rarely even showed itself, and that was all to the good as far as Gask was concerned. There weren't many demons like the ur'droch, and the few he knew about were universally shunned. They didn't take the forms of humans like most demons; they didn't take any form at all. Something in their makeup made them feel more comfortable in a substanceless form, a part of the shadows they hid within.

Not that this made them any less capable of killing.

'We're going out tonight,' he advised, his eyes flicking left and right in a futile effort to find the other. 'I want you along.'

No response. Nothing moved. Findo Gask was tempted

to have the whole house lighted from top to bottom just to expose this weasel to a clinical examination, but the effort would be pointless. The ur'droch was useful precisely because of what it was, and putting up with its shadowy presence was part of the price paid for its services.

Gask turned and walked back down the stairs and shut the door behind him. His mouth tightened as he stood in the upstairs hallway and ran his fingers over the cover of his book. Penny, Twitch, and the ur'droch. They were a strange and unpredictable bunch, but they were also what was needed.

He had learned that lesson in Salt Lake City.

*T*he biggest of the five men he had hired bent close to the hotel room door, listening. The dimly lighted hallway was empty and silent at one o'clock in the morning. Findo Gask could hear the sound of his own breathing.

The man with his ear to the door straightened, shaking his head at the other two and Gask. No snores, no heavy breathing, no television, nothing.

Gask motioned impatiently. *Go in. Get it over with.*

The big man glanced at the two who flanked him, then down the hallway to where the other two were positioned, one each in front of the elevator and the stairway doors. Then he took out the Glock with the screwed-on silencer, stepped back a pace, and carefully inserted the key in the door.

Findo Gask's search for John Ross had begun three weeks earlier with a summoning. He was in Chicago at the time, working the projects on the south side, stirring up dissension and playing on frustrations, an invisible presence in an

intellectual and cultural wasteland where hope was a mirage
and reality a hammer. The riots of summer had been his
work, as had the tenement fires of fall. Winter brought
freezing cold and no heat, good building blocks for the insti-
gation of further carnage.

The summoning came to him in the middle of the night
as a child's wailing. It was inaudible to human ears, but perfectly clear to his. He knew at once what it was. He had been
summoned before, and he recognized the feelings the call
invoked. Hunger, blood-lust, fury, and a deep and pervasive
emptiness. It was as if the Void were hollowing him out,
dredging his insides, his heart and mind and soul, with a tiny
metal scoop. The pain was excruciating, and he went quickly
from his room in search of relief.

He found it in the basement of the abandoned project in
which he had constructed his spider's web of hate, a place
where gangs carried out acts so unspeakable there were no
names for them. The wail had its source in a dark corner
where rats prowled and the detritus of expended human
lives was discarded as casually as yesterday's newspapers.
There were no windows in the concrete-block walls, but
gaps in the ceiling served the purpose. Streetlamps lent just
enough illumination to the chamber for Findo Gask to pick
his way to where the summoning originated.

The wail died to a rustle as he appeared, a voice speaking
to him not from the shadows but from inside his head. The
Void's presence was unmistakable, cold, empty, and lifeless,
a whisper of the passing of all things and the beginning of
none.

Listen carefully, the rustle cautioned. *A gypsy morph has been cap-*

tured by a Knight of the Word at a place called Cannon Beach, Oregon.
The Knight's name is John Ross. He is a seasoned, dangerous veteran of
our wars. He seeks to unlock the morph's magic. He must be found and
destroyed. Findo Gask. Findo Gask.

The words echoed and died into silence. The dark of
the basement shifted and tightened about him as he waited
for the rest.

Bring me the morph. Findo Gask. Findo Gask.

Something like an electric shock jolted him, lifting him
clear of the floor, filling his vision with red fire, then retreating in a light as clear as glass. Within the light was a vision
of John Ross and the gypsy morph on a day as hard and gray
as slate. They emerged onto a beach from a cavern cut into
the side of an embankment of stone and brush, the morph
caught in a strange netting, all bright lights and speed, the
Knight of the Word already beginning to check for the enemies he knew would be coming for him.

The vision faded, and Findo Gask found himself
slumped on his knees on the cold concrete basement floor,
rats skittering away in the dark, shadows again gone still,
silence everywhere.

Not many demons were summoned, Findo Gask knew.
Only the oldest and most experienced, the ones the Void
depended on most. A gypsy morph was rare and dangerous.
Formed of loose, wild magics come together in the ether, a
morph had the potential of becoming a weapon of incredible power. How a Knight of the Word had managed to
capture one was unimaginable. It must have taken an incredible stroke of luck. Whatever the case, the Knight's luck was
about to change.

Findo Gask left the basement and the projects and Chicago that night. One or two other demons would be dispatched by the Void as well. But Findo Gask knew he was the one who would have the best chance of succeeding.

In the beginning, tracking John Ross was not difficult. Every time the gypsy morph underwent a new transformation, which was sometimes hourly, it emitted a pulse of expended magic. Like a beacon, the pulses could be homed in on, leading a hunter to his target. But human behavior was complex, and John Ross would know he was being hunted and that the gypsy morph was giving them away. He would be evasive. He would not stand around waiting to be caught.

Findo Gask tracked John Ross for eighteen days before he found him. He read the pulse of the gypsy morph at each change and relied on his instincts to tell him what Ross would do. He found the Knight of the Word in Salt Lake City ten days before Christmas in a seedy hotel at the north edge of the downtown area. With five very tough, well-paid thugs in tow, he entered the empty lobby of the hotel on the night shift, walked up to the clerk, produced his fake U.S. marshal's identification, and asked for the key to Ross's room. The clerk, young and stupid and scared, handed it over without a word.

'There's not gonna be no trouble, is there?' he asked.

Gask smiled reassuringly. 'Tell me what Mr. Ross brought with him to his room,' he ordered.

The clerk stared at him dumbly, trying to figure out what was being asked of him. 'I dunno. A duffel bag and a knapsack's all. Came in off a bus.' He paused, thinking. 'Oh, yeah, he's got a ferret, too. Must be some sort of pet.'

Gask took the men up to the third floor where Ross was staying. One man would position himself at the elevator, one by the stairs, and the other three would go in after Ross. They had been told Ross was a dangerous man, a traitor and a spy. They were not to try to subdue him; they were to kill him. He would be armed, and he would kill them if they did not kill him first. They had been issued Glocks with silencers and sworn in as deputy U.S. marshals. They would face no adverse consequences for their actions. All were under the protection of the United States government. Everything they did was fully sanctioned.

A demon could persuade violent men of anything, and Findo Gask had no trouble with these. Kill John Ross, he emphasized, but under no circumstances harm the ferret. Leave the ferret to him.

Standing at the far end of the hall in the shadows, Findo Gask watched it all. The room key went into the lock smoothly, the door cracked open, the big man kicked out the chain, and the three primary assailants burst through the opening, their weapons firing—*phfft, phfft, phfft*. One heartbeat later, there was a brilliant flash of light, as if a thousand cameras had all gone off at once. The wall separating the room from the hallway shattered as the broken bodies of two of the assailants hurtled through it. The third assailant, he discovered later, was thrown through the window to the street.

Then John Ross came through the door in a crouch, his staff ablaze with magic, his knapsack slung over his shoulder, his duffel abandoned. For just an instant he looked in Findo Gask's direction, but the demon remained in the shadows, holding himself perfectly still.

The man by the elevator began firing his weapon. Ross knocked him twenty feet through the air with a single surge of power from the staff, and when his head struck the metal-bound edge of the wall where it angled around the main heating vent, Gasko heard the vertebrae crack. By now, the last man was firing as well, but Ross knocked him down with a sweep of his staff and was past him so quickly he might as well have been armed with a flyswatter.

In less than two minutes, the Knight of the Word had disposed of all five assailants and disappeared through the fire door. Four of the five were dead, and Findo Gask finished off the last on his way out, pausing as he passed through the lobby to silence the night clerk as well.

It was a messy business, and it netted him nothing. What he learned, however, was that if he was to have any chance at all with John Ross, he would need help of a special sort.

Help of a kind only other demons could supply.

But three days earlier, while he was continuing his search for Ross, something unexpected happened.

That the morph continued to change shape on a regular basis not only provided a way to trace it, but showed that it hadn't settled on a form or been revealed. John Ross had not found the key to unlock its magic. His time was running out. A morph, on average, survived for only thirty days before it began to break up. If Ross was to solve its riddle, he must do so quickly. The odds against his succeeding were enormous. Only on a handful of occasions in the course of history had the servants of either the Word or the Void found a way to unlock the magic.

But then, sometime in the middle of the night three days ago, the gypsy morph had found the shape it wanted. It had not changed since, not once, not even for the briefest moment. Findo Gask had searched the power lines that embraced the earth carefully for any disturbance, and there had been none.

Even more unexpected than the morph's settling into a permanent shape was that it had spoken. A morph lacked a voice. It was energy, pure and simple. But somehow it had communicated, one word only, spoken three times. Undoubtedly, the word had been meant for the ears of John Ross alone, yet it was delivered with such intensity of purpose and need that it snagged on the lines of power that conveyed all the magics of the world and filtered through the ether in a whisper that Findo Gask overheard.

The word was *Nest*.

Findo Gask walked down the hallway of the old Victorian toward the stairs, musing over his good fortune. No other demon had heard, he was certain; no other had his talent and instincts. The find was his alone, and he would be the one to make use of it. John Ross would come to Hopewell because he would draw the same conclusion as Findo Gask. He would come in the hope that Nest Freemark could provide the clue that would unlock the secret of the gypsy morph's magic. He would come to seek help

from someone he trusted and respected. He would come
because he had nowhere else to go.

When he did, Findo Gask would be waiting.

Chapter 6

I've come home.

The words didn't register for a moment, Nest struggling with the idea that it was really Bennett Scott standing in front of her, no longer a little girl, but someone so far removed from the child she remembered she could barely bring herself to accept that such a transition was possible.

'Home?' she echoed in confusion.

Bennett looked embarrassed. 'Yeah, well, I know it's been a long time since I lived here. I should have written or called or something. But you know me. I was never much good at keeping in touch.'

Nest stared at her, still trying to make sense of the fact that she was here at all. 'It's been almost ten years,' she said finally.

Bennett's smile faltered slightly. 'I know. I'm sorry.' She brushed at her lank hair. 'I was hoping it would be all right if I just showed up.'

Her words had taken on a defensive tone, and there was

an unmistakable hint of desperation in her voice. She looked
used and worn, and she did not look well. Nest suddenly felt
the cold and grayness of the day more acutely. The sun had
slipped all the way west, and darkness hung in the bare-
limbed trees like a shroud.

'Of course, it's all right,' she told Bennett softly.

The smile returned. 'I knew it would be. You were always
my big sister, Nest. Even when I was back with Big Momma
and the other kids, moved to that southern Indiana redneck
farming town . . .'

Her voice tightened, and she shivered with more than the
cold.

'Mommy?' the little girl at her side said, tugging on her
sleeve.

Bennett reached down and touched her round cheek.
'Hey, pumpkin, it's okay. This is your Aunt Nest. Nest, this
is my baby girl, Harper.'

Nest came forward and dropped to one knee in front of
the little girl. 'Hello, Harper.'

'Say hello to Aunt Nest, baby,' Bennett encouraged.

The little girl lifted her eyes doubtfully. 'Lo, Neth.'

Bennett picked her up and hugged her close. 'She's kind of
shy at first, but once she gets to know you, she's real friendly.
Talks all the time. She can say a lot of words, can't you,
baby?'

Harper dug her face into her mother's shoulder, entwin-
ing her tiny fists in Bennett's dark hair. 'Appo juss.'

Nest straightened. 'I might have some apple juice in the
fridge. Come on inside.'

Bennett picked up a small satchel sitting to one side and,

still carrying Harper, followed Nest through the back porch door and into the house. Nest took them into the kitchen and sat them down at the table. She accepted a baby cup from Bennett and filled it with apple juice. The baby began to suck the liquid down with steady, hungry gulps.

Nest busied herself with emptying the dishwasher while Bennett bounced Harper gently on one knee. Every so often Nest would glance over, still trying to convince herself that it was really Bennett Scott. Piercings and tattoos aside, the young woman sitting at her kitchen table didn't look anything like the girl she remembered. All of the softness and roundness was gone; everything was sharp and angular. Bennett had been full of life and bright-eyed; she had been a repository of fresh possibilities. Now she looked hollowed out, as if her life had been reduced to harsh truths that boxed her in.

'Would you like something to eat?' she asked impulsively, still worried about the way Bennett looked.

'What have you got?' Bennett Scott asked.

'How about some chicken noodle soup for you and Harper? It's only Campbell's, but it might take the edge off the chill.' She looked over. 'Are you hungry?'

'Sure.' Bennett was looking down at Harper. 'We haven't had anything to eat . . .'

Nest put on a can of chicken noodle soup, made some peanut butter and jelly sandwiches, and peeled an orange. She didn't take any for herself, which was just as well. Harper and Bennett ate everything.

As she watched them eating, Nest found herself recalling how long it had been since she had seen Bennett. Bennett had

lived with her for almost two years while her alcoholic
mother drifted in and out of rehab facilities and struggled to
get her life together. Fifteen years ago, when Nest was fourteen, Enid Scott's boyfriend had beaten her oldest boy,
Nest's close friend Jared, so badly he had almost died. The
result was a court action that stripped Enid of her children
and put them in foster homes. Old Bob was still alive then,
and Nest had begged him to bring little Bennett, who was
only five, home to live with them. Old Bob, perhaps remembering Gran's promise to Enid to do what she could for her,
applied for temporary custody of the little girl, and the
court agreed to give it to him.

It was a hard time in everyone's life. Nest and Bennett had
gone through a traumatic and life-altering experience over a
Fourth of July weekend that saw John Ross come and go
from Hopewell like a one-man wrecking crew. Gran was
dead. Enid was in recovery. All of the Scott children were in
separate homes. Something of what they had survived
brought them closer together. They became like sisters in the
weeks and months that followed, and Nest remembered even
now how happy Bennett had been living with her.

But eventually Enid returned, sufficiently dried out and
stable to reclaim her children from their foster homes. It was
a wrenching ordeal for both Bennett and Nest, and Old Bob
even asked Enid to reconsider moving Bennett back until she
was older. But Enid was determined to reunite her family, and
it was hard to blame a mother for wanting that. Bennett went
home with the others, and after a year's probation, Enid was
allowed to move the children out of state to a small town in
Indiana where a handful of Enid's relatives lived.

There were letters from Bennett at first, but she was only nine, and nine-year-olds don't make it a point to write without encouragement. After a time, the letters stopped coming. Nest continued to write on her own, then tried calling. She found out that Enid was back in detox and the children were living with relatives. She began getting cards from Bennett again. Then the cards stopped for good.

When Old Bob died, Nest lost all track of Bennett Scott. Her own life was consumed with training for the Olympics and the demands of college. The relationship, like so many in her life, just drifted away.

Nest cleared the dishes from in front of Bennett and Harper. The little girl had fallen asleep in her mother's lap, moppet's head buried in a deep crease in the leather jacket. Nest motioned for Bennett to pick Harper up and led the way to one of the spare bedrooms in back. Together, they deposited Harper on the king-size bed, slipped off her shoes and parka, covered her with a blanket, and tiptoed out the door.

'I'll make us some tea,' she advised, placing Bennett back at the kitchen table.

As she boiled water and fished about in the cupboard for some herbal tea bags, she wondered what had happened to Bennett Scott in those ten years gone. Nothing good, she suspected; very little remained of the child Bennett had been when she lived in Hopewell. She looked used and worn and hard. The tattoos and piercings suggested things Nest would rather not think about.

But maybe she was being small-minded and jumping to conclusions; she brushed the thoughts away angrily.

'Is Harper's father traveling with you?' she asked, handing Bennett a cup of the tea and sitting down across from her.

Bennett shook her head. 'It's just Harper and me.'

'Are you meeting him for Christmas?'

'Not unless they decide to let him out of the pen.'

Nest stared.

'Sorry, Nest, that's a lie.' Bennett looked away, shaking her head. 'I tell it all the time. I tell it so often, I get to believing it. Bobby thinks he's the father 'cause I told him so once when I needed money. But he isn't. I don't know who Harper's father is.'

The old clock in the hallway ticked in the ensuing silence. Nest sighed wearily. 'Why didn't you write me to come for you, Bennett?' she said finally. 'I would have.'

Bennett nodded. 'I know that. You were my big sister, Nest. You were the only one who cared about me, except for Jared. He ran off as soon as he turned sixteen. I haven't seen him since. I should have called you when I had the chance. But I wasn't sure. I just wasn't. Big Momma kept telling me that everything was going to be all right, even after she started drinking again and bringing home trash from the bars. And I kept right on believing, because I wanted it to be true.'

She put her teacup down and stared out the window. 'She's dead, you know. Drank herself to death, finally. Five years ago. Pneumonia, they said, but I heard the doctor tell Uncle Timmy that every organ in her body was ruined from her drinking.

'So I did what Jared did. I ran away from home. I lived on the streets, in the parks, on beaches, anywhere I could. I grew up real fast. You can't imagine, Nest. Or if you can, you don't want to. I was alone and scared all the time. The people I was with did things to me you wouldn't do to a dog. I was so hungry I ate out of garbage cans. I was sick a lot. Several times I was in hospitals, then farmed out to foster homes. I always ran away.'

'But not here,' Nest said quietly.

Bennett Scott blew out a short breath and laughed. 'You got a cigarette, Nest?' Nest shook her head. Bennett nodded. 'Didn't think so. World champion runner like you wouldn't smoke, would you? Bet you don't drink, either?'

'Nope.'

'Do any drugs?'

'Why didn't you come here, Bennett?'

Bennett stretched, then slipped out of her leather jacket. She was wearing a sleeveless cotton sweater that hugged her body and retained almost no warmth. Nest got up, took the throw from behind the couch, walked over, and placed it over her shoulders. Bennett pulled it around her without a word, staring down at her teacup on the table.

'I've done a lot of drugs,' she said after a minute, still not looking up. She sipped at the tea. 'I've done just about every drug you could name and a few besides. For a while I was doing them all at once sometimes, just to get away from myself and my crappy life. But the high never lasts; you always come down again, and there you are, the old you, and nothing's changed.'

She looked up now. 'I was sixteen when I was doing all of it at once, but I started a lot earlier.' She shook her head slowly. 'That's why I didn't call you or write you or try to come see you. I didn't want you to see me like that. I didn't want you to know what I'd become. My life was ...' She shrugged.

'It wouldn't have mattered to me, you know,' Nest said.

Bennett shook her head reprovingly. 'Pay attention, Nest. I know it wouldn't have mattered to you. But it would have mattered to me. That's the whole point.' She shivered inside the throw, her slim body hunching down and tightening into stillness. 'When I got pregnant with Harper, I tried to stop using. I couldn't do it. I wanted to stop, I wanted it bad. I knew what my using might do to her, but I couldn't help myself. I tried a couple of programs, but they didn't work out. Nothing worked.'

She brushed back her dark hair. 'When Harper was born, I checked into Hazelden. You've probably heard of it, big drug-rehab program out of Minneapolis. I got into a treatment center for new mothers, something long term. It was better there. We were all women on drugs with children just born or about to be born. I went there because Harper was born clean, and that was a real miracle. My higher power gave me another chance, and I knew I'd be a fool not to take it. I was turning into Big Momma.' She snorted. 'Who am I kidding? I was already there, worse than she ever was. You got any more of that tea, Nest?'

Nest got up and brought over the hot water and fresh tea bags. She poured them both another cup, then sat down again. 'Are you better now?' she asked.

Bennett laughed bitterly. 'Better? No, I'm not better! I'll never ever be better! I'm an addict, and addicts don't get better!'

She glared at Nest angrily, defiantly. Nest waited a moment, then said, 'You know what I mean.'

Bennett's sigh was sad and empty. 'Sorry. I'm not mad at you. Really, I'm not. I'm mad at me. Twenty-four hours a day, seven days a week, all year long, I'm mad at me. Loser me.' She shrugged. 'Anyway, I'm not better. I'm "between treatments" again. I stay good for a while, then I fall off the wagon. Look under *relapse* in the dictionary and you'll find a picture of me. It's pitiful. I don't want it to happen, but I'm just not strong enough to stop it. Each time I go in for help, I think maybe this is the time I'll get off drugs for good. But I can never quite manage it.'

'I guess it's not easy,' Nest said.

Bennett Scott smiled. 'Nope.' She exhaled sharply and set down the tea. 'It wasn't so much of a problem when it was just me. But now there's Harper, and she's almost three, and she hasn't ever seen me clean for more than a few months in a row. First year or so, I got into rehabs where they'd let me keep her with me. Now they won't do that. I don't have many friends so I have to leave her with anyone who will take her.'

She looked down at her hands where they rested on the tabletop. They were cracked and dry, and the nails were dirty. She folded them together self-consciously. 'I just got out again a couple of weeks ago. I don't plan on going back.'

'If you needed to,' Nest said quietly, 'you could leave Harper with me.'

Bennett's eyes lifted. For a moment, she didn't say anything. 'Thanks, Nest. That's nice of you to offer.'

'She would be safe here.'

'I know that.'

Nest looked out the window into the crisp black night. It

was almost five in the afternoon. 'Would you like to stay for dinner?' she asked.

Bennett Scott looked down again at her hands. 'We wouldn't want to be any trouble.'

In those few words, Nest heard a plea so desperate that she knew things were much worse than she believed. Then she remembered the dilapidated satchel Bennett was carrying. It was sitting inside the back door where Bennett had left it. Nest had thought it was just a baby bag, but now she wondered if it might not contain everything they had.

'Maybe you'd like to stay over for the night, too,' she said carefully, feeling her way across this treacherous ground. 'Is someone else expecting you? Are you visiting anyone here?'

Bennett shook her head. 'No. No one.' She was quiet for a long moment, as if she was making up her mind about something, and then she looked up. 'The truth is, Harper and me came here because we don't have anywhere else to go.'

Tears glistened at the corners of her eyes, and she looked down again quickly. Nest reached across the table and put her hand over Bennett's. 'I'm glad you came. You're welcome to stay as long as you need to.'

She rose and walked around the table. 'Come on,' she urged, gently drawing the other to her feet. 'I want you to go in and take a long, hot bath, soak everything out, just let it all go. I'll look after Harper. When you're done, we'll talk some more.'

She walked Bennett into the guest bathroom, helped her out of her clothes, and deposited her in the big claw-foot tub that used to be Gran's. Leaving Bennett to soak, she looked in on Harper, then went back out into the kitchen to clean up. Feeling as she did about herself, it must have taken a strong mix of courage and desperation for Bennett to come back to her after all this time. It made Nest wonder how much of what had happened to her she couldn't bring herself to talk about and was keeping hidden somewhere deep inside.

When she finished the dishes, she began preparing dinner. She put together a tuna and noodle casserole and stuck it in the refrigerator so Bennett could heat it up later on. Nest had agreed to accompany the church youth group as a chaperone while they went caroling to the elderly sick and shut-in, and she would have to leave soon. She would get herself something to eat when she returned.

Finished with her preparations, she stood at the sink and stared out the window at the darkness. The park lay directly in front of her, just across the backyard, but the moon and stars were masked by clouds, so there was little to see. The temperature had dropped to well below freezing, and she doubted that it would snow tonight. When she lifted her hand and placed her fingers against the window glass, the cold pierced her skin like needles.

How did Pick stay warm on a night like this? Did he burrow down in a tree somewhere or was his bark skin impervious to cold? She had never asked him. She must remember to do so.

She thought about the ways in which magic ruled both their lives, its influence pervasive and inexorable. Sometimes she wished she could talk about it with someone, but for the whole of her life there had been only Pick and Gran. Gran had been willing, but Pick regarded talk of magic the same

way he regarded talk about the weather—a pointless exercise.
He would instruct, but he didn't know how to empathize.
Having magic didn't mean the same thing to him that it did
to her. To him, it was a natural condition of who and what
he was. To her, in spite of her heritage, it was an aberration.

The back porch light clicked on at the Peterson house,
and she was reminded of her promise to herself to look in
on them. She walked to the kitchen doorway and listened
down the hall for signs of stirring from Bennett or Harper.
All was quiet, so she went back into the kitchen and set
about baking sugar cookies. Gran had taught her how to
cook when Nest was still a girl, and she had made it a point
to stay in practice even after she was living alone. She baked
all the time for the church and the neighbors. There was
something comforting and satisfying in baking; it always
left her feeling good about herself.

The cookie sheets went into the oven, and the sweet,
doughy smell wafted through the kitchen. She took down the
red and green sprinkles and set them on the counter.
Hawkeye came in through the cat door and padded to his
food bowl, pointedly ignoring her. He ate noisily, tossing
bits of food around as he nosed about his bowl, chewing
each bit loudly. When he was done, he left the way he had
come without so much as a glance in her direction.

Moments later, Harper Scott appeared in the kitchen
doorway, all sleepy-eyed and lost-looking. 'Mommy?' she
asked.

Nest walked over and gathered her up. 'Mommy's taking
a bath, pumpkin. She'll be right out. How would you like a
fresh-baked sugar cookie while you're waiting?'

Great dark eyes regarded her solemnly. A small nod followed. Nest sat her down at the table, poured milk into her baby cup, and went to work on the first batch of cookies, taking them from the oven and off the cookie sheet, stacking them on a plate. She gave one to Harper when it had cooled enough to hold and watched the little girl nibble around the edges as she held the cookie carefully in both hands.

Oh, child, child.

Fifteen years ago, she had saved Bennett Scott's life when the feeders had lured the frightened sleepy child to the top of the bluffs at the turnaround. When Pick and Nest found her, she had been close to walking off the edge of the cliffs. Terrified and confused, the little girl had barely known where she was.

That was a long time ago, Nest thought, watching Harper eat her cookie. Bennett hadn't been much older than her daughter then—just a little girl herself. It was hard to reconcile the grownup with the child. She remembered how Bennett had looked back then and how she had looked an hour earlier when Nest had helped her step into the old bathtub. How had Bennett gotten so far away from herself? Oh, it was easy to rationalize when you factored in drug usage and child abuse. But it was emotionally jarring nevertheless; the memory of who she had been was not easy to dismiss.

By the time Harper was working on the last few bites of her sugar cookie, Bennett reappeared, wrapped in the old terry cloth robe Nest had left for her by the tub. She gave Harper a hug and sat down to share a cookie with her. Her

pale skin looked translucent in the kitchen light, and her
dark eyes were sunken and depthless. Beneath the robe,
needle tracks walked up and down her arms and legs; Nest
had seen them, and the image flashed sharply in her mind.

She smiled at Nest. 'You were right about the bath. I feel
a lot better.'

Nest smiled back. 'Good. Stick Harper in the tub next.
Borrow anything you need in the way of clothes. There's a
casserole in the fridge for dinner; just heat it up. I have to go
out with the church youth group, but I'll be back around
eight or nine.'

She finished up with the cookies, shutting down the oven
and washing up the metal sheets. She glanced at the clock.
Five-fifty. Allen Kruppert and his wife, Kathy, were picking
her up in their big Suburban at six-thirty. She had just
enough time to take a plate of cookies over to the Petersons.

She picked up the phone and called to see if they had
started dinner, which they hadn't.

'I've got to be going,' she called over her shoulder to
Bennett as she finished putting together her cookie offering.
'Don't worry about the phone; the answer machine will pick
up. And don't wait up. You need to get some sleep.'

She went out into the hall to pull on her parka, scarf, and
gloves, then came back for the cookies and whisked them out
the back door.

The cold was hard and brittle against her skin as she
tromped down the porch steps, and she shivered in spite of
herself. The clouds were breaking up, and moonlight illuminated the stark, skeletal limbs of the trees, giving them a
slightly silver sheen. All about her, the darkness was hushed

and still. She blew out a breath of white vapor, tucked her chin into her chest, and hurried across the backyard toward her neighbors' home.

She had gone only a few steps when she saw the feeders. They were gathered at the lower end of her yard, tucked up against the hedgerow in formless clumps, their yellow eyes blinking in the night like fireflies. She slowed and looked at them. She hadn't seen any feeders this close to her home in months. She glanced in either direction from the hedgerow and found others at the edges of the house and garage, shadowy forms creeping stealthily, silently through the cold night.

'Get out of here!' she hissed in a low voice.

A few disappeared. Most simply moved off a bit or shifted position. She glanced around uneasily. There were too many for coincidence. She wondered suddenly if they knew about John Ross, if the prospect of his coming was drawing them.

More likely it was just the stink of the demon who had visited her earlier that was attracting them.

She brushed the matter aside and hurried on across the frosted carpet of the lawn.

She saw nothing of the figure who stood at the top of her walk in the deep shadow of the cedars.

CHAPTER 7

Findo Gask waited for Nest to cross the lawn to the Petersons', then for her to come out again when the big Suburban pulled into her driveway. He stood without moving in the darkness, virtually invisible in his black frock coat and black flat-brimmed hat, his leather-bound book held close against his chest. The night was bitter cold, the damp warmth of the sunny day crystallized to a fine crust that covered the landscape in a silvery sheen and crunched like tiny shells when walked on. Even the blacktop in front of the Freemark house glimmered in the streetlight.

When Nest Freemark climbed inside the Suburban and it backed out of her driveway and disappeared down the street, Findo Gask waited some more. He was patient and careful. He watched his breath cloud the air as it escaped his mouth. A human would have been freezing by now, standing out there for better than an hour. But demons felt little of temperature changes, their bodies shells and not real homes. Most of Findo Gask's human responses had been shed so long ago that he no longer could recall how they made him feel. Heat or cold, pain or pleasure, it was all the same to him.

So he waited, unperturbed by the delay, cocooned within the dark husk to which he had reduced himself years ago, biding his time. It had taken a bit of effort to find out Nest would be gone this evening. He didn't want that effort to be wasted.

He passed the time keeping watch on the house, intrigued by the shadowy movements inside. There were lights on in a few of the rooms, and they revealed an unexpected presence. Nest had left someone at home. The wrinkled old face creased suddenly with smile lines. Who might that someone be?

When everything was silent with the cold and the dark and there was no longer any reasonable possibility that Nest Freemark might be returning for something she had forgotten, Findo Gask left his hiding place and walked up onto the front porch and knocked softly.

The door opened to reveal a young woman wrapped in a terry cloth bathrobe. She was rather small and slender, with lank hair and dark eyes. It was the eyes that caught his attention, filled with pain and disappointment and betrayal, rife with barely concealed anger and unmistakable need. He knew her instantly for what she was, for the life she had led, and for the ways in which he might use her.

She stood looking out through the storm door, making no move to admit him. 'Good evening,' he said, smiling his best human smile. 'I'm Reverend Findo Gask?' He made it a question, so that she would assume she was supposed to be expecting him. 'Is Nest ready to go with me?'

A hint of confusion reflected on her wan face. 'Nest isn't here. She left already.'

Now it was his turn to look confused. He did his best. 'Oh, she did? Someone else picked her up?'

The young woman nodded. 'Fifteen minutes ago. She went caroling with a church group.'

Findo Gask shook his head. 'There must have been a mix-up. Could I use your phone to make a call?'

His hand moved to the storm-door handle, encouraging her to act on his request. But the young woman stayed where she was, arms folded into the robe, eyes fixed on him.

'I can't do that,' she announced flatly. 'This isn't my house. I can't let anybody in.'

'It would take only a moment.'

She shook her head. 'Sorry.'

He felt like reaching through the glass and ripping out her heart, an act of which he was perfectly capable. It wasn't anger or frustration that motivated his thinking; it was the simple fact of her defiance. But the time and place were wrong for acts of violence, so he simply nodded his understanding.

'I'll call from down the road,' he offered smoothly, taking a step back. 'Oh, by the way, did Mr. Ross go with her?'

She pursed her lips. 'Who is Mr. Ross?'

'The gentleman staying with her. Your fellow boarder.'

A child's voice called to her from somewhere out of view, and she glanced over her shoulder. 'I have to go. I don't know Mr. Ross. There isn't anyone else staying here. Good night.'

She closed the door in his face. He stood staring at it for a moment. Apparently Ross still hadn't arrived. He found himself wondering suddenly if he had been wrong in coming to Hopewell, if somehow he had intuited incorrectly. His instincts were seldom mistaken about these things, but perhaps this was one of those times.

He couldn't afford to have that happen.

He turned around and walked back out to the street. The ur'droch joined him after a dozen paces, all shadowy presence and rippling movement at the edges of the light.

'Anything?' he asked.

When the shadow-demon gave no response, he had his answer. It was not unexpected. It wasn't likely Ross was there if the young woman hadn't seen him. Who was she, anyway? Where had she come from? *Another pawn on the board, waiting to be moved into position,* he thought. It would be interesting to see how he might make use of her.

He walked back down the road to where he had left the car parked on the shoulder and climbed inside. The ur'droch slithered in behind him and disappeared onto the floor of the backseat. He would give Ross another three days, until Christmas, before he gave up his vigil. It wasn't time to panic yet. Panic was for lesser demons, for those who relied on attributes other than experience and reasoning to sustain them.

He started the car and wheeled it back onto the roadway. It was time to be getting home so that he could enjoy the little surprise he had prepared for Nest Freemark.

Nest climbed in beside Kathy Kruppert, squeezing her over toward her husband on the Suburban's bench seat. In the back, somewhere between six and nine teens and preteens, two of them Krupperts, jostled and squirmed while trading barbs and gossip. She exchanged hellos with everyone, then leaned back against the padded leather while Allen backed the big Chevy onto Woodlawn and headed for the next pickup.

Her thoughts drifted from John Ross and Findo Gask to Bennett and Harper Scott and back again.

'Everything okay, Nest?' Kathy asked after a few minutes of front-seat silence amidst the backseat chaos. She was a big-boned blond carrying more weight than she wanted, as she was fond of saying, but on her the weight looked good.

Nest nodded. 'Sure, fine.'

'You seem awfully quiet tonight.'

'For a basically noisy person,' Allen added, straight-faced.

Nest gave him a wry grin. 'I'm just saving myself for later, when the singing starts.'

'Oh, is that it?' Allen said, nodding solemnly. He glanced at her over the top of his glasses, beetle-browed and balding. 'You know, Kath, it's always the quiet ones you have to look out for.'

They hit a bump where weather and repeated plowing had hollowed out a section of the roadway. *Ouch! Hey, watch it!* the kids all began yelling at once in back, offering myriad, unnecessary pieces of driving advice.

'Quiet down, you animals!' Allen shouted over his shoulder, giving them a mock glare. When they did, for what must have been a nanosecond, he declared with a smirk, 'Guess I showed them.'

Kathy patted his leg affectionately. 'Father always knows best, honey.'

Allen and Kathy had been married right out of high school, both graduating seniors, six or seven years older than Nest. Allen began working as a salesman with a realty firm and found he had a gift for it. Ten years later, he was running his own business. Ten years earlier, he had approached Nest with an offer for her house at a time when she was seriously considering selling. Even though she had decided against doing so, she had been friends with the Krupperts ever since.

'How are the Petersons?' Kathy asked her suddenly.

'Pretty frail.' Nest dug her hands into her parka pockets with a sigh. The truth was, time was running out on the Petersons. Their health was deteriorating, there was no one to look after them, and nothing anyone said or did could convince them to consider moving into a care facility.

'You do the best you can for them, Nest,' Kathy said.

Allen shifted his weight in the driver's seat and brushed back his thinning black hair. 'They're determined people. You can only do so much to help them. There's no point in fussing about it. They'll go on, just like they have been, until something happens to force them to change their way of life. You have to respect that.'

'I do, but I worry anyway. It's like sitting around waiting for the other shoe to fall.'

'Sure enough,' Kathy agreed with a sigh. 'My uncle Frank was like that.'

'Gran, too,' Nest said.

Allen chuckled. 'Good thing you two understand the problem so well. That way, you won't become part of it later on. That'll sure be a relief to a lot of folks.'

They picked up two more teens from the Moonlight Bay area, then headed back into town for a rendezvous with a vanload of kids driven by Marilyn Winthorn, one of the older ladies who still worked assiduously with the youth groups. From there, they started on their rounds, following a list of names and addresses supplied by Reverend Andrew Carpenter, who had taken over the ministry after Ralph Emery retired three years ago. At each stop, they sang a few carols at the front door, deposited a basket of Christmas goodies supplied by the ladies' guild, exchanged Merry Christmases and Happy New Years, and moved on.

By the twelfth visit, Nest had stopped thinking about anything but how good this was making her feel.

It was sometime around eight-thirty when they pulled into the driveway of an old Victorian home on West Third, an area of fallen grandeur and old money gone elsewhere. The name on the list for this home was smudged, and no one could quite make it out. Hattie or Harriet something. It wasn't a name or address anyone recognized, but it might be a church member's relative. They climbed out of the vehicles, walked to the front entry, and arranged themselves in a semi-circle facing the door.

There were lights on, but no one appeared to greet them. Allen stepped up to the door, knocked loudly, and waited for a response.

'Creepy old place, isn't it?' Kathy Kruppert whispered in Nest's ear.

Nest nodded, thinking that mostly it seemed rather sad, a tombstone to the habitation it had once been. She glanced around as the kids whispered and shuffled their feet, waiting impatiently to begin. It was a neighborhood of tombstones. Everything was dark and silent along the rows of old homes and corridors of ancient trees. Even the street they bracketed was empty.

Someone came to the door now and inched back the curtain covering the glass. A face peeked out, its features vague and shadowy in the gloom.

The door cracked open, and a frail voice said, 'Goodness.'

Taking that as a cue to begin, Allen stepped off the porch, and the youth group began singing 'Joy to the World.' Their voices rang out through the darkness and cold, and their breath clouded the air. The door remained cracked, but no one appeared.

They had begun the refrain, 'Let heaven and nature sing,' when the door burst open with such force that it shattered the glass pane, and a huge, hulking figure stormed through the opening and down the steps. Albino white and hairless, he stood seven feet tall and weighed three hundred pounds, but he moved with such quickness that he was on top of the group almost as quickly as their singing turned to shrieks of fear and shock.

'Joy to the world! Joy to the world! Joy to the world!' the big man shouted tunelessly.

The kids were scattering in every direction as he reached Allen Kruppert, knotted one massive fist into the startled realtor's parka, and snatched him right off his feet. Holding him aloft with one arm extended, he shook Allen like a rag doll, yelling at him in fury.

'Joy to the world! Joy to the world! Joy to the world!'

Fists pressed against her mouth, Kathy Kruppert was

screaming Allen's name. Marilyn Winthorn was herding the kids back toward the vehicles, intent on loading them in as quickly as she could manage, her face tight and bloodless.

Allen was kicking and shouting, but the big man held him firm, continuing to shake him as if he meant to loosen all his bones and empty out his skin.

'Joy to the world! Joy to the world!'

It all happened in seconds, and for the brief length of time it took, Nest Freemark was frozen with indecision. Her first impulse was to use her magic on the big man, the magic that caused people to lose control of their muscles and collapse in useless heaps, that she had used on Danny Abbott and Robert Heppler all those years ago, that she had used on her father.

But if she invoked it now, she risked setting Wraith loose. It was the reality she had lived with since she was nineteen. She could never know what might trigger his release. She had discovered that three years ago at the Olympics, and she had not used her magic since.

Now, it seemed, she had no choice.

She shouted at the big man, striding toward him, small and inconsequential in his shadow. He barely looked at her, but his shaking movement slowed, and he let Allen sag slightly. He was all misshapen, she saw, as if he had not been put together in quite the right way and his parts did not fit as they should, some too large and some too small. He had the look of something formed of castoffs and leftovers, the detritus of the human gene pool.

Nest shouted harder, and now the strange pink eyes fixed on her. Screwing up her courage and tightening her hold on Wraith, who was already awake and pressing for release inside her, she hammered at the big man with her magic, trying to make him take a sudden misstep in her direction, to lose his balance and release Allen. But it was as if she had run into a wall. He shrugged aside her magic as if it weren't even there, and in his eyes she found only an empty, blank space in which nothing human lived.

Nothing human . . .

He tossed Allen aside, and the realtor collapsed in a crumpled heap, head lowered between his shoulders like a broken fighter as he struggled to his hands and knees, Kathy racing over to kneel next to him, tears streaming down her cheeks.

The big man wheeled on Nest. 'Joy to the world! Joy to the world!'

He came at her, and she hit him with another jolt of magic, eyes locked on his. This time he slowed, staggered slightly by the force of her attack. The kids were still scream-ing in the background, some of them calling to her to run, to get away, thinking she was paralyzed with fear and inde-cision. She stood her ground, watching as Kathy tried in vain to pull a battered Allen to his feet.

The big man snarled at her, an animal sound, a deep, throaty growl that brought Wraith right up into her throat, so close to breaking free she could see the tiger striping of his wolfish face and feel the thick, coarse fur of his powerful body. She backed away, trying to keep him in check. If she failed to do so, everyone would discover the truth about her. Whatever else happened, she could not permit that.

'Joy to the world!' the big man howled as he lumbered toward her. 'Joy to the world!'

'Twitch!' a voice shrilled.

The big man stopped as if he had been reined in by invisible wires, jerking upright, his strange, misshapen head lifting like a startled bird's.

'You come right into this house!' the voice ordered. 'You are so bad! I mean it! Right now!'

On the porch stood a solitary figure bundled in a heavy coat and scarf, frizzy red hair sticking out all over. It was the young woman who had introduced herself at church that morning, the one called Penny. At the sound of her voice, the giant slowly turned away and trudged back toward the old house. Nest took a deep, calming breath as the screaming behind her died away into hushed whispers and sobs.

The young woman stood aside as the giant lumbered past her sheepishly and disappeared inside. Then she came down the porch, shaking her head in exasperation.

'Nest, I'm really, really sorry about this.' She came up and took Nest's gloved hand in her own and held it. 'That's my brother. He isn't right in the head. He doesn't mean any harm, but he doesn't know how strong he is.'

She looked over at Allen, who was finally climbing back to his feet. 'Are you all right, mister? Did he hurt you at all?'

Allen Kruppert looked as if he had just climbed out of a working cement mixer. He tried to speak, coughed hard, and shook his head.

'I think he's okay,' Kathy offered quietly, bracing him against her with both arms wrapped tightly about his bulky form. 'That was a very scary thing your brother did, miss.'

Penny nodded quickly in agreement. 'I know. I should

have been watching him more closely, but I was upstairs working. My grandmother answered the door, but she is so old and feeble she can't do anything with him. He just pushed her aside and came out.' She looked quickly from Nest to the Krupperts. 'He just wanted to play. That's what he thought all this was about. Playing.'

Nest gave her a brief, uncertain smile. She had the oddest queasy feeling. Penny seemed sincere in her apology, but there was just a hint of something in her voice that suggested maybe she wasn't.

Nest glanced up at the house. 'Do you live here, Penny?' she asked conversationally.

'Sometimes.' Penny's red hair gave her the look of something that had shorted out. Her green eyes glittered. 'Right now I'm just visiting.'

'With your brother?'

'Yeah. With Twitch. We call him Twitch.'

'Is it your grandmother who belongs to the church?'

Penny shrugged. 'I suppose.'

'What is your grandmother's name?'

Penny smiled. 'I better get back inside, Nest. I don't like leaving Twitch alone after an episode. You know how it is. Thanks for coming by with the church group, though. It was really nice of you.'

She walked back up the steps and through the broken door, closing the windowless frame carefully behind her. Nest watched until she was gone, then gave the windows a casual sweep as she swung back toward the others.

The interior of the house had gone completely dark.

*　*　*

She helped Kathy get Allen back in the Suburban, settling him into the passenger seat and buckling him in. He
insisted he was all right, and it seemed he was. The youth
group was noticeably subdued, and there was talk of calling
it a night. But Allen wouldn't hear of it. There were four
more names on the list, including the Northway Nursing
Home. All those people were counting on them. Allen wasn't
the sort to let anyone be disappointed on account of him.
He insisted they finish what they started.

It was nearing ten o'clock when Nest finally got home.
Everyone else, Allen included, seemed to have put the incident on West Third behind them, but she was still uneasy
about it. Two encounters in one day with Penny Whoever-
she-was seemed a bit of a stretch for coincidence and two
encounters too many in any case. The whole business troubled her, particularly since it had forced her to confront
anew what it meant to employ her magic as a weapon. It was
something she had hoped never to have to do again.
Tonight's incident suggested her thinking was incredibly
naive.

She walked up the drive and slipped in through the back
door. There were lights on, but the house was quiet.
Hawkeye was curled up on his chair in the kitchen, the one
he had adopted for this week anyway, and he did not even
open his eyes as she passed through. She left her coat, scarf,
and gloves in the hall closet and eased down the hall to the
den, where the television was playing. Bennett was dozing in
her grandfather's big leather easy chair.

She opened her eyes as Nest entered. 'Hi,' she murmured.

'Hi,' Nest replied, sitting at the desk chair. 'Harper asleep?'

Bennett stretched and yawned. 'About an hour ago. She was pretty worn out.' She stood up. 'Me, too. I'm going to bed. Did Reverend Gask ever catch up with you? He was here earlier.'

Nest went cold, her whole body stiffening. She had forgotten to warn Bennett about Gask. But then, what could she have said? 'No, he must have missed me.'

'He said he was here to pick you up. He wanted to come in, but I told him I couldn't let anyone in someone else's house. I hope that was all right.'

Nest responded to the wave of relief that washed through her by giving the other a big hug. 'You did good.'

'Thanks.' Bennett trundled toward the door. 'Oh, I almost forgot. He was looking for someone named John Ross, too. Said he thought he was staying here, but I told him I didn't think so.'

'You told him right,' Nest assured her, growing angry again with Gask. 'Go on to bed. I'll see you in the morning.'

Alone, she sat thinking anew of John Ross and Findo Gask and what their conflict meant. Gask was not going to give up. He would keep coming around until he found Ross and whatever it was that he thought Ross was hiding from him. Demons are persistent. Time means nothing to them; they operate on a schedule as foreign to humans as life on Mars. She had dealt with demons half her life, and she had a pretty good idea what she was in for.

She got up and turned off the television, then sat down again, staring out the window into the darkness. At times like this, she wished Gran was still alive. Gran, with her no-nonsense approach to life's problems and her experience with the ways of demons and forest creatures, would know better than she how to deal with this mess. Gran might have some thoughts about what to do with Bennett and Harper, too. Nest would have to try her best to think like Gran and hope that would be enough to see her through.

After a time, she went out into the kitchen and made herself some dinner. She ate a small portion of the leftover tuna and noodle casserole and drank a glass of milk, sitting at the kitchen table, listening to the ticking of the clock and to the whisper of her scattered thoughts. It wasn't as if John Ross wouldn't show, she realized. Too much of what Gask had told her suggested he would. The problem was what to do about him when he did. Or, more specifically, what to do about the fact that he was coming to find her, which was really the only reason he would come back.

She shook her head at the idea. So much time had passed with no contact between them. What would bring him to her now? What did he need?

Surrounded by memories of her past, of a childhood and girlhood linked inextricably to him, she searched in vain for an answer.

She was still awake at midnight when the knock on the front door came. She had turned off most of the lights and moved to the living room. She was sitting there in the dark, staring out the window once more, her thoughts drifting through the frosty landscape of the park. She was not sleepy, her mind spinning out possibilities that might explain the day's events, her magic alive and singing in her blood with strange energy. Sitting there, working her way through the past to conjecture on the future, she found herself wanting to do what Gran had done as a girl, to go out into the park and run with the feeders who lived there, wild and uninhibited and free. It was a strange feeling, and she was mildly shocked by the idea that after all she had gone through to escape her grandmother's past, she was still somehow drawn to it.

The knock brought her to her feet and scattered her thoughts. There was never any doubt in her mind as to who it was. She walked quickly through the darkness of the living room to the hallway, where a solitary light glimmered weakly from farther down the corridor. The porch light was on as well, but she never even bothered to look out the peephole. She knew who it was. She knew who it had to be. She simply opened the door to confirm it, and there he was.

'Hello, Nest,' he said.

He stood in the halo of the porch light, clear-eyed and expectant, looking younger and fitter than when she had seen him last in Seattle, ten years ago. She was astonished at the transformation, and immediately suspicious of what it meant.

A small, slender boy of maybe four or five years stood at his side, honey-colored hair tousled and shaggy, blue eyes bright and inquisitive. He stared at her with such intensity that she was momentarily taken aback.

She looked from the boy to Ross, and for just a moment Findo Gask's dark warning whispered from the closet in the back of her mind to which she had consigned it. She stood at the edge of a precipice, and she could feel a tremendous mix of attraction and repulsion roiling within her. Whichever way she turned, whatever choice she made, her life would never be the same again.

She cracked the storm door wide open. 'Come on inside, John.' She gave him a warm smile. 'I've been expecting you.'

Monday,

December 22

CHAPTER 8

After he awoke from the dream of the Knight on the cross, John Ross began his search for the gypsy morph.

It wasn't so much the Knight's words of advice that guided him in his efforts. He had forgotten those almost immediately, shards of sound buried in the wave of emotion he experienced on seeing that the Knight bore his own face. But in the Knight's eyes, in eyes that were undeniably his own, he found a road map he would never forget. In a moment's time, that map became indelibly imprinted on his consciousness. All the Knight's memories of where and how the gypsy morph could be found were made his. To recall them, to remember what they showed, he need only look inside himself.

It was early summer when he set out, the weather still mild almost everywhere. In Pennsylvania, where he began his journey, the air smelled of new grass and leaves, the green beginnings of June fresh and pungent. By the time he reached the west coast, the July heat had settled in, all scorched air and damp heat, thick and barely breathable, an ocean of suspended condensation bearing down with suffocating determination. On the colored weather charts that appeared in *USA Today*, seven-eighths of the country was shaded in deep reds and oranges.

The sole exception was the Pacific Northwest, where Ross had gone to await the morph's coming. In Oregon, where he would make his preparations, the heat was driven inland by the breezes off the ocean, and the coastal bluffs and forests west of the Cascades stayed green and cool. Like a haven, the windward side of the mountains gave shelter against the burning temperatures that saturated everything leeward to the Atlantic, and the coast was like a world apart.

John Ross knew what he had to do. The crucified Knight's memories of what was needed were clear and certain. He could not tell if the dream had shown him his own fate, if he was the Knight on the cross and he had witnessed his own death. He could not know if by being told of the morph he was being given a second chance at changing his own life. To accept that his dream had allowed him to step outside himself completely in bearing witness to the future he was working so hard to prevent, he must conclude that there was an extraordinary reason for such a thing to happen because it had never happened before.

It was easier to believe that seeing his own face on the crucified Knight of the Word was a trick of his imagination, a deception wrought by his fear that he would fail as this other Knight had failed and come to a similar end. It was not difficult to believe. The odds against his successfully capturing and exploiting a gypsy morph were enormous. It had been done only a handful of times in all of history. The methods employed and the differing results had never been documented. There was no standard procedure for this. But if necessity was the mother of invention, John Ross would find a way.

The stories of gypsy morphs were the stuff of legends. Ross had heard tales of the morphs during the twenty-five-odd years he had served the Word. Mostly they were whispered in awe by forest creatures, stories passed down from generation to generation. When the consequences of an intervening magic were particularly striking, either for good or evil, it was always suggested that it might have been due to the presence of a morph. No one living, as far as Ross could tell, had ever seen one. No one knew what they looked like at the moment of their inception. No one knew what they would turn out to be because no two had ever turned out the same. There were rumors of what they might become, but no hard evidence. One, it was said, had become an antibiotic. Another had become a plague. Gypsy morphs were enigmas; he had to be able to accept that going in.

What John Ross knew for sure when he went to Oregon was that whoever gained control over a gypsy morph acquired the potential to change the future in a way no one else could. It was a goal worth pursuing, even knowing it was also virtually impossible to achieve. He had little working for him, but more than enough to know where to begin. The crucified Knight's memories had told him the morph would appear in a low-tide coastal cave on the upper coast of Oregon near the town of Cannon Beach three days after

Thanksgiving. In those memories he found a picture of the cave and the landscape surrounding it, so he knew what to look for.

What his dream of the crucified Knight had revealed to him was not so different from what his dreams usually told him—a time and a place and an event he might alter by his intervention. But usually he knew the details of the event, the course it had taken, and the reason things had gone amiss. None of that was known to him here. He did not know the form the gypsy morph would take when it came into being. He did not know how to capture it. He did not know what would happen afterward, either to the morph or to himself.

It was reassuring in one sense to have it so. Not knowing suggested he was someone other than the Knight on the cross, their resemblance notwithstanding. But it was odd, too, that the Knight's memories ceased with the moment of the morph's appearance, as if the slate afterward had been wiped clean or never come into being. Clearly the Knight felt he had failed in his attempt to secure the morph's magic and unlock its secret. Was this because he had failed even to capture the morph? Or was it because he was hiding the truth of what had happened afterward, not wanting Ross to see? There was no way for Ross to know, and speculation on the matter yielded nothing.

Cannon Beach was a small, charming oceanfront town a little more than an hour directly west of Portland. Bustling with activity generated by the annual appearance of summer vacationers, the town's shops and residences were clustered along a bypass that looped down off Highway 101 to run parallel to the edge of the ocean for about three miles. A second, smaller town, called Tolovana Park, which was really less town and more wide spot in the road, occupied the southernmost end of the loop. Together the two communities linked dozens of inns, hotels, bed-and-breakfasts, and vacation cottages through a tangle of shingle-shake and wood-beam restaurants and fast-food emporiums, souvenir and craft shops, art galleries, and clothing stores. There was a theater, a bakery, two wine shops, a gas station, a general store, a post office, and a whole clutch of real estate agencies. To its credit, Cannon Beach seemed to have resisted the pervasive onslaught of name-brand chains that had invaded virtually every other vacation spot in the country, so that the familiar garish signs touting burgers and tacos and chicken and the like were all blessedly missing.

Ross arrived on a Sunday, having caught a ride west out of Portland with a trucker hauling parts for one of the lumber mills. He was dropped five miles inland and walked the rest of the way to the coast on a sunny, pleasant afternoon. It was still light when he arrived. Cannon Beach was so busy that Ross judged it impossible to differentiate Sunday from any other day of the week. Vacationers thronged the streets, pressing in and out of the shops, eating ice cream and chewing fudge, with shopping bags, small children, and dogs in hand.

Carrying his duffel and his backpack, he limped down the sidewalk with the aid of his black walking stick, the sun glinting off its bright surface and etching out in shadowed nuance the rune carvings that marked its otherwise smooth surface. He looked a transient, and the impression was not far from wrong. He was not indigent or bereft of hope or purpose, but he was homeless and rootless, a citizen of the world. He had lived this way for twenty-five years, and he had become used to it. His service to the Word required that he travel constantly, that he be able to respond to his dreams by moving to wherever they directed him, that when he had finished acting on them he be prepared to move again. It was a strange, wearing existence, and if he did not believe so strongly in the work he was doing, it would have quickly done him in.

Once, ten years earlier, he had lost his faith and given up on himself. He had settled in one place and tried to make a life as other men do. He had failed at that. His past had caught up with him, as he now understood it always would, and he had gone back to being what he now understood he must always be.

Thoughts of that past and this present drifted through his mind as he walked the business district of Cannon Beach. Hemlock, its main north-south street, was the center of almost everything of note, and he did not deviate from its path in the forty minutes his walk required. He was looking for a beginning, as he always did. Sometimes when he was in a larger city, he would simply take a room at a YMCA and go from there. That approach would not do in a vacation town or in the circumstances of his present endeavor. He would be in Cannon Beach until close to the end of November. He needed more than just a six- or seven-day room at the Y.

He found what he was looking for more quickly than he had expected. A small, hand-lettered sign in the window of the Cannon Beach Bookstore, which was located at the south end of Hemlock where the shops and galleries began to peter out, read HELP WANTED. Ross went into the store and asked what sort of help they were looking for. The manager, a sallow-faced, pleasant man of fifty named Harold Parks, told him they were looking for summer sales help. Ross said he would like to apply.

'That's summer sales, Mr. Ross,' Harold Parks said pointedly. 'It doesn't extend beyond, oh, maybe mid-September. And it's only thirty, thirty-five hours a week.' He frowned at Ross through his beard. 'And it only pays seven-fifty an hour.'

'That suits my purposes,' Ross replied.

But Parks was still skeptical. Why would John Ross want a job for only two months? What was his background concerning books and sales? How had he found out about the position?

Ross was ready with his answers, having been through this many times before. He was a professor of English literature, currently on leave so that he could try his hand at writing his own work of fiction, a thriller. He had decided to set it on the Oregon coast, and he had come to Cannon Beach to do the necessary research and to begin writing. He needed a job to pay expenses, but not one that would take up too much of his time. He admitted to having almost no sales experience, but he knew books. He gave Parks a small demonstration, and asked again about the job.

Parks hired him on the spot.

When asked about lodging, Parks made a few calls and found Ross a room with an elderly lady who used to work at the store and now supplemented her own small retirement income with rent from an occasional boarder. At present, both rented rooms were open, and Ross could have his pick.

So, by Sunday evening he had both living quarters and a job, and he was ready to begin his search for the gypsy morph—or, more particularly, for the place the morph would appear just after Thanksgiving. He knew it was somewhere close by and that it was a cave the elements and time's passage had hollowed into the side of the bluffs that ran along the ocean beaches. He knew the cave was flooded at high tide. He knew what the cave looked like inside and a little of what it looked like from without.

But the beaches of the Oregon coast ran all the way from Astoria to the border of California in an unbroken ribbon of sand, and there were thousands of caves to explore. For the most part, the caves lacked identifiable names, and in any case, he didn't know the name of the one he was searching for. He believed he would have to walk the coast for a dozen miles or so in either direction to find the right one.

He began his search during his off hours by walking north to Seaside and south to Arch Cape. He did so during low tide and daylight, so his window of opportunity was narrowed considerably. It took him all of July and much of August to complete his trek. When he was done, he had nothing to show for it. He had not found the cave.

His progress as a bookseller was meeting with better results. He had a gift for selling, and since he was familiar with and a believer in the value of his product, he was able to impress Harold Parks with his effort. His landlady, Mrs. Staples, liked him well enough to give him the run of the house, including the use of her own refrigerator, and she came to visit him frequently at work, always insisting that Mr. Ross be the one to help with her buying selections.

It was Mrs. Staples who suggested he talk with Anson Robbington.

By now it was nearing September, and he was beginning to be concerned about his lack of success. He had not found the cave in which the gypsy morph would appear, and he still had no idea what the morph would look like or how he would capture it. He had not asked for help from anyone, thinking that he could manage the search on his own and not involve others. When it became clear his plan was not working, he then had to decide how to ask for the help he needed without revealing what he was really up to.

So he mentioned to a few carefully chosen people, rather casually, that he was looking for someone to talk to who knew the Oregon coast around Cannon Beach.

'The man you want,' Mrs. Staples advised at once, 'is Anson Robbington. He's explored every inch of the coastline from Astoria to Lincoln City at one time or another in his life. If there's something you want to know, he's the one who can tell you.'

Ross found Robbington two mornings later holding down the fort at Duane Johnson Realty, where he worked part-time as a salesman. He was big and weathered and bearded, and he dressed like the prototypical Northwest iconoclast. He was slow talking and slow moving, and he seemed lost in his own thoughts during much of their conversation, rather as if he were busy with something else entirely and could give Ross only a small portion of his time and attention.

Ross approached his inquiry in a circumspect manner, asking a few general questions about the geological

underpinnings of the bluffs, offering a short synopsis of
his imaginary book's premise, then detailing, as if it were his
personal vision for his writing, a description of the cave he
was thinking of including.

'Oh, sure,' Robbington said after a long pause, gray eyes
wandering back from whatever country they'd been viewing.
'I know one just like it. Just like you described.' He nodded
for emphasis, then went away again for a bit, leaving Ross to
cool his heels. 'Tell you what,' he began anew when he
returned, 'I'll take you out there myself Monday morning.
Can you get some time off?'

The bright, sunny Monday morning that followed found
them driving south along the coast in Robbington's rackety
old Ford pickup, motoring out of Cannon Beach, past
Tolovana Park, the turnoff to Arcadia Beach, and onward
toward Arch Cape. The cave he was thinking of, Anson
Robbington advised, lay just below Arch Cape on the other
side of the tunnel, cut into the very rock that the tunnel bur-
rowed through. It was six o'clock in the morning, and the
tide was out. At other times, when the tide was either coming
in, all the way in, or going out, you wouldn't know the cave
was even there.

When they reached their destination, they parked the
truck, climbed out, and worked their way along the bluff
edge to a narrow trail, so hidden in underbrush it was invisible until they were right on top of it. The trail led
downward toward the beach, winding back and forth amid
outcroppings and ledges, switchbacking in and out of pre-
cipitous drops and deep ravines. It took them almost fifteen
minutes to get down, mostly because of the circuitous route.

Robbington admitted they could have gone farther down the beach to an easier descent and then walked back, but he thought Ross ought to experience something of the feel of bluffs if he was going to be writing about their features. Ross, making his way carefully behind the old man, his bad leg aching from the effort, held his tongue.

When they reached the cave, Ross knew immediately it was the one he was looking for. It was cut sideways into the rock where the bluff formed a horseshoe whose opening was littered with old tree trunks, boulders, and broken shells. It was farther south by less than a half mile from where Ross had given up his own search, but he might not have found it even if he had kept on, so deep in shadow and scrub did it lie. You had to get back inside the horseshoe to see that it was there, warded by weather-grayed cedar and spruce in various stages of collapse, the slope supporting them slowly giving way to the erosion of the tides. It bore all the little exterior landmarks he was looking for, and it felt as it had in the eyes of the crucified Knight of the Word.

They went inside with flashlights, easing through a split in the rock that opened into a cavern of considerable size and several chambers. The air and rock were chill and damp and smelled of dead fish and the sea. Tree roots hung from the ceiling like old lace, and water dripped in slow, steady rhythms. The floor of the cave rose as they worked their way deeper in, forming a low shelf where the rock had split apart in some cataclysmic upheaval thousands of years ago. On the right wall of the chamber into which the shelf disappeared, a strange marking that resembled a bull's head had been drawn over time by nature's deft hand.

Ross felt a wave of relief wash through him at the discovery. The rest, he felt, would come more easily now.

He explored the cave with Robbington for twenty or thirty minutes, not needing to, but wishing to convince his guide that he was working on descriptive material for the book. When they departed, they walked the beach south to a more gentle climb, and then returned along the shoulder of the highway to where they had left the pickup.

As they climbed into the cab, Ross thanked Anson Robbington and promised he would make mention of him in the book when it was published. Robbington seemed content with the fact that he had been of help.

John Ross worked in the bookstore that afternoon, and that night he treated himself and Mrs. Staples to dinner out. He was feeling so good about himself that he was able to put aside his misgivings and doubts long enough to enjoy a moment of self-congratulation. It was little enough compensation for the agonizing burden of his life. All the while he had been engaged in this endeavor, his dark dreams of the future had continued to assail him on a regular basis. Once or twice, they had shown him things he might otherwise have acted upon, but he had not, for fear of jeopardizing his search for the morph. It was difficult to ignore the horror of the future he lived each night in his dreams, and his first impulse each morning on waking was to try to do something about what he had witnessed. But there was only so much he could do with his life, only so much one man could accomplish, even as a Knight of the Word, even with the magic he could summon. He must make his choices, stand his ground, and live with the consequences.

In the days that followed, he returned to the cave many times, seeking something more that would help him when the gypsy morph finally appeared. He studied the configuration and makeup of the walls, of the separate chambers, of the entry. He tried to figure out what he might do to trap something found in that cave. He did his best to imagine in what way he might win over the creature he would snare so that it might trust him enough to reveal itself.

It was a hopeless task, and by the close of September, he was no closer to finding answers to his questions than he had been on waking from his dream. He had thought he might have the dream again, that he might see once more the Knight on the cross and be given further insight into what he must do. But the dream never returned.

He was beginning to despair when, on a dark still night as he thrashed awake from a particularly bad dream of the future, a tatterdemalion appeared to him, sent by the Lady, and summoned him to Wales.

CHAPTER 9

John Ross paused in his narrative and took a long, slow drink of his coffee. His gaze drifted to the curtained windows, where the sunrise burned with a golden shimmer through the bright, hard, cold December dawn.

Nest Freemark sat across from him at the kitchen table, her clear, penetrating gaze fixed on him, assessing his tale, measuring it for the consequences it would produce. She looked pretty much as he remembered her, but more self-assured, as if she had become better able to cope with the life she had been given. He admired the calm acceptance she had displayed the night before on finding him on her doorstep after ten long years, taking him in, asking no questions, offering no conditions, simply giving him a room and telling him to get some sleep. She was strong in ways that most people weren't, that most couldn't even begin to approach.

'So you went to Wales,' she prodded, ruffling her thick, curly hair.

He nodded. 'I went.'

Her eyes never left his face. 'What did you learn there?'

'That I was up against more than I had bargained for.' He smiled ruefully and arched one eyebrow. 'It works out that way more often than not. You'd think I'd learn.'

The big house was quiet, the ticking of the old grandfather clock clearly audible in the silences between exchanges of conversation. The sun was just appearing, and darkness cloaked the corners and nooks with layered shadows. Outside, the birds were just waking up. No car tires crunched on the frosted road. No voices greeted the morning.

The boy who had come with him to Nest Freemark—the boy the gypsy morph had become only a handful of days ago—knelt backward on the living room couch, chin resting on folded arms as he leaned against the couch back and stared out the window into the park.

'Is he all right?' Nest asked softly.

Ross shook his head. 'I wish I knew. I wish I could tell. Something. Anything. At least he's quit changing shapes. But I don't have a clue about what he's doing or why.'

Nest shifted in her high-backed wooden chair, adjusting her robe. 'Didn't the Lady give you any insight into this?'

'She told me a little of what to expect.' He paused, remembering. 'She gave me a kind of netting, so light and soft it was like holding a spiderweb. It was to be used to capture the morph when it appeared in the cave after Thanksgiving.'

He cleared his throat softly. 'She told me how the morph was formed, that it was all wild magic come together in shards to form a whole. It doesn't happen often, as I've said. Very rare. But when it does, the joining is so powerful it can become almost anything. I asked her what. A cure or a plague, she said. You could never tell; it was different each time and would seek its own shape and form. She wouldn't elaborate beyond that. She said wild magic of this sort was so rare and unstable that it only held together for a short time before breaking up again. If it could find a form that suited it, it would survive longer and become a force in the war between the Word and the Void. If not, it would dissipate and go back into the ether.'

He twisted his coffee cup on its saucer, eyes dropping momentarily. 'The gypsy morph is not a creation of the Word, as most other things are, but a consequence of other creations. It comes into being because the world is the way it is, with its various magics and the consequences of using them. The Word didn't foresee the possibility of the morph, so it hasn't got a handle on its schematic yet. Even the Word is still learning, it seems.'

Nest nodded. 'Makes sense. There are always unforeseen consequences in life. Why not for the Word as well as for us?'

Hawkeye wandered in from outside, trudged through the hallway and into the kitchen for a quick look around, then moved on to the living room. Without pausing, he jumped onto the couch next to the boy and began to rub against him. The boy, without looking, reached down absently and stroked the cat.

'I've never seen Hawkeye do that with anyone,' Nest said quietly. Ross smiled faintly, and her gaze shifted back to him. 'So, she gave you a net?'

He nodded. 'When the gypsy morph appeared for the first time, she told me, it would materialize in a shimmer of lights, a kind of collection of glowing motes. As soon as that happened, I was to throw the net. The light would attract it, and the net would close about it all on its own, sealing it in. Immediately, she warned, the morph would begin to change form. When it did, I was to get out of there as quickly as possible because the expenditure of magic that resulted from the morph's changes would attract demons from everywhere.'

'And did it?'

He lifted the coffee cup from its saucer and held it suspended before him.

*H*e remembered how it had begun, his words as he spoke them recalling the moment. He had gone to the cave at sunrise on the day of the event, having rehearsed his role many times, having explored the grotto and its surroundings so thoroughly he could detail everything with his eyes closed. It was bitter cold and damp that day, the rains of the past two having ceased sometime during the night, leaving the chill and the wet to linger in the earth and air. Mist clung to the edges of the beach and the surface of the water in a thick, impenetrable curtain. Clumps of it had broken away from the main body and wandered inland to hunker down among the trees and rocks like fugitives in hiding. The ocean surf, calm this windless morning, rolled in a steady, monotonous *whoosh* onto the beach, advancing and receding, over and over in hypnotic motion. Gulls screamed their strange, challenging cries as they flew in search of food, smooth and bright against the gray.

He had once again borrowed Mrs. Staples's Chevy. It had carried him back and forth to the cavern often enough over the past three months that it probably could find the way on its own. Leaving it on the shoulder of the road where the beach access was easiest, he descended through the mist and gray and damp, a solitary hunter in the dim dawn light, and made his way back along the broad, sandy expanse to his destination.

Inside, it was dark enough that he was required to use his flashlight to find his way to the rock shelf, where he began his vigil. He did not know exactly how long he would have to wait, only that the morph would appear this day before sunset. Besides his flashlight and the spiderweb netting given to him by the Lady, he carried a blanket and a small basket of food and drink. The dead Knight's memories carried with them a clear image of where the morph would appear, and so Ross knew how to position himself.

After a time, he began to see the feeders. There were only a couple at first, then a couple more, then half a dozen, all of them hanging back in the darkened corners and nooks, eyes glinting as they kept watch. Ross was not surprised to see them; feeders were always watching him, drawn by his magic, waiting in anticipation of its expenditure. He could not think of a time when there hadn't been feeders close by, so he thought nothing of seeing them now.

But as midmorning crawled toward noon, their numbers increased, and soon there were so many he could not begin to count them. They sensed that something unusual was going to happen. Perhaps they even sensed what it was. But so many gathered in one place was not a good thing. Other creatures of magic would sense their presence and be drawn as well.

Ross rose and stalked from one end of the cave to the other, chasing the feeders back into the darkness. Their eyes winked out, then reappeared in the wake of his passing. Light from the midday sun, hazy and weak, brightened the entrance to the cave through the leafy curtain of tree branches and scrub. He peered out cautiously at the beach, open and flat and empty. There was no sign of life beyond the gulls. The ocean rolled in a low smooth surf of white noise.

At midday, he ate his lunch and drank a bottle of water, growing increasingly uneasy with the long wait. The number of feeders was now immense, and people were beginning to appear on the beach, strolling, walking dogs, playing with children, all of them passing by without stopping or even pausing, but all of them worrisome nevertheless. He knew now from the crush of feeders and his own heightened sense of a foreign magic's presence that the morph was going to appear. Wild magic was present, careening through the ether in waves that shocked his conscience and sharpened his instincts.

He was on his feet, the netting in hand, his parka cast aside, when the magic finally came together. It did so in a rush of wind and sound that brought him to his knees as it tore through the rock chamber with ferocious purpose. Damp spray flew into his face, and the eyes of the feeders gleamed and closed. Hunching his shoulders, he squinted at the movement he saw materializing above the shelf of rock, a darkness at first, then a slow brightening. It was happening! He crept forward amid the sound and fury, the gossamer netting clutched tightly to his chest. The wind alone would rip it to shreds, he feared. But it was all he had and what the Lady had given him to use.

The brightening grew more intense, a kind of wash in the air that slowly began to coalesce. Motes appeared, whirling through the shimmering haze, taking incandescent form against the backdrop of shadows and gloom. Ross was on his feet, ignoring the deep whistle of the wind, the spray of dampness, and the thrust of movement from the magic's gathering. He must be ready when the moment came, he knew. He must not falter.

When the dancing motes tightened suddenly, beginning to take form in the air before him, he cast the net. It billowed in the wind as if it had become a sail, taking shape as it flew through the darkness to close about the gathering light.

Instantly, the wind died away and the light went out. An abrupt, blanketing silence descended over everything. John Ross stood frozen in place, his ears still ringing and his shoulders hunched, his eyes trying to readjust to the sudden change in light. He breathed slowly and deeply, listening, watching, and waiting.

Then the eyes of the feeders began to reappear, lantern bright against the gloom in which they crouched. Outside, the screams of gulls and the roll of the surf could be heard. He edged forward on the rock shelf, feeling his way over the smooth, cold, wet rock. He did not want to turn on the flashlight, afraid of the reaction the light might bring.

He found the netting with its prize nestled in a hollow at the center of the shelf. The netting was opaque and still until he touched it, and then its captive moved and light emanated from within. He picked it up and carried it to the cave's entrance, where the dim sunlight fell upon and revealed it.

The netting was changing shape with such rapidity that he could barely follow what was happening. It squirmed and shook and twitched, and with each movement, a small amount of light escaped.

A quick check of the beach outside the cave revealed it was momentarily deserted. Clutching the netting and its writhing contents to his chest, he started back down the beach at a rapid walk.

He had almost reached his car when the first demon appeared.

A young woman and a little girl appeared suddenly in the kitchen doorway, and John Ross went silent. The young woman was thin and worn looking, and she had the look of someone with problems sleep alone could not solve. Her dark eyes fixed boldly on Ross and stayed there, assessing him, reading him, seeing him in some secret way.

Nest, her back to the entry, turned in her chair. 'Good morning,' she said, smiling at them. 'Did you sleep well?'

The young woman nodded, her dark, intense eyes still on Ross. 'Did we miss breakfast?'

'No, we were waiting for you.' Nest glanced at Ross. 'This is John Ross. John, this is Bennett Scott and her daughter, Harper.'

Ross nodded. 'Nice to meet you.'

'Nice to meet you,' Bennett Scott replied, but looked doubtful about it. 'Guess you got in late.'

'After midnight sometime.'

'Is that your son?' She gestured toward the living room,

where the boy who was the gypsy morph kneeled on the sofa and stared into the park.

Ross hesitated, not sure what to say. 'Yes.'

'What's his name?'

Ross glanced at Nest. 'John Junior. We call him Little John.'

'Little John,' Bennett repeated thoughtfully.

'Kind of corny, I guess.' Ross gave her a rueful smile.

'Appo juss,' Harper said softly, tugging on her mother's hand.

Nest rose to retrieve the container from the refrigerator and pour some into one of the sealed cups the little girl drank from, leaving Ross to deal with Bennett, who continued to stare boldly at him.

'How old is Little John?' she asked casually, but there was an edge to her voice.

'Four years and two months.' Ross held the smile. 'We're just visiting for a few days, and then we'll be on our way.'

Bennett Scott pursed her lips. 'There was a minister here last night looking for you. Findo Gask. Odd name. I told him I didn't know you. But now I kind of think maybe I do.'

He shook his head, holding her gaze. 'I don't think so.'

She brushed at her lank hair, then folded her arms under her breasts. 'Nest doesn't seem to think much of this minister. I guess I don't either. He was kind of pushy.'

Ross stood up slowly, levering himself to his feet by leaning on the tabletop. 'I'm sorry if he caused you any trouble, Miss Scott. I don't know who this man is or what he wants.' *But I can guess,* he thought to himself.

The young woman pointed at him suddenly. 'I do know

who you are. I remember now. You were here, oh, fifteen years ago or so. I was just a little girl. You came to see Nest's grandparents. You knew her mother, didn't you?'

His throat tightened. 'Yes. That was a long time ago.'

'Sit down,' she urged, concern mirrored in her dark eyes. Her hands gestured, and he did as she asked. 'I shouldn't expect you to remember me after all that time. I guess I wasn't sure where . . .'

She trailed off, looking around quickly for Harper, who was sucking on her juice cup. 'Are you hungry, sweetie?'

Harper's eyes were on the boy in the living room. 'Boy,' she said, not seeming to hear her mother. She trundled past Bennett into the living room and climbed up on the couch next to the gypsy morph. She knelt as he did, drinking her juice and staring out at the park. The morph did not look at her.

'Why don't you get dressed,' Nest suggested to Bennett, coming back to the table. 'Harper can play with Little John. I'll keep an eye on her. She'll be fine. When you come out, we'll have breakfast.'

Bennett considered the matter, then nodded and went down the hallway to her bedroom, closing the door softly behind her. Ross watched her go without comment, wondering why she had been so worried about who he was. It was more than uneasiness she had demonstrated; it was fear. He recognized it now, considering her response to him, to the possibility that their paths had crossed somewhere before. Yet once the mystery of their previous encounter was cleared up, she seemed fine. Perhaps *relieved* was a better word.

Nest reseated herself at the table. 'Little John?' she inquired, arching one eyebrow.

He shrugged: 'It was all I could come up with on the spur of the moment. He's only been a boy for four days. I haven't had any reason to think of a name for him before.'

'Little John will do. Tell me about the demons before Bennett gets back.'

Pushing the empty coffee cup away from him as if to distance himself from his narrative, he did as she asked.

*H*e hadn't even reached the car before the first demon appeared. Carrying the netting that contained the morph in one hand and gripping his walnut staff with the other, he clambered awkwardly up the sandy trail from the beach to the shoulder of Highway 101 and immediately caught sight of the longhaired young man standing several dozen feet away, occupying the space between himself and the car. He was paying Ross no attention whatsoever, his eyes directed out at the ocean. But Ross felt his instincts prickle, the magic that warded him surfacing in a rush, and he knew what was coming.

He walked up the road as if indifferent to the young man's presence, keeping close to the paving so as to pass behind the other. He saw the young man's posture shift, then watched him step back and shade his eyes as if to get a better look at something on the beach. When Ross came abreast of him, the young man wheeled to attack, but Ross was already moving, bringing his staff around to catch the other squarely across the forehead. Fire lanced from the rune-scrolled wood, and the young man's head exploded in a shower of blood. Revealed for what it was and stripped of its disguise, the demon's ruined shell went backward over the bluff and tumbled from view.

Wiping away the blood with an old rag, Ross climbed hurriedly into the car, backed onto the road, and drove toward Cannon Beach. They would be waiting for him at Mrs. Staples's by now, converging from all directions to intercept him. But he had anticipated this and had no intention of returning to Cannon Beach. He hadn't stayed alive this long by being predictable.

He drove past the turnoff without slowing and caught Highway 26 east toward Portland. In the seat beside him, the morph continued to change shape and emanate light, the magic pulsing like a beacon with each re-forming, leading his enemies right to it. Ross knew that if he was to have any chance at all, he needed to lose himself in a large population. If he remained in Cannon Beach or tried to find sanctuary in any other small town, the demons would find him in a heartbeat. But in a city he could disappear. The number and frequency of the morph's changes would diminish after a time, and while he could not hope to avoid entirely the demons seeking him, he could make it harder for them to determine where he was. When the morph was not changing, it was less identifiable; the Lady had advised him of this. Gradually, Ross would become the focus of their hunt. As one among thousands, he would not be so easy to find.

But he had to get to Portland to have any chance at all, and the demons were already in place. A logging truck ran him off the road just above the turnoff to Banks. He escaped into the woods, found a dirt road farther in, and caught a ride with an old woman and her daughter to a town so small he didn't even see a sign with a name. He felt bad about Mrs. Staples's car, but there was nothing he could do. He felt bad about the car he stole in the nameless town, too, but there was nothing he could do about that either. He abandoned it outside Portland and caught a metro bus into the city.

In a cavernous train station on the west side, while waiting to board a train south to San Francisco, he was attacked again. Two men came at him in the men's room, armed with iron pipes and buttressed by lives of willful destruction. He took them both out in seconds, but the demon who had dispatched them and was waiting outside surprised him as he tried to sneak out the back. The demon was savage and primal, but intelligent as well. It picked a good spot for an ambush, and if it had been a little luckier, it might have succeeded in its effort. But his instincts saved John Ross once more, and the demon died in a fiery conflagration of magic.

Ross called Mrs. Staples from the bus station after the cab dropped him off to tell her of the car and apologize for what he had done. He told her he would send her money. She took it very well, considering. Then he picked up his ticket, boarded the bus, waited until it was ready to leave, and got off again. He walked out of the station and down the street to a used-car agency, took a clunker out for a test drive after leaving the salesman the purchase price in cash as security, and kept going. He drove north to Vancouver, abandoned the car, caught another bus south, and was in California the next day.

He continued on like this for more than a week, twisting and turning, dodging and weaving, a boxer under attack. Over and over again he picked up and moved, sometimes not even bothering to unpack. He slept infrequently and for brief periods, and he was tired and edgy all the time, his energy slowly draining away. It did not help that he was forced to defend himself so often that he was spending all of his time in his dreams of the future without protection, a fugitive there as well, constantly on the run, hunted and at risk. That he stayed alive in both worlds was impressive. That he managed to hold on to the gypsy morph was a genuine miracle.

The morph continued to change rapidly for the first seven days before finally slowing down. It stayed in the netting all this time, never even trying to venture forth, going through its multitude of transformations. It was animal, vegetable, insect, bird, reptile, and a whole slew of other things that Ross was unable or unwilling to identify. At one point it seemed to disappear entirely, but when he peeked inside, he found it was a slug. Another time, it was a bee. A third time it was some sort of mold. Ross quit looking after that and, until it took the shape of something possessing bulk, just assumed it was in the net. It never made a sound and never seemed in need of food or drink. Somehow it had the capacity to sustain itself during this early period, so he didn't need to be concerned for its well-being beyond keeping it safe and alive.

By the time of the incident in Salt Lake City in mid-December, it was changing on the average of only once a day. For two days during that period, it was a cat. For a day and a half, it was a chimp. Once, for a matter of only a few hours, it was a wolf with a tiger-striped face, an uncanny reminder of Wraith.

Shortly after that, it changed into the little boy it was now and spoke a single word—*Nest*. When it said her name twice more in the space of a single day, Ross decided to take a chance and come back to Hopewell.

'*B*ecause he said "Nest" and you thought he was talking about me,' she said quietly.

'Because I thought he *might* be talking about you, yes.' She watched his face grow intense and troubled. 'Because I had just watched him turn into a miniature Wraith, and it made me wonder. But mostly because I was at my wits' end—am at my wits' end still, for that matter—and I had to try something.'

He leaned back in his chair. 'I am exhausted and almost out of time, and I haven't gotten anywhere. I've been with him for twenty-two days, and I don't have a clue how to reach him. I thought I would learn something in that time, thought I would tip to some secret about his magic. But all I've managed to do is to keep the two of us alive and running. There's been no communication, no exchange of information, no discovery of any sort at all. Your name was the first breakthrough. That, and the fact that he's stayed a little boy for four days now. Maybe it means something.'

She nodded, then rose to pour them both a fresh cup of coffee and reseated herself. Outside, the day was bright and clear and cold, the early morning frost still visible in the shadowed spaces and on the tree trunks in crystalline patches. Ross could hear the oil furnace thrum as it pumped out heat to ward against the freeze.

'He doesn't seem especially interested in me now that he's here,' she observed carefully.

He sipped at the coffee. 'I know. He hasn't spoken your name either. Hasn't said a single word. So maybe I was wrong.'

'How much time is left?'

'Before he disappears altogether?' Ross shook his head. 'Several days, I guess. They give a morph on the average of thirty days of life, and that leaves this one down to eight.'

'Interesting,' she said, 'that he's become a little boy.'

'Interesting,' he agreed.

They talked a bit longer about the propensities of gypsy morphs, but since morphs came without blueprints and tended to be wholly inconsistent in their development, there was really little to conclude about the intentions of this one. Nest would have liked to understand more about the strange creatures, but the fact remained that she understood little enough even about Pick, whom she had known for most of her life. Creatures of the forest and magic tended to be as foreign to humans as plankton, even to those as attuned to them as she was.

Bennett reappeared wearing jeans and an old sweatshirt she'd pulled from Nest's closet and a pair of her walking shoes, so they set about making breakfast. It was served and consumed at the larger dining room table, with everyone eating except the morph, who picked at his food and said nothing.

'Lo, boy,' Harper said to him midway through the meal. The gypsy morph studied her solemnly.

'Is he always this quiet?' Bennett asked Ross, frowning.

He nodded. 'He understands everything, but he doesn't speak.' He hesitated. 'The fact is, we're on our way to Chicago after the holidays to see a specialist on the matter.'

'Better have his appetite checked at the same time,' she advised pointedly. 'He hasn't eaten a thing.'

'He ate some cereal earlier,' Nest said.

'Mommy?' Harper asked, looking up, big eyes curious. 'Boy talk?'

'Maybe later, sweetie,' Bennett said, and went back to her breakfast.

Afterward, she bundled up Harper and told Nest they were going for a walk in the park. She asked Ross if Little John wanted to come with them, but Ross said he hadn't seemed well and should probably stay in. Her intentions were good, but he couldn't take a chance on letting the gypsy morph out of his sight.

Bennett and Harper went out the back door, across the lawn, and into the frozen expanse of the park. It was still not even noon. From his position on the couch, the gypsy morph watched them go, staring out the window anew. Ross stood beside him for a time, speaking in low tones, eliciting no response at all.

Finally he walked back into the kitchen and picked up a towel to help dry the dishes Nest was washing.

'You have a dishwasher,' he pointed out, indicating the machine in front of her.

'I like doing it by hand. I like how it makes me feel.'

They worked in silence for a while, falling into a comfortable rhythm. Then Ross said, 'They'll come looking for me, you know.'

She nodded. 'They already have. One of them, at least. Findo Gask, minister of the faith.'

'There will be more. It will be dangerous if I stay.'

She looked at him. 'No duh, as Robert would say.'

He didn't know who Robert was, but he got the message. 'So maybe I should go after tonight.'

'Maybe you should. But maybe coming here was the right thing to do. Let's give it some time and see.' She handed him a juice glass. 'Let's get one thing straight, John. I'm not asking you to leave. We crossed that bridge last night.'

He finished drying all the glasses, stacking them on a towel spread out atop the counter. 'It means a lot. I don't know when I've been this tired.'

She smiled. 'It's funny, but I thought I was going to end up spending Christmas all alone this year. Now I have a house full of people. It changes everything.'

'Life has a way of doing that.' He smiled ruefully. 'It keeps us from becoming too complacent.'

They had just finished putting away the dishes when a knock sounded at the front door. Nest exchanged a quick glance with Ross, then walked down the hall to answer it. He stayed in the kitchen for a few minutes listening to the slow drift of conversation that ensued, then walked to the kitchen window and looked out.

A county sheriff's car was parked in the drive.

CHAPTER 10

Bennett Scott walked out of Nest Freemark's backyard and into Sinnissippi Park, head lowered, wincing against the brightness of the sun. A crystalline coating of frost lingered in shadowed patches of brittle grass and crunched beneath her boots when she walked on it. She watched Harper skip ahead of her, singing softly to herself, lost in that private child's world where adults aren't allowed. She recalled it from her own childhood, a not-so-distant past tucked carefully away in her memory. It was a world she had gone into all the time when growing up, often when she was seeking escape from Big Momma and the unpleasantness of her real life. She supposed Harper did the same, and it made her want to weep.

'Mommy, birdies!' the little girl called out, pointing at a pair of dark shadows winging through the trees.

'Robins,' Bennett guessed, smiling at her daughter.

'Obbins,' Harper parroted, and skipped ahead once more, watching the fluid movement of her shadow as it stretched out beside her.

Bennett tossed back her dark hair and lifted her face bravely against the sunlight. It would be better here, she thought. Better than it had been on the streets, when she was using all the time. Better than in the shelters, where she always kept her switchblade in one hand and Harper's wrist in the other. Better, even, than in the rehab units where she always felt used up and hopeless, where she went through the litany of recovery and still craved a fix all the time. She had tried to shield Harper, but the truth was, everything originated with her. There was no protection without separation, and she couldn't bear that.

But it had happened a few times, just because it was necessary if she was to survive. That was behind her now, so she could bear to think of it again, if only just. But she had left Harper in places rats called home and with people she wouldn't trust a dog with if she were thinking straight, and it was something of a miracle that nothing bad had happened to her baby. Coming back to Hopewell and to Nest was an attempt to set all that straight, to prevent any more incidents, to stop exposing Harper to the risks her mother had chosen to embrace. The men, the sex, the sickness, the drugs, the life—all rolled up into one big ball of evil that would drag her down and bury her if she gave it enough space in her life.

No more, she thought. *Not ever.*

They crossed the ball diamonds to the roadway fronting the bluffs and walked to the crest of the slope to look down over the bayou and the river beyond. Harper had found a stick and was dragging it through patches of frost, making designs. Bennett took out a cigarette, lit it, inhaled deeply,

and sighed. She was a mess. She wasn't using, but her health
was shot and her head was all fuzzy inside where reason
warred with need and emotions fragmented every few days in
a fireworks display that was truly awesome. She thought of
her mother and hoped she was burning in hell, then immediately regretted the thought. Tears filled her eyes. She had
loved her mother, loved her desperately, the way she hoped
Harper loved her. But her mother had abandoned her, disappointed her, and rejected her time and again. What was
left for her when it happened so often but to flee, to try to
save herself? Her flight had saved her life, perhaps, but had
cost her in measurable increments her childhood innocence
and sense of self-worth and any chance of escaping her
mother's addict life.

But it would be different for Harper. She had made that
vow on the morning she had learned at the free clinic she was
pregnant and had decided whatever higher power had given
her this one last chance at something good, she wasn't going
to mess it up.

So here she was, come back to where she had started,
back to where a few things still seemed possible. She was
dressed in another woman's clothing, and the clothes her
child wore had been stolen from or discarded by others, but
even so she felt new and hopeful. Nest Freemark had been so
good to her in the past. If anyone could help her find a way
back from the dark road she had traveled, it was Nest.

A train whistle sounded, distant and forlorn in the
midday silence, echoing across the gray, flat surface of the
Rock.

'Choo choo,' Harper said, and she made some train noises.

She shuffled around in a circle, dragging her stick, chuffing out clouds of breath into the sunshine.

I can make this work, Bennett thought, staring off into the distance, out where the whistle was still echoing through the winter silence.

'Hi, there, cutie,' a voice behind her said. 'You are about the sweetest little muffin I've ever seen.'

Bennett turned quickly, shifting in a smooth, practiced motion to place herself between the newcomer and Harper. The young woman facing her smiled and shrugged, as if apologizing for her abrupt appearance while at the same time saying, so what? She was close to Bennett's age, tall and lanky, with wild red hair that stuck out. Her bright, green eyes fastened on Harper with an eagerness that was disconcerting. 'Hey, you.'

Then she glanced at Bennett, and the look cooled and hardened. 'You are one lucky mom, to have someone like her. How are you doing? My name is Penny.'

She stuck out her hand. Bennett hesitated before accepting it. 'I'm Bennett. This is Harper.'

Penny shifted her stance without moving her feet, loose and anticipatory. 'So, are you from around here or just passing through, like me?' Penny grinned. 'I'm visiting my granny for the holidays, but you can believe me when I tell you this place is in a time warp. Nothing to do, nowhere to go, no one to see. I can't wait to get out. You?'

'I'm from here, back for a visit with a ... friend, an old friend.' Bennett held her ground, watchful, the hand in her pocket fastened on the switchblade. 'We're staying on awhile.'

Penny sniffed. 'Whatever. I'm outta here December twenty-sixth and good riddance.'

She looked off into the distance as the freight train swung into view out on the levee, wheeling down the tracks with a slow-building rumble of iron wheels and pistons. They stood motionless, the three of them, staring out at the train as it bisected the horizon in a seemingly endless line of cars, a zipper motion against the still backdrop of water and winter woods. When it disappeared, the sound faded gradually, still audible when the train was several miles up the track.

'So, you having fun here in the park, Harper?' Penny asked suddenly, shifting her gaze once more.

Harper nodded wordlessly and edged closer to Bennett. She sensed the same thing about this woman her mother did, that something wasn't quite right. Bennett felt suddenly exposed and vulnerable, standing at the edge of the wooded slope, away from everyone and everything in the hard edge of the winter chill. Clouds had crept out of the northwest, obscuring the sun, and the gray sky was melting down into the backdrop of the skeletal trees.

'We've got to be going,' Bennett advised, reaching down for Harper's hand, keeping her eyes on Penny.

'Oh, sure,' Penny replied, smiling cheerfully, the light in her green eyes dancing, shrugging her shoulders and shifting away. 'You go, girl, you need to. But, hey, you look a little uptight. Know what I mean?'

'No.' Bennett shook her head quickly, not wanting to hear any more, already sensing what was coming. 'I'm fine.'

She started away, but Penny moved with her. 'Well, you

can say you're fine if you want, but you are most definitely not, you know? I can tell. And I don't blame you. I wouldn't be fine if I didn't have a little something to help me get by, let me tell you.'

Bennett wheeled on her. 'Look, I don't know who you are—'

'Hey, I'm just another victim of life, just another sister fighting to make it through another day.' Penny held up her hands placatingly. 'You don't need to worry about me. You think I'm the law? I'm not, girlfriend. Not hardly.' She winked. 'Hope you're not the law either, because I got something for you, you want it, something to make you feel a little better.'

Bennett heard the blood pounding inside her head. She felt the familiar pumping of adrenaline, her body's automatic response to the possibility of a fix. Everything seemed to kick in at once, all the familiar expectancies, all the insatiable needs. She was surprised at how strong they were, even in the face of her resolve to put them aside.

Penny eased closer to her, eyes bright. 'What I got, is a little white dust that doesn't take but a single whiff to sweep you away to la-la land, smooth and easy and cream-puff sweet. You can live on this stuff for days, girl. Keeps you sharp and strong and focused, but takes the edge off, too. I got it before I came to Dullsville, knowing what it would be like. I used it day before last, and I'm still flying high.'

'No, thanks,' Bennett told her abruptly, shaking her head, starting off again. It took everything she had to say it, to make her feet move, to keep her mind focused, but she managed. 'We've got to go.'

'Hey, wait up, Bennett!' Penny came after her quickly, keeping pace as she walked. 'Don't be mad. I wasn't trying to jerk you around or anything. I was just trying to be nice, trying to make conversation. Hey, I'm lonely here, I admit it. You seem like me, that's all. I was just looking for some company.' She paused. 'I wasn't going to ask you for money, you know. I was going to share, to give it to you for free.'

Bennett kept walking, trying to shut the words out, trying to make Penny go away. *Even here,* she was thinking. *Even here, someone's got the stuff and wants me to use.* She was walking faster, practically dragging Harper, needing to escape and not wanting to, both at once.

'We could meet later and do some together,' Penny was suggesting, keeping pace effortlessly. 'My place, maybe. You know, just the two of us. Granny doesn't know what's going on anyway, so she won't be a bother.'

'Owee, Mommy,' Harper was complaining, trying to pull free from her mother's grip.

Bennett shifted her hand on the little girl's arm and looked over at Penny angrily. 'I can't—'

'What do you say?' Penny cut her short. 'You want a little now? Just a taste to see if it's worth doing some more later?'

Bennett stopped and stood with her head lowered and her eyes closed. She wanted nothing more. She wanted it so bad she could hardly wait for it to happen. She felt empty and sick inside, and she found herself thinking, *What the hell difference does it make after all the other drugs I've done?*

Penny's hand was on her shoulder, and her frizzy red head was bent close. 'You won't be sorry, babe, I promise.

Just a taste to get you by until, oh, maybe tonight, okay? Come on. I know the signs. You're all strung out and uptight and you want a little space for yourself. Why shouldn't you have it?'

Bennett felt her defenses shutting down and her addictive needs sweeping through her with relentless purpose. The itch was working its way up her spine and down her throat, and she thought—knew—that if she didn't take what was being offered, she would self-destruct in spectacular fashion. Besides, a taste was not so much, and Nest could help her later, give her the strength she lacked now so she could start over again.

'Come on, I'll do a little with you,' Penny persisted, whispering now, so close that Bennett could hear her breathing.

Her eyes were still closed, but now, on the verge of capitulating, on the edge of a hunger so intense she could not find words to define it, she opened them.

It was then she saw the Indian.

*N*est Freemark opened her front door and found Deputy Sheriff Larry Spence waiting, his big hands clasped around his leather gloves. He was dressed in his uniform, brown over tan, and he wore a leather jacket with the collar and cuffs trimmed in dark fur. Bits and pieces of metal stays and accents glinted dully in the graying light, giving him that armored look that lawmen and the military favor.

'How you doing, girl,' he greeted pleasantly.

She glanced past him to the empty sheriff's car. He had come alone. 'Can I help you, Larry?'

He shoved his gloves into his coat pocket, eyes shifting away. 'I'd like to speak with you for just a minute, if it's okay.' She studied him pointedly, waiting. He flushed. 'It's business, you know, not personal.'

She smiled, but held her ground. 'Sure. Go right ahead.'

He cleared his throat, looking past her for just a moment. 'I wonder if we might speak inside?'

The last thing she wanted was Larry Spence in her house. On the other hand, it was rude to make him stand out in the cold and she couldn't come up with a good reason for not inviting him in long enough to tell her what he wanted.

She stood aside. 'Sure.'

He moved into the entry, and she shut the door behind them. He glanced around, nodding appreciatively. 'You have a very nice home. Very warm. Sort of reminds me of my folks' old two-story.'

'Would you like some hot tea?' she asked. 'We can sit in the kitchen.'

She led him down the hall and through the kitchen doorway. John Ross stood with his back to the sink, leaning on his staff, a mix of curiosity and wariness mirrored in his green eyes. But it was the look on Larry Spence's face that surprised her, changing from friendly to antagonistic and back again so fast she almost missed it. Something was very wrong, but she had no idea what it was.

'John, this is Larry Spence,' she said. 'Larry, my friend John Ross. He's visiting for the holidays with his son.'

The men shook hands, a firm, measured sort of greeting that lacked warmth and advised caution. Nest put Larry

Spence at the old wooden table and gave both men fresh cups of tea. Leaving Ross at the sink, she sat down across from Spence. 'So, tell me what you need, Larry.'

He cleared his throat and straightened. 'There's been some rumors of drug dealing in the park, Nest. I'm making a few inquiries, just in case anyone's seen anything unusual this past week or so. You haven't noticed any strangers around, have you?'

This was the first Nest had heard about the matter. If there was any drug dealing going on in Sinnissippi Park, Pick would have noticed and said something. She frowned. 'Pretty hard for anyone to hide out there in the park at this time of the year, Larry.'

'Maybe. What you need to know is that these people are pretty dangerous.'

She shrugged. 'I haven't seen anyone.'

He looked at Ross. 'How about you, Mr. Ross? Do you know anything about this business?'

His tone of voice and the emphasis he gave to his words turned his question into an accusation. Nest was stunned.

John Ross merely shook his head.'I just got here last night.'

'Didn't see anyone out in the park when you drove up?'

'I came in on the bus.'

'Are you from around here, Mr. Ross?'

'No, I—'

'Just a minute, John.' Nest had had enough. She fixed Larry Spence with a withering look. 'As a sheriff's deputy, you make a great Nazi, Larry. What are you doing? John is an old friend and a guest in my house. I invited you in out of kindness, not to give you a chance to practice your interrogation skills.'

The big man nodded, a gesture intended to placate, as if anything else might invite further attack. He brushed at his mop of blond hair. 'His name came up during my investigation, Nest.'

'What?' She stared. 'How?'

He shrugged. 'Anonymous source.'

'Anonymous source? How convenient!'

He took a slow, steadying breath. 'I'm just doing my job, girl, asking these questions. And I'm concerned about your safety. Mr. Ross is a stranger, and I just want to be sure—'

She came to her feet abruptly, incensed. 'You don't have to be sure in my house, Larry. You just have to be courteous. I think you better go.'

He rose reluctantly, then nodded at Ross. 'I apologize for any rudeness, Mr. Ross. I didn't come here to make trouble.'

John Ross nodded back. 'You don't need to apologize to me, Deputy.'

Larry Spence looked down at the floor. 'Nest, I'm sorry. But I worry about you. Rumors have a way of sneaking up on you, if you don't keep an eye on them. If there's drug dealing going on in the park, I don't want you to be associated with it.'

Nest stared at him. For just an instant she sensed that he was talking about something else entirely, that he was trying to tell her something. She shook her head slowly and stepped up to him. 'Larry, I appreciate your concern. But drugs have never been a part of my life and certainly not of John's. I promise you, if we see anything suspicious, we'll give you a call.'

The big man nodded, turned, and started back down the hall. He caught sight of Little John perched on the sofa, staring out at the park, and turned back to Ross. 'Your son?'

Ross nodded.

Spence looked at the boy, puzzlement etched in his rough features, as if he found the boy's presence difficult to accept. Then he continued down the hall to the front door, where he paused.

'The offer for Christmas is still open. Kids would love it.'

'I don't think so, Larry,' she replied, wondering what in the world he was thinking.

He nodded, opened the door, and went back outside. Nest stood in the doorway and watched as he climbed into his sheriff's car and drove slowly off. Her hands were clenched and her throat was tight with anger.

Larry Spence, she decided, was an idiot.

The Indian seemed to come out of nowhere, appearing amidst the bare trees in a wooded stretch behind the toboggan slide, all size and dark shadows in the graying light. He was big all over, dressed in camouflage pants, ribbed army sweater, mesh vest, and combat boots. His black hair glistened with a gunmetal sheen, braided and drawn tight against his scalp, and his coppery skin shone like orange fire. He carried a rucksack and a rolled blanket over one shoulder, and his eyes, even from so far away, were bright pinpricks beneath his heavy brow.

Bennett Scott forgot about Penny and the drugs and everything else, and simply stared at him as he approached, his slow, heavy steps carrying him steadily closer, until he seemed to take up all the space in her screen of vision.

At the last minute, Penny, still whispering sweet enticements and urgent pleas, realized something was wrong. She backed away quickly and turned as the Indian loomed over her. Bennett heard her gasp of surprise and shock turn an instant later to a hiss of warning.

'Afternoon,' the Indian said, his copper face expressionless, his deep voice smooth. He was addressing Bennett and Harper, looking right through Penny. 'Beautiful day for a walk in the park.'

No one replied. The women and the little girl stood frozen in place, as if turned to ice. The Indian glanced from Bennett to Harper, unperturbed. 'Ah, little one,' he said softly to the child. 'Do you wait for tonight's snow so that tomorrow you might go out and build a snowman with Mama?'

Harper gave a slow nod. 'Yeth.'

The Indian smiled faintly. 'Mama,' he said to Bennett, speaking past a seething Penny as if she weren't even there. 'Do you know a woman named Nest Freemark?'

Bennett swallowed against the dryness in her throat, so frightened she could barely bring herself to do that much. The Indians she had encountered had mostly been street people, drunks and indigents and welfare dependents, barely able to get from street corner to soup line. This one was a different sort entirely, big and powerful and self-assured. He had not threatened Harper or her, but he seemed capable of anything.

'Do you know Nest Freemark?' he pressed gently.

Bennett nodded. 'She lives right over there,' she managed, suddenly in control of herself again, her mind clear.

'She is your friend?'

'Yes. I'm staying with her.'

'Would you go to her and tell her Two Bears is waiting in the park to speak with her?'

It was an odd request. Why didn't he just walk over there and tell her himself? But she didn't feel inclined to argue the matter, and it gave her the excuse she needed to get away from Penny. 'Okay,' she said. 'Come on, Harper.'

She reached for the little girl's hand, but Penny moved instantly to block their way, wheeling back on the Indian. 'Why don't you just push off, Tonto? Run your own errand. We were talking.'

For the first time, he looked at her. And Penny, well, Penny with her drugs and smart-ass talk, looked as if she might turn into a pillar of salt. She shrank from him as if struck, retreating into a protective crouch. Then something ugly and dark surfaced in her eyes, and she took on the appearance of a feral creature. She lunged at the Indian, snake-quick. There was a glint of metal, but the metal went spinning out into the gray, and Penny shrieked and dropped to one knee, holding her wrist and baring her teeth at Two Bears. A knife lay on the ground a dozen feet away, knocked free from her hand. Bennett had never even seen the Indian move.

'You should be more careful,' the big man told Penny, then dismissed her as if she were already gone. He bent to Harper. 'Come, little one,' he said, taking her tiny hand in his. 'I will walk part of the way with you.'

Harper went obediently, saying nothing. Bennett followed, leaving Penny kneeling on the ground where the Indian had put her. She did not look back.

CHAPTER 11

Nest Freemark pulled on her parka, not bothering with snaps or zippers, and banged her way out through the storm door onto the back porch, down the steps, and into the yard. She exhaled her frustration in a frothy cloud, her mind racing. First Larry Spence comes by with his bizarre story about drug dealing in the park and now O'olish Amaneh reappears. Today was turning into a replay of yesterday, and she wasn't sure she was up to it.

She was already scanning the park, searching for the Indian's familiar silhouette when Pick dropped onto her shoulder.

'Getting to be old home week around here, isn't it?' he offered brightly, fastening on her collar with both twiggy hands. 'Hey, watch what you're doing!'

She was hunching down into the coat, jostling Pick as she did so, working the Gore-Tex into a more protective position. It was colder out than she had believed. The temperature was dropping again, the afternoon chill deepened by the sun's disappearance behind a thick bank of clouds, the morning's brightness faded to memory.

'Try thinking about someone besides yourself!' Pick snapped, regaining his balance.

'Quit griping.' She was in no mood for sylvan nonsense. Pick meant well, but sometimes he was an out-and-out annoyance. She had enough to deal with. 'You saw him, I gather?'

'Which one do you mean? That deputy sheriff, John Ross, or the Indian? I saw them all. What's going on?'

She shook her head. 'I'm not sure.'

She pushed through the bushes and onto the service road separating the Freemark property from the park. Ahead, the dead grass of the ball diamonds and central play area stretched away in a gray and windburned carpet. Beyond, along the ridge of the bluffs ahead, right toward Riverside Cemetery, and left past the toboggan slide, the bare trunks and limbs of the broad-leaves were framed like dark webbing against the steely sky.

Two Bears was nowhere in sight.

'I don't see him,' she said, casting about as she proceeded.

'He's there,' Pick insisted. 'He was there early this morning, sitting all by himself at one of the picnic tables.'

'Well, I don't see him now.'

'And you want *me* to stop griping? Criminy!' He rode her shoulder in silence for a moment. 'What does he want this time? Did the Scott girl say?'

'Nope. I don't think she knows.'

Nest's boots crunched and skidded against the frosty dampness that had melted earlier and was now refreezing.

She'd left both children with Bennett, who seemed confused and out of sorts from her encounter with Two Bears. There's an Indian waiting outside in the park, she'd reported. Bear Claw, she'd called him. Ross was in the shower. Maybe he didn't need to know about this. Maybe he didn't even have to find out O'olish Amaneh was there. Maybe cows could fly.

She wasn't kidding herself about what the Indian's appearance meant. When Two Bears showed up, it meant trouble of the worst kind. She could have predicted his coming, she realized, if she had let herself. With Findo Gask sniffing around in search of the gypsy morph, John Ross bringing the morph to her in an effort to save it, and a deadly confrontation between the paladins of the Word and the Void virtually assured, it was inevitable that O'olish Amaneh would be somewhere close at hand.

A dog came bounding across the park, a black Lab, but its owner's whistle brought it around and back toward where it had come from. She glanced behind her at the house, shadowed in the graying light and heavy trees, remote and empty-seeming. She found herself wondering anew about the unexpected appearance of Larry Spence. One thing was certain. He had come to her for something more than a warning about drug sales in the park, and it clearly had to do with John Ross. Larry didn't like Ross, but she couldn't figure out why. She didn't think they had even met when Ross had come to Hopewell fifteen years ago. Even if they had, Larry wouldn't be carrying a grudge that long, not without more reason than she could envision. It was something else, something more recent.

'There he is,' Pick said.

Two Bears stood next to the toboggan slide, a dark
shadow within the heavy timbers. He was O'olish Amaneh in
the language of his people, the Sinnissippi. He had told
Nest once that he was the last of them, that his people were
all gone. She shivered at the memory. But Two Bears was
much more than a Native American. Two Bears was another
of the Word's messengers, a kind of prophet, a chronicler of
things lost in the past and a seer of things yet to come.

He moved out to meet her as she approached, as imper-
turbable as ever, big and weather-burnt, black hair braided
and shining, looking for all the world as if he hadn't aged a
day. Indeed, even after fifteen years, he didn't seem to have
aged at all.

'Little bird's Nest,' he said with that slow, warm rumble,
hands lifting to clasp her own.

'O'olish Amaneh,' she said, and placed her hands in his,
watching them disappear in the great palms.

He did not move to embrace her, but simply stood looking at her, dark eyes taking her measure. She was nearly as tall
as he was now, but she felt small and vulnerable in his presence.

'You have done much with your life since we spoke last,'
he said finally, releasing her hands. 'Olympics, world cham-
pionships, honors of all sorts. You have grown wings and
flown far. You should be proud.'

She smiled and shook her head. 'I have a failed marriage,
no family, no future, a ghost wolf living inside me, and a
house full of trouble.' She held his steady gaze with her own.
'I don't have time for pride.'

He nodded. 'Maybe you never did.' His eyes shifted to

Pick. 'Still have your shy little friend, I see. Mr. Pick, the park looks tended and sound, the magic in balance. You are a skilled caretaker.'

Pick frowned and gave a small *humph*, then nodded grudgingly. 'I could use a little help.'

Two Bears smiled faintly. 'Some things never change.' His eyes shifted back to Nest. 'Walk with me. We can talk better down by the river.'

He started away without waiting for her response, and she found herself following. They moved beyond the slide and down into the trees, edging slowly toward the icy skin of the bayou. The temperature was dropping quickly as the afternoon lengthened and the skies darkened further, and their breath formed white clouds in the air before them. Nest was tempted to speak first, to ask the obvious, but Two Bears had asked to speak with her, so she thought it best to wait on him.

'It feels good to hear you speak my name, to know that you have not forgotten it,' he said, looking off into the distance.

As if she could, she thought without saying so. As if it were possible. She had encountered Two Bears only twice, but both times her life had been changed forever. O'olish Amaneh and John Ross, harbingers of change: she wondered if they ever thought of themselves that way. Both served the Word, but in different ways, and their relationship was something of a mystery. Two Bears had given Ross the rune-carved staff that was both the talisman of his power and the chain that bound him to his fate. Ross had tried at least once to give the staff back and failed. Each had come to Nest both as savior and executioner, but the roles had shifted back and forth between them, and in some ways they remained unclear. They were fond of her, but not of each other. Perhaps their roles placed restrictions on their feelings. Perhaps fondness for her was allowed, while fondness for each other was not.

She was not certain how she felt about them. She guessed she liked Ross better for having witnessed his vulnerability ten years ago in Seattle, when a demon had almost claimed him through misguided love. He had lost almost everything then, stripped of illusion and hope. In a few seconds of blinding recognition, he discovered how deeply pervasive evil was and how impossible it would be to walk away from his battle against it. He had taken up the black staff of his office once more, reclaimed his life as a Knight of the Word, and gone on because there was nothing else for him to do. She found him brave and wonderful because of that.

By the same token, she guessed, she had distanced herself from Two Bears. It wasn't for what he had done, but for what she had discovered he might do. In Seattle, he had come to observe, to see if she could change the direction in which John Ross had drifted and by doing so enable him to escape the trap that was closing about him. Two Bears had come to watch, but if she had failed in her efforts, he had come to act as well, to make certain that whatever else happened, John Ross would not become a servant of the Void. He had made that clear to her in urging her to go to Ross, even after John had rejected her help, and it had given her an understanding of Two Bears that she would just as soon not have.

But that was long ago, she thought, walking through the park with him, *and these are different times.*

'I'm surprised you showed yourself to Bennett,' she said finally, abandoning her resolve to wait longer on him.

'She needed someone to protect her from evil spirits.' He kept his gaze directed straight ahead, and she could not determine if he was serious.

'I had a visit from a demon named Findo Gask,' she said.

'An evil spirit of the sort I was talking about. One of the worst. But you already know that.'

She scuffed at the frozen ground impatiently. 'John Ross is here as well. He brought a gypsy morph to me.'

'A houseful of trouble, as you claim, when you add in the young woman and her child.' He might have been talking about the weather. 'What will you do?'

She made a face. 'I was hoping you might tell me.' On her shoulder, Pick was muttering in irritation, but she couldn't tell who or what he was upset with.

Two Bears stopped a dozen yards from the riverbank in a stand of winter grasses and gray hickory. He looked at her quizzically. 'It is not my place to tell you what to do, little bird's Nest. You are a grown woman, one possessing uncommon strength of mind and heart and body. You have weathered difficult times and harsh truths. The answers you seek are yours to provide, not mine.'

She frowned, impatient with his evasiveness. 'But you asked to speak to me, O'olish Amaneh.'

He shrugged. 'Not about this. About something else.' He began walking again, and Nest followed. 'A houseful of trouble,' he repeated, skirting a stand of hackberry and stalks of dried itch weed, moving toward the ravine below the deep woods, following a tiny stream of snowmelt upstream from the bayou. 'A houseful of trouble can make a prisoner of you. To get free, you must empty your house of what is bad and fill it with what is good.'

'You mean I should throw everybody out and start over?' She arched one eyebrow at him. 'Bring in some new guests?'

Still walking steadily ahead, as if he had a destination in mind and a firm intention of reaching it, he did not look at her. 'Sometimes change is necessary. Sometimes we recognize the need for it, but we don't know how to achieve it. We misread its nature. We think it is beyond us, failing to recognize that our inability to act is a problem of our own making. Change is the solution we require, but it is not a goal that is easily reached. Identifying and disposing of what is troubling to us requires caution and understanding.'

He was telling her something in that obscure, oblique way he employed when talking of problems and solutions, believing that everyone must resolve things on their own, and the best he could do was to offer a flashlight for use on a dark path. She struggled with the light he had provided, but it was too weak to be of help.

'Everyone in my house needs me,' she advised quietly. 'I can't ask them to leave, even if allowing them to stay places me in danger.'

He nodded. 'I would expect nothing less of you.'

'So the trouble that fills my house, as you put it, will have to be dealt with right where it is, I guess.'

'You have dealt with trouble in your house before, little bird's Nest.'

She thought about it a moment. He was speaking of Gran and Old Bob, fifteen years earlier, when John Ross had come to her for the first time, and she had learned the truth about her star-crossed family. But this was different. The secrets this time were not hers, but belonged to the gypsy morph. Or perhaps to John Ross.

Didn't they?

She looked at him sharply, sensing suddenly that he was talking about her after all, that he was giving her an insight into her own life.

'Not all the troubles that plague us are ours to solve,' Two Bears advised, walking steadily on. 'Life provides its own solutions to some, and we must accept those solutions as we would the changing of the seasons.' He glanced at her expectantly.

'Well, I'm not much good at sitting back and waiting for life to solve my problems for me.'

'No. And this is not what you should do. You should solve those problems you understand well, but leave the others alone. You should provide solutions where you are able and accept that this is enough.' He paused, then sighed. 'In a houseful of trouble, not everything can be salvaged.'

Well, okay, she was thinking, you save what you can and let go of the rest. Fair enough. But how was she supposed to save anything if she didn't know where to start?

'Can you tell me something about the gypsy morph?' she tried hopefully.

He nodded. 'Very powerful magic. Very unpredictable. A gypsy morph becomes what it will, if it becomes anything at all, which is rare. Mostly it fails to find its form and goes back with the air, wild and unreachable. Spirits understand it, for they occupy space with it. They brush against it, pass through it, float upon it, before it becomes a solid thing, while it is still waiting to take form.' He shrugged. 'It is an enigma waiting for an answer.'

She blew out a cloud of breath. 'Well, how do I go about finding out what that answer is? This morph has become a little boy. What does that mean? Is that the form it intends to take? What does it want with me? It spoke my name to John Ross, but now that it's here it doesn't even look at me.'

They stopped on the rickety wooden bridge that crossed the nearly frozen trickle of the winter stream. Two Bears leaned on the railing, hands clasped.

'Talk to him, little bird's Nest.'

'What?'

'Have you said anything to him? This little boy, have you spoken to him on your own?'

She thought about it a moment. 'No.'

'The solution is often buried somewhere in the problem. If the gypsy morph requires you, it may choose to tell you so. But perhaps it needs to know you care first.'

She thought about it a moment. The gypsy morph was a child, a newborn less than thirty days formed, and as a four-year-old boy, it might be necessary that he be reassured and won over. She hadn't done that. She hadn't even tried, feeling pressed and rushed by Ross. The morph might need her badly, but needing and trusting were two different things entirely.

'All right,' she said.

'Good.' He lifted away from the bridge, straightening.

'Now I will explain my reason for asking to speak with you. It is simple. I am your friend, and I came to say good-bye. I am the last of the Sinnissippi, and I have come home to be with my people. I wanted you to know, because it is possible I will not see you again.'

Nest stared, absorbing the impact of his words. 'Your people are all dead, O'olish Amaneh. Does this mean you will die, too?'

He laughed, and his laugh was hearty and full. 'You should see your face, little bird's Nest! I would be afraid to die with such a fierce countenance confronting me! Mr. Pick! Look at her! Such fierce resolution and rebuke in her eyes! How do you withstand this power when it is turned on you?'

He sobered then, and shook his head. 'This is difficult to explain, but I will try. By joining with my ancestors, with my people, who are gone from this earth, I do not have to give up my own life in the way you imagine. But I must bond with them in a different form. By doing so, I must give up something of myself. It is difficult to know beforehand what this will require. I say good-bye as a precaution, in the event I am not able to return to you.'

'Transmutation?' she asked. 'You will become something else.'

'In a sense. But then, I always was.' He brushed the matter off with a wave of his big hand. 'If I leave, I will not be gone forever. Like the seasons, I will still be in the seeds of the earth, waiting.' He shrugged. 'My leaving is a small thing. I will not be missed.'

She exhaled sharply. 'Don't say that. It isn't true.'

There was a long silence as they faced each other in the

graying winter light, motionless in the cold, breath clouding the air before their intense faces. 'It isn't true for you,' he said finally. 'I am grateful for that.'

She was still fighting to accept the idea that he would not be there anymore, that he would be as lost to her as Gran and Old Bob, as her mother and her father, as so many of her friends. It was a strange reaction to have to someone she had encountered only twice before and had such mixed feelings about. It was an odd response no matter how she looked at it. The closest parallel she could draw was to Wraith, when he had disappeared on her eighteenth birthday, gone forever it seemed, until she discovered him anew inside her.

Would it be like that with O'olish Amaneh?

'When will this happen?' she asked, her voice tight and small.

'When it is time. Perhaps it will not happen at all. Perhaps the spirits of my people will not have me.'

'Perhaps they'll throw you back when they find out you talk in riddles all the time!' Pick snapped.

Two Bears' laughter boomed through the empty woods. 'Perhaps if they do, I will have to come live with you, Mr. Pick!' He glanced at Nest. 'Come, walk with me some more.'

They retraced their steps down the ravine toward the bayou, then along the riverbank where the woods hugged the shoreline, the dark, skeletal limbs crisscrossing the graying skies. The air was crisp and cold, but there was a fresh dampness as well, the smell of incoming snow, thick and heavy. The Rock was frozen solid below the toboggan run, and there would be sleds on the ice by nightfall.

When they reached the edge of the woods and were in sight of the wooden chute where it opened onto the ice, Two Bears stopped.

'Even when I am with my people, you may see me again, little bird's Nest,' he said.

She wrinkled her nose. 'Like a ghost?'

'Perhaps. Are you afraid of what that might mean?'

She gave him a look. 'We're friends, aren't we?'

'Always.'

'Then I have no reason to be afraid.'

He shook his head in contradiction. 'If I come to you, I will do so as my ancestors did for me in the park fifteen years ago—in dreams. They came to you as well that night. Do you remember?'

She did. Fifteen years ago, her dreams of the Sinnissippi had shown Gran as a young girl, running with a demon in the park, feeders chasing after her, a wild, reckless look in her dark eyes. They had revealed truths that had changed everything.

'There is always cause to be afraid of what our dreams will show us,' he whispered. One hand lifted to touch her face gently. 'Speak my name once more.'

'O'olish Amaneh,' she said.

'No one will ever say it and give me greater pleasure. The winds bear your words to the heavens and scatter them as stars.'

He gestured skyward, and her eyes responded to the gesture, searching obediently.

When she looked back again, he was gone.

'Just tell me this,' Pick said after a long moment of

silence. 'Do you have any idea what he was talking about?'

John Ross came down the hallway to the living room and found Bennett Scott sitting in a chair reading a *Sports Illustrated* while Harper colored paper on the floor. The gypsy morph knelt on the couch and stared out the window as if turned to stone.

Bennett looked up, and he asked, 'Where's Nest?'

She shrugged. 'Out in the park, talking with some Indian.'

A cold space settled in the pit of his stomach. Two Bears. He leaned heavily on his staff, thinking that it was all going to happen again, a new confrontation between the Word and the Void, another battle in an endless war. What was expected of him this time? To unlock the secret of the morph, he knew. But if he failed . . .

He brushed his thoughts aside, finding they spiraled down into a darkness he didn't care to approach. He thought back suddenly to the Fairy Glen and the Lady, to his last visit there, and to the secret he had discovered and could never share with anyone. Thinking on it made him suddenly weary of his life.

'Are you all right?' Bennett Scott asked him.

He almost laughed, thinking that he would never be all right, thinking the question strange coming from her. 'Yes,' he said, and walked into the kitchen.

He had poured himself a fresh cup of coffee and was halfway through it when the doorbell rang. When it rang a second time, he walked to the kitchen entry and looked into the living room. Harper was in her mother's lap, a storybook in her hands. Bennett glanced up and shrugged indifferently, so Ross limped down the hallway instead.

When he opened the front door, Josie Jackson was waiting.

CHAPTER 12

It had been fifteen years since they had seen each other, but it might just as easily have been yesterday. Physically, they had changed, weathered and lined by the passing years and life's experiences, settled into midlife and aware of the steady approach of old age. But emotionally, they were frozen in time, locked in the same space they had occupied at the moment they had spoken last. Their feelings for each other ran so deep and their memories of the few days they had shared were so vivid and immediate that they were reclaimed instantly by what they had both thought lost forever.

'John?' Josie said his name softly, but the shock mirrored in her dark eyes was bright and painful.

She was older, but not enough so that it made more than a passing impression on him. Mostly, she was the way he remembered her. She still had that tanned, fresh look and that scattering of freckles across the bridge of her nose. Her blond, tousled hair was cut shorter, but it accentuated her face, lending it a soft, cameo beauty.

Only the smile was missing, that dazzling, wondrous

smile, but he had no reason to expect she would be inclined to share it now with him. When he met her, the attraction was instantaneous and electric. Even though he knew that a relationship with her would be disastrous, particularly one in which he fell in love, he let it happen anyway. For two days, he allowed himself to imagine what it would be like to have a normal life, to share himself with a woman he cared about, to pretend it might lead to something permanent. Together, they spent an evening in Sinnissippi Park at a picnic and dance. When he was attacked and beaten by men who believed him someone other than who he was, she took him home, washed him, bandaged him, soothed him, and gave herself to him. When he left her in the morning for a final confrontation with the demon who was Nest Freemark's father, walking away from her as she sat in her car looking after him, he had thought he would never see her again.

'Hello,' she said, and he realized he hadn't said anything, but was simply standing there in the doorway, staring.

'Hello, Josie,' he managed, his own voice sounding strange to him, forced and dry. 'How are you?'

'Good.' The shock in her eyes had eased, but she didn't seem to be having any better luck than he was with conversation. 'I didn't know you were here.'

'My coming was kind of unexpected.'

He felt slow and awkward in her presence, aware of his ragged appearance in old jeans, plaid work shirt, and scuffed boots. His long hair, tied back from his face and still damp from his shower, was shot through with gray and had receded above his temples. He bore the scars from his battles with the minions of the Void across his sun-browned face and forearms, and the damage to his leg ached more often these days. He found Josie as fresh and youthful as ever, but believed that to her he must look old and used up.

He glanced down at the plate of cookies she was holding in her hands, seeing them for the first time.

Her eyes lowered. 'I brought them for Nest. She always bakes cookies for everyone else, so I thought someone ought to bake some for her. Can I come in?'

'Of course,' he said hurriedly, stepping back. 'Guess my mind is somewhere else. Come in.' He waited until she was inside and then closed the door. 'Nest is out in the park, but she should be back in a few minutes.'

They stared at each other in the shadowed entry, hearing the ticking of the grandfather clock and the low murmur of Bennett reading to Harper.

'You look tired, John,' she said finally.

'You look wonderful.'

The words were out of his mouth before he could stop them. Josie flushed, then released that blinding smile, and he felt as if nothing on earth would ever be more welcome.

'That smile—now there's something I've thought about often,' he admitted, shaking his head at what he was feeling inside, knowing already he shouldn't allow it, unable to help himself.

She held his gaze, the smile in place. 'I've missed you, too. Isn't that remarkable?'

'It's been a long time,' he said.

'Not so long that you felt the need to call or write?'

He gave her a rueful look. 'I've never been much good at either. I tell myself to do it, but I just don't follow through.

I don't really know what to say. It feels strange trying to put down what I'm thinking on paper or to say it into a phone. I don't know. Ask Nest. I haven't called or written her either.'

The smile faded, and she shook her head slowly. 'It's all right. I guess I never really thought you would.' She handed him the plate of cookies. 'Here, hold these for a moment, will you?'

She shrugged out of her coat and hung it on the coatrack, draping her scarf on top and shoving her gloves into the pockets. She brushed back her hair self-consciously, smoothed her blouse where it tucked into her pants, and took the cookies back.

'Pour me a glass of milk and I'll share,' she offered, the smile back in place again.

They walked down the hall past the living room, and Bennett and Harper looked up. Little John, kneeling on the couch, never moved. Josie leaned around Ross to say hello and asked if anyone would like a snack. The women didn't seem to know each other, but neither made an effort to introduce herself, so Ross let the matter alone. He went into the kitchen with Josie, helped her with glasses of milk, then remained leaning against the counter looking off into the tree-shrouded distance while Josie carried a tray for Bennett and the children into the living room.

When she returned, he sat with her at the old wooden table, the cookies and milk between them. For a moment, no one spoke.

'Do you still have the coffee shop?' he asked finally.

'Yep. Mostly the same customers, too. Nothing changes.' She arched one eyebrow. 'You?'

'Traveling,' he said. 'Working odd jobs here and there, trying to make sense of my life. You know. How's your daughter?'

'Grown up, married, two kids. I'm a grandmother. Who would have thought?'

'Not me. I don't see you that way.'

'Thanks. How long are you here for?'

He shook his head. 'I don't know yet. Through Christmas, I guess. It depends.'

She nodded slowly. 'On them?' She indicated the living room with a nod of her head.

'Well, on the boy, at least.'

She waited, watching him carefully. When he didn't say anything, she asked, 'Who is he?'

He cleared his throat softly. 'He's my son. I'm taking him to Chicago to see a specialist. He doesn't speak.'

She went very still. 'Is that your wife and daughter with him?'

'What?'

'The woman and the little girl?'

He blinked. 'No. Why would you—No, she's barely twenty, and I don't . . .'

'You seemed a little awkward about introducing them,' she said.

'Oh, well, maybe so.' He shook his head. 'I don't know them, is the problem. I just got here last night, and they were already here, and I don't know much more about them than you do.'

She took a bite of cookie and sip of milk, eyes shifting away. 'Tell me about your son. Where is his mother?'

He shook his head again. 'I don't know.' He caught himself too late, the lie already spoken, and quickly added, 'He's adopted. Single-parent adoption.' His mind raced. 'That's another reason I'm here. I'm not much good at this. I'm hoping Nest can help.'

He was getting in deeper, but he couldn't seem to stop himself. He had never thought he would have to explain the gypsy morph to anyone except Nest, that he would slip in at night, tell her why he was there, then wait for something to develop, and slip out again. Instead, he found himself in a situation where he was forced to make things up almost faster than he could manage.

'What is it you think Nest can do?'

He stared at her wearily. 'I don't know,' he admitted, realizing he was saying the same thing over and over, but this time speaking the truth. 'I'm in over my head, and I don't know who else to turn to.'

Her face softened instantly. 'John, you can ask Nest for anything. You know that. If she can help you, she will.' She paused. 'I hope you know that you can ask me, as well.'

He grinned ruefully. 'It helps hearing you say it. I wasn't sure how things stood between us.'

She nodded slowly. 'They stand the way they have always stood. Can't you tell?'

The way she looked at him when she said it, he guessed maybe he could.

Deputy Sheriff Larry Spence pulled over at the Quik Stop and went inside to buy some gum. When he came out,

hunching down into his heavy leather coat for warmth,
taking note of the graying skies and gusting winds, he
paused at the pay phone attached to the side of the building
and dialed the number FBI Agent Robinson had given him.
He still wasn't sure about this whole business, but he didn't
want to take any chances with Nest.

He drummed his fingers on the metal phone shell while
he waited for someone to pick up. He didn't much like
Robinson or that woman agent, especially after their visit to
his house. His kids didn't seem to like them much either.
Neither had slept very well last night, and Billy had come
awake half a dozen times screaming about knives. No, he
didn't much like it. It seemed to him they might have found
a better place to talk to him about John Ross. He'd thought
about calling the bureau, checking up on the agents, but he
was afraid it would make him look foolish to do so. Anyway,
all they wanted to know was whether or not Ross was out
there. Once he told them that, he was done with the matter.

Then, maybe, the buzzing in his ears would lessen and the
headaches would go away and he wouldn't be spending all his
time arguing within himself about what he should do.

The phone picked up on the other end, and a man said,
'Yes?'

The buzzing stopped. 'Agent Robinson?'

'Good afternoon, Deputy Sheriff Spence.' Robinson's
voice was smooth and reassuring. 'What do you have for
me?'

Spence looked off into the distance, unsure once more.
Ross didn't seem like much of a threat to him. Hell, he
could barely walk with that bum leg. Nest didn't seem all

that taken with him either, not in the way Robinson had suggested she was. He was pretty old for her, more like a father. It just didn't feel right.

'Deputy?'

'Sorry, I was checking on something.' He brushed his concerns aside, hearing whispers of derision and urgency that warned him of the dangers of equivocation. He was anxious to get this over with. 'I was out at Nest Freemark's house just a little while ago. John Ross was there.'

'Good work, Deputy. What did you tell them was the reason for your visit?'

'Oh, I made something up about checking on drug sales in the park, said it was a rumor we were investigating. I just asked if they'd seen anything, either of them.' He flashed on the angry response he'd gotten from Nest when he'd pushed the matter with Ross, and decided not to say anything about that part.

There was a pause on the other end. 'Did you notice anything unusual? Was Ross carrying anything?'

Spence frowned. 'Like what?'

'I don't know, Deputy. I'm asking you.'

Spence flushed at the rebuke. 'He was carrying a walking stick. He's got a bad leg.'

'Yes. Anything else?'

'Not that I could see.' His breath clouded the air in front of him. The buzzing returned, working its way around inside of his head, making him crazy. He pushed hard at his temples. 'I don't get it. What am I supposed to be looking for?'

Robinson's voice was iron sheathed in velvet. 'You know

better than to ask me that, Deputy. This is an ongoing investigation. I'm not at liberty to reveal everything just now.'

The whispers burned their way past the buzzing, filling
Larry Spence's head with sound and pain. Don't ask stupid
questions! Don't go into places you don't belong! Do what
you're told! Remember what's at stake!

Nest! Nest was at stake!

He pictured her in his mind, upset with him now, and it
was all because of John Ross. He pressed at his temples
anew and leaned into the shelter of the call box, suddenly
angry and belligerent. It wasn't right, the way she protected
him. What was he doing here, anyway? He was taking up all
the space in her life, so that there was no room for anyone
else.

Like me! She should be with me!

Just do as you're told, and everything will be all right,
someone seemed to say. Then he heard Robinson add, 'I'll be
in touch.'

He caught his breath. 'But I thought that was all you
wanted me to do,' he said, and the line went dead.

Ross and Josie finished their cookies and milk, waiting
on Nest's return. Josie talked about life in Hopewell, about
working still at Josie's, about the people who came in and the
way they were. Ross mostly listened, not having much he
could tell her that wouldn't reveal things he wanted kept
secret. He did say he had gone back to university a couple of
times, audited some courses, taught a few classes. He talked
a little of some of the places he had been. Josie listened and

didn't press, taking what he would give her, giving him the space he required when he chose to back away.

'I'd better be going,' she said finally. 'You can tell Nest I dropped by.'

She rose, and he stood with her, levering himself up with his staff. 'You sure you don't want to wait?'

'I don't think so.' She carried their glasses and the empty plate to the sink and began rinsing them. 'Will I see you again before you leave?' she called over her shoulder.

The question startled him. 'I don't know,' he said automatically. Then he added, 'I hope so.'

She turned, her eyes meeting his. 'Would you like to come to dinner tomorrow night?'

The back door opened and closed, and they both looked toward the hall. A moment later Nest appeared, rubbing her hands briskly. 'Cold out there. Hi, Josie.' She looked from one to the other. 'Have I missed anything?'

'We were just visiting,' Josie Jackson offered brightly. 'I stopped by with some cookies, Nest. John was keeping me company.' She hesitated only a moment. 'I was just asking if he might like to come to dinner tomorrow night.'

Nest never looked at John Ross. She walked over to the sink, picked up a cookie from the tray, and began munching on it. 'Sounds like a good idea to me. Why don't you go, John?'

Ross felt himself transfixed by Josie's eyes. 'You're all invited, of course,' she added, her smile warm and encouraging.

'No, thanks anyway,' Nest interjected quickly. 'I have a Christmas party to attend. I was planning on taking Bennett and Harper with me. I'll just take Little John, too. There will be lots of other kids there.'

She looked at Ross. 'John, you go to Josie's.'

Ross was thinking that he shouldn't do this. He wanted to, but it could only lead to the same sort of problem he had encountered with Josie Jackson fifteen years ago. It didn't make any sense to let history repeat itself when he knew he couldn't change it. Besides, it meant leaving the morph alone with Nest, which was dangerous for her. It meant taking a risk of the sort he should never even consider.

On the other hand, Nest Freemark seemed to be the gypsy morph's only hope. He had brought the morph to her in an effort to save it. He would have to give it up to her at some point, and time was running out. Maybe it would help if they could spend some time together without him.

'John?' Nest said quietly.

He was still looking at Josie, taking in her familiar features, her face and body, so much of it remembered so well after all these years. Everything about Josie was just right, a composite so perfectly formed that he couldn't imagine her being any other way. Being with her made him feel as if anything was possible and none of it mattered. Only her, and only now.

Fifteen years, and she still made him feel like this. A sweet ache filled him, then a small whisper of despair. No matter how she made him feel, it would end in the same way.

'I'd better take a rain check.'

Josie stared at him without speaking for a moment. 'All right, I understand.' She started for the kitchen entry, her eyes lowered. 'Bye, Nest.'

She went down the hall, stopped to pull on her coat, scarf, and gloves, and went out the front door. Her car started up in the drive and pulled out onto Woodlawn.

Nest busied herself at the kitchen counter, putting away the rest of the cookies. When she looked at Ross again, her expression was neutral. 'Sit down, and I'll tell you what happened in the park.'

He did as she asked and listened patiently as she talked about her meeting with Two Bears. But his mind drifted like smoke on the wind.

Outside, it was beginning to snow.

CHAPTER 13

By nightfall, eight inches had fallen and more was on the way. Local forecasts called for as much as two feet by morning, and a second storm was expected by Christmas. Ross listened to the weather report on the radio and stared out the kitchen window at the thick white fluff that blanketed everything for as far as the eye could see—which wasn't far, because snow continued to fall in big, swirling flakes that reflected the street and porch lights in gauzy yellow rainbows and curtained away the night.

Bennett Scott was sitting on the living-room floor with Harper, working on an old wooden puzzle. Harper would lift each piece and study it, then set it down again and move on. The puzzle had only twelve pieces, but she seemed to regard the preparation process as more important than actually building anything. Little John had turned away from the window and was sitting on the floor beside them, watching intently. He still wasn't saying anything. He still barely paid attention when he was spoken to. He was still a complete enigma.

Nest put together a stew for dinner, chopping up pota-
toes, onions, carrots, and celery, adding frozen peas, and
throwing the whole mess in with chunks of browned chuck
roast and some beef broth. She worked on memory and
instinct, not from a recipe, and every now and then she
would hesitate and consider before choosing or passing on
an ingredient. She spoke sparingly to Ross, who sat there
with his gaze directed out toward the snowfall and his
thoughts drifting to Josie.

It bothered him that he found himself so obsessed with
her. It wasn't as if he hadn't thought of her before he'd seen
her this afternoon; he'd done so often. But his memories of
Josie had seemed part of a distant past that was uncon-
nected to his present. He supposed that seeing her again
and remembering how strongly he felt about her simply
pointed up the emptiness of his life. Bereft of family and
friends, of loved ones, of relationships, of an existence of
the sort other people enjoyed, he was one of the homeless he
had worked with years ago in Seattle. It was only natural, he
supposed, that he should want those things that others had
and he did not.

Once or twice he pondered the appearance of Two Bears,
but there was nothing he could make of the Sinnissippi that
wasn't self-evident. A pivotal moment in the war between the
Word and the Void was at hand, and Two Bears was there to
monitor what happened. Perhaps he was there to attempt to
tip the balance, as he had done twice before in Nest
Freemark's life, but Ross knew it was pointless to try to
guess what O'olish Amaneh intended. The Indian lived in a
sphere of existence outside that of normal men, and he

would do what was required of him. For Ross to dwell on the matter was a waste of time.

But so was thinking of Josie. So there he was.

It was after six and dark two hours already when Robert Heppler called. He wanted to know if Nest would go tobogganing in the park. A check of the ice by the park service people revealed it was strong enough to take the weight of an eight-man sled, and with the snow packed down on the chute, the slide was slick and ready. Robert was taking Kyle while Amy stayed home with his parents, but he needed a few more bodies for weight. How about it?

While she was listening to Robert and before Ross even knew the nature of the conversation, he saw her do something odd. She started to say it probably wasn't a good time or something of the sort, and then she looked off into the living room where Harper and Little John were sitting with Bennett, hesitated a moment, her gaze lost and filled with hidden thoughts, and then said she would come if she could bring her houseguests, two adults and two children. Robert must have said yes, because she said they would meet him at the slide at eight, and hung up.

She relayed the conversation to Ross, then shrugged. 'It might be good for the children to get out of the house and do something kids like.'

He nodded, thinking she was jeopardizing the morph's safety by taking it out where it would be exposed and vulnerable, but thinking as well that the morph was useless if she couldn't get close enough to it to discover what it wanted of her and that maybe doing something together would help. There was no rational reason to believe going down a toboggan slide would make one iota of difference to any-thing, but nothing else seemed to be working. Nest had gone out to Little John several times before starting dinner, sitting with him, trying to talk to him, and there had been absolutely no response. She was as baffled by the morph's behavior as he was, and trying something different, anything, no matter how remote any chance of it working might seem, was all that was left.

'Maybe Little John will like Kyle,' she offered, as if read-ing his thoughts. 'Maybe he'll talk with someone closer to his age.'

Ross nodded, moving to help with silverware and napkins as she carried plates to the table and began arranging the place settings. The morph had taken the form of a child for a reason, so treating it like a child might reveal something. He thought it a long shot at best, but he couldn't think of anything better. He felt drained by the events of the past twenty-odd days, and the gypsy morph was a burden he wasn't sure he could carry much longer.

They sat at the table and ate stew with hot rolls and butter and cold glasses of milk, the morph eating almost nothing, Harper eating enough for three. Then they cleared the dishes and bundled into sweaters, parkas, boots, scarves, and gloves, and headed out into the night. Nest had enough extra clothing that she was able to outfit everyone, even Ross, who wore spares she had kept from her days with Paul. The night was crisp and still, and the wind had died away. Snow continued to fall in a hazy drifting of thick, wet flakes, and the ground squeaked beneath their boots. No other tracks marred the pristine surface across her backyard and into the ball diamonds, so they blazed their own trail, heads bent to the snowy carpet, breath pluming the air before them.

Ross limped gingerly at the rear of the group, his staff making deep round holes where he set it for support. All the while, he glanced around watchfully, still not trusting Little John's safety. As they crossed the service road, he caught a flicker of movement out of the corner of his eye. An owl winged its way through the trees bordering the residences, lifting away across the park, a tiny shadow attached to its neck—Pick, on patrol.

'Mommy, look!' Harper called out, dancing this way and that with her mouth open and her tongue out, trying to catch snowflakes. 'Mmmm, stawbury! Mmmm, 'Nilla!'

They crossed the open spaces of the ball diamonds toward the east end of the park and the toboggan slide. Lights blazed from the parking area, which was filled with cars, and shouts and screams rose from the slopes where the sleds were making their runs. Ross peered through the snow-fall, which was slowing now, turning to a lazy drifting of scattered flakes against a stark backdrop of black sky and white, snow-covered earth. The toboggan slide came into view, timbers blocky, dark struts against the haze of lights, looking like the bones of a creature half-eaten.

'Mommy, Mommy!' Harper was calling excitedly, pulling on Bennett's arm, trying to get her to move faster.

They found Robert waiting with the toboggan and Kyle throwing snowballs at another boy. Nest made quick introductions. Robert seemed pleased to see Bennett Scott and Harper and wary of Ross. Ross didn't blame him. Robert Heppler had no reason to remember him with any fondness.

But Robert shook his hand firmly, as if to prove his determination to weather the unexpected encounter, and beckoned them onto the slide.

The toboggan slide had been in Sinnissippi Park since Nest was a small child. Various attempts had been made to dismantle it as unsafe, a climbing hazard that would eventually claim some unfortunate child's life or health and result in a serious lawsuit against the park district. But every time the subject came up for discussion, the hue and cry of the Hopewell populace was so strident that the park board let the matter drop.

The slide was built on a trestle framework of wood timbers fastened together by heavy iron bolts and sunk in concrete footings. A fifteen-foot-high platform encircled by a heavy railing was mounted by ladder. Two teams could occupy the platform at any given time, one already loaded and settled in the chute, the other waiting to take its place. The slide ran down from the top of the bluff to the edge of the bayou, where it opened onto the ice. A space had been cleared of snow all the way to the levee and the railroad tracks. A good run with enough weight could carry a sled that far.

At the top of the slide, a park district employee stood just to the right of the chute with a heavy wooden lever that locked the sled in place while it was being loaded and released to free the sled when it was ready to make its run.

When he got a close look at how it all worked, Ross took Nest aside. 'I can't do this,' he told her quietly. 'Getting up there is just too hard.'

'Oh.' She glanced at his staff. 'I forgot.'

His eyes shifted to the others. 'I'd better wait here.'

She nodded. 'Okay, John. I'll watch him.'

He didn't have to ask who she was talking about. He stood aside as Robert got the rest of them in line, carrying the toboggan tipped on end with its steering rope hanging down the bed. When they reached the ladder and began to climb, Nest took the lower end of the toboggan to help boost it up. Ross glanced downhill to where the toboggan chute rested comfortably in its cradle of support timbers, lowering toward the earth as it neared the ice in a long, gradual incline. Lights brightened the pathway, leaving the chute revealed until it reached the ice. On the ice, everything was dark.

Robert's group climbed the platform and stood waiting for the sled ahead of them to load and release. Ross shifted his weight in the snow, leaning on his staff, his eyes wandering off into the trees. A pair of feeders slid like oil through the shadows. He tensed, then shook his head admonishingly. *Stop worrying*, he told himself. There were lights and people everywhere. A few feeders creeping around in the darkness didn't necessarily mean anything.

He glanced skyward for Pick, but didn't see him.

Moments later, Robert's group was climbing onto the sled, Robert steering, Kyle behind him, then Bennett, Harper, Little John, and Nest. They tucked themselves in place. Except for Robert, each had legs wrapped around the waist of the person ahead, hands and arms locked on shoulders. Kyle and Harper were laughing and shouting. Little John was staring off into the dark.

When the lock bar was released, the sled slid away from the loading platform into the night, picking up speed as it went, the sound of its flat runners on the frozen snow and ice a rough, loud *chitter*. Down the sled went, tearing through a wave of cold and snow, of freezing air, of shouts and screams. Ross watched until it reached the ice and disappeared from view.

All around him, families were lining up for another run.

One run, however, was more than enough for Bennett Scott. Harper, crazy little kid, was eating it up, screaming and howling like a banshee all the way down the run, laughing hysterically when it was over, then begging all the way back up the slope to do it again.

'Mommy, Mommy, go fast, go fast!' she trilled.

If the ride wasn't enough to give Bennett heart failure, the climb would finish the job, and by the time she'd reached the top again, she was gasping for breath and desperate for a cigarette.

'Mind if I sit this one out?' she asked Nest as they lined up for another run. That creepy guy Ross was standing off to the side, looking like he was about to be jumped or something, and if he didn't have to go with his kid, then Bennett didn't see why she should feel obligated to go with hers.

'Sure,' Nest agreed, peering at her. 'Are you okay?'

Bennett shrugged. 'Define *okay*. I just need a cigarette, that's all.' She looked at Harper. 'Honey, can you go with Nest, let Mommy take a break?'

The little girl gave her a questioning look, then nodded and turned away to say something to Kyle. He appeared to have hit it off with her, even if Little John hadn't. Creepy kid for a creepy father. She felt sorry for him, but that's the way things worked out. She should know.

Deliberately avoiding John Ross, who was looking somewhere else anyway, she moved away as the others took their place in line. She took a deep breath, her lungs aching with cold and fatigue, fished in her pocket for her cigarettes, knocked one loose from the pack, and reached for her lighter.

Someone else's lighter flared right in front of her face, and she dipped her cigarette tip to catch the fire. Drawing in a deep lungful of heat and smoke, she looked into Penny's wild green eyes.

'Hey, girlfriend,' Penny said, snapping shut the lighter.

Bennett exhaled and blew smoke in her face. 'Get away from me.'

Penny smiled. 'You don't mean that.'

'Try me.' Bennett began to move away.

'Wait!' Penny caught up to her and kept pace as she walked. 'I got something for you.'

'I don't want it.'

'Sure you do. It's good stuff. White lightning and mellow smoke. It'll make you fly and glide all night. I took some earlier. Let me tell you, this town becomes a better place in a hurry.'

Bennett sucked on her cigarette and kept her gaze turned away. 'Just leave me alone, all right?'

'Look, you hate it here as much as me. Don't pretend you don't.' Penny brushed at her wild hair, eyes darting everywhere at once, feral and hungry. 'This town is for losers. It's nowhere! I keep trying to find something to do besides sit around listening to Grandma snore. There's not even a dance club! Bunch of bars with redneck mill workers and farmers. "How's the crop this year, Jeb?" "Oh, pretty fair, Harv." Like that. Only way to get past losing your mind is doing a little something to keep sane.'

'I'm off drugs.' Bennett stopped at the edge of the trees where the darkness grew so heavy she couldn't make out even the trunks. She was already too far away from the light. 'I'm clean and I'm staying clean.'

'State of mind, girl,' Penny sniffed. 'There's clean and there's clean. You do what you want, what you need. You still stay clean.'

'Yeah, right.'

Penny shrugged. 'So now what? You gonna go back up there for more toboggan fun?' Her eyes were on the platform, clearly outlined in the light. 'Gonna join your friends?'

Bennett glanced up. Nest, Robert, and the children were standing on the platform, waiting to go next. 'Maybe.'

Penny laughed, her angular frame twisting for emphasis. 'You lie like a rug. You wouldn't go back up there on a bet! But you make believe all you want, if it gets you through your pain. Me, I got a better way. Have a look at this.'

She took out a plastic pouch filled with brilliant white powder, took a little of the powder on her finger, and snorted it in. She gasped once, then grinned. 'Mother's milk, girl. Try a little?'

Bennett wet her lips, eyes fixed on the pouch. The need inside her was so strong she didn't trust herself to speak or move. She wanted a hit so bad she could hardly stand the thought. Just a little, she was thinking. Just this one time. Penny was right. She was all twisted up inside, fighting to stay straight and not really believing there was any hope for it.

It wouldn't hurt anything. I've used before and kept going. Besides, Harper will be all right, no matter what. Nest is here. Nest is looking after her, probably better than me. Harper likes Nest. She doesn't need me. Anyway, doing a little coke would probably give me some focus. Just a little. I can take as much as I want and stop. I've always been able to do that. I can quit anytime. Anytime I want.

Oh, God, she thought, and squeezed her eyes shut until it hurt. *No. No.* She folded her thin arms against her body and looked back at the toboggan slide. 'You keep it.'

Penny kept looking at her for a minute, then tucked the pouch back into her coat pocket. She glanced up at the platform, where Nest and the others were climbing onto the sled.

Her smile was a red slash on her pale face. 'Better get back with your friends, take another ride down the chute,' she said. She smiled in a dark sort of way, giving Bennett a look that whispered of bad feelings and hard thoughts.

Then she walked over to the edge of the rise and looked down at the bayou. 'Be a good mom, why don't you? Keep your kid company.' She reached into her pocket, brought out a flashlight, pointed it downhill, and clicked it on and off twice.

She turned back to Bennett, stone-faced. 'Maybe later, girlfriend,' she said. 'There's always later.'

She waved casually over her shoulder as she walked off.

*S*tanding in the shelter of the big oaks and scrub birch bordering the bayou's edge, back where the lights from the toboggan run didn't penetrate, Findo Gask watched Penny

Dreadful's flashlight blink twice from the top of the rise and smiled. Time to start demonstrating to Nest Freemark the consequences of engaging in uncooperative behavior. He'd wasted enough time on her, and he wasn't inclined to waste any more.

He stepped from the shadows to walk down to the water's edge. The water was all ice just now, of course. But everything was subject to change. It was just a matter of knowing how to apply the right sort of pressure. It was a lesson that Nest Freemark would have done well to learn before it was too late.

Garbed in his black frock coat and flat-brimmed hat, he might have been a preacher come to the river to baptize the newly converted. But the demon had something more permanent in mind than a cleansing of the soul. Baptism wasn't really up his alley in any case. Burial was more his style.

Aware of the clutch of feeders creeping hungrily out of the shadows to be close to him, he knelt beside the ice. Feeders were fond of Findo Gask; they could always depend on him for a good meal. He saw no reason to disappoint them now.

He reached down and touched the ice with his fingers, eyes closing in concentration. Slowly, a crack in the surface appeared, broadened and spread, then angled off into the darkness toward the clearing on the ice where the sleds usually ended their runs, close to where the levee that supported the railroad tracks rose like a black wall. He lifted his hand away from the ice and listened carefully. Out in the darkness where the crack had gone, dispatched by his magic, he could hear snapping and splintering, then the soft slosh of water.

A nice surprise would be waiting for Nest Freemark and her friends when they came down this time.

He stood up in time to catch a glimpse of a large bird streaking out of the trees behind him, bolting from cover toward the slide.

Atop the loading platform, the locking lever released.

The toboggan slid out of the starting gate with a crunching of ice crystals under wood runners, easing down the chute, quickly picking up speed. There were only five of them riding the sled now, Robert in front, gloved hands fastened on the steering ropes, Kyle behind him, Harper and Little John next, and Nest in the rear. Hunched close against each other, legs looped over hips and around waists, arms clasped about shoulders, and heads bent against the rush of wind and cold and snow, they watched the landscape of dark trees and hazy trail lights gradually begin to blur and lose shape.

'Hang on!' Robert shouted gleefully, grinning back over his shoulder.

'Hang on!' Harper repeated happily.

The chittering sound of runners pounding over packed snow, ice, and wooden boards grew louder as their speed increased, mixing with a rush of air until they could only barely hear themselves shouting and yelling in response to their excitement. Nest clutched at Little John, trying for a response, but the boy continued his stoic silence, blue eyes fastened on something out in the night, his pale child's face expressionless and distant.

'Eeeeek!' Harper screamed in mock horror, burying her face in Kyle's parka. 'Too fast! Too fast!'

They were halfway down the slide, the darkness of the ice drawing steadily closer, the toboggan flying over the packed surface of the chute. Nest grinned, the burn of the wind on her cheeks sharp and exhilarating. It was a good run. Even with only five of them to give the sled weight, they were getting a smooth, fast ride, one that should carry them all the way to the levee. Ahead, Robert was bent all the way forward toward the sled's curled nose, trying to cut down wind resistance, anxious for more speed.

'Go, Robert!' she yelled impulsively.

They were almost to the end of the chute when a dark, winged shadow streaked out of the night, angling close, pulling even with Nest as she rode the sled. Huge wings and a barrel body hove into view, barely within her line of sight, and Pick's voice cried out in her ear, 'Get off the sled, Nest! Gask's cracked the ice right ahead of you! Get off!'

At first she thought she was imagining things—catching a blurred glimpse of the owl, listening as Pick yelled at her out of nowhere, hearing words that sounded crazy and dangerous. She turned her head in response, half expecting the shadow and the words to disappear, to prove a figment of her imagination. Instead the shadow swung closer, barely clearing the heads of riders pulling their sleds uphill for another run, shouts of surprise breaking out as the sled on the chute and the trailing shadow swept past.

'Nest, get off now!' Pick screamed.

She felt a jolt of recognition, a moment of deep shock. She wasn't mistaking what she saw or heard. It was real.

The toboggan launched itself clear of the chute and onto the ice, tearing away through sudden darkness as the trail lights disappeared behind.

'Robert, turn the sled!' she screamed at him.

Robert glanced over his shoulder, confused. She reached forward with a lunge, jamming all three children together as she did so, grabbed Robert's right arm, and hauled back, causing him to jerk sharply on the steering rope and yank the sled out of its smooth run. But the ropes gave only minimal control, and the sled continued to rush ahead, skidding slightly sideways, but still on track.

'Nest, stop it!' Robert shouted back, yanking his arm free. 'What are you doing?'

The darkness ahead was a black void beneath the clouded, snowy sky, and only a pair of very distant track lights provided any illumination. Nest felt her stomach clutch as she imagined what waited, and she yanked on Robert's arm anew.

'Robert! There's a hole in the ice!'

Finally, in desperation, she grabbed him by both shoulders, the children locked between them, shouting and screaming in protest, and launched herself sideways off the sled, pulling all of them with her. The toboggan tipped wildly, careened on its edge for a moment, then went over, spilling them onto the ice. Riders and sled separated, the former skidding across the ice into a snowbank, the latter continuing on into the dark.

Lying in a pile of bodies, gasping for breath and fighting for purchase on the bayou's slick surface, with Harper crying and Robert cursing, Nest heard a sudden sloshing of water.

A dark premonition burned through her.

'Hush!' she hissed at the others, grabbing at them for emphasis, needing their silence in order to hear what was happening, but fearful of what might be listening for them as well. 'Hush!'

They responded to the urgency of her words and went still. In the silence that followed, there was a rush of freezing wind across the open expanse of the bayou, and the temperature dropped thirty degrees and what little warmth the night had provided was suddenly sucked away. Ice cracked and snapped, shifting and reforming as the cold invaded its skin. Swiftly, the gap closed. There was a crunching of wood as the ice seized the toboggan, trapped it like a toothpick in a giant's dark maw, and sealed it away.

Nest took Harper in her arms and soothed her with soft words and a hug, quieting her sobs. Kyle was staring out into the darkness with eyes the size of dinner plates. Little John was staring with him, but with no expression on his face at all.

'Damn!' Robert whispered softly as the last of the terrifying ice sounds died away. 'What was that?'

You don't want to know, Robert, Nest thought in the dark silence of her anger and fear.

CHAPTER 14

They trudged back up the slope from the now empty ice, Nest and Robert herding the children in front of them, no one saying much of anything in the aftermath of the spill. Toboggan runs had been suspended after they went over. Now the slide attendant, a twenty-year park employee named Ray Childress, a man Nest had known since she was a little girl, had dropped the locking bar across the chute, emptied the loading platform of people, and hurried down the hill to find out what had happened. On reaching them, he fell into step beside Robert, warned off of Nest, perhaps, by the look on her face. Robert did his best to explain, but the truth was he didn't understand either, so the best he could do was improvise and suggest that further runs that night probably weren't safe and the park service could investigate the matter better in daylight.

Bennett was next on the scene, bounding down the slope in a flurry of arms and legs, snatching up Harper with such force that the little girl cried out.

'Baby, baby, are you all right?' Still hugging and kissing

her, she wheeled angrily on Nest. 'What did you think you were doing out there? She's just a little girl! You had no right taking chances with her safety, Nest! I thought I could trust you!'

It was an irrational response, fueled by a mix of fear and self-recrimination. Nest understood. Bennett was an addict, and she viewed everything that happened as being someone else's fault, all the while thinking deep inside that it was really hers.

'I'm sorry, Bennett,' she replied. 'I did the best I could to keep Harper from any danger. It wasn't something I planned. Anyway, she did very well when we tipped over. She kept her head and held on to me. She was a very brave little girl.'

'Sorry, Mommy,' Harper said softly.

Bennett Scott glanced down at her, and all the anger drained away in a heartbeat. 'It's okay, baby.' She didn't look up. 'Mommy's sorry, too. She didn't mean to sound so angry. I was just scared.'

When they arrived at the top of the slope, Ray Childress told those still standing around to go home, that the slide was closed for the evening and would open again tomorrow if things worked out. The adults, already cold and thinking of warmer places, were just as happy, while the kids grumbled a bit before shuffling away, dragging their sleds behind them. Cars started up and began to pull out of the parking lot, headlights slashing through the trees, tires crunching on frozen snow. Flurries blew sideways in a sudden gust of wind, but the snowfall had slowed to almost nothing.

Nest checked the sky for some sign of Pick, but the sylvan had disappeared. Undoubtedly, Findo Gask was gone as well. She chastised herself for being careless, for thinking that the demon wouldn't dare try anything in a crowd—no, she corrected herself angrily, wouldn't dare try anything *period*, because that had been the level of arrogance in her thinking. She had been so stupid! She had believed herself invulnerable to Gask, too seasoned a veteran in the wars of the Word and the Void for him to challenge her, too well protected by the magic of Wraith. Or perhaps it had simply been too long since anything had threatened her, and she had come to believe herself impervious to harm.

'You look like you could chew nails,' Robert said, coming over to stand beside her.

She put a hand on his shoulder and leaned on him. 'Maybe I'll just chew the buttons off your coat. How about that?'

'I don't have any buttons, just zippers.' He sighed. 'So tell me. What happened down there? I mean, what really happened?'

She shrugged and looked away. 'There was a hole in the ice. I caught a glimpse of it just in time.'

'It was pitch-black, Nest. I couldn't see anything.'

She nodded. 'I know, but I see pretty well at night.'

He brushed at his mop of blond hair and looked over at John Ross, who was kneeling in front of Little John, speaking softly to him, the boy looking somewhere else. 'I don't know, Nest. Last time something weird like this happened, he was here, too. Remember?'

'Don't start, Robert.'

'Fourth of July, fifteen years ago, when the fireworks blew up on the slope right below us, and you went chasing after him, and I went chasing after you, and you coldcocked me in the trees . . .'

She stepped back from him. 'Stop it, Robert. This isn't John's fault. He wasn't even with us on the sled.'

Robert shrugged. 'Maybe so. But maybe it's too bad that he's here at all. I just don't feel good about him, Nest. Sorry.'

She shook her head and faced him. 'Robert, you were always a little on the pigheaded side. It was an endearing quality when we were kids, and I guess it still is. Sort of. But you'll understand, I hope, if I don't share your one-sided, unsubstantiated, half-baked judgments of people you don't really know.'

She took a deep breath. 'Try to remember that John Ross is a friend.' He looked so chastened, she almost laughed. Instead, she shoved him playfully. 'Take Kyle and go home to Amy and your parents. I'll see you tomorrow night.'

He nodded and began to move away. Then he looked back at her. 'I may be pigheaded, but you are too trusting.' He nodded at Ross, then toward Bennett Scott. 'Do me a favor. Watch out for yourself.'

She dismissed him with a wave of her hand and walked over to Ross, who rose to greet her. 'Are you all right?' he asked.

She glanced around to make sure they were out of earshot. Little John stood next to them, but his gaze was flat and empty and directed out at the night. She put a comforting hand on the boy's shoulder, but he didn't respond.

'Gask opened the ice in front of us on that last run,' she said quietly. 'Pick warned me in time, and I tipped the sled over and threw us into a snowbank. The sled went into the water, and the ice closed over it and crunched it into kindling. I think. It was dark, and I didn't care to go out for a closer look. My guess is that what happened to the sled was supposed to happen to us.' She shook her head. 'I'm sorry. I know this is my fault. I'm the one who talked us into coming. I just didn't think Gask would try anything.'

Ross nodded. 'Don't blame yourself. I didn't think he would, either.' His gaze wandered off toward the trees. 'I'm wondering who this attack was directed at.' He paused and looked back at her. 'Do you see what I mean?'

She kicked at the snow with her boot, her head lowering. 'I do. Was Gask after us or Little John?' She thought about it a moment. 'Does he know Little John is a gypsy morph, and if he does, would he try to destroy him before finding a way to claim the magic for himself?'

Ross exhaled wearily, his breath clouding the air between them. 'Demons can't identify morphs unless a morph is using its magic, and that usually happens only when it's changing shape. Little John hasn't changed since we got here.' He frowned doubtfully. 'Maybe Gask guessed the truth.'

Nest shook her head. 'That doesn't feel right. This attack was a kind of broadside intended to take out whoever got in the way. It was indiscriminate.' She paused. 'Gask warned me what would happen if I tried to help you.'

A tired and distraught Bennett came up with Harper, saying the little girl was cold and wanted to go home. Harper stood next to her, looking down at her boots and saying nothing. Nest nodded and suggested they all head back to the house for some much needed hot chocolate.

Tightening collars and scarves against the deepening chill,

they walked back across the snowy expanse of the ball diamonds toward Sinnissippi Townhomes, pointing for the
lights and the thin trailers of smoke from chimneys illuminated by a mix of street and porch lights reflected off the
hazy sky. The last of the car lights trailed out of the park
and disappeared. From the direction of the homes bordering
the service road, someone called out a name, waited a
moment, then slammed a door.

Nest cast about for Pick once more, but there was still no
sign of him. She worried momentarily that something had
happened, then decided it was unlikely and that if it had, she
would have sensed it. Pick would show up by morning.

They reached the house and went in, dumped boots, coats,
gloves, and scarves by the back door, and moved into the
kitchen to sit around the table while Nest heated milk and
added chocolate mix and put out more of Josie's cookies. She
was still irritated with herself for being so incautious, but
she was angry as well with Findo Gask and wondered what
she could do to stop him from trying anything else. If he was
willing to attack them out in the open, with other people all
around, he might be willing to attack them anywhere.

They ate the cookies and drank the hot chocolate, and
Bennett took Harper off to bed. When she came back, Nest
had finished cleaning up and was sitting alone at the table.

Bennett walked to the sink and looked out the kitchen
window. 'I'm going out for cigarettes.'

Nest kept her expression neutral. 'It's pretty late.' She
wanted to say more, to dissuade Bennett from going anywhere, but she couldn't think of a way to do it. 'Maybe you
should wait until morning.'

Bennett looked down at her feet. 'It won't take long. I'll just walk up to the gas station.'

'You want some company?' Nest started to rise.

'No, I need some time alone.' Bennett moved away from the counter quickly, heading for the door. 'I'll be right back.'

Nest stood staring after her. A moment later, the back door opened and closed again, and Bennett was gone.

*B*ennett Scott walked up the drive and turned onto the shoulder of Woodlawn Road, working on the zipper of her coat as the cold burned against her skin, her boots plowing deep furrows through the new-fallen snow. She breathed in the biting air and folded her arms against her slender body. She had never liked the cold. Snowplows hadn't gotten this far out yet, and Woodlawn was still carpeted in white. A few cars eased past, locked in four-wheel drive, but mostly the road was empty and the night silent.

Bennett lowered her head against the cold and hugged her body. She knew she wasn't being rational. She didn't know what had brought her outside again, just knew she had to get away for a while. When she realized the sled had gone over and Harper was out there somewhere in the dark where she couldn't see her, maybe hurt, maybe worse, she just lost it. That was why she had attacked Nest, almost without thinking about it, reacting instinctively to her own fear. She couldn't bear the thought of losing Harper. The little girl was really all she had, the only thing in her life she hadn't managed to screw up. She would do anything to protect her, and she expected everyone else to do the same, though she didn't really think they would, and that was what ate at her. But she'd had confidence in Nest; she'd trusted her big sister.

She trudged through the snow, head lowered, eyes fixed on a moving point in space several feet in front of her boots. It hurt her to be angry then realize her anger was misplaced and wrong. She would walk awhile, wait for things to cool down. Nest wasn't angry with her and wouldn't hold it against her that she had blown up. Not Nest. Never Nest.

When she reached the gas station, she went inside and bought two packs of cigarettes and a coffee. The cold burned her anew when she came back out and started across the parking area toward Woodlawn Road. She lit a cigarette, shielding it in the cup of her hands, and drew the hot, acrid smoke deep into her lungs. Her head swam momentarily with the sensation, and the misery of her life faded to a manageable level. Maybe this would work for her, coming to Nest with Harper, trying to get a new start. Maybe she would find what she needed here, back in good old Hopewell. It wouldn't take all that much to stay straight, if she just worked at it hard enough. Get a job, a little apart-ment, put Harper in day care, make a few friends. She could do it.

Yeah, right. She shook her head angrily. Like there was any chance at all for someone like her. Who was she kidding? She cried a little, at how messed up her life was and how little chance she had of ever getting it straightened out again.

'It's cold out here, girlfriend,' Penny Dreadful said, ma-terializing next to her out of nowhere. 'Hey, my car's right over there. Come on. Let me give you a ride.'

Bennett looked at her dully, as if she were an inevitability, a constant in her life that refused to change or disappear. She suddenly felt tired and worn and alone. The cold numbed and deadened her, but that wasn't how she wanted to feel. She wanted to feel good about something. Just for a little while. Just for a bit.

Dropping her cigarette into the snow, she allowed Penny to take her by the arm and lead her away.

*D*eputy Sheriff Larry Spence sat alone in his living room at one end of the big couch, staring at the television set across the way. He was watching it without paying attention to what he was seeing, his mind trying to focus on the voice speaking to him through the telephone receiver he held against his ear. His kids were in bed, asleep or pretending to be, getting ready for a final day and a half of school before the Christmas break, anticipating what Santa was going to bring them. Billy was sleeping better again, not having those nightmares about severed fingers, but he still had a haunted look in his eyes that was troublesome.

'You have to go back out there in the morning and check on him,' Special Agent Robinson was saying through the phone, the words resonating inside Spence's confused and distracted mind. 'You have to be sure he doesn't hurt her.'

'Why would he do that?' Spence asked, staring at nothing. 'He doesn't have any reason to.'

Robinson paused thoughtfully. 'He's dangerous, and dangerous men will do anything. He uses her to give himself a place to hide. He is a drug dealer, and he is here to do business. If she discovers this, what do you think he will do?'

'But she doesn't want me to come there. She practically threw me out. What am I supposed to do?'

'You visit officially, just like you did today. You have every right to conduct an investigation.'

'Into what? What am I supposed to be investigating?'

'What do you think, Deputy? What seems possible to you?'

Larry Spence blinked and shook his head. 'He's a dealer. So he's here to make a sale. There must be something going down in the park, right?'

'Seems like a good place to start.'

'I can say someone saw something, try that out and see if I get a reaction.'

'Maybe someone did see something. Someone usually does.'

Spence shifted on the couch, his big frame leaning forward. 'I can't let that girl be hurt. She doesn't understand how people are. She believes the best about everyone, but she doesn't know.'

'Someone has to open her eyes to the truth,' Robinson agreed. 'She would be very grateful to anyone who did, don't you think?'

Larry Spence nodded slowly. 'I could do that for her. I could help her see how things really are. All I have to do is get him to slip up, say the wrong thing. I just have to keep after him, that's all. Yeah, just stay on it.'

He didn't know that Findo Gask was listening to him with the same amount of interest that young children evidence when they watch ants before stepping on them. He didn't know that he was just another wild card in a game being played by others, ready to be used when needed. *If nothing else*, the demon thought, *the good deputy sheriff will help distract the troublesome Miss Freemark.* The young lady was proving to be a much larger obstacle than he had anticipated.

But all that would change in the next twenty-four hours. Tonight's events had dictated the need for that.

'It's the right thing to do,' Larry Spence was mumbling to himself, nodding for emphasis.

The demon yawned. Bored, he sent a fresh nightmare into the head of the young boy sleeping in the deputy sheriff's back bedroom, then listened idly through the phone as the boy woke, screaming, to run for his father's reassuring arms.

Scattered snowflakes swirled on cold night winds across the mostly darkened expanse of Sinnissippi Park. Like white moths drawn by the incandescent brightness of the pole lights bracketing the roadways, they spun and twisted in small explosions of white. Elsewhere, moonlight peeked through breaking clouds to sparkle off frosted iron stanchions and crusted patches of road ice. Snow drifts climbed tree trunks and hedges, a soft white draping against the velvet black.

Ray Childress finished locking down the toboggan slide, placing chains across steps and loading ramps, hooking warning signs in place, and closing up the storage shed with its equipment and parts. It was quiet in the park, the last of the cars dispersed, the last of the people gone home. Trail lights still burned down the length of the slide and out along the bayou's edge where the ice had been cleared for skating, but only shadows shifted in the glare.

Ray paused in the act of padlocking the shed and stared out at the darkness below. Damned odd, he was thinking, ice breaking apart like that, all at once. He'd tested it himself earlier in the afternoon. He'd gotten four inches, solid, on several bores and no indication at all of a weakening on the run.

Damned odd.

He had been a park employee for a lot of years, and he'd run this slide during the winter months for most of them. He had seen a lot of strange things in that time, some of them of the head-scratching variety, but never anything like this.

A hole in the ice for no reason.

Standing there, thinking it over, he heard the unmistakable sound, sharp and penetrating in the stillness of the night, of ice tightening—a slow, almost leisurely crackling, like glass crunching underfoot.

He turned and looked. Twenty years, and this had never happened before.

He was a thorough, methodical man, one who followed through on what he started and made sure the job was done right. When something difficult arose in his work, he made it a point to understand the nature of the problem so that it wouldn't happen again, or so that if it did, he would be ready.

Impulsively, almost stubbornly, he snatched up his four-cell flashlight and started down the slope. He took his time, picking his way carefully over the icy spots, finding solid footing with each step. He just couldn't help himself—he had to have a look. He was being silly, doing it now, when it was so dark, instead of waiting for morning. But he wanted to see what had happened before someone else did so he could have a chance to think about it. It wouldn't take long, after all, just to take a look.

Myriad pairs of lantern eyes followed his descent toward the bayou, peering out from the gloom of the surrounding trees, tracking his movements, but he didn't see them.

His breath clouded the air before him as he eased down along the toboggan slide to the riverbank and made his way past the chute where it opened onto the ice. Carol was off with the church guild and wouldn't be back anytime soon, so there was no hurry about getting home. He shuffled his way across the ice with slow, steady steps, keeping to the edges of the shoveled area so that his boots could find purchase. The beam of his flashlight stabbed the darkness, reflecting off the hard, black surface of the frozen river.

It's so quiet, he was thinking. Not even the wind was—

He stopped abruptly, several hundred feet out, and stared at the tombstone shape of the Heppler toboggan where it jutted from the ice, cocked slightly to one side, its curled nose pointing skyward, its lower half trapped in the frigid waters. Parts of the sled were splintered and cracked, slats sticking out in jagged relief, bindings torn and shredded.

Ray shook his head. He had never seen anything like it. A hole opening and then closing again, crushing a toboggan into kindling. Damn, this was weird!

He started forward, intending to go only another few steps, but the ice gave way beneath him all at once, breaking

and snapping apart as if formed of the thinnest crust. Ray
threw himself backward toward safety, but he was already
sliding down into the freezing waters, the shock of the cold
taking his breath away. He went all the way under, then
fought his way back to the surface, gasping for breath. His
heavy boots and coat dragged at him, and he kicked his way
out of them, shucking off his gloves as well, all the while
groping desperately for a solid piece of ice on which to find
a grip.

'Help!' he screamed, his voice thin and high-pitched.
'Help! For God's sake!'

Thrashing wildly in the freezing waters, he tried to reach
the edge of the ice. But his flashlight was lost, its light gone
out, and he could not find the edge of the hole.

'Help me!' he cried in a long, desperate wail.

Then he saw the eyes, yellow and bright and all around,
slipping through the darkness just at the edge of his vision,
watching him struggle.

Waiting.

The ice began to shift. He heard it crack and snap, then
felt the water about him lift in a slow wave. The crunching
that followed was deep and resonant and filled the whole of
the night's silence. He screamed anew, but something was
dragging at his legs, pulling him under. He went down, then
flailed back to the surface, gasping for air. *No!* he was screaming inside his head. *Oh, please, no!*

He went down again, and this time when he came back to
the surface, the ice was in his face, closing over him. He
groped for the edge of the hole and managed to get one arm
out before the ice locked about his wrist, trapping everything

but his hand beneath the surface. He kicked and lunged frantically from beneath, but the ice would not give way.

From above, just where he could see them, the strange yellow eyes peered down at him hungrily.

For a few moments longer, his bare hand groped and twitched in the night air. When it finally quit moving, frost began to form on the skin until it looked as if the hand wore a white glove.

The eyes watched a little while longer, then disappeared.

TUESDAY,

DECEMBER 23

Chapter 15

It was dark the next morning when Nest rose to go running. Light from streetlamps pooled on the snow outside, and the luminous crystals of her bedside clock told her it wasn't yet five. She dressed in the dark, pulling on tights and running shoes, adding sweats, then tiptoed down the hall to the back entry where she picked out a rolled watch cap, gloves, and a scarf. A glance at the coatrack revealed no sign of Bennett's parka. Apparently, she hadn't come home.

The early morning air was so cold it took her breath away. She jogged up the drive, highstepping through drifts to the road, and began to run. The snowplows had been out early, and Woodlawn was already scraped down to the blacktop in a broad swath that cut like a river through the snow. Somewhere in the distance, the plows were still working, the growl of the big engines and the harsh scrape of the metal blades clearly audible in the windless silence. Nothing moved on the road ahead, and she ran alone down its center, picking her way along the cleanest sections, avoiding patches of ice and frozen snow, breathing deep and slow as she moved out toward the country.

Out where, in the solitude and silence, in the deep midwinter calm, she could be at peace.

Streetlights illuminated her path until she was past Hopewell's residences and into the farmland beyond. By then, the eastern sky was showing the first traces of brightness, and the black of night was lightening to deep gray. Stars glimmered in small, distant patches through breaking clouds, and the snow-covered fields reflected their silvery sheen.

She picked up her pace, the adrenaline surging through her body, a humming in her ears, the warmth of her blood pushing past the night chill until she didn't feel it anymore. Her mind worked in response to her body's energy, and her thoughts whirled this way and that, like kids waving their hands in a classroom, eager to ask questions. She wrestled with them in silence as she listened to the pounding of her shoes on the pavement, working through the mix of emotions the thoughts triggered. She should have been smarter about last night, taking them all to the toboggan run and putting them at risk. She should have been smarter about Bennett and not let her go out alone afterward. She probably should have been smarter about a lot of things—like running alone in the early morning hours when she was vulnerable to an attack by the demons stalking John Ross and the gypsy morph, almost as if daring them to try something.

And perhaps, she thought darkly, she was. Let them try contending with Wraith.

She shook off her bravado quickly, recognizing it for what it was, knowing where it led. Reason and caution would serve her better. But it was anger that drove her thinking. She had not asked to be put in this position, she kept telling herself. She had not wanted Ross to come back into her life, bringing trouble in the form of a four-year-old boy who wouldn't communicate with anyone. That he had spoken her name, bringing them to her, was bad enough. But that her name alone seemed to be the extent of his ability to respond to her, a boundary beyond which he could not go, was infuriating.

*L*ast night, when Ross and Harper were asleep and she was waiting up for Bennett, just beginning to worry that perhaps everything was not as it should be, he had come out of his room to sit with her. As soundless and fluid as a shadow, he had taken a place on the couch next to her. He had looked at her for just a moment, his blue eyes sweeping her face, and then he had turned his attention to the darkness that lay outside, staring once more through the window into the park. She had watched in silence for a time, then turned around to kneel next to him. The lights were all off, save for a nightlight in the hallway, so there was no reflection in the window, and the snowy sweep of the park, its broad expanse white and shimmering, lay revealed beyond the jagged wall of the hedgerow.

'What are you thinking, Little John?' she had asked, again trying out Two Bears' advice. Then added, 'What do you see?'

No answer. The boy's features were delicate and fragile, his body slender. His mop of dusky blond hair hung over his forehead and about his ears in ragged wisps. He needed a haircut, she thought, wondering if she should give him one. He needed food and love and a sense of belonging. He was too frail, in danger of fading away.

'Can't you say something, Little John?' she pressed. 'Can't you talk to me just a little? You spoke my name once. John told me so. You said "Nest." That's my name. Did you know about me? Tell me if you did, Little John. Tell me what you need, and I will try to give it to you.'

No answer. The boy's eyes remained fixed on the park.

'I have magic, too,' she said finally, easing so close they were touching. She half expected him to flinch or move away, but he stayed perfectly still. 'I was born with magic, just like you. It isn't easy having magic, is it? Magic does things to you that you don't always like. It makes you be something you don't necessarily want to be. Has that happened with you?'

She waited, then continued. 'I have a magic living inside me that I don't want there. It's my father's magic, and he gave it to me when I was very little. I didn't know it for a long time. I found out when I was fourteen. This magic is a ghost wolf called Wraith. Wraith is very big and scary. When I was little, he followed me everywhere, watching over me. Now he lives inside me. I don't really know how it happened . . .'

She trailed off, not liking how it made her feel to think about Wraith and magic. Flashes of Seattle and her battle with the demon who was trying to subvert John Ross roiled through her mind. It was her confrontation with the demon that had brought Wraith out of her, had revealed his presence. In her memories she felt him rise anew, taking who and what she was with him, sealing them together, so that she felt a part of his dark rage, his terrible power.

He had appeared again, unbidden and unwelcome, at the last race she had ever run . . .

She closed her eyes for a moment and then opened them to the window-framed night. 'If you could tell me about your magic, Little John, maybe we could help each other. Maybe we could make each other understand something about what's happened to us. I don't like living with myself like this. Do you?' She placed her hand gently on his thin wrist, feeling his warmth and the beat of his pulse beneath her fingertips. 'Maybe we could make each other feel a little better if we talked about it.'

But the gypsy morph did not answer, and although she stayed next to him talking for a long time afterward, there was no response, and at last she went to bed, leading him down the hall to his own room. She was tired and dejected, her perceived failures magnified by the lateness of the hour and her inability to make even the smallest progress in unlocking his voice.

She was running smoothly now, the roadway straight and open ahead, leading her on toward Moonlight Bay and the river. Her worries disappeared into the rhythm of her pace, fading away as she ran, left behind as surely as the place she had started from. When she returned, of course, they would be waiting. But they wouldn't seem so bad then;

they would be more manageable. That was how running worked.

At the five-mile mark, she turned around and started back again, feeling loose and easy and clearheaded. Her breath clouded the air before her, and her arms and legs pumped smoothly in the cold. She ran almost every day the weather allowed her to, ran because running was what she had done all her life to make herself feel better. It was what had given her strength when she needed it as a girl. It was what had led her to the Olympics and her eight-year professional career as a runner. It was what had, on more than one occasion, saved her life.

Sometimes, she wondered what she would have done without it. It was hard to imagine; running defined who she was, defined her approach to life. It wasn't that she ran from life, but all through it and around it to gain perspective and to find the answers she needed to deal with it. Mostly, she believed, she ran toward it. She was direct in her approach to things, a lesson she had learned from Gran years ago. Nest didn't mind. She thought, on balance, that Gran's way was probably best.

But, at the moment, she was having trouble making that approach to life work.

As she turned up the drive, she saw a fresh set of footprints in the snow. Bennett had returned. She came in the back door quietly, not knowing if anyone was awake yet, and heard voices from the living room. Shucking off her cap, scarf, gloves, and running shoes, she eased quietly down the hallway and peeked around the corner.

'So Little Bear went home to his mother and never, ever

went out into the woods again without asking first. The end.' Bennett Scott closed the book she was reading to Harper and put it aside. 'That's a good lesson for little girls, too. Never go out of your home without asking your mother first. You remember that, sweetie. Okay?'

''Kay, Mommy.'

Harper sat on her mother's lap, still in her pajamas, nestled in the folds of an old throw Bennett had wrapped about them both. Bennett still wore last night's clothes, and her face was haggard and pale.

''Cause Mommy would feel so bad if anything happened to her baby girl. You know that, Harper?' Bennett hugged her. 'Mommy just wants to keep you safe always.'

'Owee, Mommy,' Harper complained, as her mother squeezed too tightly.

'Sorry, sweetie.' Bennett rumpled her hair. 'Hey, look, the sun's coming up! Look, Harper! It's all gold and red and lavender and pink! Look at all the pretty colors!'

They shifted on the couch, turning to look east out the window where the sun's early light was just cresting the treeline of the park. Nest watched in silence as Bennett drew Harper's small body close to her own and pointed.

'You know what that is, Harper?' she asked softly. 'Remember what I told you? That's angel fire. Isn't it beautiful?'

'Bootiful.'

'Remember what Mommy told you about angel fire? At the beginning of every day, the angels go all over the world and gather up a little bit of the love that mommies have for their babies. They take bits and pieces, just scraps of it really, because mommies need most of it for themselves, to keep their babies safe. But the angels gather as much as they can, and they bring it all together, before anyone's awake, and they use it to make the sunrise. Sometimes it's really bright and full of colors, like today, because there is more love to spare than usual. But there is always enough to make a sunrise, enough to begin a new day.'

She went silent then, lowering her head into Harper's thick hair. Nest slipped past them down the hall to her bedroom. Once inside, she stripped off her running clothes and went into the bathroom. She took a long shower, washed her hair, dressed, and put on makeup, wondering all the while what she was going to say to Bennett. Maybe nothing, she kept thinking. Maybe it was better to just leave things alone.

She was just about to go out and start breakfast when she noticed the message light blinking on her answer machine.

There was one message.

'Hi. It's Paul. I thought I might catch you in, but I guess you're already up and about. Or maybe sleeping, but I bet not. Not you. Anyway, I just wanted to say "Hi" or maybe "Merry Christmas." I've been thinking about you lately. Haven't talked with you for a while, so I decided to call. Hope you're doing okay. Anyway, I'll try again later. Bye.'

The machine offered its programmed choices, delete, save, or replay, and she hung up. She stared at the phone, still sitting on the bed. She hadn't heard from Paul in months. Why was he calling her now? Maybe he just wanted to talk, like he said. Maybe it was something else. She wasn't sure she wanted to know.

She went out of her bedroom and down the hall to the

kitchen. She was pulling out pots and pans and cooking utensils, trying to decide on a breakfast menu, when Bennett came in and took a seat at the old kitchen table.

Nest glanced over. 'Morning.'

'Morning,' Bennett replied, holding her gaze only a moment before her eyes slid away. She looked a wreck, much worse than Nest had thought earlier. 'Can I do something?'

Nest saw Harper playing alone in the living room, content for the moment. 'Make yourself some coffee, why don't you?'

Bennett rose and walked over to the machine. She was pulling down the box of filters and opening the coffee tin when her hands began to shake. She couldn't seem to stop them, but continued to try to set the filter in place in the machine, dropping it to the floor in the process.

Nest walked over and took her hands, holding them firmly in her own. 'Nobody said this was going to be easy.'

Bennett's face turned sullen and stiff. 'I'm all right. Leave me alone.'

'Where were you last night, Bennett?'

'Out, Nest. Look, I don't want to talk about it, okay. Just leave me alone!'

She wrenched her hands away and threw herself back down at the table, biting her lip. Nest stayed where she was, watching. Then she turned away and began to make the coffee herself.

'You want me to leave?' Bennett asked after a moment, head lowered in the veil of her dark hair. 'Just say the word. Harper and I can be gone in a flash. We don't have to stay here.'

'I want you to stay,' Nest said quietly.

'No, you don't! You want me out! Admit it, okay? Don't lie to me! You want your life back the way it was before I showed up!'

Nest finished with the coffee and walked back to the stove, deciding on pancakes and sausage. 'Well, we don't always get what we want in life, and sometimes what we get is better than what we want anyway. Gran used to say that all the time. I think having you and Harper and John and Little John for Christmas is a good example of what she meant. Don't you?'

She waited a minute and then turned around. Bennett was crying, her head buried in her hands, her shoulders hunched and still. Nest walked over and knelt beside her.

'I don't even have a present for her!' Bennett's voice was a whisper of despair and rage. 'Not one shitty present! I don't even have the money to buy one! What kind of mother does that make me?'

Nest put her arm around Bennett's shoulders. 'Let's make her one, then. You and me. Something really wonderful. I used to do that with Gran, just because Gran liked making presents rather than buying them. She felt they were more special when you made them. Why don't we do that?'

Bennett's nod was barely perceptible. 'I'm such a loser, Nest. I can't do anything right. Anything.'

Nest leaned closer. 'When the holiday is over, Bennett, you and I are going to see a man who works with addicts. He's very good at it. He runs a program out of a group home he supervises. You can live there if you want, but you don't have to. I like him, and I think you will, too. Maybe he can help you get straight.'

Bennett shook her head. 'Sure, why not?' She didn't sound like she believed it. She sighed and buried her face in her hands, the sobs ending. 'God, I hate my life.'

Nest left her and went back to the stove. She worked on breakfast until the coffee was ready, then poured a cup and carried it over to Bennett, who hadn't moved from the table. Bennett drank a little, then rose and began setting the dining-room table. After a while, John Ross and Little John appeared, the boy going straight to the couch to kneel facing out the window once more. Harper stared at him for a while from where she sat on the floor, then went back to playing.

They ate breakfast in the dining room with the lights on. The sky clouded over again and the sun disappeared from view until it was only a pale hazy ball, the air turned gray and wintry in its absence. Outside, cars moved on the street like sluggish beetles, the whine of snow tires and the rattle of chains marking their passage. Andy Wilts came by from the Texaco station to plow out the drive with his four-by-four. Bennett talked with Harper about snow angels and icicle lollipops, and Nest talked about driving out to get a Christmas tree, now that she had company for the holiday. Ross ate in silence, and the gypsy morph looked off into space.

When they were clearing off the table and putting the dishes in the dishwasher, there was a knock at the front door. Nest glanced out the curtained window and saw a county sheriff's car parked in the drive. *Not again*, she thought immediately. Leaving Bennett to finish loading the dishes, she walked down the hall, irritated at the prospect of having to deal with Larry Spence yet again. What could he possibly want this time? Ross was in his room, so maybe she could avoid another confrontation.

'Good morning, Larry,' she said on opening the door, fighting down the urge to tell him what she really wanted to say.

Larry Spence stood stiffly in front of her, hat in hand, bundled up in his deputy sheriff's coat. 'Morning, Nest. Sorry to have to bother you again.'

'That's all right. What can I do for you?'

He cleared his throat. 'Well, it might be better if I could come in and we could talk about it there.'

She shook her head. 'I don't think so. We tried that yesterday, and it didn't work out very well. You better tell me what you want right here on the porch.'

His big frame shifted. 'All right. We'll do it your way.' His tone of voice changed, taking on a slight edge. 'It's about the drug dealing in the park. It's still going on. There was a major buy last night. Witnesses saw it going down and called it in. It's possible that someone staying in your house was involved.'

She thought at once of Bennett Scott, missing all night. Had Bennett been involved in a drug transaction? She stared at Larry Spence, trying to read his face. How would Bennett have paid for 'a major buy' of drugs? She didn't have any money.

'Who did your witnesses think they saw?' she asked quickly.

'I can't tell you that.'

'Who are your witnesses?'

'I can't tell you that, either.'

'But there are witnesses and they did see someone

involved in this drug buy that they can identify, is that right?'

'Right.'

But Nest didn't believe it. He was fishing for something. Otherwise, he wouldn't be here asking questions of her. He would be holding a warrant for Bennett's arrest.

'Look, Larry.' She closed the door behind her, moved out onto the porch, and stood with her arms folded across her chest. 'My guests were all here last night, tucked in their beds, asleep. If you have someone who says differently, trot them out. Otherwise, go investigate someone else.'

His face began to redden. 'You don't have to be so defensive about this. I'm just doing my job. Drug dealing is a mean business, and the people involved are dangerous. You might be smart to think about that.'

'What are you talking about, Larry? I don't know anyone involved in drug dealing, and I'm not friends with people who do. I have four guests in my house—friends I've known for a long time and a couple of small children. I hardly think they are the kind of people you're talking about.'

He shook his head stubbornly. 'Maybe you don't know them as well as you think.'

'Well, maybe that's so. But what makes you think you know them any better? This is the second time in two days you've been out here, ladling out large helpings of innuendo and unsubstantiated accusations.' Her anger surfaced in a rush. 'If you know something I don't, why not just tell me instead of waiting for me to break down and confess?'

'Look, Nest, I don't—'

'No, you tell me what you know, or you get the hell off my porch!'

He took a deep breath, his face bright red. 'John Ross is a dangerous man. There are people here investigating him. I'm trying to keep you out of it, girl!'

She stared at him. 'John Ross? This is about John?' She realized then that this had never been about Bennett, that Larry Spence had been talking about John all along. About John Ross dealing drugs. She wanted to laugh.

Larry Spence looked confused. 'Hey, you better wake up about Ross. The people investigating him . . .'

Something clicked in the back of her mind. 'What people?' she asked quickly.

'I can't tell you that.'

'You don't seem to be able to tell me much of anything. It makes me wonder how much you actually know.' She took a step toward him. 'Who do these people say they are, Larry? Have you checked them out? Because *I* have a feeling about this.'

His mouth tightened. 'It's an official investigation, Nest. I've already said more than I should, and I—'

'Is one of them an older man with gray eyes and a leather book, looks like an old-time preacher?'

Larry Spence stared at her, his sentence left unfinished. She sensed his uncertainty. 'Listen to me, Larry,' she said slowly, carefully. 'You're in way over your head. Way over. You stay away from this man, you understand? He isn't who you think. He's the one who's dangerous, not John Ross.'

The big man's mouth tightened. 'You do know something about this drug-dealing business, don't you?'

'There isn't any drug-dealing business!' she snapped, furious. 'Can't you get it through—'

His portable radio squawked sharply in his coat pocket, and he turned away from her as he pulled it out. He spoke softly for a minute, shielding his voice from her, listened, and turned back. 'I've got to go. We'll talk about this later. You be careful, girl. I don't think you're clear about what's going on.'

Without waiting for her response, he walked off the porch to his car, climbed in, and drove off. She wheeled away as he did so, went back inside, and stood seething in the entryway. Larry Spence was a fool. Findo Gask was using him, that much was certain. But what was he using him for? She thought of the ways the demons she had encountered before had used humans as pawns to get what they wanted. She remembered her father, come back to claim her for his own. She remembered Stefanie Winslow.

History always repeats itself, she thought angrily. *There is nothing you can do to change that. Even in the small things in our lives, we make the same mistakes.* How could she avoid that happening here?

She rubbed her arms through her heavy sweater, chasing away the last of the winter chill from her skin. But the cold that had settled in the pit of her stomach remained.

CHAPTER 16

When she had calmed down enough to think about something else, Nest loaded everyone into the Taurus and drove them to a tree farm north of town. Picking up a bow saw from the farmer, she marched them out into the Christmas tree forest in search of an acceptable tree. Other customers prowled the long rows, searching for trees of their own. The air was cold and dry against their skins, and a west wind whipped across the snowy fields, kicking up sudden sprays. Heavy clouds rolled in from across the Mississippi, and Nest could taste and smell the impending snow.

Exhilarated, she breathed in the winter air. If she was going to celebrate Christmas, she was going to do it right. Sitting around the house might be the easier choice, but it was also apt to drive her insane. Better to be out doing something. Ever since she was a little girl, she had handled her problems by getting up and doing something. It seemed to help her think, to come to terms with things. It was why she had begun running.

Harper raced ahead, darting in and out of the shaggy trees, playing hide-and-seek with anyone who would do so, leaping out unexpectedly and laughing as the adults feigned surprise and shock. Little John watched her for a time, his face expressionless, his blue eyes intense. He did not join in or respond, but he was not disinterested either. Something about the game seemed to engage his curiosity, and once or twice he slowed long enough to give Harper a chance to spring out at him and run away. Nest watched him do it several times, puzzled by what it meant. Once she encouraged him to join in, but he just walked away.

They found a fat little five-foot fir that Harper hugged and jumped up and down over, so they cut it down and hauled it out to where the farmer measured it and collected their payment. After loading the tree in the trunk and tying down the lid to hold it in place, they drove back to the house. It was not yet noon, and after consuming such a big breakfast, no one was ready to eat again. Nest wanted to keep everyone occupied, so she suggested they stick the tree in a bucket of water on the back porch to give it a chance to relax, and go for a walk.

With snow beginning to fall in fat, lazy flakes, they struck out into the park, Harper in the lead, racing this way and that, Nest, Ross, and Little John following. Smoking a cigarette and hunching her thin shoulders against the cold, Bennett, trailing everyone, had the look of someone who would just as soon be somewhere else. She had grown increasingly moody as the morning progressed, slowly withdrawing from all of them, Harper included. Nest had tried to make conversation, to bring her out of whatever funk

she had fallen into, but nothing worked. Bennett's eyes
drifted away each time she was addressed, as if she had gone
off in search of something. Whatever had happened last
night, Nest thought darkly, it was not good.

But she decided to wait on saying anything more. Bennett
was already in such a black place that it didn't seem to Nest
that it would do much good to emphasize it. After Christmas, maybe she would say something.

They drifted across the snow-covered ball diamonds
toward the toboggan slide, drawn at first by their lingering
curiosity over last night's accident and then by a clutch of
police, fire, and ambulance vehicles that came into view.
The deputy sheriff's car belonged to Larry Spence. Nest
glanced at Ross, but he shook his head to indicate he had
no idea what was happening. Nest moved to the front of
the group, directing them west of the parking lot and its
knot of traffic, crossing the road farther down. People were
gathered along the crest of the slope leading down to the
bayou, all of them whispering or standing silent, eyes fixed
on a knot of firemen and ambulance workers clustered on
the ice.

Nest's group slowed beside the others. The first thing she
saw was the twisted length of Robert's toboggan lying to one
side. A dark, watery hole glimmered where the ice had been
chopped apart by picks and axes to free it. But then she saw
that it wasn't the sled they had worked to free. The firemen
and ambulance techs were working over a sodden, crumpled
form.

'What's going on?' she asked a man standing a few feet
away.

The man shook his head. He had owlish features and a beard, and she didn't know him. 'Someone fell through the ice and drowned. Must have happened during the night. They just fished him out.'

Nest took a steadying breath and looked back at the tableau on the bayou. A body bag was being unrolled and unzipped, its bright orange color brilliant against the dull surface of the ice. 'Do they know who it is?' she asked.

The man shrugged his heavy shoulders. 'Don't know. No one's been up yet to say. Just some poor slob.' He seemed unconcerned.

Someone who fell through the ice, she repeated carefully, trying out the sound of the words in her mind, knowing instantly Findo Gask was responsible.

'They had to chop right through the ice to get him,' the man said, growing chummy now, happy to be sharing his information with a fellow observer. 'His hand was sticking out when they found him. Ice must have froze right over him after he drowned. The hand was all he got out. Maybe he was a sledder. They found him next to that toboggan. It was froze up, too.'

Who was he? Nest wondered. Someone who had ventured out onto the ice while the demon magic was still active? The magic would probably have responded to anyone who got close enough.

The man next to her looked back at the ice. 'You'd think whoever it was would have been smarter. Going out on the ice after the slide was shut down and the lights turned off? Stupid, if you ask me. He was just asking for it.'

A woman a little farther down the line turned toward

them. Her voice was low and guarded, as if she was afraid someone would hear. 'Someone said it's a man who works for the park system. They said he was working the slide last night until an accident shut it down, and he must have gone out on the ice afterward to check something and fallen in.' She was small and sharp-featured and wore a blue stocking cap with a bell on the tassel. Her eyes darted from the man's face to Nest's, then away again.

Ray Childress, Nest thought dully. *That's Ray down there.*

She turned away and began walking back toward the road. 'Let's go,' she said to the others.

'Mommy, what's wrong?' Harper asked, and Bennett hushed her softly and took her hand.

Nest kept her eyes lowered as she walked, sad and angry and frustrated. Ray Childress. Poor Ray. He was just doing his job, but he was in the wrong place at the wrong time. This whole thing was her fault. It had happened because she had insisted on bringing everyone out for sledding, even knowing Findo Gask was a danger to them, even after she had been warned not to help John Ross. It wasn't enough that she had saved them on the ice. She should have anticipated that others would be in danger, too. She should have warned Ray. She should have done something. Her eyes teared momentarily as she remembered how long she had known him. Most of her life, it seemed. He had been there when her grandfather had almost died in the fireworks explosion fifteen years ago. He had been one of the men who had dragged Old Bob clear.

Now he was dead, and a pretty good argument could be made that it was because of her.

'Nest!' Ross called sharply.

At first she ignored him, not wanting to talk to anyone, still wrapped in her grief. But then he called to her again, and this time she heard the urgency in his voice and looked up.

Findo Gask stood a dozen yards away at the edge of a clump of alder and blue spruce. He had materialized all at once, his black-garbed form barely distinguishable from the dark, narrow trunks of the alder trees and the slender cast of their shadows. He wore his familiar flat-brimmed black hat and carried his worn leather book. His eyes glittered from beneath his frosted brows as they fixed on her.

'A tragic turn of events, Miss Freemark,' he said softly. 'But accidents happen sometimes.'

She stared at him without speaking for a moment, frightened by his unexpected appearance, but enraged as well. 'Who would know that better than you?' she said.

His smile did not waver. 'Life is uncertain. Death comes calling when we least expect it. It is the nature of the human condition, Miss Freemark. I don't envy you.'

She glanced over her shoulder at Ross, Bennett, Harper, and Little John, who stood in a loose clutch, watching. Then she looked back at the demon. 'What can I do for you, Mr. Gask?'

He laughed softly. 'You can give me what I want, Miss Freemark. You can give me what I've come here for. You and Mr. Ross. You can give it to me, and I'll go away. Poof—just like that.'

She came forward a few steps and stopped, distancing herself from the others. 'The gypsy morph?' she asked.

He nodded, cocking his head slightly.

'Just hand it over, and you'll be gone? No more unexpected accidents? No more visits to my home by deluded law
enforcement officials inquiring into drug buys in the park?'

His smile broadened. 'You have my word.'

She matched his smile with her own. 'Your word? Why is
it I don't find that particularly reassuring?'

'In this case, you can rely on it. I have no interest in you
or your friends beyond finding the morph. Where is it, Miss
Freemark?'

His eyes locked on hers, probing, and she was struck with
a flash of insight. He doesn't know it's Little John he's looking for, she realized. That was the reason for the threats and
the attacks; he was stymied unless he could compel her cooperation. He couldn't identify the morph without her.

She almost laughed aloud.

'You seem perplexed by my request, Miss Freemark,'
Findo Gask said jovially, but there was an edge to his voice
now. 'Is there something about it you don't understand?'

She shook her head. 'No, I understand perfectly. But you
know what? I don't like being threatened. Especially by
someone like you. Especially now, when I'm not in a very
good mood and I'm feeling angry and hurt, and it's mostly
because of you. I've known that man you let die on the ice
for most of my life. I liked him. He didn't do anything to
you, but that wasn't enough to save him. That doesn't matter
to you, does it? You don't care. You don't care one bit.'

Findo Gask pursed his lips and shook his head slowly. 'I
thought we were beyond accusations and vitriol. I thought
you understood your position in this matter better than it
appears you do.'

'Guess you thought wrong, huh?' She came forward another step. 'Let me ask you something. How safe do you feel out here?'

He stared at her in surprise. His smile disappeared, and his seamed face suddenly lost all expression.

She came forward another step, then two. She was only a few paces away from him now. 'I'm not afraid of demons, Mr. Gask. I've faced them before, several times. I know how to stand up to them. I know how they can be destroyed. I have the magic to make it happen. Did you know that?'

He did not give ground, but there was a hint of uncertainty in his frosty eyes. 'Don't be foolish, Miss Freemark. There are children to be considered. And I did not come alone.'

She nodded slowly. 'That's better. Much better. Now I'm seeing you the way you really are. Demon threats are all well and good, but they work best when they are directed toward children and from behind a shield of numbers.'

Her words were laced with venom, and hot anger burned through her. Wraith was awake and moving inside, all impatience and dark need, her bitterness fueling his drive to break free and attack. She was tempted. She was close to letting him go, to willing him out of her body and onto the hateful form of the creature in front of her. She wasn't sure how that would end, but it might be worth finding out.

'I made a mistake with you when you came to my house two days ago, Mr. Gask,' she said. 'I should never have let you leave. I should have put an end to you then and there.'

His mouth twisted. 'You overestimate yourself, Miss Freemark. You are not as strong as you think.'

She smiled anew. 'I might say the same for you, Mr. Gask. So now that we know where we stand on matters, why don't we just say good-bye and go our separate ways?'

He considered her silently for a moment, his eyes shifting to Ross and the others, then back again. 'Perhaps you should take a closer look at yourself, Miss Freemark, before you expend all of your energy judging others. You are not an ordinary, commonplace member of the human race with which you are so quick to identify. You are an aberration, a freak. You have demon blood in your body and demon lust in your soul. You come from a family that has dabbled more than once in demon magic. You think you are better than us, and that your service to the Word and the human cause will save you. It will not. It will do exactly the opposite. It will destroy you.'

He lifted the leather-bound book in front of him. 'Your life is a charade. All that you have accomplished is a direct result of your demon lineage. Most of it you have repudiated over the course of time, until now you have nothing. I know your history, Miss Freemark. I made it a point to find out. Your family is dead, your husband left you, and your career is in tatters. Your life is empty and useless. Perhaps you think that by allying yourself with Mr. Ross, you will find the purpose and direction you lack. You will not. Instead, you will continue to discover unpleasant truths about yourself, and in the end your reward for doing so will be a pointless death.'

His words were cutting and painful, and there was enough truth in them that she was not immune to their intended effect. But they were the same words she had spoken to herself more than once in the darker moments of her life, when acceptance of harsh truths was all that would save her, and she could hear them again now without flinching. Findo Gask would break down her resolve with fear and doubt, but only if she let him do so.

He smiled without warmth. 'Better think on it, Miss Freemark. Should it come to a test of magics between you and me, you are simply not strong enough to survive.'

'Don't bet against me, Mr. Gask,' she replied quietly. 'It may be that this is a battle you will win, that the magic you wield is more powerful than my own. But you will have to find out the hard way. John Ross and I are agreed. We will not hand over the gypsy morph—not because you say we must or because you threaten us or even if you hurt us. We won't cede you that kind of power over our lives.'

Findo Gask did not reply. He simply stood there, as black as ink and carved from stone. The wind gusted suddenly, whipping loose snow across the space that separated them. The demon stood revealed for an instant longer before the blowing snow screened him away.

When the wind died again and the loose snow settled, he was gone.

Some lessons you learn early in life, and some of those lessons are hard ones. Nest learned an important one when she was twelve and in the seventh grade. She had only just the year before experienced the consequences of using magic after Gran had warned her not to do so, and she was still coming to terms with the fact that she would always be

different from everyone else. She had taken a book from the
school library and forgotten to check it out. When she tried
to slip it back in place without telling anyone, she got caught.
Miss Welser, who ran the library with iron resolve and an
obvious distrust of students in general, found her out,
accused her of lying when she tried to explain what had
happened, and sentenced her to after-school detention as
punishment. Nest had been taught not to challenge the
authority exercised by adults, particularly teachers, so she
accepted her punishment without complaint. Day after day,
week after week, she came in after school to perform whatever service Miss Welser required—shelving, stacking,
cataloguing, and cleaning, all in long-suffering silence.

But after a month of this, she began to wonder if she
hadn't been punished enough for a transgression she didn't
really believe she had committed in the first place, and she
screwed up her courage sufficiently to ask Miss Welser when
she would be released. It was almost March, and spring training for track would begin in another few weeks. Running was
Nest's passion then as now; she did not believe she should
have to give it up just because Miss Welser didn't believe her
about the book. But Miss Welser didn't see it that way. She
told Nest she would be on detention for as long as it took,
that sneaking and lying were offenses that required severe
punishment in order to guarantee they would not happen
again.

Nest was miserable, trapped in a situation from which it
did not seem she could extricate herself. Everything had begun
to revolve around Miss Welser's increasingly insufferable
control over her life. If Gran noticed what was happening,

she wasn't saying, and Nest wasn't about to tell her. At twelve, she was beginning to learn she had to work most things out for herself.

Finally, with only a week to go before the start of track season, she told her coach, Mr. Thomas, she might not be able to compete. One thing led to another, and she ended up telling him everything. Coach Thomas was a big, barrel-chested man who preached dedication and self-sacrifice to his student athletes. Winning wasn't the only thing, he was fond of saying, but it wasn't chopped liver either.

He seemed perplexed by her attitude. 'How long have you been going in after school?' he asked, as if maybe he hadn't heard her correctly. When she told him, he shook his head in disgust and waved her out the door. 'Tell Miss Welser that track begins on Monday next and Coach Thomas wants you out here training with everyone else and not in the library shelving books.'

Nest did what she was told, thinking she would probably end up being sentenced to the library for life. But Miss Welser never said a word. She just nodded and looked away. Nest finished out the week and never went back. After a while, she realized she should have spoken up sooner, that she should have insisted on a meeting with the principal or her adviser. Miss Welser had kept her coming in because she hadn't stood up for herself. She had given Miss Welser power over her life simply by accepting the premise that she wasn't in a position to do anything about it. It was a mistake she did not make again.

Staring at the space Findo Gask had occupied only moments before, she thought about that incident. If she

gave the demon power over her by conceding that she was
frightened, she lost any chance of ever being free of him.

Of course, there was a certain amount of risk involved in
standing up for yourself, but sometimes it was a risk you had
to take.

Ross, Bennett, and the children came up to her, Ross's
hands knotted about his rune-scrolled staff as he limped
past her a few steps to study carefully the tree-thrown shadows. Far back in the hazy gloom of the conifers, there was a
hint of movement. Ross started toward it. He looked so
tightly strung that Nest was afraid he would lash out at anything that moved.

'John,' she said quietly, drawing his dark gaze back to
hers.'Let him go.'

Ross shook his head slowly. 'I don't think I should. I
think I should settle this here and now.'

'Maybe that's what he's hoping you'll try to do. He said
he wasn't alone.' She paused to let the implication sink in.
'Leave it for another time. Let's just go home.'

'I don't like that old man,' Bennett muttered, her thin face
haunted as she pulled Harper close. 'What was he talking
about, anyway? It was hard to hear.'

'Scary man,' her daughter murmured, hugging her back.

'Scary is right,' Nest agreed, ruffling the little girl's parka
hood in an effort to lighten the mood. Her eyes found
Bennett's, and she spoke over the top of Harper's head. 'Mr.
Gask thinks we have something that belongs to him. He's
not very rational about the matter, and I can't seem to persuade him to leave us alone. If he comes to the house again,
don't open the door, not for any reason.'

Bennett's mouth tightened. 'Don't worry, I won't.' Then she shrugged. 'Anyway, Penny said he—'

She caught herself and tried to turn away, but Nest moved quickly in front of her. 'Penny? Penny who? What did Penny say?'

Bennett shook her head quickly. 'Nothing. I was just—'

It can't be, Nest was thinking, remembering the strange, wild-haired girl at the church. 'Penny who?' she pressed, refusing to back off.

'Leave me alone!'

'Penny who, Bennett?'

Bennett stopped moving, head lifting, eyes defiant. She brushed at her lank hair with one gloved hand. 'Get over yourself, Nest! I don't have to tell you anything!'

'I know that,' Nest said. 'You don't. But this is important. Please. Penny who?'

Bennett took a deep breath and looked off into the distance. 'I don't know. She didn't tell me her last name. She's just a girl I met, that's all. Just someone I talked to a couple times.'

'Someone who knows Findo Gask?'

Bennett flicked her fingers in a dismissive gesture. 'She says he's her uncle. Who knows?' She fumbled in her pockets for her cigarettes. 'I don't think she likes him any more than we do. She makes fun of him all the time.'

'All the time,' Nest repeated, watching as Bennett lit a cigarette and inhaled deeply. *Like all last night, maybe. Because that's who you were with.* 'What did she say about Findo Gask?' she asked again.

Bennett blew out a thin stream of smoke. 'Just that he was

leaving town in a day or so and wouldn't be back. Said it was the only thing they'd ever agreed on, him leaving this pissant little town.' She sighed. 'I just thought that meant we probably wouldn't be seeing him again because he'd be gone, that's all. What's the big deal?'

Ross was staring at both of them, eyes shifting from one to the other.

'Does Penny have wild red hair?' Nest asked quietly.

Bennett's gaze lifted. 'Yeah. How did you know that?'

Nest wondered how she could explain. She decided she couldn't. 'I want you to listen to me, Bennett,' she said instead. 'I can't tell you how to live your life. I won't even try. It's not my job. You're here with Harper because you want to be, and I don't want to chase you off by giving you a lot of orders. But I won't look the other way when I think you're in danger. So here it is. Stay away from Penny and Gask and anyone you think might be friendly toward them. You'll have to trust me on this, just like I have to trust you on some other things. Okay?'

'Yeah, okay.' Bennett took a last drag on her cigarette and dropped it into the snow. 'I guess.'

Nest shook her head quickly. 'No guessing. I know a few things you don't, and this is one. These are dangerous people. Penny as much as Gask. I don't care what she says or does, she isn't your friend. Stay away from her.'

Ross glanced past her to where they were bringing up Ray Childress from the bayou. 'Maybe we ought to get back to the house,' he said, catching her eye.

Nest turned without another word and started walking. *Maybe we ought to dig ourselves a hole, crawl into it, and pull the ground up over our heads instead,* she thought. *Because not much of anywhere else is looking very safe.*

But she kept the thought to herself.

CHAPTER 17

They had crossed the park road onto the flats and were starting for home when Nest changed her mind and told the others to go on without her. It was a spur-of-the-moment decision, but she felt a compelling need to visit the graves of her grandparents and mother. She hadn't been up that way recently, although she had intended to go more than once, and her encounter with Findo Gask lent new urgency to her plans. There was a danger in putting things off for too long. Ross, Bennett, and the children could go back to the house and get started on decorating the tree. Everything they needed was in labeled boxes in the garage. She would catch up with them shortly.

Bennett and the children were accepting enough, but Ross looked worried. Without saying so, he made it clear he was concerned that Findo Gask might still be somewhere in the park. Nest had considered the possibility, but she didn't think there was much danger of a second encounter. The park was full of families and dog walkers, and there would be other visitors to the cemetery as well.

'This won't take long,' she assured him. 'I'll just walk up, be by myself for a few moments, and walk back.' She glanced at the sky. 'I want to get there before it snows again.'

Ross offered to accompany her, rather pointedly she thought, but she demurred. He would be needed to help with the Christmas tree, she told him just as pointedly, nodding toward Bennett and the children. Ross understood.

She set off at a steady pace across the flats until she reached the road again, then began following its plowed surface west toward the bluffs. The sky was blanketed with clouds, and the first slow-spiraling flakes of new snow were beginning to fall. West, from where the weather was approaching, it was dark and hazy. The storm, when it arrived, would be a big one.

A steady stream of vehicles crawled past her, going to and from the parking lot. Some had brought toboggans lashed to the roofs of cars and shoved through the gates and back windows of SUVs. Apparently the word hadn't gotten around yet that the slide was closed. There were sledders on the slopes leading down to the bayou, and kids ran and cavorted about the frozen playground equipment under the watchful, indulgent eyes of adults. Futile efforts to build snowmen were in progress; it was still too cold for the snow to pack.

Watching the children play, Nest was reminded how much of her life had been lived in Sinnissippi Park. When she was little, the park had been her entire world. She had known there were other places, and her grandparents had taken her to some of them. She understood that there was a world outside her own. But that world didn't matter. That world was as distant and removed as the moon. Her family and friends lived at the edge of the park. Pick lived in the park. Even the feeders appeared to her mostly in the park. The magic, of course, had its origins in the park, and Gran and the Freemark women for five generations back had cared for that magic.

It wasn't until the summer of her fourteenth birthday, when her father came back into her life, that everything changed. The park was still hers, but it was never again the same. Her father's deadly machinations forced her to give up her child's world and embrace a much larger one. Perhaps it was inevitable that it should happen, later if not then. Whatever the case, she made the necessary adjustment.

But even after growing up and moving away for a time, even with all she had experienced, she never lost the sense of belonging that she found in the park. She marveled at it now, as she walked down the snow-packed road in the wintry gray light—the way she felt at peace in its confines, at home in its twenty acres of timber and playground and picnic areas. Even now, when there was reason to be wary of what might be lurking there, she did not feel threatened. It was the legacy of her childhood, of her formative years, spent amid magic and magic's creatures, within a world that few others even knew existed.

She wondered if she would ever lose that. She couldn't be sure, especially now. Findo Gask was a powerful and intrusive presence, and his intent was to undo everything in her life. To take her life, she corrected herself quickly, if he could find a way to do so. She looked off across the river, where smoke from fireplace chimneys lifted in the air like streamers. It was the John Ross factor again. Every time she connected with him, her life changed in a way she hadn't imagined was possible. It would do so again this time. It was foolish to believe otherwise.

She shook her head at the enormity of this admission. It would crush her if she tried to accept its weight all at once. She would have to shoulder it a little at a time, and not let herself be overwhelmed. Maybe then she could manage to carry it.

The wind gusted hard and quick down the road, sending a stinging spray of ice needles against her skin and down her throat. The cold was raw and sharp, but it made her feel alive. Despondent over the death of Ray Childress and angered by her confrontation with Findo Gask, she felt exhilarated nevertheless. It was in her nature to feel positive, to pull herself up by her emotional bootstraps. But it was her symbiotic relationship with the park as well. There was that link between them, that tie that transcended every life change she had experienced in her twenty-nine years.

Maybe, she mused hopefully, she could save her connection with the park this time, too. Even with the changes she knew she must undergo. Even with the return of John Ross.

She crossed the bridge where the road split off and curved down to the bayou and to the caves where the feeders lived, making instead for the summit of the cliffs and the turnaround. The parking area was empty, and the snow stretched away into the trees, undisturbed and pristine. In the shadowed evergreens, a handful of feeders crouched, their flat, empty eyes watchful. They had no particular interest in her now, but that could change in a heartbeat.

She found the gap in the cemetery fence that had opened

two years ago and not yet been repaired, and she squeezed herself through. Riverside's tombstones and monuments stretched away before her, their bumpy, rolling acres dissected by roads that meandered in long, looping ribbons through clusters of old hardwoods and shaggy conifers. The roads were plowed, and she trudged to the nearest and followed it on toward the edge of the bluffs. The wind had picked up, and the snowflakes were falling more quickly, beginning to form a curtain against the gray backdrop of failing light. It would be dark by four o'clock, the evening settling in early during the winter solstice, the days gone short and the nights made long. She pulled up her collar and picked up her pace.

When she reached the plots of her grandparents and of her mother, she knelt in the snow before them. Snow layered the rough-cut tops of the marble and the well-tended grounds beneath, but the vertical surface of the stone was clear and legible. She read the names to herself in silence. ROBERT ROOSEVELT FREEMARK. EVELYN OPAL FREEMARK. CAITLIN ANNE FREEMARK. Her grandparents and her mother, laid to rest in a tree-shaded spot that overlooked the river. One day she would be there, too. She wondered if she would see them then. If she did, she wondered how it would feel.

'Kind of a cold day for paying your respects to the dead,' a voice from behind her remarked.

From her kneeling position, she glanced over her shoulder at Two Bears. He stood a few paces back, beefy arms folded over his big chest. Snowflakes spotted his braided black hair and his ribbed army sweater. One arm encircled his bedroll and gripped his rucksack, which hung down against his camouflage pants and heavy boots. For as little clothing as he wore, he did not seem cold.

'Don't you ever wear a coat?' she asked, swiveling slightly without rising.

He shrugged. 'When it gets cold enough, I do. What brings you to visit the spirits of your ancestors, little bird's Nest? Are you lonesome for the dead?'

'For Gran and Old Bob, I am. I think of them all the time. I remember how good they made me feel when they were around. I miss them most at Christmas, when family is so important.' She cocked her head, reflecting. 'I miss my mother, too, but in a different way. I never knew her. I guess I miss her for that.'

He came forward a few paces. 'I miss my people in the same way.'

'You haven't found them yet, I guess.'

He shook his head. 'Haven't looked all that hard. Calling up the spirits of the dead takes a certain amount of preparation. It takes effort. It requires a suspension of the present and a step across the Void into the future. It means that we must meet halfway between life and death.' He looked out across the river. 'No one lives on that ground. Only visitors come there.'

She came to her feet and brushed the snow from her knees. 'I took your suggestion. I tried talking with the gypsy morph. It didn't work. He wouldn't talk back. He just stared at me—when he bothered looking at me at all. I sat up with him last night for several hours, and I couldn't get a word out of him.'

'Be patient. He is just a child. Less than thirty days old.

Think of what he has seen, how he must feel about life. He
has been hunted since birth.'

'But he asked for me!' she snapped impatiently. 'He came
here to find me!'

Two Bears shifted his weight. 'Perhaps the next step
requires more time and effort. Perhaps the next step doesn't
come so easily.'

'But if he would just tell me—'

'Perhaps he is, and you are not listening.'

She stared at him. 'What does that mean? He doesn't
talk!' Then she blinked in recognition. 'Oh. You mean he
might be trying to communicate in some other way?'

Two Bears smiled. 'I'm only a shaman, little bird's Nest,
not a prophet. I'm a Sinnissippi Indian who is homeless and
tribeless and tired of being both. I give advice that feels
right to me, but I cannot say what will work. Trust your own
judgment in this. You still have your magic, don't you?'

Her mouth tightened reproachfully. 'You know I do. But
my magic is a toy, all but that part that comprises Wraith
and belonged to my father. You're not trying to tell me I
should use that?'

He shook his head. 'You are too quick to dismiss your
abilities and to disparage your strengths. Think a moment.
You have survived much. You have accomplished much. You
are made more powerful by having done so. You should
remember that.'

A smile quirked at the corners of her mouth. 'Isn't it
enough that I remember to speak your name? O'olish
Amaneh. I say it every time I feel weak or frightened or too
much alone. I use it like a talisman.'

The copper face warmed, and the big man nodded approvingly. 'I can feel it when you do so. In here.' He tapped his chest. 'When you speak my name, you give me strength as well. You remember me, so that I will not be forgotten.'

'Well, I don't know that it does much good, but if you think so, I'm glad.' She sighed and exhaled a cloud of frosty air. 'I better be getting back.' She glanced skyward. 'It's getting dark fast.'

They stood together without speaking over the graves of her family, flakes of snow swirling about them in gusts of wind, the dark distant tree trunks and pale flat headstones fading into a deepening white curtain.

'A lot of snow will fall tonight,' Two Bears said in his deep, soft voice. His black eyes fixed her. 'Might be a good time to think about the journeys you have taken in your life. Might be a good time to think back over the roads you have traveled down.'

She did not want to ask him why he was suggesting this. She did not think she wanted to know. She did not believe he would tell her anyway.

'Good-bye, little bird's Nest,' he said, backing off a step into the white. 'Hurry home.'

'Good-bye, O'olish Amaneh,' she replied. She started away, then turned back. 'I'll see you later.'

He did not respond. He simply walked into the thickly falling snow and disappeared.

*F*rom the concealing shelter of a thick stand of spruce, Findo Gask watched Nest Freemark converse with the big

Indian. He watched them through the steadily deepening curtain of new snow until Nest began walking back toward the park, and then he turned to an impatient Penny Dreadful.

'Let's go get her,' Penny suggested eagerly.

Findo Gask thought a moment, then shook his head. 'I don't think so. Not just yet.'

Penny looked at him as if he were newly arrived from Mars. Her red hair corkscrewed out from her head in a fresh gust of wind. 'Gramps, are you going soft on me? Don't you want to hurt her after the way she talked to you?'

He smiled indulgently. 'I want to hurt her so badly she will never be well again. But the direct approach isn't necessarily the best way to accomplish this.'

She made a face. 'I'm sick and tired of playing around with Little Miss Olympics, you know that? I don't get the point of these mind games you love so much. If you want to play games, let's try a few that involve cutting off body parts. That's the way to hurt someone so they won't forget.'

Findo Gask watched Nest Freemark begin to fade into the white haze of falling snow. 'If we kill her now, John Ross will take the morph and go to ground, and we might not find him again. He is the more dangerous of the two. But he relies on her. She has something he needs. I want to know what it is.'

He signaled into the trees behind him where Twitch and the ur'droch were waiting. Then he began walking, Penny right on his heels.

'We're going after the Indian instead,' he told her.

She quickened her pace to get close to him. 'The Indian? Really?' She looked excited.

He slid through the spruce, shadowy in his dark clothing, his eyes scanning the snow-flecked land ahead. He had heard stories of an Indian who was connected in some way to the Word, either as a messenger or prophet, a powerful presence in the Word's pantheon of magics. He would be the most powerful of Nest Freemark's allies, so it made sense to eliminate him first. It was his plan to strip away Nest Freemark's friends one by one. He wasn't doing this just to weaken her and thereby gain possession of the morph. He wasn't even doing it because he was afraid that killing her outright would scare off John Ross. He was doing it because there was something about her that disturbed him. He couldn't identify it, but it had revealed itself in the way she stood up to him, so confident, so determined. She knew he was dangerous, but she didn't seem to care. Before he killed her, he wanted to find out why. He wanted to break down her defenses, strip away her confidence and determination, and have a close look at what lay beneath.

He would have the morph, of course. It didn't matter what Nest Freemark or John Ross tried to do to stop him. He would have the morph, and their names in his book, before the week was out.

And in the process, he would have their souls as well.

The big Indian was already out of sight, disappeared into the white curtain of blowing snow. But Findo Gask did not need to see the Indian to find him. There were other senses he could call upon besides his sight. There were other ways to find what was hidden.

He glanced left and right, catching just a glimpse of Twitch and the ur'droch to either side. Penny stalked next to him, eyes darting this way and that, pale face intense. She was whispering, 'Here, Tonto. Here, big fella. Come to Penny.'

Wind gusted and died away, snow swirled and drifted, and Riverside Cemetery was a surreal jungle of dark trunks and ice-capped markers. They were closing on the bluffs overlooking the bayou, where the cemetery ended at a chain-link fence set just back from the cliffs. There was still no sign of the Indian, but Findo Gask could sense him, not far ahead, still moving, but seemingly in no great hurry. The demon's mind was working swiftly. He might lose one or two of his allies in this effort, but demons were replaceable.

All but him, of course.

There was no one else like him.

They came out of the blowing snow on a tree-sheltered flat, close back against the edge of the bluffs, and the Indian was waiting.

*N*est made her way out of the maze of tombstones to the cemetery road and followed it back toward the park. The wind was gusting heavily and the snow blowing so hard it was impossible to see much more than a dozen yards. Banks of storm clouds rolled across the sky, and the light had dimmed to an iron gray that turned the landscape hazy and colorless.

'O'olish Amaneh,' she whispered to herself.

A dark shadow whizzed by her head, and she flinched from it automatically, dropping to a guarded crouch. The shadow was gone a moment and then it was back again, appearing out of the whirling snow in a rush of darkness. It was an owl, winging low across the tombstones and monuments, flattened out like a big kite. Without a sound, it flew right at her. At the last minute it banked away, and Pick dropped onto her shoulder with a grunt.

'Criminy, I can't see a thing!' he grumbled, latching on to her collar and pulling himself into the warmth of its folds. 'Cold up there, too. I might be made of twigs and leaves, but I'm frozen all the way through!'

'What are you doing?' she asked, coming back to her feet, looking at the white space where the owl had been a moment before.

'What does it look like I'm doing? I'm patrolling the park!'

'In this weather?' She exhaled sharply. 'What is that supposed to accomplish?'

'You mean, besides possibly saving your life?' he snapped irritably. 'Oh, right, I forgot. That was yesterday, wasn't it? Guess I'm just wasting my time out here today.'

'Okay, okay, I'm sorry.' She hadn't seen him since last night's incident and had forgotten that she hadn't thanked him. 'What can I say? I'm an ingrate. You did save my life. All of our lives, for that matter.'

She could feel him puff up. 'You are entirely welcome.'

'I mean it. It's belated, I know, but thanks.'

'It's okay.'

'I'm just a little distracted.'

He gestured impatiently. 'Start walking. It's freezing out here, and I have to see you safely home before I can take cover myself. Mr. Gask is still out here, and he has a couple

of his demon cronies with him. They were watching you talk
with the Indian.'

'With Two Bears?' She glanced around quickly.

'Don't worry, they didn't follow you. I was watching to
make sure. Come on, keep moving, don't be looking around
like you didn't know the way. I'll keep watch for the both of
us.'

She made her way to the fence and squeezed through the
gap to the other side. Ahead, the park was a white blur. The
residences to her left and the bayou and railroad tracks to her
right had disappeared completely. But even in weather conditions as bad as this, she could find her way, the park as
familiar to her as her own bedroom in darkest night. Head
lowered against the stinging gusts of frozen snow and bitter
wind, she moved down the road past the Indian mounds.

'Tell me what you know about last night,' she suggested,
striding steadily forward.

'Not much to tell.' Pick was so light she could barely tell
he was there. 'I was patrolling the park on Jonathan, just like
I always do when there's trouble about. After what you'd
told me about Mr. Gask, I knew he'd be back. Sure enough,
I found him down by the ice, hiding in the trees. He didn't
seem to be doing anything, so I took Jonathan high up and
out of sight. You went down the toboggan slide once or
twice, and Mr. Gask watched. Then someone flashed a light
up top by the loading platform, and our demon friend went
down to the ice and touched it with his hand. When I saw
the cracks start out toward the center, I could see where
things were heading. You were already coming down, so I
flew out to warn you.'

'Good thing,' she told him.

He grunted. 'There's the understatement of the month. That was a pretty wicked magic he concocted. Lethal stuff. It missed you, but it got that park guy.'

'Ray Childress. I know. It makes me sick.'

Pick was silent for a time. 'You better watch out, Nest,' he said finally. 'There are bad demons and there are worse-than-bad demons. I think Findo Gask is in a class by himself. He won't give up. He'll keep coming after you until he has what he wants.' He paused. 'Maybe you ought to just give it to him.'

Nest shook her head. 'I won't do that. I already told him so.'

Pick sighed. 'Well, no surprises there. Is John Ross with you on this?'

'Right to the bitter end.'

'Good choice of words. That's likely how it will turn out.' Pick squirmed on her shoulder to get more comfortable. 'Wish this was happening in the summer, when it was warmer. It would make my job a lot easier.'

She glanced down at him. 'You be careful yourself, Pick.'

He snorted. 'Hah! You don't have to worry about me. I've got eyes in the back of my head, and Jonathan's got them in his wing tips. We'll be safe enough. You just keep your own instincts sharp.'

She swallowed against the cold, moistening her lips. Some Chap Stick was definitely in order. 'How come you call him Jonathan? And before that, it was Benjamin and Daniel. What kind of names are those for owls? Can't you come up with something . . . I don't know, not so common?'

He straightened, twiggy hands tightening in her collar. 'Those names are only common to you, not to me. I'm a sylvan, remember? We don't use names like Daniel and Benjamin and Jonathan in the normal course of things. Cripes! Try to remember, we're not like you!'

'Okay, already.'

'Sometimes, you appall me.'

'All right!'

'Well, criminy!'

She trudged on into the snowy gloom, following the dark ribbon of the road as the snow slowly began to hide it away.

*F*indo Gask was surprised. The Indian was just standing there, watching them. He must have known they were following him, and yet he hadn't tried to escape or hide. Why was that?

'Looky, looky, Gramps,' Penny teased. 'Someone wants to play.'

Gask ignored her, slowing his approach to study his adversary. The Indian was bigger than he had looked earlier, his copper skin dark, his black hair damp and shiny, his eyes hard-edged and penetrating. He had dropped the bedroll and rucksack in the snow, as if anticipating the need to keep his hands free.

'Are you looking for me?' he rumbled softly.

Findo Gask stopped six yards away, close enough that he could see the other's eyes, not so close that he was within reach of those big hands. The Indian did not look at Penny.

He did not look to either side, where Twitch and the ur'droch had melted into the trees.

'Hey, Tonto,' Penny called out to him. 'Remember me?'

Gask let his eyes shift momentarily. She was standing closer to the Indian than he was. She had knives in both hands, their metal blades glinting as she moved them in small circular motions.

The Indian glanced at her, then dismissed her with a shrug. 'What is there worth remembering? You are a demon. I have seen many like you before.'

'Not like me,' she hissed at him.

The Indian looked back at Findo Gask. 'Why do you waste my time? What do you want with me?'

Gask brought the leather book in front of him, gripping it with both hands. 'What is your name?' he asked.

The Indian was as still as carved stone. 'O'olish Amaneh, in the language of my people, the Sinnissippi. Two Bears, in the language of the English. But should you choose to speak my name, it will sear your tongue and scorch your throat all the way down to where your heart has turned to coal.'

Findo Gask gave him a considering look. Out of the corner of his eye, he could see Twitch sliding along the fenceline behind the Indian, his movements smooth and silent in the snowfall, his big form barely visible. He could not see the ur'droch, concealed somewhere back in that spruce grove, but he knew it was there. Penny was giggling with anticipation. She was unpredictable, apt to do almost anything in a given situation, this one especially, and it made her useful.

Two Bears seemed oblivious of them. 'You are a demon

who prides himself on his understanding of humans,' he said, studying Gask. 'But what you understand is limited by what you feel. Demons feel so little. They lack empathy. They lack the kinder emotions. In the end, this will be your undoing.'

Findo Gask smiled without warmth. 'I don't think my undoing is the issue at hand, do you?'

'Isn't it?' The Indian's weathered face stayed expressionless. 'You would do well not to misjudge your enemies, demon. I think maybe in this case, you have done so.'

Gask held the other's dark gaze. 'I make it a point never to misjudge my enemies. I think it is you who have misjudged in this instance. You've made a big mistake taking sides in this dispute with Miss Freemark. It is a mistake I intend to correct.'

Twitch was behind the Indian now, less than ten paces away. Gask knew the ur'droch would be on his other side. Two Bears was hemmed in, with no place to go. Snow blew in a steady slant out of the northwest. The storm clouds seemed to have dropped all the way down to the treetops, and the light had gone cloudy and gray.

Two Bears shifted his weight slightly, his big shoulders swinging toward Gask. 'How would you make this correction, Mr. Demon?'

Findo Gask cocked his head. 'I would remove you from this place. I would make you go away so that you could never come back.'

Now it was the Indian who smiled. 'What makes you think I was ever really here?'

Twitch rushed across the space that separated them and

launched himself at the Indian. A flurry of shadowy movement marked the ur'droch's attack from the other side. Penny
screamed in glee, dropping into a crouch, right arm cocked
for throwing, her knives catching the light.

But in the same instant, snow funneled all about Two
Bears, blown straight up out of the earth on which he stood,
a cloud of white particles that filled the air. The wind
whipped and tore about him, and for a split second everything disappeared.

When the snow settled and the winter air cleared, Two
Bears was gone. His rucksack and bedroll lay on the ground,
but the Indian had vanished. Big head swiveling left and
right, Twitch crouched in the space the Indian had just occupied. The ur'droch was a dark stain sliding back and forth
across the rutted snow, searching futilely for its quarry.

Penny hissed in rage as the knives disappeared back into
her clothing. 'Is this some sort of trick? Where is he?'

Findo Gask stood without moving for a moment, testing
the air, casting all about for some indication. 'I don't know,'
he admitted finally.

'Did we kill him or not?' Penny shrieked.

Gask searched some more, but nothing revealed itself,
not a trace, not a whisper. The Indian had simply vaporized.
His last words whispered in the demon's mind. *What makes you
think I was ever really here?* But, no, he had been here in some
sense. He had been more than just an image.

Ignoring Penny's rantings, Findo Gask opened the leather-
bound book and read the last entry burned onto its
weathered pages.

There was nothing after the name of Ray Childress.

He closed the book slowly. A pang of disappointment tweaked his pride. The Indian would have been a nice addition.

'Gone is gone,' he said. 'A neat trick, but you don't come back for a while after executing it. He's removed himself from the picture, wherever he is.' He shrugged dismissively, and his weathered face creased in a slow smile. 'Let's go to work on the others.'

CHAPTER 18

J ohn Ross was standing at the living-room window, keeping watch for her, when Nest emerged from the whirling snowfall. She appeared as a dark smudge out of the curtain of white, pushing through the skeletal branches of the hedgerow and trudging across the backyard toward the house. He could tell by the set of her shoulders and length of her stride she was infused with determination and her encounter with Findo Gask had not dampened her resolve. Whether she'd changed her mind regarding her insistence on protecting the gypsy morph remained to be seen. He was inclined to think not.

He limped toward the back door as she came through. Bennett and Harper were already decorating the tree, which had been placed in its stand in the corner across the room from the fireplace. Ross had helped with that and with carrying in the boxes of ornaments, then stood back. Little John had resumed his place on the couch, staring out into the park.

'Whew, it's bad out there now,' Nest declared as he came

up to her. She stamped her boots on the entry rug and brushed the snow from her coat. 'You can hardly see in front of your nose. How's everyone here?'

'Fine.' He shifted to let her walk past and followed her down the hall. 'They're decorating the tree.'

She glanced over her shoulder in surprise. 'Little John, too?'

'Well, no.' He gave a little shrug. 'Me either, actually.'

'What's your excuse?'

'I guess I don't have one.'

She gave him a look. 'That's what I thought. Try to remember, John, it's Christmas. Come on.'

She led him back into the living room and put him to work with the others. She brought Little John off the couch and spent time trying to show him how to hang ornaments. He stared at her blankly, watched Harper for a few minutes, hung one ornament, and went back to the couch. Nest seemed unperturbed. She strung tinsel and lights for a time, then went over to sit with him. Kneeling at his side, she began speaking softly to him. Ross couldn't quite catch what she was saying, but it was something about the park and the things that lived in it. He heard her mention Pick and the feeders. He heard her speak of tatterdemalions, sylvans, and the magic they managed. She took her time, not rushing things, just carrying on a conversation as if it was the most natural thing in the world.

When the tree was decorated, she brought out cookies and hot chocolate, and they sat around the tree talking about Santa Claus and reindeer. Harper asked questions, and Nest supplied answers. Bennett listened and looked off into space, as if marking time. Outside, it was growing dark, the twilight fading away, the snowstorm disappearing into a blackness punctured only by the diffuse glow of streetlamps and porch lights, flurries chasing each other like moths about a flame. Cars edged down the roadway, slow and cautious metal beasts in search of their lairs. In the fireplace, the crackling of the burning logs was a steady reassurance.

It was nearing five when the phone rang. Nest walked to the kitchen to answer it, spoke for a few minutes, then summoned John. 'It's Josie,' she said. She arched one eyebrow questioningly and handed him the receiver.

He looked at her for a moment, then placed the receiver against his ear, staring out the kitchen window into the streetlit blackness.

'Hello.'

'I don't mean to bother you, John,' Josie said quickly, 'but I didn't like the way we left things yesterday. It felt awkward. It's been a long time, and seeing you like that really threw me. I can't even remember what I said. Except that I asked you to dinner tonight, and I guess, thinking it over, I was a little pushy.'

'I didn't think so,' he said.

He heard her soft sigh in the receiver. 'I don't know. It didn't feel that way. You seemed a little put off by it.'

'No.' He shifted his weight to lean against the counter. 'I appreciated the invitation. I just didn't know what to say. I have some concerns about Little John, that's all.'

'You could bring him. He would be welcome.' She paused. 'I guess that's another invitation, isn't it? I'm standing in my kitchen, making this dinner, and I end up thinking about you. So I call to tell you I'm sorry for being pushy yesterday, then I get pushy all over again. Pathetic, huh?'

He still remembered her kitchen from fifteen years earlier, when she had dressed the wounds he had suffered during his fight with the steel-mill workers in Sinnissippi Park. He could picture her there now, the way she would look, how she would be standing, what she would be looking at as she spoke to him.

'I would like to come,' he said quietly.

'But?'

'But I don't think I can. It's complicated. It isn't about you.'

The phone was silent for a moment. 'All right. But if you want to talk later, I'll be here. Give your son a kiss for me.'

The line went dead. Ross placed the receiver in its cradle and walked back into the living room. Harper and Bennett were sitting by the tree playing with old Christmas tins. Nest got up from the sofa where she was sitting with Little John.

'I've got to take some soup over to the Petersons,' she said, heading for the kitchen. 'I'll be back in twenty minutes.'

She made no mention of the call and was out the door in moments. Ross stood looking after her, thinking of Josie. It was always the same when he did. It made him consider what he had given up to become a Knight of the Word. It made him realize all over again how empty his life was without family or friends or a lover. Except for Stefanie Winslow, there had been no one in twenty-five years besides Josie Jackson. And only Josie mattered.

Twice, he walked to the phone to call her back and didn't

do so. Each time, the problem was the same—he didn't know what to say to her. Words seemed inadequate to provide what was required. The emotions she unlocked in him were sweeping and overpowering and filled with a need to act, not talk. He felt trapped by his circumstances, by his life. He had lived by a code that allowed no contact with others beyond the carrying out of his duties as a Knight of the Word. Nothing else could be permitted to intrude. Everything else was a distraction he could not afford.

When Nest returned, rather more quiet than before, she took Bennett down the hall to the project room to work on a Christmas present for Harper and left Ross to watch the children. With Harper sitting on the sofa next to Little John and pretending to read him a book, Ross moved over to the fireplace and stood looking into the flames. His involvement with the gypsy morph and his journey to find Nest Freemark had been unavoidable, dictated by needs and requiring sacrifices that transcended personal considerations. But his choices here, in Hopewell, were more suspect. The presence of Findo Gask and his allies was not unexpected, but it was disturbing. It foreclosed a number of options. It required pause. Nest was threatened only because Ross was here. If he slipped away, they would lose interest in her. If he took the gypsy morph someplace else, they would follow.

That was one choice, but not the logical one. Another darker and more dangerous one, the one that made better sense, was to seek them out and destroy them before they could do any further damage.

That would allow the morph to stay with Nest. That would give her a better chance of discovering its secret.

For a long moment, he considered the possibility of a preemptive strike. He did not know how many demons there were, but he had faced more than one before, and he was equal to the task. Track them down, turn them to ash, and the threat was ended.

He watched the logs burning in the hearth, and their fire mirrored his own. It would be worth it, he thought. Even if it ended up costing him his life . . .

He recalled his last visit to the Fairy Glen and the truths the Lady had imparted to him. The memory flared in the fire's embers, her words reaching out, touching, stroking. *Brave Knight, your service is almost ended. One more thing you must do for me, and then I will set you free. One last quest for a talisman of incomparable worth. One final sacrifice for all that you have striven to achieve and all you know to have value in the world. This only, and then you will be free . . .*

His gaze shifted to where the children sat upon the couch. Little John had turned around and was looking at the picture book. He seemed intent on a particular picture, and Harper was holding it up to him so that he could better see.

Ross took a deep breath. He had to do something. He could not afford to wait for the demons to come after them again. It was certain they would. They would try a different tactic, and this time it might cost the life not of a park employee but of someone in this house. If it did not come tomorrow, it would come the next day, and it would not end there, but would continue until the demons had possessed or destroyed the gypsy morph.

Ross studied the little boy on the couch. A gypsy morph. What would it become, if it survived? What, that would make it so important? He wished he knew. He wished the Lady had told him. Perhaps it would make choosing his path easier.

Nest and Bennett came out of the work area a few minutes later with a bundle of packages they placed under the tree. Nest was cheerful and smiling, as if the simple act of wrapping presents had infused her with fresh holiday spirit. She went over to the couch to look at the picture book Harper was reading, giving both Harper and Little John hugs, telling them Santa wouldn't forget them this Christmas. Bennett, in contrast, remained sullen and withdrawn, locked in a world where no one else was welcome. She would force a smile when it was called for, but she could barely manage to communicate otherwise, and her eyes kept shifting off into space, haunted and lost. Ross studied her surreptitiously. Something had happened since yesterday to change her. Given her history as an addict, he could make an educated guess.

'We have to get over to Robert's party,' Nest announced a few minutes later, drawing him aside. 'There will be lots of other adults and kids. It should be safe.'

He looked at her skeptically. 'I know what you're thinking,' she said. 'But I keep hoping that if I expose Little John to enough different situations, something will click. Other children might help him to open up. We can keep a close watch on him.'

He accepted her judgment. It probably didn't make any difference what house they were occupying if the demons chose to come after them, and he was inclined to agree that they were less likely to attempt anything in a crowd. Even last night, they had worked hard to isolate Nest and the children before striking.

Nest mobilized the others and began helping the children with their coats and boots. As she did, Ross walked back to the kitchen and looked out the window. It was still snowing hard, with visibility reduced and a thick layer of white collecting on everything. It would be difficult for the demons to do much in this weather. Even though the cold wouldn't affect them, the snow would limit their mobility. In all likelihood, they would hole up somewhere until morning. It was the perfect time to catch them off guard. He should track them down and destroy them now.

But where should he look for them?

He stared out into the blowing white, wondering.

When they were all dressed, they piled into the car and drove down Woodlawn Road to Spring Drive and back into the woods to Robert's house. A cluster of cars was already parked along the drive and more were arriving. Nest pulled up by the front door, and Bennett and the children climbed out and rushed inside.

Ross sat where he was. *If I were Findo Gask, where would I be?*

Nest was staring at him. 'I have to do something,' he said finally. 'It may take me a while. Can I borrow the car?'

She nodded. 'What are you going to do?'

'A little scouting. Will you be all right alone with the children and Bennett? You may have to catch a ride home afterward.'

There was a long pause. 'I don't like the sound of this.'

He gave her a smile. 'Don't worry. I won't take any chances.'

The lie came easily. He'd had enough practice that he could say almost anything without giving himself away.

Her fingers rested on his arm. 'Do yourself a favor, John. Whatever it is you're thinking of doing, forget it. Go have dinner with Josie.'

He stared at her, startled. 'I wasn't—'

'Listen to me,' she interrupted quickly. 'You've been running for weeks, looking over your shoulder, sleeping with one eye open. When you sleep at all, that is. You're so tightly strung you're about to snap. Maybe you don't see it, but I do. You have to let go of everything for at least a few hours. You can't keep this up.'

'I'm all right,' he insisted.

'No, you're not.' She leaned close. 'There isn't anything you can do out there tonight. Whatever it is you think you can do, you can't. I know you. I know how you are. But you have to step back. You have to rest. If you don't, you'll do something foolish.'

He studied her without speaking. Slowly, he nodded. 'I must be made of glass. You can see right through me, can't you?'

She smiled. 'Come on inside, John. You might have a good time, if you'd just let yourself.'

He thought about his plan to try tracking the demons, and he saw how futile it was. He had no place to start. He had no plan for finding them. And she was right, he was tired. He was exhausted mentally, emotionally, and physically. If he found the demons, what chance would he have of overcoming them?

But when he glanced over at the Hepplers' brightly lit

home, he didn't feel he belonged there, either. Too many
people he didn't know. Too much noise and conversation.

'Could I still borrow the car?' he asked quietly.

She climbed out without a word. Leaning back in before
closing the door, she said, 'She still lives at the same address,
John. Watch yourself on the roads going back into town.'

Then she closed the door and disappeared inside the
house.

*I*t took him a long time to get to where he was going. It
was like driving through an exploded feather pillow, white
particles flying everywhere, the car's headlights reflecting
back into his eyes, the night a black wall around him. The
car skidded on patches of ice and through deep ruts in the
snow, threatening to spin off the pavement altogether. He
could barely make out the roadway ahead, following the
tracks of other cars, steering down the corridor of streetlamps that blazed to either side. Now and again, there would
be banks of lights from gas stations and grocery stores, from
a Walgreens or a Pizza Hut, but even so, it was difficult to
navigate.

He thought again of going after the demons, of making
a run at them while they were all gathered together somewhere, waiting out the storm. It remained a tempting image.
But Nest was right. It was a one-in-a-million shot, and it
required energy he did not have to spare.

More debilitating than his exhaustion was his loneliness
and despair. He had denied it for a long time, shrugging off
the emptiness inside, pretending that for him such things

didn't matter. But they did. He was a Knight of the Word, but he was human, too.

It was seeing Josie again that triggered the feelings, of course. But it was returning to Hopewell and Nest Freemark as well, to a town that seemed so much like the one he had grown up in and to the last member of a family that seemed so much like his own. Just being here, he found himself trying to recapture a small part of his past. He might tell himself that he wasn't here for that, but the truth was simple and direct. He wanted to reaffirm his humanity. He wanted to step outside his armor and let himself feel what it was to be human again.

He drove down Lincoln Highway until it became Fourth Avenue, then turned left toward the river. He found his way without effort, the directions still imprinted on his memory, fresh after all these years. He steered the Taurus down the dead-end street to the old wooden two-story and parked by the curb. He switched off the headlights and engine and sat staring at the house, thinking over what he was about to do.

It isn't as if you have to decide now, he told himself. *How can you know what will happen after so long?*

But he did. His instincts screamed it at him. The certainty of it burned through his hesitation and doubt.

He got out of the car, locked it, limped through the blowing snow and drifts, climbed the porch steps, and knocked. He had to knock twice more before she opened the door.

She stared at him. 'John?'

She spoke his name as if it were unfamiliar to her, as if she had just learned it. Her blue eyes were bright and

wondering, and gave full and open consideration to the fact
that he was standing there when by all rights he shouldn't be.
She was wearing jeans and a print shirt with the sleeves
rolled up. She had been cooking, he guessed. He did not
move to enter or even to speak, but simply waited.

She reached out finally with one hand and pulled him
inside, closing the door behind him. She was grinning now,
shaking her head. He found himself studying the spray of
freckles that lay across the bridge of her nose and over both
cheeks. He found himself wanting to touch her tousled
blond hair.

Then he was looking into her eyes and thinking he was
right, there had never been anyone like her.

She brushed snow from his shoulders and began unzip-
ping his coat. 'I shouldn't be surprised,' she said, watching her
fingers as they worked the zipper downward. 'You've never
been predictable, have you? What are you doing here? You
said you weren't coming!'

His face felt flushed and heated. 'I guess I should have
called.'

She laughed. 'You didn't call for fifteen years, John. Why
should you call now? Come on, get that coat off.'

She helped him pull off the parka, gloves, and scarf, and
bent to unlace his boots as well. In stocking feet, leaning on
his still-damp staff for support, he followed her from the
entry into the kitchen. She motioned him to a chair at the
two-person breakfast table, poured him a cup of hot cider,
and spent a few moments adjusting various knobs and dials
on the stove and range. Savory smells rose from casseroles
and cooking pans.

'Have you eaten?' she asked, glancing over her shoulder at him. He shook his head. 'Good. Me, either. We'll eat in a little while.'

She went back to work, leaving him alone at the table to sip cider. He watched her silently, enjoying the fluidity of her movements, the suppleness of her body. She seemed so young, as if age had decided to brush against her only momentarily. When she looked at him and smiled—that dazzling, wondrous smile—he could barely believe that fifteen years had passed.

He knew he loved her and wondered at his failure to recognize it before. He did not know why he loved her, not in a rational sense, because looking at the fact of it too closely would shatter it like glass. He could not parcel it out like pieces of a puzzle, one for each part of the larger picture. It was not so simply explained. But it was real and true, and he felt it so deeply he thought he would cry.

She sat with him after a while and asked about Nest and Bennett and the children, skipping quickly from one topic to the next, filling the space with words and laughter, avoiding close looks and long pauses. She did not ask where he had been or why he had a child. She did not ask why she had not heard from him in fifteen years. She let him be, perhaps sensing that he was here in part because he could expect that from her, that what had drawn them together in the first place was that it was enough for them to share each other's company.

She set the breakfast table for dinner, keeping it casual, serving from the counter and setting the plates on the table. The meal was pot roast with bread and salad, and he ate it hungrily. He could feel his tension and emptiness drain away, and he found himself smiling for the first time in weeks.

'I'm glad you came,' she told him at one point. 'This will sound silly, but even after you said you couldn't, I thought maybe you would anyway.'

'I feel a little strange about that,' he admitted, looking at her. He wanted to look at her forever. He wanted to study her until he knew everything there was to know. Then he realized he was staring and dropped his gaze. 'I didn't want to be with a lot of people I didn't know. I didn't want to be with a lot of people, period. In a strange house, at Christmas. I thought I would go looking for . . .' He trailed off, glancing up at her. 'I don't know what I thought. I don't know why I said I wouldn't come earlier. Well, I do, but it's hard to explain. It's . . . it's complicated.'

She seemed unconcerned. 'You don't have to explain anything to me,' she said.

He nodded and went back to eating. Outside, the wind gusted about the corners and across the eaves of the old house, making strange, whining sounds. Snow blew past the frost-edged windows as if the storm were a reel of film spinning out of control. Ross looked at it and felt time and possibility slipping away.

When he finished his meal, Josie carried their plates to the sink and brought hot tea. They sipped at the tea in silence, listening to the wind, exchanging quick looks that brushed momentarily and slid away.

'I never stopped thinking about you,' he said finally, setting down the tea and looking at her.

She nodded, sipping slowly.

'It's true. I didn't write or call, and I was sometimes a long way away from here and lost in some very dark places, but I never stopped.'

He kept his eyes fixed on hers, willing her to believe. She set her cup down, fitting it carefully to the saucer.

'John,' she said. 'You're just here for tonight, aren't you? You haven't come back to Hopewell to stay. You don't plan to ask me to marry you or go away with you or wait for you to come back again. You aren't going to promise me anything beyond the next few hours.'

He stared at her, taken aback by her directness. He felt the emptiness and solitude begin to return. 'No,' he admitted.

She smiled gently. 'Because I'd like to think that the one thing we can count on from each other after all this time is honesty. I'm not asking for anything more. I wouldn't know what to do with it.'

She leaned forward slightly. 'I'll take those few hours, John. I'll take them gladly. I would have taken them anytime during the last fifteen years of my life. I thought about you, too. Every day, I thought about you. I prayed for you to come back. At first, I wanted you to come back forever. Then, just for a few years, or a few months, or days, minutes, anything. I couldn't help myself. I can't help myself now. I want you so badly, it hurts.'

She brushed nervously at her tousled hair. 'So let's not spend time offering each other explanations or excuses. Let's not make any promises. Let's not even talk anymore.'

She rose and came around to stand over him, then bent to kiss him on the mouth. She kept her lips on his, tasting him, exploring gently, her arms coming around his shoulders, her fingers working themselves deep into his hair. She kissed him for a long time, and then she pulled him to his feet.

'I guess you remember I was a bold kind of girl,' she whispered, her face only inches from his own, her arms around his neck, and her body pressed against him. 'I haven't changed. Let's go upstairs. I bet you remember the way.'

As it turned out, he did.

CHAPTER 19

Bennett Scott stayed at the Heppler party almost two full hours before making her break, even though she had known before coming what she intended to do. She played with Harper and Little John, to the extent that playing with Little John was possible—such a weird little kid—and helped a couple of butter-wouldn't-melt-in-their-mouths teenage girls supervise the other children in their basement retreat. She visited with the adults—a boring, mind-numbing bunch except for Robert Heppler, who was still a kick—and admired the Christmas decorations. She endured the looks they gave her, the ones that took in her piercings and tattoos and sometimes the needle tracks on her arms, the ones that pitied her or dismissed her as trash. She ate a plate of food from the buffet and managed to sneak a few of the chicken wings and rolls into her purse in the process, knowing she might not get much else to eat for a while. She made a point of being seen and looking happy, so that no one, Nest in particular, would suspect what she was about. She hung in there for as long as she could, and much longer than she had believed possible, and then got out of there when no one was looking.

She said good-bye to Harper first.

'Mommy really, really loves you, baby,' she said, kneeling in front of the little girl in the darkened hallway leading from the rec room to the furnace room while the other children played noisily in the background. 'Mommy loves you more than anything in the whole, wide world. Do you believe me?'

Harper nodded uncertainly, dark eyes intense. 'Yeth.'

'I know you do, but Mommy likes to hear you say it.' Bennett fought to keep her voice steady. 'Mommy has to leave you for a little while, baby. Just a little while, okay? Mommy has to do something.'

'What, Mommy?' Harper asked immediately.

'Just something, baby. But I want you to be good while I'm gone. Nest will take care of you. I want you to do what she tells you and be a real good little girl. Will you promise me?'

'Harper come, too,' she replied. 'Come with Mommy.'

The tears sprang to her eyes, and Bennett wiped at them quickly, forcing herself to smile. 'I would really like that, baby. But Mommy has to go alone. This is big-people stuff. Not for little girls. Okay?'

Why did she keep asking that? *Okay? Okay?* Like some sort of talking Mommy doll. She couldn't take any more. She pulled Harper against her fiercely and hugged her tight. 'Bye, baby. Gotta go. Love you.'

Then she sent Harper back into the rec room and slipped up the stairs. Retrieving her coat from the stack laid out on the sofa in the back bedroom, she made her way down the hallway through the crowds to the front door, telling anyone who looked interested that she was just going to step out for a cigarette. She was lucky; Nest was nowhere in evidence, and she did not have to attempt the lie with her. The note that would explain things was tucked in Nest's coat pocket. She would find it there later and do the right thing. Bennett could count on Nest for that.

She was not anxious to go out into the cold, and she did not linger once the front door closed behind her. Trudging down the snowy drive with her scarf pulled tight and her collar up, she walked briskly up Spring to Woodlawn and started for home. She would travel light, she had decided much earlier. Not that she had a lot to choose from in any case, but she would leave everything Nest had given her except for the parka and boots. She would take a few pictures of Harper to look at when she wanted to remind herself what it was she was trying to recover, what it was she had lost.

What it was that her addiction had cost her.

All day her need for a fix had been eating at her, driving her to find fresh satisfaction. What Penny had given her last night hadn't been enough. It was always surprising how quickly the need came back once she had used again, pervasive and demanding. It was like a beast in hiding, always there and always watching, forever hungry and never satisfied, waiting you out. You could be aware of it, you could face it down, and you could pass it by. But you could never be free of it. It followed after you everywhere, staying just out of sight. All it took was one moment of weakness, or despair, or panic, or carelessness, and it would show itself and devour you all over again.

That was what had happened last night. Penny had given her the opportunity and the means, a little encouragement, a friendly face, and she was gone. Penny, with her unkempt red hair, her piss-on-everyone attitude, and her disdain for everything ordinary and common. Bennett knew Penny; she understood her. They were kindred spirits. At least for the time it took to shoot up and get high, and then they were off on their own separate trips, and Bennett was floating in the brightness and peace of that safe harbor drugs provided.

By this morning, when she was alone again and coming down just enough to appreciate what she had done, she understood the truth about herself. She would never change. She would never stop using. Maybe she didn't even want to, not down deep where it mattered. She was an addict to the core, and she would never be anything else. Using was the most important thing in the world to her, and it didn't make any difference how many chances she was offered to give it up. It didn't matter that Nest would try to help her. It didn't matter that she was in a safe place. It didn't even matter that she was going to lose Harper.

Or at least it didn't matter enough to make her believe she could do what was needed.

What she could manage, she decided, was to leave Harper with Nest. What she could manage was to give her daughter a better chance at life than she'd been given. Maybe something good would come of it. Maybe it would persuade her to find a way at last to kick her habit. Maybe. Maybe not. Either way, Harper would be better off.

She had been thinking about it all day. She could stand the bad things that happened to her, but not when they spilled over onto Harper. Especially if she was at fault because she was using. She could not bear it; she could not live with it. She was haunted by the possibility. To prevent it from happening, to remove any chance of it, she had to give Harper to Nest.

She shivered inside the parka, the wind harsh and biting as it swept over her in sudden gusts, particles of frozen snow stinging her exposed skin and making her eyes water. Cars lumbered by in the haze, and she wished one would stop and offer her a ride, but none did. When she got to the house, she would be able to get warm for a few minutes before Penny came. Penny would bring drugs and a ride downtown. She would catch the ten o'clock bus out and by morning she would be in another state.

She regretted that she'd had to steal money from Nest to make the break possible, but that was the least of the sins she had committed in her addict's life and the one most likely to be forgiven first. Nest was her big sister, and a good person, and more family to her than Big Momma and the kids, all of whom were lost to her as surely as her childhood, and good riddance. Sometimes, she missed Jared, though. She remembered how sweet Nest had been on him. *Sweet.* She laughed aloud. Where had she picked up that word? She hoped Jared was all right somewhere. It would be nice to know he was.

Big Momma was a different matter. She hoped Big Momma was burning in hell.

It took a long time to reach the house. Her face stung and

her fingers and toes were numb with cold. She extracted the house key, unlocked the door, and got herself inside. She stood in the entry and breathed in the warmth, waiting for the cold that had settled in her bones to melt. She was coughing, and her chest rattled. She was sick, but she wondered how sick she really was. It had been a long time since she had been to a doctor. Or Harper. Nest would do a better job with things like that.

Harper's stuffed teddy was sitting by the Christmas tree, and Bennett started to cry. *Harper,* she whispered soundlessly. *Baby.*

She called the number Penny had given her. Penny answered and said she'd be right there, and Bennett hung up. Her bag was already packed, so once the call was made there was little to do but wait. She walked out into the living room from the kitchen and stood looking into space. After a moment, she plugged in the tree. The colored lights reflected in the window glass and hall mirror and made her smile. Harper would have a nice Christmas. She glanced down at the present she had made for Harper—a rag doll with her name stitched on the apron, a project Nest had found in a magazine and helped her finish. She wished she could be there to see Harper's face when she opened it. Maybe she would call from the road, just to say Merry Christmas.

She closed her eyes and hugged herself, thinking of how much better she would feel once Penny came with the drugs. She would do just enough to get her through the night and save the rest for later. She would buy all she could. It was great stuff, whatever it was, some sort of crystal, really smooth. She didn't know how Penny had found anything so good, but it just took you up and up and up. Penny had said she would give it to her for free, but Bennett didn't believe her. You gave it for free the first time, which was last night. Today it would cost. Because it was costing Penny. It had to be.

The phone rang once, but she left it alone. No one would be calling her. She began to worry that Nest would miss her and come after her before Penny arrived. She brought her small bag to the front door and stood looking out at the streetlit darkness. Cars came and went, a few, not many, indistinct and hazy lumps in the blowing snow. She wondered if it would snow all night. She wondered if the bus would be on time. She wished she had a fix.

By the time a car finally pulled into the driveway her anticipation and need were so high she could feel her skin crawl. She peeked out from behind the window curtain, uncertain who it was, torn between hiding and charging out. When the driver's door opened and Penny's Little Orphan Annie head appeared, she let out an audible gasp of relief and rushed to the front door to let her in.

'Ohhh, little girl, you are in some kind of state!' the redhead giggled as she came inside, slamming the door on the wind and the cold and throwing off her coat. 'Let's get you back together again right now!'

They shot up right there in the front entry, sitting crosslegged on the wooden floor, passing the fixings back and forth, heads bent close, whispering encouragement and laughing. It didn't matter what was said, what words were used, what thoughts were exchanged. Nothing mattered but the process of injecting the drug and waiting for that first, glorious rush.

Bennett had no idea how much of the stuff she used, but it hit her like a sledgehammer, and she gasped with shock as it began to take hold. She threw back her head and let her mouth hang open, and everything in the world but what she was feeling disappeared.

'There you go,' Penny whispered from somewhere far, far away, her voice distant and soft, barely there at all, hardly anything more than a ripple in the haze. 'Bring it on, girl. Momma needs her itch scratched good!'

Bennett laughed and soared and watched everything around her change to cotton candy. She was barely awake when Penny climbed to her feet and opened the front door. She was barely aware of the black-clad old man who walked through and stood looking down at her.

'Hey, girlfriend,' Penny hissed, and her tone of voice was suddenly sharp-edged and taunting. 'How's this for an unexpected surprise? Look who's joining the party!'

Bennett lifted her eyes dreamily as Findo Gask bent close.

It was after nine-thirty before Nest missed Bennett Scott. She was having a good time talking with friends, some of them people she had known since childhood, sharing stories and swapping remembrances. Robert was very much in evidence early on, trying to make up for last night's provocative comments about John Ross by being overly attentive. She tolerated his efforts for a while because she knew he meant well, but sometimes a little of Robert went a long way. Fortunately, Amy was up and about, though not feeling very much better, and when Nest made a point of beginning a discussion with her about pregnancies and babies, Robert quickly disappeared.

Now and then, Nest would drift down to the rec room to see how the children were doing. She had played in this house as a little girl, so she knew the floor plan well. The rec room was safe and secure. A single entry opened down the stairs from the main hallway. There were no exterior doors or windows. The girls who were baby-sitting knew that only parents and friends were allowed to visit and were instructed to ask for help if there was any problem.

Harper fit right in with the other kids, but Little John parked himself in a corner and wouldn't move. She kept checking on him, hoping something would change over the course of the evening, but it never did. Her attempts to persuade him to join in proved futile, and eventually she gave up.

Once or twice she caught sight of Bennett, but since her concerns were primarily for the children and Bennett seemed to be doing all right, she didn't stop to worry about her.

But finally she realized it was getting late and they had to think about making arrangements to get home, and it was then she realized she hadn't seen Bennett for a while. When she had gone through the house twice without finding her, she tracked down Robert and drew him aside.

'I don't want to make too much of this, but I can't find Bennett Scott,' she advised quietly. From her look, he knew right away this wasn't good.

He raised and lowered one eyebrow in a familiar Robert gesture. 'Maybe she went home.'

'Without Harper?'

He shrugged. 'Maybe she got sick. Are you sure she's not here somewhere? You want me to ask around?'

She wheeled away abruptly and went back downstairs to the rec room. Kneeling next to Harper as the little girl worked to make something out of Play-Doh, she asked if her Mommy was there.

Harper barely looked up. 'Mommy go bye-bye.'

Nest felt her throat tighten in panic. 'Did she tell you this, Harper? Did she tell you bye-bye?'

Harper nodded. 'Yeth.'

Nest climbed back to her feet and looked around helplessly. When had Bennett left? How long had she been gone? Where would she go without taking Harper, without telling anyone, without a car? She knew the answer before she finished the question, and she experienced a rush of anger and despair.

She bounded back up the stairs to find Robert. She would have to go looking, of course—even without knowing where to start. She would have to call John home to watch the children while she took the car and conducted a search.

In a snowstorm where everything was shut down and cars were barely moving? On a night when the wind chill was low enough to freeze you to death?

She felt the futility of what she was proposing threaten to overwhelm her, but she shoved aside her doubts to concentrate on the task at hand. She found Robert coming down the stairs from the second floor, shaking his head.

'Beats me, Nest. I looked everywhere I could think—'

Nest brushed the rest of what he was going to say aside

with a wave of her hand. 'She's gone. I got that much out of Harper. She left sometime back. I don't know why.'

Robert sighed wearily. 'But you can guess, can't you? She's an addict, Nest. I saw the tracks on her arms.' He shook his head. 'Look, I know this is none of my business, but—'

'Don't start, Robert. Just don't!' She clenched his wrist so hard he winced. 'Don't lecture me about the company I keep, about Bennett and John Ross and all the strange things happening and how you remember it was just like this fifteen years ago on the Fourth of July! Just warm up your car while I get the children into their coats and boots and then drive us home!'

She let go of his wrist. 'Do you think you can manage that?'

He looked mortified. 'Of course I can manage it! Geez!'

She leaned in and gave him a peck on the cheek. 'You're a good guy, Robert. But you require a lot of maintenance. Now get going.'

*T*he demons bundled Bennett Scott into her parka and took her out of the house and into the night, letting the drugs in her system do the job of keeping her in line. Snow was flying in all directions, the wind was blowing hard, and it was so cold that nose hairs froze, but Bennett Scott was floating somewhere outside her body, barely aware of anything but the pleasant feeling of not really being connected to reality. Every so often, something around her would come sharply into focus—the bite of the wind, the white fury of the snow, the skeletal shadow of a crooked tree limb, or the faces of Findo Gask and Penny Dreadful, one on either side, propping her up and moving her along. But mostly there was only a low buzzing in her ears and a wondrous sense of peace.

Findo Gask had left everything in the house as he found it, closing the front door behind them without locking it. He wanted Nest Freemark to return home without suspecting he had been there, so he had been careful not to do anything that would scare her off. If she grew too cautious, it would spoil the surprise he had left for her.

With Penny laughing and talking nonstop, they climbed into the car, backed out of the driveway onto Woodlawn, drove to the park entrance, parked in front of the crossbar, and set off on foot. Sinnissippi Park was a black hole of cold and sleet, the darkness unbroken and endless across the flats and through the woods, the snow freezing to ice in the grip of the north wind howling up the river channel. The lights that normally lit the roadway had been lost earlier when a power line went down, and the curtain of blowing snow masked the pale glimmerings of the nearby residences and townhomes. Tonight, the park might as well have been on the moon.

Bennett Scott stumbled and mushed through the deepening snowdrifts, her feet dragging, her body listless, her progress made possible by the fact that the demons who clutched either arm were dragging her. She gulped blasts of frigid air for breath and ducked her head for warmth, automatic responses from her body, but her mind told her almost nothing of what she was doing. She remembered Penny being there, the sharing of drugs that gave her such relief, and the thin, tenuous thread of hope she clung to that some-how, someday, she would find her way back to Harper. Now and again, she would hear her daughter's voice calling to her, small words, little noises, bits and pieces of memories retrieved from the haze of her thoughts.

She saw nothing of the eyes that began to appear in the dark, bright pairs of yellow slits coming out of nowhere in twos and threes until there were dozens.

They crossed the park to the bluffs, then continued west past the Indian mounds to the turnaround and the cliffs. The road had disappeared in the snow, and the entire area was a white carpet beneath the ragged limbs of the leafless hardwoods. Findo Gask was unconcerned about being inter-rupted; there was no one else in the park. Together with Penny, he nudged Bennett Scott toward the cliff edge, maneuvering her forward until she was only a few yards from the drop.

The feeders pressed closer, eager to become involved.

'Let her go, Penny,' Gask ordered.

They stepped back from Bennett, leaving her alone at the cliff's edge, facing out toward the river, her head lolling and her arms hanging loose. The feeders closed on her, touching her softly, cajoling her voicelessly, urging her to give them what they needed.

Bennett stood without moving, her mind in another time zone, gliding through valleys and over peaks, the land all white-edged and golden bright, the singing of her blood in her veins sustaining and comforting. She soared unfettered for a long time, staring at nothing, and then remembered suddenly that she had not come alone.

'Penny?' she managed.

The wind howled at her.

'Penny?'

A child's voice called sharply. 'Mommy!'

Bennett lifted her head and peered into the snow and darkness. It was Harper!

'Mommy, can you hear me?'

'Baby, where are you? Baby?'

'Mommy, I need you! Please, Mommy!'

Bennett felt the cold suddenly, a taste of its bite ripping past the armor of her stupor, leaving her shaking and breathing hard. She licked at her dry lips and glanced around. She saw the eyes now, close and watchful and hungry, and she jerked away in shock and fear.

'Harper!' she screamed.

'Mommy, run!' she heard Harper call out.

She saw her daughter then, a faint image just ahead of her in the darkness, lit by a pale white light that brightened and faded with the beating of her own heart, with the pulsing of her blood. She saw Harper and reached for her, but Harper was already moving away.

'Harper!' she wailed.

She couldn't go to her, knew she couldn't, knew there was something very wrong with trying to do so. She had a vague memory of having been in this situation once before, but she could not remember when or why.

'Mommy!' Harper begged, stumbling as she retreated.

Something was pulling at the little girl, dragging her away—something dark and shapeless and forbidding. It was too much for Bennett Scott. She cast off her lethargy and fear and burst through the knot of eyes that pressed against her, lunging after her daughter.

She was close enough to touch Harper, to see the fear in her daughter's eyes, when the ground disappeared beneath her feet and she fell away into the dark.

CHAPTER 20

Robert Heppler pulled the big Navigator into the empty driveway and put it in park, leaving the engine running. Nest gave a quick sigh of relief. It was blowing snow so hard that the driveway itself and all traces of tire tracks that might have marked its location had long since disappeared, so it was a good thing he knew the way by heart or they could easily have ended up in the front yard. She stared at the lighted windows of the house, but could see no movement. There were more lights on now than when she had left for the party, so someone must have gotten there ahead of her. She felt a surge of hope. Maybe she was wrong about Bennett. Maybe Bennett was waiting inside.

'Do you want me to come in with you?' Robert asked. She shifted her eyes to meet his, and he gestured vaguely. 'Just to make sure.'

She knew what he meant, even if he wasn't saying it straight out. 'No, I can handle this. Thanks for bringing us back, Robert.'

He shrugged. 'Anytime. Call if you need me.'

She opened the door into the shriek of the wind and climbed out, sinking in snow up to her knees. *Criminy*, as Pick would say. 'Watch yourself driving home, Robert!' she shouted at him.

She got the children out of the backseat, small bundles of padded clothing and loose scarf ends, and began herding them toward the house. The wind whipped at them, shoving them this way and that as they trundled through its deep carpet, heads bent, shoulders hunched. It was bitter cold, and Nest could feel it reach all the way down to her bones. She heard the rumble of the Navigator as it backed out of the driveway and turned up the road. In seconds, the sound of the engine had disappeared into the wind's howl.

They clambered up the ice-rimmed wooden steps to the relative shelter of the front porch, where the children stamped their boots and brushed snow from their shoulders in mimicry of Nest. She tested the front door and found it unlocked—a sure sign someone was home—and ushered Harper and Little John inside.

It was silent in the house when she closed the door against the weather, so silent that she knew almost at once she had assumed wrongly; no one else was there, and if they had been, they had come and gone. She could hear the ticking of the grandfather clock and the rattle of the shutters at the back of the house where the wind worked them against their fastenings, but that was all.

She glanced down and noticed Bennett's small bag packed and sitting by the front door. Close by, she saw the damp outline of bootprints that were not their own. Then she caught sight of a glint of metal in the carpet. She bent slowly to pick it up. It was a syringe.

She felt a moment of incredible sorrow. Placing the syringe inside a small vase on the entry table, she turned to the children and began helping them off with their coats. Harper's face was red with cold and her eyes were tired. Little John looked the way he always did—pale, distant, and haunted. But he seemed frail, too, as if the passing of time drained him of energy and life and was finally beginning to leave its mark. She stopped in the middle of removing his coat, stared at him a moment, and then pulled him against her, hugging him close, trying to infuse him with some small sense of what she was feeling, trying once again to break through to him.

'Little John,' she whispered.

He did not react to being held, but when she released him, he looked at her, and curiosity and wonder were in his eyes.

'Neth,' Harper said at her elbow, touching her sleeve. 'Appo jus?'

She glanced at the little girl and smiled. 'Just a minute, sweetie. Let's finish getting these coats and boots off.'

She dropped the coats on top of Bennett's bag to hide it from view, pulled off the children's boots, and laid their gloves and scarves over the old radiator. Outside, a car wearing chains rumbled down the snowy pavement, its passing audible only a moment before disappearing into the wind. Shadows flickered across the window panes as tree limbs swayed and shook amid the swirling snow. Nest stood by the door without moving, drawn by the sounds and movements, wondering if Bennett had been foolish enough to go out. The packed bag by the door suggested otherwise, but the house felt so empty.

'Come on, guys,' she invited, taking the children by the hand and leading them down the hallway to the kitchen.

She glanced over her shoulder. It was dark in the back of the house. If Bennett was there, she was sleeping. Her gaze shifted to the shadowy corners of the living room as they passed, and she caught sight of Hawkeye's gleaming orbs way back under the Christmas tree, behind the presents.

Then she looked ahead, down the hall. The basement door was open. She slowed, suddenly wary. That door had been closed when she left. Would Bennett have gone down there for some reason?

She stopped at the kitchen entry and stared at the door. There was nothing in the basement. Only the furnace room, electrical panels, and storage. There were no finished rooms.

Outside, the wind gusted sharply, shaking the back door so hard the glass rattled. Nest started at the sound, releasing the children's hands.

'Go sit at the table,' she ordered, gently shooing them into the kitchen.

Standing by the doorway, she picked up the phone to call John Ross, but the line was dead. She put the receiver back in its cradle and looked again at the basement door.

She was being silly, she told herself as she walked over to it swiftly, closed it without looking down the stairs, and punched the button lock on the knob. She stood where she was for a moment, contemplating her act, surprised at how much better it made her feel.

Satisfied, she walked back into the kitchen and began setting out cider and cookies. When the cider and cookies were distributed, she took a moment to check out the bedrooms, just to be sure Bennett was not there. She wasn't. Nest returned to the kitchen, considering her options. Only one made any real sense. She would have to get a hold of the police. She did not like contemplating what that meant.

She was sipping cider and munching cookies with the children when the shriek of ripping or tearing of metal rose out of the bowels of the house. She heard the sound once, and then everything went silent.

She sat for a moment without moving, then rose from her chair, walked out of the kitchen and down the hallway a few steps, and stopped again to listen. 'Bennett?' she called softly.

An instant later, the lights went out.

John Ross dreams of the future. The day is gray and clouded, and the light is poor. It is morning, but the sun is only a spot of hazy brightness in the deeply overcast sky. The walls of partially collapsed buildings hem him in on all sides, shutting away the world beyond and giving him the feel of what it must be like to be a rat in a maze. He moves down passageways and streets with quick, furtive movements, sliding from doorway to alcove, from alleyway to darkened corner. He is being hunted, and he feels his hunters drawing close.

He is in a village. He has been hiding there for several days, tired and worn and bereft of his magic. He carries his rune-scrolled black staff, but its magic is dormant. An expenditure of that magic in his past has left him without its use in his present. It has been more than a week since the magic was his to command, the longest time he has spent without its protection. He does not know why the magic has failed him so thoroughly and for so long, but he is running out of time. In the world of the future he has failed to prevent, a week without armor or weapons is a lifetime.

Ahead, he sees the shapes of trees through a haze that never clears. If he can make it to those trees, he may have a chance. Someone in the village has betrayed him, as someone always does. They depend on him, but they do not trust him. The magic he wields is powerful, but it is frightening as well. Sooner or later, someone always decides he is more dangerous than the once-men and the demons he battles. They arrive at the decision out of a misguided belief that by sacrificing him, they can save themselves. It is a condition of humankind brought about by the collapse of civilization. He has long since accepted it as the way of things, but he cannot get used to it. Even as he runs for his life yet another time, he is filled with anger and disgust for those he tries so hard to protect.

The sounds of pursuit are audible now, and he picks up his pace, making for the concealment of the trees. Once clear of the village and deep enough into the woods, he will be difficult to find. He is physically fit, toughened by his years of survival in the brave new world of the Void's ascendancy. He is no longer hampered by the limp that shackled him in the old world, when the Word held sway. He knows how to flee and hide as well as how to attack and fight, and he will not be easily found. He remembers how little he knew of such things in his old life. He was a Knight of the Word then, too, but in the old world there was still hope. Bitterness colors his thoughts; if he had not failed in his efforts there, his survival knowledge would not be necessary here.

Feeders shadow him as he gains the tangle of the trees and melts into their darkened mass. They are always with him, hopeful that one day they will feed on him as they have fed on so many others. Everywhere he goes, they are drawn to him. He has come to accept this, too. He is a magnet for predators of all sorts, and the feeders are only the most pervasive of the breed. Sometimes they will challenge him, but they cannot stand against his magic. It is only now, when the magic is out of his reach, that they sense they have a chance. He tries to ignore the hunger that reflects in their eyes as they keep pace with him, but he does not completely succeed.

Behind him, screams begin to rise from the village. The demons and once-men are reaping their harvest of death, reducing the village to ashes and rubble. It is unavoidable. All communities of men, whether city fortresses or unwalled villages, are targeted for this end. The destruction of humankind is the goal to which the servants of the Void are pledged. It is a goal that will be attained one day in the not-too-distant future, even though a few like himself struggle still to prevent it. It will be attained because all chance of winning has been lost in the past, and the Word has been reduced to memory and lost in time.

There are movements on his left and right, and he realizes his hunters have flanked him, moving more quickly than he has expected. He slows and listens, trying to judge what he must do. But there is little time for speculation, and after a moment he plunges on, reduced to hoping he can outdistance them. He does not succeed. They come upon him moments later, one or two at first, crying out wildly as they discover him, quickly bringing more, until soon there are so many the trees are thick with them. Still he races on, zigzagging down ravines and up hills, knocking aside the few brave enough to challenge him alone. He tries to call up the magic, hoping that it has returned, that it has not forsaken him when he needs it most, but the magic does not respond.

They catch him in a clearing where there is room enough for them to come at him from all sides. He struggles ferociously, bringing to bear all of his considerable fighting skills, but his attackers overwhelm him by sheer numbers. He is thrown to the ground and pinned fast by many hands, the stench of the once-men thick in his nostrils, their eyes bright with expectation and fever. Feeders swarm over him, finding him helpless at last, already beginning to touch him, to savor the emotions he emits while trapped and helpless.

A demon emerges from the crush of bodies and rips the black staff from his hands. No one has ever been able to do this before, but that is because he has always had the magic to prevent it and now he does not. The demon studies the staff, its twisted face bristling with dark hair and pocked with deep hollows where the leathery skin has collapsed into the bone. It attempts to snap the staff in two, using its inhuman strength, but the staff resists its efforts. Frustrated, the demon throws it down and stamps on it, but the staff will not break. Finally, the demon burns it with magic, scattering the once-men who have gotten too close, leaving the staff charred and smoking within an outline of blackened earth.

They bear him from the clearing then, dozens of hands holding him fast as they move back through the woods toward the village. The demon follows, clutching the remains of the staff. He can hear anew the shrieks and moans of the injured and dying, of the people who first harbored him and then gave him up, guilty and innocent alike. Many will be dead before the day is done, and this time, he knows, he will be one of them. The thought of dying does not frighten him; he has lived with the possibility for too long to fear it now. Nor is he frightened of the pain. There are rents and tears in his skin, and his blood flows down his arms and legs, but he does not feel it. The pain he feels most lies deep inside his heart.

His captors bear him past the village through a ruined orchard and up a small rise to a country church. The church is smoldering from a fire that has mostly burned itself out. The roof has collapsed, the walls are scorched, and the windows have been broken out. A clutch of once-men have brought a large wooden cross from within and laid it on the open ground. The brackets that secured it to the wall behind the altar are still attached, twisted and scarred. Once-men with hammers and iron spikes stand waiting, heads turning quickly at his approach.

Hands lower him roughly to the earth and hold him pinned against the wooden cross, arms outstretched, legs crossed at the ankles. They strip off his boots so that his feet will be unprotected. He does not struggle against them. There is no reason to do so. His time as a Knight of the Word is ended. He watches almost disinterestedly as the demon casts the ruined staff on the ground at his feet and the men with the hammers and spikes kneel beside him. They force one hand open and place the tip of a spike against his palm. He remembers a dream he had—long ago, when there was still hope—of being in this time and place, of hanging broken from a cross. He remembers, and thinks that perhaps the measure of any life is the joining of the past and the future at the moment of death.

Then a hammer rises and falls, and the spike is driven through the bones and flesh of his hand . . .

Ross awoke with a gasp, hands clenching the sheets and blankets, body rigid and sweating. He lay staring into the darkness of the room for several moments, trying to remember where he was. His dreams were always like this—so disturbing that waking from them left him feeling adrift and lost.

Then he felt Josie Jackson stir next to him, folding her body into his, and he remembered that he was in her house, in her bedroom, and had fallen asleep after lovemaking. A sliver of streetlight silvery with frost and cold glimmered through a gap in the window curtains. Josie put her arm around his chest, her fingers settling on his shoulder, smooth and warm. Her body heat infused him with reassurance and a sense of place.

But any contentment he felt was illusory. The dream had told him that his failure to save the gypsy morph, to breach its layers of self-protection, to discover the key to its magic and thereby bring it alive, was locking his future in place.

He lay there for a long time thinking through what that meant, of having to live the rest of his life knowing that even if he stayed alive through everything, his death was already predetermined. He did not know if he could live with that. He did know that his only chance to change things was now.

What then, he asked himself angrily, was he doing here? Nest, at least, was with Little John, monitoring his progress and seeking a way to reach him. What was he doing, away from both, fulfilling needs that had nothing to do with either?

The bitter taste in his mouth compressed his lips into a tight line. He was only human. It wasn't fair to expect more. It wasn't possible for him to give it.

He closed his eyes. Nevertheless, he conceded in the darkness of his mind, it was time to go.

Gently, he extracted himself from Josie's embrace, climbing from the bed, picking up his clothes, and slipping from the room. He dressed in the hallway and walked downstairs to retrieve his coat and boots. The clock in the kitchen told him it was closing on midnight. He glanced around. The old house was dark and silent and felt comfortable. He did not want to leave.

He took a deep breath. He was in love with Josie Jackson. That was why he was here. That was why he wanted to stay. Forever.

He remained where he was for a few moments, then walked to the bottom of the stairway and looked up into the darkness. He should go to her. He should tell her good-bye.

He considered it only briefly. Then he turned and went out the door into the night.

Nest Freemark froze in the sudden darkness, surprised and vaguely uneasy. The lights were all down. The hum of the refrigerator had gone silent. They had lost all power. All she could hear was the ticking of the grandfather clock.

She walked quickly back to the kitchen. The children were sitting at the table, staring around in confusion. 'Neth,' Harper whispered. 'Too dark.'

'It's okay, sweetie,' she said, walking to the kitchen window to peer outside. Lights blazed up and down the road. Hers were the only ones that had gone out. She glanced around the yard, seeing nothing but blowing snow and the shadows of tree limbs spidering over the drifts. 'It's okay,' she whispered.

She wished suddenly that John Ross or even Pick was there, to provide some measure of backup. She felt very alone in the old house, in the darkness, with two children to care for. It was silly, she knew. Like the basement door—

The basement steps creaked softly. She heard the sound distinctly. Someone was climbing them. For an instant she dismissed the idea as ridiculous, wanting the sound to be her imagination. Then she heard it again.

She walked to the kitchen table and bent close to the children. 'Sit right here for a moment and don't move,' she said.

She opened the drawer by the broom closet and brought out Old Bob's four-cell flashlight, the big, dependable one he always carried. She gripped it with determination, the weight of it comforting as she slipped on cat's feet from the kitchen and down the hall to the basement door. She listened a moment, hearing nothing.

Then she took a deep breath, yanked open the door, switched on the flashlight, and flooded the stairwell with its powerful beam.

She almost missed what was there because it had climbed the wall and was hanging from the ceiling. It was shapeless and black, more shadow than substance, a kind of moving stain caught in the edge of the light. When she realized it was there and shifted the light to reveal it more fully, arms and legs unfolded, eyes glimmered out of its spidery mass, a hint of claws and teeth appeared, and it came down off the ceiling in a rush.

Nest reacted instinctively, summoning the magic with which she had been born, the magic that had been the legacy of the Freemark women for six generations. Locking eyes with the dark horror scrabbling up the stairs, she sent the magic spinning into it. It was like burrowing into primal ooze, as if the creature had no bones and there was nothing about it that was solid. But it stumbled and lost its grip anyway, the magic stealing its momentum and twisting its reactions, and it tumbled away into the dark.

Nest slammed the door, punched the button lock, and rushed back into the kitchen. Grabbing one of the high-backed wooden chairs away from the table, she dragged it to the basement door, tilted it so that its back was under the knob, and jammed it in place.

Her breath came in quick gasps. She had to get the children out of there. She hurried back to the kitchen, snatched up Harper, and grabbed Little John by the arm. 'Come with me,' she urged as calmly as she could manage. 'Quick, now.'

She got them to the front door and began shoveling them into their coats. Harper was protesting, and Little John was just standing there, looking at her. She fought to keep her composure, listening for the sound of the thing in the basement, thinking, *No lights, no phone, no transportation, trapped.*

The basement door flew open with a crash, the lock giving way, the chair splintering apart.

Keeping the children behind her, she stepped into the hall to face her attacker—only it wasn't there. She speared the darkness with the flashlight, searching for it. She tried the ceiling first, then the walls. Nothing. She backed toward the children, eyes flitting left and right. It must be in the kitchen or living room. It must have ducked through one doorway or the other. She felt her insides churning, her throat and chest going tight with fear. She felt Wraith come awake inside her. In seconds, he would begin to break free. She could not afford to let that happen. Not in front of the children.

Hawkeye shot out from under the Christmas tree, a blur of orange fur as he disappeared down the hall.

She swung the beam of the flashlight back toward the kitchen, frantically searching.

Where is it?

It came from behind her, out of the darkness at the hallway's other end, from the direction of the bedrooms. She sensed it before she heard it and swung about to block its attack just before it launched itself through the beam of her light. It came at her in a rush, a black and formless mass, unexpectedly veering away at the last moment to try to get behind her. She threw the magic at it in a blanket, then swung at it with the flashlight. She saw it twist wildly and stumble, caught in the magic's grip, unable to recover. Some part of it lashed out at her in fury, catching her arms a numbing blow, and the flashlight spun away. Then it was past her and down the hall the other way, lost in shadows.

The flashlight went out and the house was plunged into darkness once more. Nest took the children by the arms and literally dragged them down the hallway to her bedroom. It was too late to get out or to try to summon help now. Her options were all gone. She needed a place where she could stand and fight. She realized something now, after this last attack, that hadn't been apparent before. The thing attacking them wasn't after her. It was after the children.

She got the children into her bedroom and slammed the door behind them, punching the lock. It was the best she could do. Her insides were twisting and roiling, and she knew Wraith would not be kept imprisoned much longer. Besides, there wasn't any choice; if they wanted to stay alive, she would have to let him out. Nothing less than the ghost wolf could protect them. Her own magic was woefully inadequate; it provided a holding action at best. Harper was sobbing, crying for her mother, but there was no time to comfort her. She hurried the children to the closet on the far side of the room, pushed them inside, and told them to get down on the floor and stay there.

She had barely closed the closet door when she heard noises in the hall outside. Her curtains were still open, and the room was brightened by light from a streetlamp. She could see everything clearly. Her eyesight had always been exceptional in any case, a gift of the magic and her heritage, Gran had told her. She could roam the park at night with Pick and see as clearly as he could. She would need that talent now.

The bedroom door flew back, the lock snapped, and the black thing heaved into the room. It didn't come at her right away this time, but floated up the wall to one side. She edged toward the center of the room, away from the bed, but with her back to the closet door, keeping herself between the attacker and the children. The black thing oozed along the wall for a moment, then dropped into a corner. Its movements were fluid and seamless, almost hypnotic.

Slowly it began to spread along the floor in a dark stain, moving toward her.

Wraith broke free then, shattering the restraints she had forged to keep him from doing so. There was no help for it; her need was too great. The big ghost wolf catapulted across the room toward the thing in the corner, tiger-striped face twisted in fury, jaws wide, teeth gleaming. Nest went with him, unable to prevent it, a part of herself trapped inside, her eyes seeing through his, her heart beating within the great sinewy chest. She felt as he did, primal and raw, all hunter and predator, caught up in his dark, compelling instinct to defend her at any cost.

The black thing counterattacked, and for a moment everything became a flurry of teeth and claws, guttural sounds and twisting bodies. Wraith fought ferociously, but the black thing, despite its shapeless, fluid mass, was immensely strong. It hammered into Wraith, and Nest felt the impact as if it was her own body under assault. Slammed violently backward, unable to hold his ground, Wraith went down in a tangle of legs and bristling hair, tiger face contorting in fury.

Up again almost immediately, he swung back to the attack, head lowered, muzzle drawn back.

But the black thing was gone.

It took Nest a moment to realize what had happened. Wraith stalked to the open doorway, gimlet eyes searching the darkness. Down the hall, the front door opened and closed. Wraith froze, a shadow silhouetted in the bedroom doorway, huge and menacing. Nest felt her connection with him unexpectedly loosen.

Then the closet door cracked softly behind her, and Little John slipped into view. He stood frozen in place for a moment, as if mesmerized by the tableau before him. His eyes shifted from Nest to Wraith and back again. Terror and despair were mirrored there; Nest could see both clearly. But there was a dark and haunting need as well. There was an unmistakable plea for contact. Nest was stunned. The gypsy morph was reaching out to her at last, groping in silent, wordless desperation. She was staggered by the depth of his voiceless cry for help. She was terrified.

She reacted instinctively, calling Wraith to her with a thought, drawing him back inside, trying to shield his presence from the boy. The ghost wolf came swiftly, obediently, knowing what was expected of him, but exuding a sense of reluctance, too, that in the heat of the moment she did not even think to question.

But Little John turned frantic. He came at her in a rush, crossing the room in a churning of arms and legs, reaching her just moments after Wraith had disappeared inside. He threw himself at her, this strange, enigmatic boy who would not be understood or revealed, and wrapped his arms around her as if she had become the most precious thing alive.

In the silence that followed, standing there in the center of her bedroom, her arms holding Little John close against her breast as she tried to reassure him that she was there for whatever need he had and would give to him whatever he required, she heard him cry softly.

'Mama,' he said in his child's voice. 'Mama.'

WEDNESDAY,
DECEMBER 24

CHAPTER 21

Nest was awake by six o'clock the next morning, dressed and ready to go. She walked up the road in the still, cold darkness to the pay phone at the all-night gas station on Lincolnway and spent twenty minutes arranging for repairmen from the electrical and phone companies to make unscheduled early morning stops at her home. Because she had lived in Hopewell all her life, she knew who to call to make this happen. Not that it was all that easy to persuade the people she knew to change things around on the day before Christmas, but in the end she got the job done.

She had taken the time to determine the extent of the damage last night before finally going off to sleep. The phone line was cut where it came into the house, so that wasn't a big deal. But the entire circuit-breaker box had been ripped out of the wall, and she had no idea how difficult it would be to fix that.

She carried back a box of doughnuts and Styrofoam cups of hot chocolate and coffee, thinking that they would at least have that for sustenance. The snow had stopped and the

wind had died, so the world around her was still and calm.
The children were sleeping, exhausted physically and emotionally from last night's events. It had taken her a long time
to get them to sleep, especially Little John, who had done a
complete one hundred eighty degree turn toward her. Instead
of distancing himself as he had before, going off to a private
world to contemplate things hidden from her, he had
attached himself so completely that it seemed any sort of
separation would break his heart. She could barely get him to
release her long enough to greet John Ross, who came
through the door less than half an hour after her battle with
the thing in the basement and found the gypsy morph clinging to her like a second skin.

She was pleased by Little John's change, but puzzled as
well. He had called her *Mama* twice, but said nothing more
since. He seemed devastated by her failure to understand
what he wanted. She held him and cooed to him and told
him it was all right, that she was there and she loved him, but
nothing seemed to help. He was disconsolate and bereft in a
way she could not understand.

'It has something to do with Wraith,' she had told John
Ross.

They sat together on the living-room couch in the aftermath of the night's events, the children asleep at last and the
house secured as best it could be. It was cold in the house
and growing colder without any heat, and she had tucked the
children into sleeping bags in front of the fireplace and built
a fire to keep them warm.

She whispered so as not to wake them. 'When he saw me
standing there, while Wraith was still across the room, he

had such excitement and hope in his eyes, John. But when Wraith came back to me, he was devastated.'

'Maybe he was frightened by what he saw.' Ross was looking at the sleeping boy, brow furrowed. 'Maybe he didn't understand.'

Nest shook her head. 'He is a creature of magic. He understood what was happening. No, it was something else. It was Wraith that bothered him so. Why would that be? Wraith has been there all along.'

'And the gypsy morph hasn't wanted anything to do with you the entire time.' Ross looked at her meaningfully.

'No,' she agreed.

'Maybe you are being asked to make a choice.'

'Between magics? Or between lives? What sort of choice?'

'I don't know. I'm just speculating. Give up one magic for another, perhaps?' Ross shook his head.

She thought about it again, walking home from the gas station. Apparently the gypsy morph couldn't find a way to tell her what it wanted. Little John was a boy, but he wasn't altogether a real boy, rather something like Pinocchio, wooden and jointed and made out of fairy dust. Perhaps he did want her to choose him over Wraith. But how was she supposed to do that? It wasn't as if she hadn't thought of ridding herself of the ghost wolf, of her father's demon magic, time and again. She didn't want that magic inside her. She was constantly battling to keep it under control. Last night she had failed, forced to release it because of a demonic presence. She knew she would never be at peace as long as Wraith stayed locked away inside her. But it wasn't as if the choice was hers.

Snowplows rumbled past her, clearing Woodlawn and the surrounding side streets, metal blades scraping the blacktop in a series of long, rasping whines. Lights glimmered from streetlamps and porches, from solitary windows and passing headlights, but the darkness was still thick and unbroken this Christmas Eve day. The solstice was only just past, and the short days would continue well into January. It would not be light until after eight o'clock, and it would be dark again by four. If the sun appeared at all, they would be lucky. Not much comfort there, if she hoped to find any. Head lowered in thought, she walked on.

Ross was awake and waiting on her return, standing in the kitchen, staring out the window. The children were still asleep. She gave him coffee and a doughnut, took the same for herself, and they sat at the kitchen table.

'I've been awake almost all night,' he told her, his gaze steady and alert nevertheless. 'I couldn't sleep.'

She nodded. 'Me, either.'

'I should never have gone to Josie's. I should have stayed with you and Little John.'

She leaned forward. 'It wouldn't have changed anything. You know that. We would have lost Bennett anyway. And if you had been here to protect us from that thing in the basement, Wraith might not have come out and Little John might not have responded to me in the way he did. John, that was the first time he's given me a second look. That was the first positive reaction I've gotten out of him. I'm this close to breaking through. I can feel it.'

'If there's time enough left.' He shook his head. 'I don't know, Nest. This has gotten entirely out of hand. Findo

Gask is all over the place, just waiting for a chance to attack us in some new way. I'm sure he was responsible for that thing in the basement. He's probably responsible for Bennett's disappearance as well.'

Nest was silent a moment. 'Probably,' she admitted.

'Did you call the police to report her missing?'

She shook her head. 'Not yet. She was gone the night before last, too, and came home on her own. I keep hoping she'll do so now.' She exhaled warily. 'But if she isn't back by the time the phone is fixed, I'll make the call.'

Ross brought the black staff around in front of him and tightened his grip on it. 'It's too dangerous for me to be here any longer,' he said softly. 'I shouldn't have come in the first place. I have to take Little John and get out of here before anything else happens—before some other horror shows up in your basement or your bedroom closet or wherever, and this time you aren't quick enough to save yourself.'

Nest sipped at her coffee, thinking the matter through. Outside, the darkness was beginning to lighten. The world glimmered crystalline and white in a faint wash of gray. She replayed last night's battle with the black thing, experiencing again the terror and rage that had overcome her, remembering how it had felt for Wraith to come out of her once again, after so long, after she had worked so hard to keep it from happening. She saw Little John's anguished look of loss and betrayal. She couldn't forget that look. She couldn't stop thinking about what it meant.

'I have an idea, John,' she said finally, looking over at him again. 'I'll have to talk to Pick about it, but it might give us some breathing space.'

Ross did not seem convinced. 'If I take Little John and go, it will give you more breathing space.'

'If you take Little John and go, we will have given up. Not to mention what effect it would have on him.' She held his gaze firmly with her own. 'Just let me talk to Pick. Then we'll see. Okay?'

He nodded wordlessly, but didn't look happy. She got up to check on the children before he could say anything else.

*T*he electrician arrived shortly afterward, a big, burly fellow named Mike who looked at the ruined breaker box, shook his head, and wanted to know how in the hell something like that could have happened. His words. Nest told him the house had been broken into and all sorts of damage had been done that didn't seem to have any purpose. Mike shrugged and went to work, apparently accepting her explanation. The phone repairman showed up while she was feeding the rest of the doughnuts and the hot chocolate and some apple juice to Harper and Little John, and fixed the line in about two minutes. The phone guy, unlike Mike, didn't seem all that concerned with being given an explanation. He simply repaired the damage and left.

Nest called the police then to report Bennett missing, making the call out of the children's hearing. This was easier than she had anticipated because Little John had gone back to ignoring her. She had hugged him on waking, and he had barely responded, eyes distant once more, that thousand-yard stare back in place. He sat on the sofa and looked into the park until she led him into the kitchen to eat, then stayed in his seat when he was done, lost in his own private world. She was too busy to be upset yet, but she knew she would be later if he didn't come back to her from wherever he had gone.

The police took down her report and said they would stay in touch. They didn't have any news at their end, which was probably all to the good. Nest still hoped that Bennett would walk through the door on her own, high on drugs or not. She still believed she could help Bennett without involving the police.

But then, while hanging up her coat, which she had tossed aside last night on coming in, she found Bennett's note in the pocket.

Dear Nest,

I am sorry to run off like this, leaving Harper with you, but I have to get away. I used last night, and I know I will use again in a little while. I don't want to, but I can't help myself. I guess I am hopeless. I don't like Harper to be around me when I am using, so I am leaving her with you. I guess maybe I planned to leave her with you all along. I can't take care of her anymore, and I can't leave her with strangers either. Guess that leaves you. Please take care of her, big sister. I trust you. Harper is all I

have, and I want to keep her safe and not
have her grow up like me. When I am better,
I will come back for her. Tell her I love her and
will think of her every day. I'm sorry for
causing so much trouble. I love you.

                                                    Bennett

Nest read the note several times, trying to think what to
do. But there was really nothing she could do. Bennett could
be anywhere, with anyone. She didn't like to speculate on the
possibilities. She did not have any difficulty with the idea of
looking after Harper, although she had no way of knowing
how the little girl would react when she found out her
mother had left her. It had happened before, but that didn't
mean it would make things any easier this time.

Mike the electrician wandered up from the basement long
enough to announce that he would have everything up and
running within the hour, so she left the children in Ross's
care, put on her parka, and went out into the park in search
of Pick.

He wasn't hard to find. As she trudged across her backyard and into the snowy expanse of the ballpark flats, he
soared out of the deep woods east aboard Jonathan. The sky
was iron gray and hard as nails. The clouds settled low and
threatening above the earth, as if snow might reappear at any
moment. Mist filtered through the woods from off the
frozen river, long tendrils snaking about the trunks and
branches and wandering off into the bordering subdivisions
and roadways. The park was empty this day, leaving Nest a

solitary watcher as the dark specks that were Pick and Jonathan slowly took on definition with their approach.

The owl swung wide of Nest, then settled in an oak bordering the roadway. Pick climbed off and began to make his way down the trunk. He moved with quick, jerky motions, like a foraging squirrel, dropping from branch to branch, circling the trunk when a better path was needed, stopping every so often to look around. Jonathan folded his broad wings into his body, tucked his head into his shoulders, and became a part of the tree.

Nest walked over and waited until Pick was low enough to jump from the branches onto her shoulder, where he sat huffing from the effort.

'Confound that owl, anyway!' he complained. 'You'd think he'd be willing to land on a lower branch, wouldn't you? For an owl, he's a bit on the slow side.'

She turned around and sat down in the snow with her back against the tree. 'I need your help.'

'So what's new?' The sylvan chuckled, pleased with his attempt at humor. 'Can you think of a time when you didn't need my help?'

He chuckled some more. It was a rather frightening sound, given that it emanated from a stick figure only six inches high.

Nest sighed, determined not to be baited into an argument. 'I need you to concoct some antidemon magic. Something on the order of what you use to protect the trees in the park when there's something attacking them.'

'Whoa, wait a minute!' Pick straightened abruptly, suddenly all business. His twiggy finger stabbed the air in her direction. 'Are we talking about Findo Gask?'

'We are.'

'Well, you can stop right there!' Pick threw up his hands. 'What do I look like, anyway? I'm just a sylvan, for goodness sake! I don't have that kind of magic! You've got a real live Knight of the Word living under your roof. Use him! He's got the kind of magic you're talking about, the kind that can strip the skin off a maentwrog in the blink of an eye. What do you need with me when you've got him?'

'Will you calm down and listen to me for a minute?' she demanded.

'Not if the rest of the conversation is going to be like this!' Pick was on his feet, arms windmilling. 'I'm a sylvan!' he repeated. 'I don't fight demons! I don't charge off into battle with things that eat me for lunch! All I do is take care of this park, and believe me, that's work enough. It takes all of my energy and magic to handle that little chore, Nest Freemark, and I don't need you coming around and asking me to conjure up some sort of . . .'

'Pick, please!'

'. . . half-baked magic that won't work on the best day of my life against a thing so black . . .'

'Pick!'

He went silent then, breathing hard from his tirade, glaring at her from under mossy brows, practically daring her to say anything more about the subject of demons and sylvan magic.

'Let me start over,' she said quietly. 'I don't really expect you to conjure up antidemon magic. That was a poor choice of words.'

'Humph,' he grunted.

'Nor do I expect you to sacrifice your time and energy in a cause where you can make no difference. I know how hard you work to protect the park, and I wouldn't ask you to do something that would jeopardize that effort.'

Her attempt at calming him seemed to be working, she saw. At least he was listening again. She gave him her best serious-business look. It wasn't all that hard considering what she had to say. She told him about what had happened during the snowstorm, with the disappearance of Bennett Scott and the attack by the black thing hiding in her base-ment. She told him about Wraith coming out to defend them, and of his struggle with their attacker.

'Findo Gask, for sure!' Pick snapped. 'You can't mistake demon mischief for anything but what it is.'

'Well, you'll understand then when I tell you I am more than a little on edge about all this.' She relaxed a hair, but kept her eye on him, waiting for his mercurial personality to undergo another shift. 'I can't have this sort of thing hanging over my head every time I walk through the door. I have to find a way to prevent it from happening again. John Ross says he should take the gypsy morph and leave Hopewell. But if he does that, we lose all chance of finding a way to solve its riddle. It will last a few more days, then break apart and be gone. The magic will be lost forever.'

Pick shrugged. 'The magic might be lost anyway, given the fact that no one knows what it is or how to use it. Maybe Ross is right.'

Now it was Nest's turn to glare. 'So you think I should just give up?'

'I didn't say that.'

'All I should worry about is helping you in the park? The rest of the world can just be damned?'

He grimaced. 'Don't swear. I don't like it.'

'Well, I don't like the idea of you giving up! Or telling me to give up, either!'

'Will you calm down?'

'Not if you're telling me you won't even try to help!'

'Criminy!' Pick was back on his feet, shuffling this way and that on the narrow ledge of her shoulder. 'All right, all right! What is it you want me to do?' He wheeled on her. 'What, that is, that doesn't involve antidemon magic?'

She lifted her hands placatingly. 'I'm not going to ask you to do anything I know you can't.' She paused. 'What I want you to create is a kind of early-warning system. I want you to spin out a net of magic and throw it over my house so that the demons can't come in again without my knowing it.'

He studied her doubtfully. 'You're not asking me to use magic to keep them out?'

'No. I'm asking you to use magic to let me know if they try to get in. I'm asking you to create a warning system.'

'Well!' he huffed. 'Well!' He threw up his hands again. 'Why didn't you say so before? I can do that! Of course, I can!' He glanced at the sky. 'Look at the time we've wasted talking about it when we could have been putting it in place. Criminy, Nest! You should have gotten to the point more quickly!'

'Well, I—'

'Come on!' he interrupted, jumping from her shoulder and scrambling back up the tree trunk toward Jonathan.

*   *   *

*H*e flew the owl back across the park to her house while she followed on foot. Midday was approaching, but it was still misty and gray, the clouds low and threatening, the air sharp with cold. The wind had not returned and no new snow had begun to fall, but the return of both seemed altogether likely. Nest stared at the houses bordering the park, indistinct and closed away, their roofs snowcapped, their walls drifted, and their eaves iced. There were cars on the roads, but not many, and they moved with caution on the slick surface. It was Christmas Eve day, but she thought people would try to confine their celebrations to their homes this year.

When she reached the house, Pick was already at work. She had seen him do this before in the park, when warding a tree. The process he used was the same in each case. Here, he flew Jonathan from tree to house, to tree, back to house, and so on, forming a crisscross pattern that draped the threads of magic in an intricate webbing. At each tree he stopped long enough to conjure up a sort of locking device and receptor, invisible to the eye, but there to serve a dual purpose—to anchor the magic in that particular place and to feed its lines of power. No materials were used and nothing of the work was visible, but the result was to render the house as secure as if a fine steel mesh had been thrown over it. All passageways in or out were covered. All entrances were alarmed. Any attempts to pass through, whatever form they took, would be detected instantly.

It took him almost an hour to complete the task, working his way slowly and carefully from point to point, all around the house, spinning out his lines of magic, making certain that nothing was missed. She stayed out of his way as he worked, watching in silence. There would be no more surprises like last night's. If the demons tried to come back again, she would know.

'Now here's the thing to remember,' Pick advised when he was done. He sat on her shoulder once more, Jonathan perched in a sycamore some distance off, awaiting his summons. 'Any attempt by a demon to get past the net and into your house will trip your alarm. This alarm isn't something that rings or honks or whistles or what have you. It's a feeling, but you won't mistake it.'

He lifted a finger in warning. 'A human entering the house won't trip the alarm. A human going out won't trip it either. But if you open up a window or door and leave it open, you invite the demon in and the system fails. So close everything up and keep it closed.'

She frowned. 'I didn't know that part.'

'Well, it hardly has any bearing in the park, when we're warding the trees, because there isn't anything living inside the net that would open it up in any case. It's different here. Keep everything shut tight. If you do that, the demons can't get past the system without you knowing. Think you can remember that?'

'I can remember.' She gave him a smile. 'Thanks, Pick.'

'Just remember what I told you. That'll be thanks enough.'

He looked exceedingly proud of himself as he jumped from her shoulder and scurried across the yard to climb back aboard Jonathan. Together, they flew off into the haze.

She watched them go, thinking that Pick, of all her friends, over all the years, was still the most reliable.

She looked at the house. There was nothing different about it; she felt nothing different inside. She was taking this entire warning system business on faith, but where Pick was concerned, faith was enough. Certainly the demons would detect the system's presence. Maybe that would be enough to keep them at bay for a day or so. Maybe that would be time enough for her to find out what it was that would unlock Little John's secret.

She found herself wondering suddenly how she had ever gotten to this point in her life. She was trapped in her home with a creature she did not understand and under attack from demons. She was struggling with her own magic and with the magics of other beings, the combination of which threatened to overwhelm her at any moment. She was hiding secrets that could destroy her. She was twenty-nine years old, adrift in both the purpose and direction of her life, her future uncertain.

What was her reason for being? Her gift of magic seemed pointless. Her life appeared to have led nowhere. She had been special since birth, but nothing of who she had been gave her insight into who she was meant to be. She was at an impasse, and the events of these past few days only pointed up how thoroughly lost she was.

If Gran were still here, would she be able to tell me what I ought to do? Would she understand the reason for all that has happened in my life? Or would she be as lost as I am?

Likely, she would just tell me to get on with it.

There was no steadying influence in her life. No parents,

grandparents, husband, or children. No family. There were friends, but that wasn't the same thing. She felt the lack of an anchor, of a touchstone that would give her a sense of belonging. The house had provided that once. And the park. All the places she had grown up in, the tapestry of her journey out of childhood. But somehow they weren't enough anymore. They served only to trigger memories that locked her in the past.

She stood thinking on the matter for a long time, staring off into space, traveling distances too far to be seen clearly.

Then the door opened, and John Ross stepped out onto the back steps. 'Better come inside, Nest,' he said quietly. 'The sheriff's office is on the phone. They've found Bennett Scott.'

CHAPTER 22

As she drove to Community General Hospital, nosing the Taurus between the dirt-and-cinder-encrusted snowbanks plowed up from the streets, Nest found herself reflecting on the cyclical nature of life. Her thinking wasn't so much about the fact of it—that was mundane and obvious—but about the ways in which it happened. Sometimes, in the course of living, you couldn't avoid ending up where you began. You might travel far distances and experience strange events, but when all was said and done, your journey brought you right back around to where everything started.

It was so in an unexpected way for Bennett Scott. She had almost died on the cliffs at Sinnissippi Park fifteen years ago, when she was only five. Nest had been there to save her then, but not this time. It made Nest wonder if the manner of Bennett's death was in some way predetermined, if saving her from the cliffs the first time had only forestalled the inevitable. It was strange and troubling that Bennett should die this way, after escaping once, after it seemed that whatever else might threaten, at least she was safe from this.

Thinking on the cyclical nature of Bennett Scott's life and death reminded Nest of her mother. Caitlin Anne Freemark had also died at the bottom of the cliffs in Sinnissippi Park, shortly after Nest was born. For years, there had been questions about how she had died—whether she had slipped and fallen, wandered off by mistake, or committed suicide. It wasn't until Nest had confronted her demon father that she had discovered the truth. He had instigated the events and emotional trauma that had led to her mother's death. Call it suicide or call it a calculated orchestration, the cause and effect were the same.

Now she wondered if demons were responsible for Bennett's death as well. Had Findo Gask and that girl Penny and whoever else might be aiding them set in motion the events that culminated in Bennett's death? Nest could not escape feeling that they had. As with her mother, as with the children in the park she and Pick had saved so often in that summer fifteen years ago, Bennett Scott had been prey to demon wiles. She could still see Bennett as a five-year-old, standing at the edge of the cliffs atop the bluff at the turnaround, feeders gathered all around her, cajoling her, urging her on, taking advantage of the fear, doubt, and sadness that suffused her life. It wouldn't have been all that different this time. Bennett Scott's life hadn't changed all that much.

It was Larry Spence who called with the news. A young woman had been found at the bottom of the cliffs below the turnaround in Sinnissippi Park, he advised. She fit the description of Bennett Scott, reported missing earlier this morning. Could Nest please come down and identify the body? Nest found herself wondering, irrationally, if anyone else worked at the sheriff's office besides Larry Spence.

She parked the car in the visitor zone of the hospital, went into the lobby, crossed to the elevators, and, following the signs, descended to the morgue.

Larry Spence was waiting when the elevator doors opened and she stepped out. 'Sorry about this, girl.'

She wasn't sure exactly what he was sorry about, but she nodded anyway. 'Let me see her.'

Spence walked her through a pair of heavy doors and down a short corridor with more doors on either side. They turned into the second one on the left. Bright light flooded a small chamber with a surgical table supporting a body draped with a sheet. Jack Armbruster, the coroner, stood sipping coffee and watching television. He turned at their entry and greeted Nest with a nod and a hello.

She walked to the table and stood quietly while he lifted the sheet from Bennett Scott's face. She looked almost child-like. Her features were bruised and scraped and her skin was very white. The metal rings and studs from her various piercings gave her the appearance of being cobbled together in some fashion. Her eyes were closed; she might have been sleeping. Nest stared at her silently for a long time, then nodded. Armbruster lowered the sheet again, and Bennett was gone.

'I want her taken over to Showalter's,' Nest announced quickly, tears springing to her eyes in spite of her resolve. 'I'll call Marty. I want him to handle the burial. I'll pay for every-thing.'

She could barely see. The tears were clouding her vision,

giving her the sense that everything around her was floating away. There was an uncomfortable silence when she finished, and she wiped angrily at her eyes.

'You'll have to wait until Jack completes his work here, Nest,' Larry Spence advised, his voice taking on an official tone. She glared at him. 'There are unexplained circumstances surrounding her death. There has to be an autopsy performed.'

She glanced at Armbruster. 'To find out how she died?'

The coroner shook his head. 'I know how she died. Prolonged exposure. But there's other concerns.'

'What he means is that preliminary blood samples revealed the presence of narcotics in her system,' Spence interjected quickly. 'A lot of narcotics. In addition, she has needle tracks all up and down her arms and legs. You know what that means.'

'She was an addict,' Nest agreed, casting a withering look in his general direction without making eye contact. 'I knew that when she came to see me. She told me she was an addict then. She came back to Hopewell with her daughter to get help.'

'That may be so,' Spence replied, shifting his weight, hands digging in the pockets of his deputy sheriff's coat. 'The fact remains she died under suspicious circumstances, and we need to learn as much about her condition at the time of death as possible. You see that, don't you?'

She did, of course. Rumors of drug sales in the park, an addict living in her house, and mysterious strangers visiting. Larry Spence had already formed his opinion about what had happened, and now he was looking for proof. It was ridiculous, but there wasn't any help for it. He would act on this as he chose, and anything she might say would do nothing to change things.

'Who found her?' she asked suddenly.

Larry Spence shook his head. 'Anonymous phone call.'

Oh, right, Nest thought.

'There's some damage to her body, but nothing that isn't consistent with her fall,' Armbruster observed, already beginning preparations for his work, laying out steel instruments and pans, spreading cloths. 'But I don't think that's what killed her. I think it was the cold. Course, I might find the drugs affected her heart, too. I can't tell, until I open her up.'

Nest started for the doors. 'Just see that she goes over to Showalter's when you're done poking around, okay?'

She was out the door and down the hall in a rush, so angry she could barely manage to keep from breaking down. She was aware of Larry Spence following, hurrying to catch up.

'There's a possibility,' he called after her, 'that the young lady didn't go over the cliffs by accident. In cases like this, we can't ignore the obvious.'

Don't get too close to me, Larry, she was thinking. *Don't even think of trying to touch me.*

She walked back through the heavy doors into the little waiting area and punched the elevator button. The doors opened, and they stepped inside. It was uncomfortably close.

'I told you about the rumors,' he persisted. His big hands knotted. 'Maybe they weren't just rumors; maybe they were fact. It's possible that this young lady was mixed up in whatever was going on.'

You are such a dolt, Larry, she wanted to say, but kept it to herself. He had no idea of what was going on. He couldn't begin to understand what was involved. He had no clue he was being used. He saw things in ordinary terms, in familiar ways, and that sort of thinking didn't apply here. His reality and hers were entirely different. She might try to educate him, but she didn't think he would listen to her. Not about demons and feeders. Not about magic. Not about the war between the Word and the Void, and the way that war used up people's lives.

'I'll have to come out to take a statement from you,' he continued. 'And from Mr. Ross.'

Her anger dissipated, replaced by a cold, damp sadness that filled her with pain and loss. She looked at him dully as they stepped off the elevator and into the hospital lobby.

'Look, Larry, everything I know is in the missing-persons report I made earlier today. If you want me to repeat it, I will. John will give you a statement, too. You come by the house, if that's what you need to do. But I'm telling you right now this isn't about drugs. You can take that for what it's worth.'

He stared at her. 'What is it about, then?'

She sighed. 'It's about children, Larry. It's about keeping them safe from things that want to destroy them.' She zipped up her parka. 'I have to be going. I have to figure out how to tell a little girl she isn't going to see her mother again.'

She stalked out of the hospital, climbed in her car, and drove home through the snowy streets and the iron gray day. That Findo Gask would kill Bennett Scott didn't surprise her. Nothing demons did surprised her anymore. But what purpose did this particular killing serve? Why even bother with Bennett? She wasn't involved in Gask's effort to recover the gypsy morph. She didn't even know what a morph was, or what a demon was, or that anything of their world existed.

Her mood darkened the more she thought about it. This whole business smacked of spitefulness and revenge. It smelled of demon rage. Gask was furious at her—first, for taking in John Ross and the morph, and second, for refusing to give them up. The attacks at the toboggan slide and her house had been designed to frighten her by threatening harm to those she cared about. She was willing to wager that killing Bennett was intended to serve the same purpose.

She was angry and unsettled when she pulled into her driveway and climbed out of the car. The first few snow-flakes were beginning to trickle out of the sky, and the light had gone darker even in the time it had taken her to drive to the hospital and back. Another storm was on the way. She hoped it would come soon. She hoped it would trap every-one inside their homes, demons included, for weeks.

Inside, she found John Ross checking the last of the locks on the doors and windows, a job she had left him to com-plete in her absence after informing him of Pick's efforts at implementing an early-warning system. When she told him about Bennett Scott, he just shook his head wordlessly. Mike the electrician had departed, his work finished, and the heat and lights were back on. She glanced into the living room where Harper and Little John were sitting cross-legged in front of the Christmas tree, playing. Colored tree lights reflected off the Mylar ribbons and paper wrapped about the scattering of presents nestled behind them. The scene had the look of a Hallmark card.

She walked into the kitchen and found the message light blinking on the answer phone. There were two messages. Both had come in this morning. The first was from Paul.

'Hi, it's me again. Just following up yesterday's call. Looks like I missed you. But I'll keep trying. Been thinking about you. Keep a good thought for me, and I'll talk with you later. Happy holidays.'

The familiar sound of his voice made her both smile and ache. She found herself wanting to talk with him, too. Just hearing those few words stirred memories and feelings that hadn't surfaced for a long time. Maybe it was because she was so lonely. Maybe it was because she missed what they'd once had more than she was willing to admit.

She closed her eyes a moment, picturing his face, then played the second message. It was a phone number. That was all. But she recognized the voice instantly. The good feelings went away, and she stared at the phone for a long moment before punching in the number.

'Miss Freemark,' Findo Gask said when he picked up the receiver on the other end. No hesitation, no greeting. 'Why don't you just give me what I want and we can put an end to this business.'

Even knowing he would be there, she felt a jolt go through her at the sound of his voice.

'That would be the easiest thing to do, wouldn't it?' she replied. She was surprised at how calm she sounded, given what she was feeling.

'Maybe you could avoid any more unpleasantness,' he

suggested pointedly. 'Maybe no one else would walk off the edge of a cliff. Maybe you wouldn't find any more surprises hiding in your basement. Maybe your life could go back to the way it used to be.'

She shook her head at the receiver. 'I don't think so. I don't think that's possible anymore.'

He chuckled softly, and she hated him so much she could barely keep from screaming it out. 'Well, life requires adapting to change, I guess. The trick is to adapt in the way least harmful to yourself and those around you. You haven't done very well with that of late, Miss Freemark. Your choices have cost you the lives of Bennett Scott and Ray Childress. They have resulted in your very nasty encounter with the ur'droch. What did you think of him, Miss Freemark? Would you like him to pay you another visit? He's very fond of children.'

She took a deep breath. 'I'll be waiting for him next time, Mr. Gask. His visit might have a different ending.'

The gravelly voice purred. 'Such stubbornness is foolish and pointless. You can't win, Miss Freemark. Don't think you can. Your allies are dropping away. Even that big Indian in the park. You've lost him, too.'

Her throat tightened, and she felt her breath catch in shock. Two Bears? No, they couldn't have done anything to him. Not him. She saw him in her mind, a rock, immovable, powerful. O'olish Amaneh. No, not him. She would know.

'I can tell you don't believe me,' Findo Gask said quietly. 'Suit yourself. What you believe or don't believe changes nothing. He's gone, and he's not coming back. Is Mr. Ross to be next? How about that little sylvan who lives in the park?

You're pretty fond of him, aren't you? What do you think about the ur'droch taking him—'

She placed the receiver gently back on its cradle, and the hateful voice died away. She stood staring at the phone, Findo Gask's words echoing in her mind. Her hands were shaking. She waited a long time for the phone to ring again, for Findo Gask to call back, but nothing happened.

Finally, she turned away. She would survive only if she kept her head. Stay busy, take things one at a time, anticipate what might happen without overreaching, and she might have a chance. Findo Gask could talk about making choices and suffering consequences all he wanted. She had made up her mind the moment she had seen Bennett Scott's dead face that she wasn't giving up the gypsy morph and its magic to the demons no matter what happened. A line had been crossed, and there was no going back. She didn't know what her decision might end up costing her, but she did know the cost of capitulating now was too great to live with.

Her resolve surprised her. It wasn't that she was brave or that she believed in the power of right over wrong. She knew Findo Gask was correct about her; she was being unreasonably stubborn. But somewhere along the way—since last night's events, she supposed—she had decided that whatever happened to her or even to those around her, she wouldn't back down. Something important was happening here, and even if she didn't understand exactly what it was, she would fight for it. She had an overpowering conviction that in this instance fighting was necessary, and that she must do so no matter what the consequences.

John Ross would understand, she believed. Certainly he

had waged similar battles over the years, championing causes when the issues weren't entirely clear to him, believing that instinct would guide him to make the right decisions when reason wasn't enough.

She glanced out the window into the park. She would have to warn Pick of Gask's threat—although Pick was probably being pretty careful already. But if even O'olish Amaneh couldn't stand against the demons, what chance did the sylvan have—or any of them, for that matter? She couldn't imagine anyone being stronger than Two Bears. She couldn't believe that he might be gone.

She put aside her thoughts on the last of the Sinnissippi and walked into the living room. Harper and Little John were still playing. She smiled at Harper when the little girl looked up. 'Come talk to me a minute, sweetie,' she said gently.

She took Harper down the hall to her grandfather's den and shut the door behind them. She led Harper over to the big leather recliner that Old Bob had favored for reading and cogitating and naps, sat down, and pulled the child onto her lap.

'When I was little, my grandfather would always bring me into this room and put me on his lap in this chair when he had something important to tell me,' she began, cradling Harper in her arms. 'Sometimes he wanted to talk about our family. Sometimes he wanted to talk about friends. If I did something wrong, he would bring me in here to explain why I shouldn't do it again.'

The little girl was staring at her. 'Harper be bad?'

'No, sweetie, you haven't been bad. I didn't bring you in

here because you did something bad. But something bad has happened to Mommy, and I have to tell you about it. I don't want to, because it is going to make you very sad. But sometimes things happen that make us sad, and there isn't anything we can do about it.'

She exhaled wearily and began to stroke Harper's long hair. 'Harper, Mommy isn't coming home, sweetie.' Harper went still. 'She got very sick, and she isn't coming home. She didn't want to get sick, but she couldn't help it.'

'Mommy sick?'

Nest bit her lip. 'No, sweetie. Not anymore. Mommy died, honey.'

'Mommy died?'

'Do you understand, Harper? Mommy's gone. She's in Heaven with all the angels she used to tell you about, the ones who make the sun bright with all the love that mommies have for their babies. She asked me to take care of you, sweetie. You and I are going to live together right here in this house for as long as you want. You can have your own room and your own toys. You can be my little girl. I would like that very much.'

Harper's lip was quivering. 'Okay, Neth.'

Nest gave her a hug and held her tight. 'Your Mommy loved you so much, Harper. She loved you more than anything. She didn't want to die. She wanted to stay with you always. But she couldn't.' She looked out the window into the park, where the hazy light was fading toward darkness. 'Did you know that my mommy died when I was a little girl, too? I was even younger than you are.'

'Wanna see Mommy,' Harper sobbed.

'I know, sweetie, I know.' Nest stroked her dark hair slowly. 'I wanted to see my mommy, too, and I couldn't. But if I close my eyes, I can see her there in the darkness inside my head. Can you do that? Close your eyes and think of Mommy.'

She felt Harper go still. 'See Mommy,' she said softly.

'She'll always be there, Harper, whenever you look for her. Mommies have to go away sometimes, but they leave a picture of themselves inside your head, so you won't forget them.'

Harper's head lifted away from her breast. 'Does L'il John got a Mommy, Neth?'

Nest hesitated, then smiled reassuringly. 'He's got you and me, Harper. We're his mommies. We have to take care of him, okay?'

Harper nodded solemnly, wiping at her eyes with her shirtsleeve. 'Harper wanna appo jus, Neth.'

Nest stood her on her feet and put her hands on the little girl's shoulders. 'Let's go get some, sweetie. Let's go get some for Little John, too.' She leaned forward and kissed Harper's forehead. 'I love you, Harper.'

'Luv 'ou, Neth,' Harper answered back, dark eyes brilliant and depthless and filled with wonder.

Nest took her hand and led her from the room. It took everything she had to keep from crying. In that moment, she felt as if her heart was breaking, but she couldn't tell if it was from sadness or joy.

CHAPTER 23

While Nest spoke with Harper Scott in the den, John Ross stood at the living-room entry watching Little John play with the pieces of his puzzle. Sitting in front of the Christmas tree, the boy picked up the pieces one at a time and studied them. He seemed to be constructing the puzzle in his mind rather than on the floor, setting each piece back when he was done looking at it, not bothering with trying to find the way in which it fit with the others. He seemed to be imitating what he had seen Harper doing a couple of days earlier. His blue eyes were intense with concentration, luminous within the oval of his pale face. He had lost color over the last twenty-four hours; there was a hollowness and a frailty about him that suggested he was not well. Of course, Little John was only a shell created to conceal the life force that lay beneath, and any outward indication of illness might be symptomatic of something entirely different from what it appeared. Little John was not a real boy, after all, but a creature of magic.

Yet sitting there as he was, lost in thought, so deeply

focused on whatever mind game he was engaged in that he was oblivious of everything else, he seemed as real as any child Ross had ever known. Were gypsy morphs really so different from humans? Little John's life force was housed in his body's shell, but wasn't that so for humans as well? Weren't their spirits housed in vessels of flesh and blood, and when death claimed the latter, didn't the former live on?

Some people believed it was so, and Ross was among them. He didn't know why he believed it exactly. He supposed his belief had developed during his years of service to the Word and had been born out of his acceptance that the Word and Void were real, that they were antagonists, and that the time line of human evolution was their chosen battleground. Maybe he believed it simply because he needed to, because the nature of his struggle required it of him. Regardless, he was struck by the possibility that humans and gypsy morphs alike possessed a spiritual essence that lived on after their bodies were gone.

He leaned on his staff, mulling it over. Such thinking was triggered, he knew, by the inescapable and unpleasant fact that time was running out on all of them. Whatever else was to happen to Little John, Nest, Harper, and himself, it should not be invited to happen here. Nest might wish to remain in her home and to make whatever stand she could in a familiar place. She might believe that the sylvan Pick could spin a protective web of magic about her fortress so that she could not again be attacked by surprise. But John Ross was convinced that their only chance for survival was to get out of there as fast as possible and to go into hiding until the secret of the gypsy morph was resolved, one way or the other. They must slip away this afternoon, as quickly as it could be managed, if they were to have any hope at all. Findo Gask would not wait for Christmas to be over or the holiday spirit to fade. He would come for them by nightfall, and if they were still there, it was a safe bet that someone else was going to die.

Ross listened to the old grandfather clock ticktock in the silence, finding in its measured beat a reminder of how ineffectual he had been in his use of the time allotted him. He knew what was required if he was to resolve the secret of the morph. He had known it from the beginning. It had taken him forever just to get this far, and he had almost nothing to show for it. That the morph had brought him to Nest Freemark was questionable progress. That she believed it wanted something from her was suspect. She was levelheaded and intuitive, but her conclusion had come in the heat of a struggle to stay alive and might be misguided. So much of her thinking was speculative. How much was generated by wishful thinking and raw emotion? Could she really believe that Wraith and the morph were somehow joined? What could Wraith have to do with the morph's interest in Nest? Why would it matter to the morph that the ghost wolf was an integral part of her magic?

Ross considered what he knew, still watching the boy. *Be fair,* he cautioned himself. *Consider the matter carefully.* It might be that there was a problem because the ghost wolf was created substantially out of demon magic. Perhaps the morph couldn't tolerate that presence. Yet morphs had the ability to be anything. Their magic could be good or bad, could be used for any purpose, so that the presence of other magics logically shouldn't have any effect. Was it something about the form of the ghost wolf that bothered the morph? Was Wraith's magic competing with its own in some way?

Ross mulled his questions through. This boy, this boy! Such an enigmatic presence, closed away and so tightly sealed, so inscrutable! Why had the morph become a boy in the first place? The answer to everything was concealed there, in that single question—Ross was certain of it. Everything that had happened flowed directly from the morph's last, final evolution into Little John, the form it had taken before asking for Nest, the form it had taken before their coming here.

His hands tightened about the smooth wood of the staff. What was the gypsy morph looking for? What, that it couldn't seem to find in the woman whose name it had spoken with such need?

The door to the den opened, and Nest came out leading Harper by the hand. Neither said anything as they passed him and went into the kitchen. Ross followed them with his eyes, keeping silent himself. He could tell they had been crying; he could guess easily enough why. Nest poured apple juice into Harper's baby cup and gave it to her, then poured a cup for Little John and carried it to the living room, Harper trailing after her. The children sat together once more and began working the puzzle anew.

Nest was bending down to help, speaking to them in a low voice, when the phone rang. She remained where she was, kneeling on the floor, Harper on one side and Little John on the other.

'John,' she called softly without looking up. 'Could you get that, please?'

He crossed the hall to the kitchen phone and picked up the receiver. 'Freemark residence.'

'I guess this just goes to prove how shameless I am, chasing after someone who leaves without a word in the middle of the night,' Josie Jackson said.

He rubbed his forehead. 'Sorry about that. I'm the one who's shameless. But I got worried about Little John. You looked so peaceful, I decided not to wake you.'

'That's probably why you decided not to call this morning either. You wanted to let me sleep in.'

'Things have been a bit hectic around here.' He considered how much he ought to tell her, then lowered his voice. 'Bennett Scott disappeared last night. They found her this morning at the bottom of the cliffs in Sinnissippi Park.'

'Oh, John.'

'Nest just finished telling Harper. It's hard to know how she's going to deal with this. I think Nest is trying to find out.'

'Should I come over?'

He hesitated. 'Let me tell Nest you offered. She can call you back if she thinks you should.'

'Okay.' She was silent a moment. 'If I don't come there, will you think about coming here?'

'To tell you the truth, Josie,' he said, 'I've been thinking about it since the moment I left.'

Not that he would go to her, he reminded himself firmly. Because he couldn't do that, not even though he was telling her the truth and badly wanted to. He had already determined what he must do. He must leave Hopewell, and leave quickly—with Little John and Nest and Harper in tow.

Maybe he could come back when this business with the gypsy morph was over. Maybe he could stay forever then. Maybe he and Josie could have a chance at a life.

But maybe not.

He was reminded anew of what had happened several months earlier when he had returned to Wales and the Fairy Glen to speak with the Lady. He was reminded anew of how deceptive hope could be.

It was early October when the tatterdemalion came to him. He was still living in Cannon Beach with Mrs. Staples and working at the Cannon Beach Bookstore. Through help from Anson Robbington, he had discovered the cave in which the gypsy morph would appear, and had returned there many times to prepare for the event. He had memorized the cave's layout and begun thinking of how he might trap the morph when it appeared. But he was still unable to conceive of a way in which to snare this elusive creature. He was hoping his dream of the Knight on the cross would come again and show him something new.

He was marking time.

The tatterdemalion appeared to him when he woke from a different dream, a particularly bad one, a dream in which he had witnessed another city's demise and the slaughter of its inhabitants. He could not remember the city's name, which troubled him considerably. He could not even remember which part of the country it was located in. There were people in the dream whose names and faces he knew, but on waking he could remember none of them. He had been fighting on a roadway leading out of the city, a group of women and children and old people under his protection and care. He had gotten them clear of the city, but they couldn't travel fast enough to stay ahead of their pursuers. Finally, Ross had been forced to turn and fight. Once-men and demons quickly surrounded them, and there was nowhere to go. Ross was still engaged in a desperate attempt to break free when he awoke.

For a moment, he could not remember where he was. His head still swam with images from the dream, and the sounds of battle rang in his ears. It was a warm, windless night, strayed somehow from the summer gone, and the windows to his bedroom were open to the air. The tatterdemalion stood by the window closest to the sea, pale and vaguely iridescent, a child of indeterminate sex, very young, with lost, haunted eyes that reflected bits and pieces of a human life best forgotten.

'Are you John Ross?' it asked in a soft, high voice.

Ross blinked and nodded, remembering his situation, the remnants of his dream beginning to fade. 'Yes.'

'I have a message for you from the Lady. She would speak with you. She wishes you to come to her.'

'To the Fairy Glen?' he asked quickly, sitting up now.

The tatterdemalion shimmered faintly. 'She wishes you to come at once.'

'To the Fairy Glen?' he repeated.

But the tatterdemalion was already fading, its luminescence failing, its lines erasing, its presence turning to memory. In seconds, it had disintegrated entirely, and Ross was alone once more.

He caught a flight out of Portland the next afternoon, flew east to New York, changed planes at Kennedy, and by midday of the following day, he was landing at Heathrow. From there, he took a train to Cardiff, then rented a car and drove north to Betwys-y-Coed. The trip cost him most of what he had earned that summer at the bookstore. He had barely managed to throw together the clothes he needed before going out the door. He was disorganized and exhausted on his arrival, and while his instincts were to go at once to the Fairy Glen, his body thought otherwise, and he collapsed in his bed and slept ten hours.

When he awoke, dream-haunted, but better able to make the decisions that might be required of him, he showered, dressed, and ate lunch in the pub downstairs. Afterward, on a typical Welsh October day—mostly cloudy, some brief rain showers interspersed with glimpses of sun, and a hint of early winter cold in the air—he drove up to the Fairy Glen and walked in from the road.

There were a pair of cars in the tiny parking area, and a handful of people in the glen, climbing over the rocks and wandering the muddied paths. The glen was green and lush, the stream that meandered along its floor swollen from recent rains. Ross descended the trail from the upper road cautiously, taking his time, placing his staff carefully for support. The familiar sounds filled him with excitement and hope—the tumble of the waterfall, the rush of the stream, the whisper of wind through the leaves, and the birdsong. He breathed in the dank rawness of the earth and plants, the rich smell laced with the fragrances of wildflowers and greenery. It was startling how much he felt at peace here, how close to everything that grew about him, as if this was where he really belonged now, as if this was his home.

He knew he would not see the Lady, or the fairy creatures that served her, in daytime. He thought he might see Owain Glyndwr in the familiar guise of a fisherman, but it didn't really matter if Glyndwr appeared to him or not. Mostly, he had come just to see the glen in daylight, to feel once again the lure of this place that had changed his life so dramatically. He descended to its floor and sat on the rocks, looking off at the waterfall and the stream, at the trees and plants and tiny wildflowers, at nothing in particular at all, just the sweep of the hollow and the colors that imbued it.

After a while, he went back to the inn and took a short nap. When he woke again, he walked around the tiny village, then returned for dinner. The innkeeper remembered him from his last visit, and they talked for a time about upheaval and unpredictability in the larger world. Betwys-y-Coed was an island of tranquillity and constancy, and it offered a sense of reassurance to its inhabitants. The innkeeper had lived in the village all his life; he couldn't understand why anyone would want to live anywhere else.

An hour before midnight, Ross returned to the Fairy Glen. The night was black and starless, and the moon peeked through the clouds like an intruder. Ross parked and walked to the gate, then descended the pathway to the glen. The damp air was chilly, and Ross tucked his chin into his heavy coat and watched his breath cloud the air before him. Using his staff, he navigated the uncertain trail to the edge of the stream and stood looking around. He breathed in the night smells and listened to the soft rush of the falls.

Almost immediately, Owain Glyndwr appeared. A Knight of the Word once and servant to the Lady now, he stood as still as stone on the other side of the stream, his greatcoat wrapped about his lean body, his wide, flat-brimmed hat shadowing his face. He held his fishing pole loosely, the line curved away into the flowing waters.

He nodded amiably toward Ross. ' 'tis a good night for watching fairies,' he said quietly. 'Come to see them, have you?'

'I have,' Ross acknowledged, realizing suddenly that it was true, it was a part of the reason he was here.

'Wait a bit, and they'll appear,' the other offered. 'Your eyes say you need their comfort. Well and good. Those who believe can always find comfort in them.'

He shifted his weight slightly, and his face lifted out of the shadows. Ross saw himself in that face, his features more closely mirrored than when he had encountered his ancestor last. He was older, of course, so their ages were closer. But it was more than that. It was as if by living lives as Knights of the Word, their resemblance to each other had increased.

Owain Glyndwr began moving slowly downstream from Ross. He stopped once, casting his line anew. Ross watched him a moment, then looked away in the direction of the falls. When he looked back again, the other man was gone.

Ross stayed where he was, waiting patiently. The glen's darkness was hard and cold about him, but it was strangely comforting as well. It enfolded and welcomed him. It gave him peace. That had not been so on his last visit, when he had returned ten years earlier to tell the Lady he could no longer serve as a Knight of the Word. The glen had felt hostile and forbidding then; it had disdained him. The Lady had not appeared, and he had gone home disconsolate and frustrated in his efforts. He had lost his way without knowing it. As a consequence, he had almost died.

Lights twinkled suddenly in the curtain of the falls, bright and pulsing as they moved through the dark waters. Hundreds of them appeared at once, as if tiny fireflies had migrated out of place and time to welcome him home. He smiled at the sight of them, at the realization the fairies were revealing themselves to him, acknowledging his presence. They grew in number until they filled the waterfall with their light, and Ross thought he would never see anything so wonderful again.

Then he heard his name called softly.

'John Ross.'

He knew her voice at once, recognized it as surely as he did the fairies dancing in the waterfall.

'John Ross, I am here.'

She was standing where Owain Glyndwr had disappeared, balanced on the surface of the water, suspended on air. She was as young and beautiful and ephemeral as ever, almost not there in the paleness of light that defined her image. She lifted her arms toward him, and the light moved with her, cloaking her in silver, trailing after her in bright streamers. She advanced in an effortless, floating motion, a shifting figure of shadows and moonlight.

'My brave knight-errant,' she whispered as she drew close. 'You have done well in my service. You are the image of your ancestor in more than appearance. You carry his blood in your veins and his heart in your breast. Six hundred years have passed since his time, but you reflect anew what was best in him.'

He was shaking, not from fear or expectation or anything he could readily define, but simply because she was so close to him that he could feel her presence. He could not answer, but only wait on her to speak again.

'John Ross,' she whispered through silky blackness and shimmering light. 'Brave Knight, your service is almost ended. One more thing must you do for me, and then I will set you free.'

He could not believe what he was hearing. He had waited more than twenty-five years for those words. He was fifty-three years old, and he had been a Knight of the Word for half of them. Ten years earlier, he had begged in vain to be released. Now she was offering him his freedom without even being asked. He was stunned.

'You must return to await the appearance of the gypsy morph,' she told him. 'As in your dream, it will come. As foretold, it will appear. When it does, you must be ready. For the time allotted to it, you must protect it from the Void. You must protect it at all costs. It is precious to me, and you must keep it safe. When it has transformed for the final time, your service to the Word is finished. Then you may come home.'

He could barely comprehend what he was being told. His voice failed him when he tried to speak; the words would not form in his mouth.

'Give me your hand,' she instructed.

Without thinking, he knelt at her approach, lifting his hand to touch hers. All that she was and all that was the

Word filled him with strength and determination. He felt something pressed into his hand, and when her own withdrew, he found himself holding a gossamer net.

'You will use this to take possession of the creature you seek. When it appears and begins to take form, cast the net. The gypsy morph will be yours then—to care for, to protect, and to shepherd as a newborn lamb.' The Lady lifted her arm to sweep the air with light. 'Give to it the shelter of your magic, your faith, and your great heart. Do not forsake it, no matter how strong the temptation or great the odds. Do this for me.'

'I will,' he said, the words coming almost unbidden, his voice returned.

'Rise,' she said to him, and he did so. 'The Word takes pleasure in you, John Ross—as do I. Go now, and serve us well.'

He did as he was bid, departing the Fairy Glen, carrying with him the gossamer net that would snare the gypsy morph, resolving that he would do what was necessary so that finally his time of service might be ended.

It was only later, when he was back at Cannon Beach, awaiting Thanksgiving and the gypsy morph's coming, that he began to ponder more closely the Lady's words, and only in the past few days, as time began to narrow down and the demons close about, that he understood how he might have mistaken their meaning.

'Do you mean that, John?' Josie's voice spoke suddenly through the receiver, interrupting his reverie. 'Because I wouldn't want you to say so if you didn't. Not to make me feel better, certainly. And not because you think it's the right thing to say after last night.'

He brushed aside his thoughts of the Lady and the Fairy Glen. 'I'm saying it because it's true, Josie.'

'Will you come see me, then? Tonight?'

'If I can.' He took a deep breath. 'I want to promise you I will. I want to promise you a lot of things. But you were right last night. I didn't come back for that. I'm not in a position to promise anything. Not yet, at least. One day, that could change. I hope it does. I suppose I hope for it more than anything.'

There was a long silence from the other end. He stood motionless by the kitchen phone, waiting for her to say something. Hawkeye appeared from somewhere in the back of the house, sauntering down the hallway and into the living room. With barely a glance at Ross, he wandered over to Little John and lay down beside him. The boy reached out at once to begin stroking him. The cat's eyes closed in contentment.

'I love you, John,' Josie said suddenly. Her voice caught. 'Big surprise, huh? But I had to say it at least once. Funny, it didn't hurt a bit. Call me later, okay?'

She hung up before he could say anything. He stared at the phone for a moment, listening to the dial tone, then placed the receiver back in its cradle. The ache he felt inside was bittersweet, and it left him wanting a resolution he couldn't have. He should call her back. He should tell her he loved her, too. But he knew he wouldn't.

He was still mulling the matter when he caught a

glimpse of movement through the kitchen window. When
he walked over for a closer look, a sheriff's cruiser was
parked in the driveway and Larry Spence was walking
toward the house.

CHAPTER 24

Just from the look on John Ross's face, Nest knew who it was even before she answered the knock at the door. Her impatience and frustration with Larry Spence crowded to the forefront of her thoughts, but she forced herself to ignore them. This visit did not concern her; it concerned Bennett Scott. Because it was necessary to talk with him about Bennett at some point anyway, she was prepared to endure the unpleasantness she was certain would follow.

'Afternoon,' he greeted as she opened the door. 'Would it be all right with you if I took those statements now?'

As if she had a choice. She managed a weak smile. 'Sure. Come on in.'

He clumped through the open doorway, knocked the snow from his boots onto the throw rug, and slipped off his uniform coat and hat and hung them on the rack. He seemed ill at ease, as if his size and authority were out of place here, as if they belonged somewhere else entirely and not in her home. She felt better for this, thinking that it wouldn't hurt for him to walk on eggshells for a while.

'Armbruster finished the autopsy,' he advised conspiratorially, lowering his voice. 'The young lady had enough drugs in her system to float a battleship. But the drugs didn't kill her. She froze to death. The marks on her body were from the fall off the bluff. I'd say she lost her way and wandered off, but it's just a guess.'

'Larry,' she said quietly, turning him with her hands on his arms so that his back was to the living room. 'I don't know anything about Bennett Scott and drugs beyond the fact she was an addict. John knows even less. I didn't even know she was coming back here until she showed up on my doorstep. John, when he came to see me, didn't either. He hasn't been back here in fifteen years. Bennett was five then. All this talk about drug dealing in the park, true or not, does not involve us. Keep that in mind, will you?'

His face closed down. 'I'll keep an open mind, I can promise you that.' He glanced over his shoulder. 'I'll need to see the young lady's room. You don't have to let me, of course, if you don't want to. But it would save me a trip down to the courthouse for a search warrant.'

'Oh, for God's sake, Larry!' she snapped. 'You can see anything you want!' She sighed wearily. 'Come with me. I'll show you where she was staying.'

They walked down the hallway past the den and Nest's room to the guest bedroom where Bennett and Harper were staying. The room was gray with shadows and silent. Bennett's clothes were still in her bag in the closet, and Nest had already picked up after Harper and made the bed. She stood in the doorway while Larry Spence poked about, checking the closet and the dresser drawers, looking under the bed and in the adjoining bathroom, and searching Bennett's worn satchel. He didn't seem to find anything of importance, and when he was done he put everything back the way he had found it.

'Guess that'll do,' he said without much enthusiasm. 'Why don't we do the interviews now, and then I'll be out of your hair?'

'All right,' she replied. 'Do you want some privacy for this?'

He shrugged his big shoulders, and she could hear the creak of his leather gun belt. 'I can interview you and Mr. Ross out in the living room. Do the both of you together. Maybe the children could play back here while we talk.'

She shook her head. 'I don't want Harper alone in this room just yet. I just finished telling her about her mother.' She hesitated. 'They can play in my bedroom.'

She went past him out the door and down the hall, irritated but resigned, already thinking about the more pressing problem of how she would manage the next twenty-four hours. It wouldn't be easy. Harper would be thinking of her mother. Little John was a weight she could barely shoulder, and yet she had to find a way to do so. Ross would probably be wanting to leave and go into hiding; he hadn't said so, but she could sense he'd made the decision. Whatever she did about any of them, she would second-guess herself later.

She collected Harper and Little John, the puzzle and a few other toys, and took them all into her bedroom. She told the children she had to talk with someone out in the living room, but she would be back to check on them. It wouldn't take long, and they could come back out when she was done.

It felt awkward, but she wanted the space and maneuver-ability that the living room offered so that she could usher Larry Spence out as soon as the interviews were con-cluded—sooner, if he started to annoy her—without disturbing the children.

Larry Spence had closed Bennett's bedroom door and was standing in the hallway, waiting for her. He continued to look ill at ease. Leaving her own bedroom door open just a crack, anxious that Harper not hear what might be said, she took him back down the hall to where Ross was waiting. They sat together in the living room, Ross and Nest on the couch, Spence in the easy chair. He produced a small note-book and pen, jotted a few notes, and then asked Nest to begin.

She did so without preamble, detailing the events from the time of their departure from the house until her discovery at Robert's that Bennett was missing. She left out anything about Ross, preferring to let him tell his own story. She also left out everything about the ur'droch, saying instead that she had come back to find the house broken into and the power and phone out.

When she finished her account, she brought out the note that Bennett had left in her coat the night before. 'I forgot about this earlier, but I found it this morning before you called. Bennett must have tucked it in my pocket last night before she slipped out of the Hepplers'.'

She handed it to Spence, who read it carefully. 'Almost sounds as if she thought something was going to happen to her, doesn't it?' he said, mostly to himself. He cleared his throat and shifted to a new position. 'Just one or two more questions. Then I'll take Mr. Ross's statement and be on my way.'

He ended up asking rather a lot of questions, she thought, repeating himself more than once in the process and annoying her considerably. But she stuck it out, not wanting to have to go through this again later. Once or twice, she got up to peek down the hallway, and each time Larry Spence quickly called her back by saying he was almost done, that he had just a few more questions, as if he was afraid she was going to walk out on him and not come back.

When he was finished with her, he interviewed Ross, a process that for all the noise he had made earlier about drug connections and shady characters took considerably less time than it had with her. He raised an eyebrow when Josie Jackson was mentioned, but said nothing. If she hadn't known better, she would have thought he'd lost interest in Ross completely.

'Guess that's it,' he announced finally, checking his watch for what must have been the twentieth time, slapping closed the notebook, and rising to his feet. 'Sorry to take so long.'

He was still nervous as Nest walked him to the front door, glancing everywhere but at her, looking as if he had something bottled up inside that he was dying to get out. At the door, he gave her a peek at what it was.

'Look, I don't want you to get the wrong idea, girl, but I'm worried about you staying here.' He seemed uncertain about where to go with this, his head lowered, his deputy sheriff's hat in his hands. 'There's things about this investigation that you don't know. Things I can't tell you.'

I could say the same, she thought. She had no time for this. 'Well, call me when you can, okay?'

He nodded absently. 'If you want to come by the office later—alone—I'll try to fill you in.' He shook his head. 'I shouldn't do this, you know, I'm not supposed to tell you anything, but I can't just leave you in the dark. You understand what I'm saying?'

She stared at him. 'Not really.'

He nodded some more. 'I suppose not. It's pretty complex, even to me. But you got yourself in the middle of something, girl. I know you don't have any part in what's happening, but I—'

'Not this again, Larry,' she interrupted quickly.

'I know how you feel, but—'

'You don't know how I feel,' she exploded, 'and if you want my honest opinion, you don't know what you're talking about, either! If this has to do with that old man in the black coat with the leather book, I'm telling you for the last time—stay away from him. Don't listen to anything he says and don't do anything he tells you to. He's dangerous, Larry. Trust me. You don't want anything to do with him.'

Larry Spence screwed up his face and straightened his shoulders. 'He's FBI, Nest!' he hissed softly.

She looked at him as if he had just climbed out of a spaceship. 'No, Larry, he isn't. He's not one of the good guys. He's not your friend and he's certainly not mine. He's not anything he seems to be. Have you checked up on him? Have you asked for proof of who he claims to be from someone else?'

'Don't tell me how to do my job, please.'

'Well, maybe someone should! Look, do yourself a favor. Call Washington or whoever. Make sure. 'Cause you know what? It's entirely possible that old man is responsible for what happened to Bennett.'

'You're way out of line, girl!' Spence was suddenly agitated, combative. 'You don't know any of this. You're just saying it to protect Ross!'

'I'm saying it to protect you!'

His face flushed dark red. 'You think I'm stupid? You think I can't see what's going on? You and Ross are—'

He caught himself, but it was too late. She knew exactly what he was going to say next. Her mouth tightened. 'Get out, Larry,' she ordered, barely able to contain her fury. 'Right now. And don't come back.'

He swept past her with a grunt and went out the door, slamming it behind him. She watched him stomp back to his cruiser, climb in, and drive off. She was so angry she kept watching until he was out of sight, half-afraid he might change his mind and try to come back.

When the phone rang, she was still seething. She stalked into the kitchen and snatched up the receiver. 'Hello?'

'Nest? Hi. You sound a little out of sorts. Did I pick a bad time to call?'

She exhaled sharply. 'Paul?'

'Yeah. Are you okay?'

She brushed back her curly hair. 'I'm fine.'

'You don't sound fine.'

She nodded at the wall, looking out the window at the empty drive. 'Sorry. I just had a visitor who rubbed me the wrong way. How are you?'

'I'm good.' He sounded relaxed, comfortable. She liked hearing him like this. 'You got my earlier messages, right?'

'I did. Sorry I didn't call back before, but I've been pretty busy. I have some guests for the holiday, and I've ...'

She ran out of anywhere to go with this, so she simply left the sentence hanging. 'Well, it's been hectic.'

'That's the holidays for you. More trouble than they're worth sometimes. Especially when you have a houseful.'

'It's not so bad,' she lied.

'If you say so. Anyway, how would you feel about having another guest, maybe sometime after the first of the year?'

She couldn't tell him how much she wanted that, how much she needed to see him. She was surprised at the depth of the feeling he invoked in her. She knew it was due in part to her present circumstances, to the loneliness and uncertainty she was feeling, to her heightened sense of mortality and loss. She knew as well that she still had strong feelings for Paul. A part of her had never really given up on him. A part of her wanted him back.

'I'd like that.' She smiled and almost laughed. 'I'd like that very much.'

'Me, too. I've missed you. Seems like a million years since I've seen you. Well, since anyone's seen you, for that matter.' His voice turned light, bantering. 'Good old Hopewell, refuge for ex-Olympians. I can't believe you're still there. Seems like the wrong place for you after all you've done with your life. You still train regularly, Nest?'

'Sure, a little.'

'Thinking about competing in the next Olympics?'

She hesitated, confused. 'Not really. No.'

'Well, either way, you've got a great story to tell, and my editor will pay a lot for it. We can talk about your career, memories, old times, flesh it out with what's happening now. I can use an old picture of you or have the photographer take a new one. It's your choice. But you might get the cover, so a new one makes sense.'

She shook her head in confusion. 'What are you talking about?'

'Of the magazine. The cover. I want to do a story on you while I'm visiting. Mix a little business with pleasure. It makes sense. Everybody wants to know what's happened to you since the last Olympics. Who can tell your story better than me? We can work on it in our spare time. They'll pay a pretty good fee for this, Nest. It's easy money.'

All the breath went out of her lungs, and she went cold all over. 'You want to do a story on me?' she asked quietly, remembering the editor from Paul's magazine she had hung up on a month or so earlier.

He laughed. 'Sure. I'm a journalist, remember?'

'That's what coming here to see me is all about?'

'Well, no. Of course not. I mean, I want to see you, first and foremost, but I just thought it would be nice if—'

She placed the receiver back in its cradle and severed the connection. She stood where she was, staring down at the phone, unable to believe what had just happened. A story. He wanted to see her so he could do a story. Had the magazine editor put him up to it? Had he thought he could get to her through Paul? Tears flooded her eyes. She fought to hold them in, then gave up. She walked to where Ross couldn't see her and cried silently. The phone rang again, but she didn't answer it. She stood alone in a corner and wished everything and everyone would just go away.

It took her a few minutes to compose herself. Outside, the day was fading quickly toward darkness, and snow was beginning to fall once more in a soft white curtain. Streetlamps and porch lights glimmered up and down Woodlawn Road, and Christmas tree lights twinkled through frosted windows and along railings and eaves. On a snow-covered lawn across the way, a painted wooden nativity scene was bathed in white light.

Ross appeared in the kitchen doorway. 'Are you all right?'

Everybody's favorite question. She nodded without looking at him. 'Just disappointed.'

The phone rang again. This time, she picked it up. 'Look, Paul,' she began.

'Nest, it's Larry Spence.' She heard him breathing hard in the receiver, as if he had run a race. His voice was breaking. 'I just wanted to tell you I'm sorry, that's all. I'm sorry. I know you'll probably never speak to me again, but Robinson is right—we can't take chances with this business. You're not thinking straight, girl. If you were, you'd see how much danger you're in and you'd get the hell out of there. I'm just doing what I have to do, nothing more. But I'm sorry it had to be me, 'cause I know you—'

'Go away, Larry,' she said, and hung up.

She stared at the phone absently. What was he talking about? She had no idea, but his tone of voice bothered her. He sounded anxious, almost frantic. Apologizing like that, over and over, for asking a few boring questions . . .

Then suddenly, unexpectedly, she thought of the children.

She had forgotten about them in the rush of events, of Larry Spence coming and going, of the phone calls. She glanced toward her bedroom. They were being awfully quiet in there.

She walked down the hallway quickly, snapping on lights as she went. She was being silly. She was overreacting. Pick's security net was in place. No one could get in or out of her house without her sensing it. She fought down the impulse to run. No, she kept saying inside her head, trying to reassure herself. No!

'Harper! Little John!'

She reached her bedroom and threw open the door. An orange blur shot past her from under the bed and disappeared down the hall—Hawkeye, hair all on end, hissing in rage and fear. Her eyes swept the room hurriedly. Shadows nestled comfortably in the corners and draped the bed in broad stripes. The puzzle and toys lay scattered on the floor. Harper's cup of apple juice sat half-empty on her nightstand.

But the children were gone.

CHAPTER 25

At first, she could not bring herself to move. She just stood, staring at the empty room, shocked into immobility, frozen with disbelief. A rush of confused thoughts crowded through her mind. The children had to be there. She had put them there herself. She just wasn't seeing them. Maybe they were playing hide-and-seek, and she was supposed to come look for them. Maybe they were under the bed or in the closet. But they couldn't have just disappeared!

She forced herself to look for them because the sound of her thinking was making her crazy. Even though she knew what she would find, she searched under the bed and in the closet and anywhere else she could think to look. As she did, her shock dissipated and her anger began to grow. They were supposed to be safe; her house was supposed to be protected! Nothing was supposed to be able to get inside without her knowing! It was the first time that Pick had let her down, and she was furious at him.

It wasn't until she searched the adjoining rooms, desperate

by now for help from any quarter, that she discovered the window in Bennett's bedroom was wide open. Then the telephone call from Larry Spence began to make sense. She had left him alone in that bedroom while she had gone to fetch the children, and he had used the opportunity to open the window from the inside. Pick had warned that the safety net was vulnerable from within. Larry was still under the sway of Findo Gask, and he had given Gask access without her knowing. He had come to her home specifically to help the demon steal the children.

Worried by the silence, Ross came down the hallway to find her. It was he who found the damp outline of the footprint on the carpet. The footprint wasn't human; it resembled that of a large lizard, three-toed and clawed at the tips.

The ur'droch took them, she realized at once. And now the demons had them.

She wanted to curl up and die. She wanted to attack someone. She was conflicted and ravaged by her emotions, and it was all she could do to hold herself together as she stood with Ross in the darkened hallway and discussed the possibilities.

'Gask has them,' she insisted quietly, her voice hushed and furtive, as if the walls would convey her thoughts to those who shouldn't hear.

Ross nodded. He stood very tall and still, another shadow carved from the night that gathered outside. 'He wants to trade for the morph.'

'But he already has the morph.'

'He doesn't realize that. If he did, he wouldn't have bothered with Harper.' Ross was staring at her, green eyes

locked on hers. 'He thinks we still have it hidden away somewhere. He's taken the children to force us to give it up.
Nothing else has worked—threats, attacks, breaking into
the house. But he knows how you feel about the children.'

She thought again of Larry Spence. 'I was a fool,' she said
bitterly. She leaned against the wall, running her fingers
through her curly hair. 'I should have seen this coming. Gask
tried for the children last night. I just didn't realize what he
was doing. I thought he was attacking them to scare me. He
was trying to steal them.'

'He was more subtle about it this time. He used the
deputy sheriff to open up the house and then distract us.'

She made a disgusted noise. 'Larry doesn't understand
what's happening. John, what are we going to do?'

'Wait.' He started back down the hall for the living room.
'Gask will call.'

The demon did so, fifteen minutes later. They were sitting
in the kitchen by then, sipping at hot coffee and listening to
the ticking of the grandfather clock in the silence. Outside,
the darkness had chased west the last of the daylight and layered the snow-shrouded landscape. Streetlamps and porch
lights blazed bravely in the blackness, small beacons illumi-
nating houses adrift in snowbanks and wreathed in icicles.
Thick flakes of snow floated through their gauzy halos as the
new storm slowly rolled out of the plains.

'Good evening, Miss Freemark,' Findo Gask greeted pleasantly when she picked up the phone on the second ring. 'I
have someone who would like to speak to you.'

There was a momentary pause. 'Neth?' Harper said in a
tiny, frightened voice.

Findo Gask came back on the line. 'No more games, Miss Freemark. Playtime is over. You lost. Give me what I want or you won't see these children again, I promise you. Don't test me on this.'

'I won't,' she said quietly.

'Good. I don't know where you've hidden the morph, but I will give you until midnight to recover it. I will call you back then to arrange a time and place for the exchange. I will call only once. Any delay, any excuses, any tricks, and you and Mr. Ross will spend a very lonely Christmas. Do we understand each other?'

She closed her eyes. 'Yes.'

He hung up. She placed the receiver back in its cradle and looked at Ross. 'You were right,' she said. 'He wants a trade. The children for the morph.'

He nodded without speaking.

'Except we don't have the morph to give him.'

'No,' he agreed softly. 'We don't.'

*F*indo Gask wrapped his fingers carefully about the Book of Names and stood staring off into empty space. Something was wrong. He couldn't put his finger on it, but something wasn't right. It wasn't in the situation, which was progressing just as he had planned, or in Nest Freemark's voice, which was suitably submissive and worried. No, it was something else, something he had overlooked.

'Gramps!' Penny snapped at him impatiently. 'What did she say?'

It wouldn't come to him, so he put the matter aside

for later consideration. 'She'll do what we want.'

Penny giggled and twirled about in mock celebration. 'Little Miss Track Shoes has run out of tricks! Too bad, too bad! No gold medal for her! Better luck next time!'

She danced around the room, frizzy red hair flying, gleefully singing *tra-la-la-la*. She danced at Twitch, who just looked at her dumbly, then at the ur'droch where it crouched hidden in a corner. Gask waited her out patiently.

'Make the children some dinner,' he said when she had calmed down sufficiently to pay attention. 'Don't get cute and don't frighten them.'

'What's the difference?' she asked, pouting. 'You'll kill them anyway. Why can't I have some fun with them first?'

'Because I say so, Penny,' he answered, giving her a steady look. 'Is that reason enough for you?'

The redhead's mouth twisted in a hard sneer. 'Sure enough, Gramps. Anything your little old heart desires.'

She disappeared into the kitchen, humming tunelessly. She was becoming increasingly unstable, less easily controlled. If she went off, as she was certain to do sooner or later, he would have to kill her. Not that he was reluctant to do so, but it was inconvenient. He still might need her help. His adversaries were resourceful, and their desperation would render them less predictable. Penny Dreadful was a valuable counter to such behavior. He might have to agree to give her the children as a reward. She would like that. If she had his promise that she could have them when this was over, she was more likely to stay in line. It was a cheap enough price.

The children were down in the basement in a big,

L-shaped recreation room containing an old Lionel train setup, a jukebox and bar, a game table and dartboard, and some couches and chairs situated around a television. There was only one way in or out, down a stairway leading from the back of the house, so it was easy to keep an eye on them.

Nevertheless, he sent the ur'droch down to stand watch without their seeing it. Twitch and Penny were too scary and more likely to do something of which he didn't approve. The ur'droch would just stay hidden.

When the phone rang, he was surprised. No one should be calling. He picked up the receiver guardedly. 'Yes?'

'Mr. Robinson?'

It was that sheriff's deputy, what's-his-name Spence. Findo Gask suppressed a grimace. 'What can I do for you?'

'We need to talk. The sooner, the better.'

'Go ahead, Deputy Sheriff. Talk.'

'No, not on the phone. In person. I just need to clarify a few things. About what's going on with John Ross and this drug business. I'm worried about those kids. I want to make sure they're safe. Where can we meet?'

Findo Gask shook his head. Gask could tell by the way Spence spoke. He had been checking, and he had found out that no one knew anything about an FBI assignment in Hopewell or an agent named Robinson. Spence was scared. On Robinson's instructions, he had opened a bedroom window in the Freemark home so that the children could be removed for safekeeping while a sting operation was implemented to collar the dangerous Mr. Ross. Spence was afraid he had facilitated the kidnapping of two children, aiding and abetting the commission of a felony, and he could see his entire career slipping away.

What to do?

'I'm going to give you an address, Deputy Sheriff.' Gask looked at Twitch, slumped on the sofa in front of the television, huge and vacant-eyed. 'I've been thinking that the children might be better off with the local authorities. If you could pick them up, I would be grateful. We can talk then.'

'Yeah, sure, that would be fine.' Spence sounded relieved.

Gask gave the deputy sheriff their address. He wasn't worried about Spence descending on him with an army of law enforcement officers; the deputy sheriff would be looking for a way to protect himself from any fallout in this business. If he could get the children back unharmed, things would be fine. That's the way he would look at it. He would come alone.

Findo Gask hung up the receiver. A picture of how this business would end took shape. Newspaper headlines and television trailers scrolled through his mind. A family tragedy was sparked by jealousy and misunderstanding. Two men and a woman were involved, the latter a well-known athlete. Multiple killings of adults and children ensued. Murder and suicide made an unwelcome appearance in tiny Hopewell.

It would make for good reading in other cities.

'What are we going to do, John?' Nest repeated, a hint of desperation creeping into her voice.

Ross limped to the kitchen counter with the aid of his staff and leaned his backside against the lower cabinets,

crossing his arms over his chest, embracing the staff posses-
sively. His lean face was lined with fatigue, but his eyes were
fierce.

'There's something I haven't told you,' he said after a
moment's reflection. 'Not because I was trying to keep it
from you or didn't trust you, but because it didn't have anything to do with you. Except that now it does. I told you that
a dream led me to the gypsy morph. But I didn't tell you
what the dream was about. In the dream, a Knight of the
Word was hung from a cross. Demons and once-men had
crucified him. He was dying. Just before I woke, I saw his
face. It was my own.'

He held up one hand to cut short her startled exclama-
tion. 'I wasn't sure at first if the Knight on the cross was me
or if I was just supposed to see myself in him. I was hoping
I would learn the answer from the Lady when she summoned me to Wales two months ago. I didn't, but I learned
something more important. I learned that if I was successful
in protecting the gypsy morph through its final transformation, I would be released forever from my commitment to
the Word.'

'John!' she breathed.

He nodded. 'I know. I fought so hard for it ten years ago
when it wasn't permitted, and then it's offered to me without my even having asked. I want it, Nest. I'll admit that.
I've seen too much, living in both the present and the future.
I'm tired of death and chaos and destruction. I'm tired of
fighting to stay alive. Hell, I'm just plain tired. I've been a
Knight of the Word for twenty-five years. Half my life. It's
all I can remember anymore. It seems like the only existence

I've ever known. I need to give it up. I need to rest.'

'But you can do that now!' she exclaimed quickly. 'You've done what was asked of you. The morph hasn't changed in days. Its time is almost up, and it's still a little boy. It's finished changing, isn't it?'

'Maybe. Maybe not. I'm not sure. It hasn't bonded with you the way I expected. It seems to be looking for something. I don't know what, but the way it responded to you last night when Wraith came out suggests it's still waiting for something to happen. It might be another change.'

She studied him a moment. 'All right. So what do we do?'

'We let Findo Gask call us back and set up the exchange. We meet with him. We find a way to separate Harper from the demons. Your job is to get her safely out of there. Mine is to do what I can to save the morph.'

She walked to the kitchen window and looked out into the night. It was snowing heavily again, thick flakes drifting out of the clouded skies, a fresh blanket of white gathering over the earth. 'They'll be expecting something like that,' she said quietly.

'I know.'

'You'll lose the morph anyway. And your life as well.'

'Maybe.'

'We'll have accomplished nothing.'

'We'll have saved Harper.'

She thought about it some more. Gask would pick a place for the exchange that would favor the demons. He would have his companions hidden all about them. He would make certain she and Ross were rendered helpless in the event they tried to surprise him. Her mind spun out possible scenarios, all bleak and hopeless. Nothing she envisioned had a happy ending.

Then a dark realization swept over her. She wasn't seeing this right. There wouldn't be any trade. There wasn't any reason for one. Why would Findo Gask leave any of them alive when he didn't have to? It made perfect sense, in demon terms, not to let them go, but to kill them.

Don't underestimate him!

She had to find a way to get one step ahead of him. Where was he now? Where was he hiding Harper and Little John? If she only knew that—

She caught herself. But she did know. She had known all along, even without realizing it. She knew exactly where they were.

The phone rang, interrupting her train of thought. She walked over and snatched it up. 'Hello?'

'Nest, it's Robert. I just heard about Bennett Scott.' He sounded shaken. 'I'm really sorry.'

She put her hand over her eyes wearily. 'Thanks, Robert.'

'I'm sorry about her dying, and I'm sorry for all the things I've said about her. And about John Ross. You didn't need to hear that kind of junk from me. I wish I'd never said any of it, but I did, and it's too late to take it back. That's been a problem for me all my life.'

'It's okay, Robert.'

'I know things must be tough over there, especially for the little ones. Amy and I want you to think about coming over here Christmas Day. All of you, Ross included. You don't have to come for the whole day, just as much of it as you want. But it would be good for the kids to have other kids to play with. It would be good for all of you to be with other people.'

She didn't say anything, her throat and chest tight with sudden grief and despair. All she could think about was losing Harper and Little John to the demons and not being able to get them safely back.

'Nest?' he said.

She felt everything break apart inside like deadwood and then come back together again, the broken pieces bound together by iron forged in the furnace of her determination. 'You're a good guy, Robert,' she said quietly. 'Tell Amy how much your invitation means to me. Let me think about it, and I'll call you tomorrow morning.'

She hung up the phone, stared off into space for a moment, and then looked at Ross. 'What do you say, John? I'm tired of being pushed around. Let's not wait on Findo Gask and his phone call. Let's go get the children back right now.'

CHAPTER 26

It took a considerable amount of effort on Nest's part to persuade Ross that she was right. If they let Findo Gask dictate the conditions of any trade, she argued, he would put them in a box. He would create a situation where they had no hope of freeing either Harper or Little John. Besides, he would not make the exchange in any case, not even if they revealed to him that he had the gypsy morph in his possession already. He would simply kill them. If they wanted to have any chance at all, they had to act now, while Gask thought them paralyzed and helpless. They had to go after the demons on their own ground.

Ross was not averse to the idea of a preemptory strike; it rather appealed to him. He had taken on a fatalistic attitude regarding his own future, and his sole concern was for the children. But he was adamant that their best approach was to keep Nest out of the picture entirely. He would go by himself, confront Gask, and free the children if he could. If there were any sacrifices required, they would come from him.

'John, you can't do it alone,' she pointed out reasonably. 'You don't even know how to get to where you need to go. I'll have to drive us. Listen to me. When we get there, one of us will have to distract the demons while the other frees the children. It will be hard enough with two of us working together. It will be impossible if you try it alone.'

There were at least four demons, she added. Findo Gask, the girl Penny, the ur'droch, and a giant albino called Twitch. That was too many for him to try to take on by himself.

'I have as much stake in this as you do, John,' she said quietly. 'Harper is my responsibility. Bennett gave her into my safekeeping. And what about Little John? He asked for me, brought you to me, and last night called me *Mama* as if I had it in me to give him the one thing he most needs. I can't ignore that. I can't pretend it didn't happen or that it doesn't mean anything, and it's wrong of you to ask me to do so.'

'You're not equipped for this, Nest,' he insisted angrily. 'You don't have the tools. The only real weapon you have is one you don't want to use. What's going to happen if you have to call Wraith out to defend you? What if you can't? The demons will kill you in a heartbeat. I have the magic to protect myself, but I don't think I can protect us both.

'Besides,' he said, shaking his head dismissively. 'You aren't the one who was asked to protect the morph. I was. This isn't your fight.'

She smiled at that. 'I think it's been my fight since the day Findo Gask appeared on my doorstep and told me what would happen if I took you in. I don't think I've got a choice.'

In the end, he agreed. They would go together, but only if she promised that once she had possession of the children she would get out of there and that she would not expose herself to any more danger than was absolutely necessary.

As *if*, she wanted to say, but agreed.

The children, she told him, were in an old house on Third Street, down by the west plant of MidCon Steel. She had gone to that house with church carolers earlier on the same night he had appeared at her door.

In the wake of everything else that had happened, Nest had all but forgotten the incident with Twitch and Allen Kruppert. She had suspected that something wasn't right with that house and the strange people in it, but she hadn't given the matter any further thought after Ross appeared with the morph. It wasn't until now she remembered Bennett saying, when pressed, that Penny claimed to be Findo Gask's niece.

'If the connection is real,' she explained to Ross, 'they're all staying in that house on Third. That's where they'll have the children. Gask wasn't there that night, or at least he didn't show himself. I think he was testing me, John, trying to see how strong I was, how easily I would frighten. But he was being careful to stay hidden from me in the process. I don't think he has any idea we know about his connection to that house.'

'Maybe,' Ross acknowledged grudgingly. 'But even if you're right, we won't be able to just walk in there. If you were smart enough to have Pick throw a protective net over your house, won't Gask have done something like it to his?'

She had to agree that he would. How would they get past whatever safeguards he had installed? For that matter, how would they even know where to look for the children? If she couldn't get to them before the demons discovered what they were about, the children's lives were over. Even a distraction by Ross probably wouldn't be enough to save them. At least one demon would get there first.

It was still snowing heavily outside, and the snowplows were beginning to make their runs up and down the nearby streets, metal blades scraping loudly in the snowfall's hushed silence. Pick might have the solution to their dilemma, knowing what he did about magic's uses, but she was unlikely to find him out on a night like this. Pick might be able to throw his voice from great distances to speak with her, but she could not do the same to summon him. Ross, when pressed, admitted he lacked any sort of magic that would enable him to bypass a demon security web. The way matters stood, if they went to the house on Third Street, any attempt at an entry would probably result in failure.

Nest felt time and opportunity slipping away. It was already edging toward eight o'clock. They had little more than four hours in which to act. The weather was worsening, the streets would soon be impassable where the snowplows hadn't reached, and even getting to where they had to go would become difficult.

Hawkeye had reappeared from wherever he had been hiding and taken up a position on the living-room couch. The hair along the ridge of his spine was spiked, and his green eyes were fierce and angry and resentful. She watched him for a time as she stood in the kitchen doorway, thinking. He must have had a close encounter with the ur'droch when it took the children out of her bedroom. He was probably lucky to be alive.

An idea came to her suddenly, but it was so strange she could barely bring herself to allow it to take shape. In fact, it was more than strange—it was anathema. Under any other circumstances, she wouldn't have even considered it. But when you are desperate, you will go down some roads you would otherwise avoid.

'John,' she said, drawing his attention. 'I'm going outside for a little bit.' She spoke quickly, before she could think better of it, before she had time to reconsider. 'I'm going to try something that might help. Wait here for me.'

She pulled on her hooded parka, scarf, gloves, and boots, and she laced, buttoned, and zipped everything up tight. She could hear Ross saying something behind her, but she didn't answer. She didn't trust herself to do so. When she was sufficiently bundled up, she went out the back door into the night.

It was cold and snowing, but the wind had died away, and the air didn't have last night's bite. Sending clouds of breath ahead of her, she walked to the hedgerow at the end of her backyard and passed through the tangle of brittle limbs to where the service road lay. Lights blazed from the windows of distant houses, but it was the eyes of the feeders who quickly gathered that drew her attention. There were dozens of them, slinking through the shadows, appearing and disappearing in the swirl of falling snow. They had come to her to taste the magic she was about to unleash, sensing in that way they had what she intended to do.

Her plan was simple, if abhorrent. She intended to release Wraith and send him into the park in search of Pick. Her own efforts would be wasted, because her presence alone would not be enough to summon the sylvan from wherever he was taking shelter. Moreover, it would take time she did not have. But Wraith was all magic, and magic of that size roaming Pick's woodland domain would alert the sylvan instantly. It would draw him out and bring him in search of her.

The problem, of course, was that this plan she had stumbled on required that she release Wraith, something she was loath to do under any circumstance and particularly where she was not personally threatened. The difficulties she faced in releasing Wraith were daunting. She did not know for certain that she could control what he might do or how far away from her he might venture once released, or if she could bring him back inside once he was out. She did not know how much energy she would have to expend on any of this, and she was looking at a night ahead when she might need that energy to stay alive.

But without Pick's help, she did not stand a chance of bypassing any security net Findo Gask might have set in place or of finding where the children were concealed. Without Pick's help, her chances of succeeding were minimal.

It was a risk worth taking, she decided anew, and hoped she was thinking clearly.

She found a patch of deep shadow amid a cluster of barren, dark trees and bushes near the far end of the Peterson yard and placed herself there. The feeders were clustered all about her, but she forced herself to ignore them. They were no threat to her if she stayed calm.

Closing her eyes, she reached down inside in search of Wraith. It was the first time she had ever done so consciously. She was not sure about what she was doing and found herself groping as if blind and deaf. There were no pathways to follow, and she lacked anger and fear as catalysts to spark his interest. She searched, and nothing happened. She hunted, but found only silence and darkness.

She opened her eyes and frowned. It wasn't working.

Briefly, she considered giving up, abandoning her search, going back into the house, and collecting Ross. But she was stubborn by nature, and she was curious about why she was struggling so. There should have been at least some sign of the ghost wolf. There should have been some small hint of his presence. Why wasn't there?

Brushing at the snowflakes that settled on her eyelashes, she tried again. But this time she went looking for what she knew she could find—her own magic, the magic she had been born with. She found it easily and called it forth with a confidence born of familiarity. A syrupy warmth spread from her body into her limbs, tingling like a charge of electricity.

Sure enough, the summoning of her own magic brought out Wraith as well. She felt him surge inside, a massive jolt that staggered her. He was there all at once, brutal and powerful, waking to confront whatever threatened, emerging to investigate, feral instincts and hunger washing through her like fresh blood.

He came out of her in a rush—without her asking him to do so, without her being under threat, without any visible danger presenting itself. In a heartbeat, her worst fears were confirmed. She could not control him. She was the vessel that housed him, but she had no power over him. Her certainty about it was visceral. It left her feeling helpless and small and torn with doubt. She wanted his protective presence, but she did not want the responsibility for what he might do. Her nearly overpowering, instinctual wish was that he might be gone from her forever. But her need for his help was stronger still and thrust her repulsion aside.

The feeders fell away from her in a whisper of scattered snow, their lantern eyes disappearing back into the night.

Wraith began to run. With a surge, he bounded into the park, a low, dark shape powering through the new snow, legs churning, lean body stretched out. She didn't ask it of him, didn't direct him to go, but he seemed to sense all on his own what was required of him and responded. Something of her went with him, feeling what he felt, seeing through his eyes. She was trapped inside his wolf's body, crossing swiftly over snowfields, past the dark trunks of trees, and over hillocks and drifts. She felt nothing of the cold and snow, for Wraith was all magic and could only wax or wane in power and presence; he would never be affected by the elements. She felt his brute strength and great heart. She felt the fury in him that burned just below the surface of his skin.

Most of all, she felt her father's magic, white-hot and capable of anything, unburdened by moral codes and reason, shot through with the iron threads of the cause for which Wraith had been created when she was still a child—to protect her, to keep her safe from harmful magic, to bring her safely to maturity, and, ultimately, to deliver her into her father's hands.

Everything had changed with time's passage, shifted around and made new. Her father was dead. She was grown and become her own person. But Wraith was still there.

He bounded on across the snow-blanketed flats and into the trees, tiger face fierce and spectral. No one was in the park to see him, and it was just as well. Nightmares are born of such encounters. Nest felt herself enveloped in a haze of emotions she could neither define nor separate, emotions born of the ghost wolf's freedom and raw power, emotions that emerged in a rush as he neared the deep woods.

Faster Wraith ran, deeper into the night.

Then, abruptly, Nest felt something snap all the way down inside her body where her joining with Wraith began. She gasped in shock, and for a long, painful moment, everything went black and silent.

When she could see again, she was back inside her own body, standing alone in the patch of shadows at the end of the Petersons' backyard. The feeders had dispersed. Snow fell wet and cold on her face, and the park stretched away before her, silent and empty.

Her realization of what had happened came swiftly and left her stunned. She could no longer see through Wraith's eyes. She was no longer connected to him.

The ghost wolf had broken free.

*L*arry Spence pulled the cruiser into the driveway of the old Victorian on West Third and shut off the engine. In the ensuing silence, he sat in the car and tried to think matters through, to decide how he should approach this business. But it was hard; his head throbbed and there was a persistent buzz in his ears. He wasn't sure how long he'd had the headache and buzzing; he couldn't remember when they had begun. But they assailed him unrelentingly, making it almost impossible for him to concentrate.

Everything seemed so difficult all of a sudden.

He knew he had made a mistake about the children. He knew he had placed his career in jeopardy by allowing Robinson to take them out of Nest's home. His betrayal of Nest was almost unbearable. It no longer mattered that he thought he was doing the right thing at the time; he had allowed himself to be manipulated and deceived. He was furious about this, but oddly impotent as well. He should do something, but even now, parked in the drive of Robinson's safe house, he was uncertain what that something should be.

He exhaled wearily. At the very least, he had to get the children back. Whatever else happened, he could not leave here without them. He did not know for sure what was going on, but he knew enough to realize he would have been better off if he had thrown Robinson out the door of his home on that first visit. Thinking back on it, he couldn't understand why he hadn't.

The headache throbbed at his temples and the buzzing hummed in his ears. He squeezed his eyes shut momentarily. He just wanted this business to be over with.

Taking a deep, steadying breath, he climbed out of the car and walked up the snowy drive to the front porch, mounted the steps and knocked on the door. Inside, it was silent. There were lights, but no movement behind the drawn curtains. The neighborhood of once-grand homes had the feel of a graveyard. The street, in the wake of the storm, was deserted.

I'll make this quick, he told himself. *I'll take those children out of here and be rid of these people.*

The door opened, and the man who called himself Robinson was standing there, smiling. 'Come in, Deputy Sheriff.' He stepped back.

Careful, now, Larry Spence warned himself. *Take it slow.*

He entered and looked around cautiously. He stood in a large entry. A stairway climbed into darkness to one side. A door stood closed on the other. The living room opened up ahead, bright and quaint with turn-of-the-century furniture and fading wallpaper that hung from wainscoting to mop-boards in a field of yellow flowers.

'Take off your coat, Deputy Sheriff,' Robinson said. It almost sounded like an order. 'Sit down for a moment.'

'I won't be staying that long.' Larry shifted his gaze to Robinson, then back to the living room, where Penny sat with her legs curled up on the couch next to a giant, nearly hairless albino, both of them staring at a television set. Penny saw him and gave a small wave and smile. He nodded stone-faced in response.

'Where are the children, Mr. Robinson?' he asked. His head was pounding, the pain much worse, the buzzing so insistent it threatened to scramble his thoughts completely.

'Playing downstairs.' The other man was watching him carefully.

'I'd like you to bring them up here, please.'

'Well, things have changed a bit.' Robinson seemed genuinely apologetic. 'I need to ask you for one more favor.'

'I think I've done enough favors for you.'

Robinson smiled anew. 'I'm not asking much. Just take a

short ride with us in a little while. The children can go, too. Afterward you can have them back.'

Larry could already feel something wrong with things, could sense a shift in attitude that signaled this was not going to go the way he wanted. He had been a sheriff's deputy for better than fifteen years, and he trusted his instincts. He needed to get the upper hand on these people right away, not take any chances.

'I've been doing some checking,' he said, deciding to force the issue. 'I called the FBI's Chicago field office and asked about you. They never heard of you. They don't know anything about a drug operation in this area.'

Robinson shrugged. 'They don't know we're here. We operate out of Washington. What is the problem, Deputy?'

'Is that one of your operatives?' Larry pressed, staying calm, pointing at the strange man on the couch.

Robinson glanced over his shoulder, then back at Spence. 'Yes, he's a local—'

Larry had his .45 out and pointed at Robinson's midsection. 'Stand easy,' he advised. 'Keep your hands where I can see them.' He reached forward and patted the old man's coat pockets and sides, then stepped away. 'I checked with Washington as well. No one there knows who you are, either.'

The man who called himself Robinson said nothing.

'So who are you?' Larry pressed.

The other man shrugged. 'It doesn't matter.'

Penny looked up from the television. When she saw the gun in Larry's hand, she started to rise.

'Sit down!' Larry ordered sharply. She hesitated, then did

so. But she was grinning broadly. 'What's going on here?' Larry demanded of everyone in general.

Robinson smiled. 'Figure it out for yourself, Deputy Sheriff. You seem pretty clever.'

'Your being here doesn't have anything to do with drugs, does it?'

Robinson pursed his lips. 'No, Deputy Sheriff, it doesn't. But it does have to do with addiction. I am a specialist in addictions, did you know that? Addictions that beset the human race. There are hundreds of them. Thousands. Human beings are enslaved by their addictions, and I find that by determining the nature of the addictions that rule them, I can influence the course of action they take.'

He cocked an eyebrow at Spence. 'Take yourself, for instance. I knew almost from the beginning that if I wanted something from you, all I had to do was link my request to your very obvious attraction to Miss Freemark. You were blinded to everything when focused on her. Silly, really, since she doesn't care the weight of a paper clip for you. But you see her as your future wife and the mother of your children and so you do the things you think will further the happening of those events.'

Larry flushed angrily. 'That's not an addiction. What the hell are you talking about?'

'Addictions come in all sizes and shapes,' Robinson continued mildly, 'and the people who have them always think they're something else. Dependencies, Deputy Sheriff. They give an illusion of control you lack. Yours is a small dependency, but deeply ingrained, and it rules you. It's why you've been so helpful to me. I give you the illusion of control

over your need to influence Miss Freemark and you're ready
to walk over coals.'

The headache and buzzing were attacking Larry Spence
with such ferocity that he could barely focus on what
Robinson was saying. 'Let's get those children up here right
now!' he snapped, suddenly furious.

'Let's not,' Robinson replied calmly.

Larry stared at him. What was he thinking? That Larry
wouldn't shoot, that he wouldn't use the gun he was holding
if the other man made even the slightest move to stop him?
Did he think Larry wasn't in charge of this situation, that he
wasn't able to do what was needed just because he had
allowed himself to be tricked earlier?

Then he looked into Robinson's eyes, and he saw the
truth. His gun didn't mean anything. Or his badge of office,
or the weight of the law, or even Larry himself. None of it
mattered. Those eyes were dead to everything. They had
been dead a long time.

Larry went cold and hot in rapid sequence, and suddenly
all he wanted to do was to get the hell out of there as quickly
as he could. But he knew it was too late, that he couldn't,
that he was trapped as surely as if Robinson was holding the
gun on him.

'Oh, my God,' he breathed softly.

His hand was frozen. Suddenly terrified, he tried to pull
the trigger, but his fingers refused to work. Robinson came
forward, took the gun out of his hand, and slipped it back
into its holster. Larry couldn't do anything to stop him.
Nothing. He was paralyzed by the buzzing in his ears and
the throbbing in his head and by a cold certainty that he was

completely helpless. He stood in front of Robinson with his hands empty and his options all used up. He wanted to scream, but he couldn't. Tears leaked from his eyes, and his big frame shook as he began to cry.

'Please,' he begged, unable to help himself. 'Please.'

Robinson smiled, but his smile held no warmth.

*S*ilence.

Nest stood paralyzed in the frigid darkness at the edge of Sinnissippi Park, trying desperately to regain her scattered thoughts. The enormity of what had just happened threatened to overwhelm her. She had lost Wraith! Somehow, some way, she had lost him. She hadn't meant to do so, hadn't even suspected it was possible. It was true that he had emerged from her body only a handful of times since he had taken up residence, but there had never been any indication that he might break free. She felt empty and bereft in a way she had never expected. She saw all her hopes of saving the children from the demons drifting away on the backs of snowflakes.

What had she done?

For a long time, she just stood there, unable to move, trying to decide what she should do. She couldn't go back into the house. She had to find Wraith and get him back under her control. She had to! She stared out at the black-and-white expanse of the park and realized how hopeless her task was. Wraith could move so much faster than she could. He would never be found if he didn't wish it. She could search forever, and she wouldn't even see him. He didn't even have to outrun her. He could simply disappear, the way he did when she was little. He could vanish as completely as last summer's warmth, and she had no way to bring him out again.

Despair staggered her; it left her frantic. She held on only through sheer force of will. She could not afford to give in to what she was feeling. If she did, there would be no chance for any of them.

Then a shadow soared out of the darkness ahead, gliding smooth and silent through the falling snow, materializing from out of the tangled limbs and trunks of the trees. She recognized Jonathan, great wings stretched wide, and as he drew closer, she saw Pick astride him. Grasping at the faint hope the sylvan's appearance offered, she detached herself from the shadows. Jonathan swept past her, circled back around, passed over her again, but closer this time, and suddenly Pick was standing on her shoulder.

'Criminy, what are you doing out in this weather?' he demanded disgustedly. But there was concern in his voice as well; he knew something wasn't right.

'Oh, Pick, everything's gone wrong!' she blurted out, cupping her gloved hands so he could jump down into them.

He did so, grumbling vehemently. 'I thought as much when I felt a disturbance in the magic of the park, and there was Wraith, running through the deep woods as if possessed. Hah, which I guess he is, in a manner of speaking!'

She started. 'You saw Wraith? Where is he? Why isn't he with you?'

'Would you settle down?' he snapped, putting up his

twiggy hands defensively. 'Since when am I in charge of keeping track of Wraith? What do I look like, anyway? He's your pet!'

'He broke away from me!' she exclaimed. 'I sent him into the park to find you, and he broke away! Why would he do that? He's gone, and I don't know how to get him back!'

She sounded like a little girl, but she couldn't help herself. Pick didn't seem to notice. He brushed at a flurry of stray snowflakes that fell into his face. 'Would you mind stepping out of the weather a bit?' he asked irritably. 'Would that be asking too much?'

She retreated back into the shelter of the trees and brush where the big limbs and trunks deflected most of the falling snow. Shadows enfolded them, and a scattering of feeder eyes appeared.

'Start at the beginning,' he ordered, 'and let's see if I can make any sense out of what you've got to say!'

She told him everything that had happened from the time Larry Spence had appeared at the house—the breaching of the sylvan's security net, the children's disappearance, Findo Gask's phone call, and her effort to send Wraith into the park in search of him. She told him that she would try to free the children from where Findo Gask had concealed them in the old house on West Third, hoping to catch the demons off guard.

'But I need someone to check for traps he might have set to warn of anyone trying to get into the house. I need someone to go inside and find out where the children are hidden. I need you, Pick.'

He was uncharacteristically silent in the aftermath of her

plea. He sat in the cup of her hands, worrying stray threads of his mossy beard with his mouth and mumbling inaudibly. She let him be; there was nothing more she could say to persuade him.

'Too bad about that fellow opening your bedroom window,' he said finally. 'But if Gask wanted the children that bad, he probably would have come after them anyway. That was what he was trying to do last night. I don't expect the security net would have stopped him.'

She nodded silently.

'Demons,' he muttered.

She waited.

'I don't like going out of the park,' he declared. He held up his hands quickly when she tried to speak. 'Not that I don't do so now and then, when there's need for it.' He huffed. 'I don't much like going into strange houses, either. You sure you don't want to let go of this thing? You might be better off if you did. Four demons are a lot to overcome, even with a Knight of the Word helping out. I know you. You're stubborn. But you can't fight everyone's battles. You can't save the entire world.'

'Pick,' she said softly, bending close to him, so she could see his pinprick eyes. 'I can't explain exactly why I have to do this, but I do. I feel it the way you feel a breach in the magic. I know it's the right thing. Harper's all alone, and there's something about Little John, something that has to do with me.'

He snorted.

'This is important to me, Pick. I have to go after those children. With or without your help, I have to.'

'Since when have you ever done anything where demons

and magic were concerned without my help?' he demanded in
exasperation. 'Look, I'll do this. I'll sweep the grounds and
walls and doors and windows for traps and snares and have a
look inside to find those kids. But when I'm finished, if I tell
you it can't be done, that's the end of it. Fair enough?'

'Deal,' she said.

He spit over his shoulder. 'Now, what's this nonsense
about losing Wraith? You can't lose magic once it's given to
you. It doesn't just go wandering off by itself. You have to
use it up or pass it on or set it free or cast it away. Did you
do any of those?'

She shook her head. 'I don't think so. I didn't do anything.
I just sent him out to attract your attention, then there was
this snapping inside, this feeling of something breaking
loose, and I couldn't feel him anymore.'

Pick shrugged. 'Well, I don't know about that, but I do
know he's standing right over there, looking at you.'

She glanced quickly to where he was pointing. Sure
enough, Wraith was standing in the shelter of the trees in the
Peterson backyard, as still as stone, tiger face lowered, bright
eyes staring at her. She stared back in surprise and disbelief.
What was he doing?

'Pick?' she said softly.

'I know, I know,' he muttered in response, fidgeting in her
palm. 'He's backed off of you for some reason. Are you sure
you didn't do anything to him?'

'What would I do?' she snapped angrily.

'I don't know! Call him! See what he does!'

She did, speaking his name softly, then more firmly. But
Wraith didn't move. Snow gathered on his dark, bristling fur,

pinpricks of white. All around, the night was silent and cold.

'Maybe he doesn't want to come back inside you just yet,' Pick mused. He shifted in her palm, a bundle of sticks. 'Maybe he wants to stay out there awhile.'

'Fine with me,' she declared quickly, frustrated and confused. 'I'm not too happy with him living inside my skin anyway. I never have been.'

Pick looked at her. 'Maybe he senses that.'

'That I don't want him to come back inside me?'

'Maybe. You made it plain enough to me. You probably made it plain enough to him.'

She shook her head. 'Then why didn't he leave sooner? Why didn't he just—'

Then suddenly she realized why. Suddenly, she knew. Her revelation was instantaneous and stunning. He had stayed not because he wanted to, but because she wouldn't let him go. He was living inside her body because she demanded it. It might not have been that way in the beginning, when she was still just a girl. He might have been responding freely to her need, which was genuine and compelling. But at some point, the relationship had changed. Subconsciously, at least, she had decided she could not give him up. She hadn't been aware of what she had done, of the chain she had forged to keep him close. She had thought him gone, after all. It wasn't until he had revealed himself in Seattle ten years ago that she had even realized he was still there.

She was staggered by the enormity of her discovery, thinking at first she must be wrong. She had wanted him gone for so long that it seemed ridiculous to believe she could have bent him to her will, even in the most subliminal way, that she could have imprisoned him inside her without realizing it. But his magic belonged to her; her father and grandmother had given it to her. It was the way Pick said: magic didn't just wander off of its own accord. Wraith was hers, and the strength of her need had persuaded her that she must keep him close, always and forever.

She stared at him now through the night shadows with fresh eyes, seeing the truth. 'It was me,' she told Pick softly.

'What are you talking about?' he demanded.

'Don't you see? I wouldn't let go of him. I didn't intend it. I didn't mean for him to become a part of me. But I made it happen without ever realizing what it was I was doing. I thought it was his choice. But it wasn't. It was mine. It was always mine.'

Pick rubbed his beard. 'That doesn't make any sense. You haven't been happy about him living inside you for years. He must have known, yet he didn't do a thing about it. So why is he standing up to you now? If he couldn't or wouldn't break free before, why is he doing so now? What's changed?'

She looked back at Wraith, at his tiger face, fierce and challenging, at his gleaming eyes fixed on her as if they could see what she could not. 'The morph,' she whispered.

'What?' Pick was confused. 'Speak up!'

'The gypsy morph,' she repeated. 'That's what's changed.'

She could almost see it then, the truth she had been searching for since John Ross and the morph had appeared on her doorstep three days ago. It was a shadowy presence that darted across her consciousness in the blink of an eye and was gone. It whispered to her of Little John, of why he took the form of a four-year-old boy and spoke her name and came to find her and called her *Mama*. It whispered to her of a revelation waiting to be uncovered if she would just believe.

She thought suddenly of the Freemark women, of the way the magic passed from one generation to the next. She thought of Gran, and the sacrifice she had made for Nest so many years ago.

When she spoke, her voice was distant and searching. 'Pick, if I set Wraith free, will I lose him? Will I lose his magic?'

Pick was silent for a long time. 'I don't know,' he said finally. 'Maybe.'

She nodded slowly. 'I'll have to chance it. I'm leaving him out there to do what he wishes. I won't take him back inside me.' She took a deep breath and turned away from the ghost wolf. No words were necessary. Wraith would know.

'Call Jonathan,' she ordered Pick. 'Fly to the house on West Third and start checking. But be careful. I'll take John in the car and meet you there.'

Pick grumbled to himself for a moment, then whistled sharply. The barn owl reappeared out of the trees, gliding past Nest's outstretched hand, his great wings brushing her shoulder softly. The sylvan jumped onto his back, and in seconds they were gone, winging away into the night.

Nest watched them fade into the snowfall, keeping her back to Wraith. When they were gone, she turned to see if he was still there. He wasn't. The ghost wolf had vanished. She stared at the space he had occupied, then glanced around quickly. There was no sign of him.

'Good hunting, Wraith,' she whispered.

Then she was running for the house and John Ross.

CHAPTER 27

They drove through the mostly deserted streets of Hopewell, Nest at the wheel and Ross beside her in the passenger seat. Neither spoke. Snow continued to fall in a curtain of thick, soft flakes, and everything was blanketed in white. The main streets had been cleared by the plows on their first pass, but the side streets were mostly untouched, the snow spilling over onto sidewalks and lawns in a smooth, unbroken carpet, the metal roofs of parked cars lifting out of the winterscape like the humped backs of slumbering beasts. Streetlights glistened off the pale crust in brilliant bursts that spread outward in halos of diminishing radiance. Everywhere, there was a deep, pervasive, and enveloping silence.

As she steered through the shaken-snow-globe world, Nest was shot through with doubt. She could not fathom doing what she knew she must without Wraith to stand beside her, even though she had accepted that it might be necessary. She tried not to dwell on the enormity of the task that lay ahead—getting into the demon lair, finding the children, and getting them out safely, all without having Wraith's magic to aid her. She tried not to question her belief that giving up Wraith was somehow necessary in order to discover the secret of the gypsy morph, even though that belief was essentially blind and deaf and paper thin. She had not told Ross of it. She had not told him of freeing Wraith. If he had known, he would never have let her come with him. She had told him only what she felt necessary—that Pick had gone on ahead to scout the grounds and entrances to the demon house in order to find a way in. What happened from here forward must be on her conscience and not made a burden on his.

When they reached the intersection of West Fourth Street and Avenue G, Nest pulled the Taurus into the mostly invisible parking lot of a dry-cleaning service two blocks away from and out of sight of their destination. From there, they walked through the deep snow, down unplowed walks and across deserted side streets until the old Victorian came in sight. West Third was plowed, but empty of traffic, and the old houses were mostly dark at the ends of their snow-covered lawns and long drives. Even the one in which Findo Gask and his demons took shelter had only a few lights burning, as if electricity were precious and meant to be rationed.

They were almost in front of the house, keeping to the shadows and away from the pale glow of the streetlamps, when they saw the sheriff's cruiser parked in the drive.

Nest shook her head at Ross as they paused beneath a massive old hickory. 'Larry Spence.' She spoke his name with disgust and frustration. 'He just can't manage to keep out of this.'

Ross nodded, eyes fixed on the house. 'We can't do anything about him now. We have to go in anyway.'

She took a deep breath, thinking of all the chances she'd had to put Larry out of the picture, to scare him so badly he wouldn't dream of involving himself further. It might have spared them what they were about to go through. It might have changed everything. She sighed. That was the trouble with hindsight, of course. Always perfect. She hadn't even considered doing harm to Larry. She had always thought he would lose interest and drop out of the picture on his own. But maybe that was never an option. Maybe the demons had gained too tight a hold over him for that to be possible.

She glanced at the cruiser one final time and dismissed the matter. She would never know now.

They worked their way along the edge of a hedgerow separating the old Victorian from an English manor knock-off that was dark and crumbling. They drew even with the front entry and paused, kneeling in the snow, staying low to the ground and the shadows.

If I'm wrong about this, Nest kept thinking, unable to finish the thought, but unable to stop repeating herself either.

She didn't see where Pick came from. He just appeared, dropping out of nowhere to land on her shoulder, giving her such a fright that she gasped aloud.

'Criminy, settle down!' the other snapped irritably, grasping her collar to keep from being shaken off. His mossy beard was thick with snowflakes, and his wooden body was damp and slick. 'Took your time getting here, didn't you?'

'Well, navigating these streets isn't like sailing along on the open air!' she snapped back, irritated herself. She exhaled a cloud of breath at him. 'What did you find?'

He sniffed. 'What do you think I found? There's traps and trip lines formed of demon magic all over. The place stinks of them. But those are demons in there, not sylvans, so they tend to be more than a little careless. No pride of workmanship at all. There are holes in that netting large enough to fly an owl through—which is exactly what I did. Then I slipped through a tear in the screen on the back porch, which they forgot about as well, and got inside through the back door. They've got the children down in the basement in a big playroom. You can get to them easy.'

He scrunched up his face. 'The bad news is that something's down there with them. I don't know what it is. Might be a demon, might be something else. I couldn't see it, but I could sure as heck smell it!'

Nest nodded. She knew what it was. She glanced at Ross, then back at Pick. 'Could you tell exactly where it was? I mean, where in the room?'

'Of course I could!' he snapped. 'You could tell, too, if you had my nose!'

'Which is my point,' she went on quickly. 'Will you go back inside with me and show me exactly where it's hiding?'

There was a long silence as he considered the matter, rubbing at his beard and muttering to himself furiously. *Don't say anything about Wraith,* she begged him silently, knowing he would be thinking about doing exactly that.

He surprised her by merely shrugging and saying instead, 'Well, you probably can't do it by yourself. Let's get on with it.'

They conversed in low tones for a few moments more, she and the sylvan and John Ross, setting up their plan of attack. It was agreed that Nest would slip in through the back door with Pick, then hide while Pick checked out the basement once more, located whatever was down there, and gave Nest whatever chance he could to reach the children first. Twenty minutes would be allotted. At the end of that time, Ross would come in through the front door and attack the demons, distracting them long enough for Nest and the children to escape out the back.

They stood staring at the old house for long moments, statues in the falling snow. Its walls rose black and solitary against the backdrop of the steel mill and the river, rooflines softened by the snowfall, eaves draped in icy daggers. Nest wondered if she was committing suicide. She believed that Wraith would come if she needed him, that he would not deny her the protection of his magic. She believed it, yet she could not be certain. Not until it was too late to do anything about it if she was wrong. Everything she was about to do was built upon faith. Upon trust in her instincts. Upon belief in herself.

'Okay, Pick,' she said finally.

They skirted the hedgerow to where it paralleled the back of the old house, then cut swiftly across the snow. Pick guided her, whispering urgent directions in her ear, keeping her clear of the snares the demons had set. They reached the back porch, where Pick directed her to the gap in the screen. She widened it carefully, rusted mesh giving way easily to a little pressure, and climbed through. She stood on the porch, a dilapidated, rotted-out veranda that had once looked out on what would have been a long, flowing, emerald green lawn. She moved to the back door, which was closed, but unlocked. With Pick settled on her shoulder, she stood listening, her ear pressed against the door.

She could just make out the faint sound of a television playing in the background. She checked her watch. She had used seven of her twenty minutes.

Cautiously, she opened the back door and stepped inside. She was at the end of a long hallway in an entry area that fed into the rest of the house. Coat hooks were screwed into an oak paneled wall, and a laundry room opened off to the left. Ahead and to the right, a stairwell disappeared downward into the basement. Light shone from the room below, weak and tiny against the larger, deeper blackness of the well.

She looked for Pick to tell him to be off, but he was already gone. She stood motionless and silent in the entry, listening to the sounds of the house, creaks that were faint and muffled, the low hum of the oil furnace, and the drip of a faucet. She listened to the sounds of a program playing on the television set, and once or twice, to one of the demons speaking. She could tell the difference between the two, the former carrying with it a hint of mechanical reproduction, the latter low and sharp and immediate. She forced herself to breathe slowly and evenly, glancing at her watch, keeping track of the time.

When Pick reappeared, she was down to three minutes. He nodded and gestured toward the basement. He had found the children and whatever watched over them.

It was twenty-five minutes to midnight.

She took off her boots, coat, gloves, and scarf, and in her

stocking feet, she started down the stairs. Slowly, carefully, placing one foot in front of the other to test her weight on the old steps, she proceeded. Carpet cushioned and muffled her stealthy advance, and she made no sound. Pick rode her shoulder in silence, wooden face pointed straight ahead, eyes pinprick bright in the gloom.

At the bottom of the stairs, she was still in darkness. A solitary table lamp, resting atop an old leather-wrapped bar, lit the large L-shaped room before her. The children sat together in an easy chair close by, looking at a picture book. Harper was pretending to read, murmuring softly to Little John, who was looking directly toward the stairs at Nest.

He knows I'm here, she thought in surprise.

Pick motioned toward the darkness at the open end of the bar, back and behind where the children sat. Whatever stood guard was concealed there. Nest felt a sudden rush of hope. Her path to the children lay open.

She took a deep, slow breath. What to do now?

The problem was solved for her by the explosion that ripped through the house upstairs.

John Ross stood watching as Nest and Pick crept down the concealing wall of the hedgerow, across the side yard and into the back of the house. He listened carefully for any response from within, but there was none. He waited patiently for ten of the twenty minutes allotted, then made his way across the yard to the sheriff's cruiser and crouched next to it in the darkness. He had been in a lot of battles in his time as a Knight of the Word, both in the present and in the future, awake and in his dreams, and he knew what to expect. The demons would react instinctively, but for a few moments at least, they would be confused. If he struck at them quickly enough, they would not be able to use their numbers to overwhelm him.

He studied the windows of the house for movement. There was none. He looked at his watch. He had less than five minutes. A whisper of fear swept through him, and he tightened his grip on the black staff. The house would be warded by demon magic; he could not hope to get past it as Nest had done. His best bet was to get as close as possible, then move quickly from there. He tried to think where the warding would begin. At the edge of the porch, he decided. It probably did not extend out into the yard.

But there was only one way to find out.

He waited until he had two minutes remaining, then left the cover of the sheriff's cruiser and advanced quickly toward the front entry. He crossed the yard to the lower steps and stopped, watching the house and its windows as he did. Nothing moved. Nothing changed.

His watch said Nest's twenty minutes were up. He braced himself. There was no more time to think, and nothing left to think about.

He went up the steps swiftly, using the railing and his staff to lever himself onto the porch, set himself in place, and hurled his magic into the door with such force that he blew it right off its hinges. He was through the opening and into the house in seconds, taking in the scene beyond. A living room was visible directly ahead through a veil of smoke, lights bright against the entry darkness. A television

screen flickered with muted images. Figures moved through
the roiling haze, swift and purposeful. In a wing chair to his
right, Larry Spence sat stiff and unmoving in his sheriff's
uniform, staring at nothing.

Ross slid to one side of the entry, crouching low. The girl
Penny flashed across his vision, face contorted, eyes wild,
throwing knives in both hands. She flung them at him with
a shriek but, deflected by the staff's magic, they sailed wide.
He turned the magic on her then, knocking her backward.
She tumbled away, her cry high-pitched and laced with rage.
Frock coat trailing as he slid along the wall, Findo Gask
moved to attack. Ross struck out at the demon instantly,
caught him a solid blow and knocked him flying, flat-
brimmed hat sailing away, arms windmilling helplessly.

Then Twitch, materializing from the other side of the
entry, was on top of him, voice booming as he lumbered forward. The giant slammed into Ross, knocking the wind
from his lungs, sending him sprawling against the wall. Ross
scrambled up, fighting for air, and sent the staff's fire ham-
mering into the albino. Enraged, Twitch was shouting
unintelligibly as he advanced. Ross burned him with the
magic again, more fiercely this time, and the giant reeled
away in pain and anger, clawing at the air.

Ross went by him quickly, into the living-room light, determined to place himself where he could keep them from
reaching Nest. But Gask was back on his feet, white hair wild,
a cottony halo about his leathery face. He gestured toward
Ross, throwing his arms forward, and Ross brought up his
staff protectively. But it was Larry Spence who responded,
grabbing him from behind, pinning his arms and staff to his

sides. A puppet to Gask's gestures, the deputy sheriff turned Ross toward Penny, as she uncoiled from the wall, both arms cocked. Another pair of the slender throwing knives streaked through the air so swiftly there was barely time to register their presence. With Spence still clinging to him, Ross twisted desperately, hands tightening about the staff, and the Word's magic flared protectively. Larry Spence grunted in pain, released him abruptly, and staggered back, Penny's blades buried in his shoulder and side. Dropping to one knee, he fumbled for his .45, dragged it from his holster, and began shooting at everything around him, people and furniture alike. Ross caught a glimpse of his face as he did so. His eye sockets were bleeding and empty. The eyes had been gouged out.

Then Penny catapulted out of the haze, another deadly knife in hand. Screaming and spitting, she raked at his midsection. Buttressed by demon magic, the slender blade broke through his defenses and pierced his side. He gasped from the force of the blow and the sudden pain. Penny yanked the knife free and stabbed at him again, but he deflected the second blow and sent her spinning away.

Almost immediately, Twitch reappeared. Reaching down, he fastened both massive hands about Ross's neck and began to squeeze.

When she heard the front door explode off its hinges, Nest called to Pick, 'Hang on.'

She broke from the darkness of the stairwell into the light and raced for the children. But she had forgotten she had removed her shoes, and she couldn't find sufficient purchase in her stocking feet. She was sliding on the tile floor almost instantly.

Harper was clinging to Little John, both of them frozen in place, uncertain what was happening.

'Run!' she shouted at them.

She was expecting the guard demon to come at her, had readied her magic to combat it, and still wasn't prepared when the ur'droch hurtled out of the shadows. A blur of darkness, it crossed in front of the children to intercept her, pushing through her magic as if it wasn't there. It slammed into her with stunning force, unexpectedly solid for something that seemed so insubstantial. The blow spun her sideways into the wall, where she sagged to her knees. Pick went flying off her shoulder and disappeared.

Wheeling back, keeping to the shadows until the last moment, the ur'droch attacked again. Dazed and gasping for air, she sent her small magic lancing into it, to gain a moment's respite. The demon was staggered this time, and it careened into the sofa, knocking it askew. Swiftly, it slid back into the gloom.

Nest looked quickly for the children. Harper and Little John were hanging on to each other only a few yards away.

'Run!' she screamed again.

Overhead, the ceiling shuddered from the impact of colliding bodies and expended magic. The lamp shade on the bar counter tilted crazily, and its dim light sprayed the darkness, casting strange shadows that rocked and swayed.

Nest braced herself against the wall, willing herself to remain upright. Everything in her body felt broken. The children were running to reach her, arms outstretched. The ur'droch shot out of the darkness in pursuit, a roiling black shadow. Nest threw her magic at it, trying again to keep it at bay. But she had little strength left and almost no focus she could bring to bear, and she could feel both crumble in the face of the other's determined assault.

Then Wraith appeared, suddenly, explosively, in response to her desperate need, in answer to her unspoken prayer, launched from the layered darkness as if from a nightmare's epicenter. Tiger-striped muzzle drawn back, the big ghost wolf hammered into its enemy and sent it flying into the shadows. Barely pausing, it gave pursuit. Seconds later, they emerged in a ball of dark fury, tearing at each other, emitting sounds that were primal and blood-chilling. Across the shadowy room they surged, back and forth, locked in their life-and-death struggle.

The children reached Nest safely and latched on to her legs. She was so weak, she almost went down again. Her head spun. She had to get them out of there, but she had no strength to do so.

And she couldn't leave Wraith. Not after he had come back for her. Not without trying to help.

The ghost wolf and the ur'droch wheeled and lunged through the pale spray of tilted lamplight, through the hazy gloom, back and forth across the furniture's debris.

Harper was sobbing and clutching tightly at her legs, and Little John was saying, 'Mama, Mama,' over and over.

Get them out! Wraith is only something made of magic! He isn't real! It doesn't matter what happens to him! Get the children out!

She hugged them against her in paralyzed confusion, eyes riveted on the battle taking place before her.

Do something!

The ur'droch continually tried to carry the fight into the shadows, to maneuver at every opportunity toward the room's shadowy edges. It dragged at Wraith, hauling him out of the light . . .

Impulsively, Nest stumbled toward the stairway and the bank of wall switches she had passed coming in. When she reached them, she threw them all on.

Light blazed the length and breadth of the rec room, flooding through the shadows, and suddenly there was no more darkness to be found. The ur'droch wheeled about in confusion, and Wraith took advantage. Boring in with single-minded fury, he fastened his jaws on some part of the demon that Nest could not identify and began to shake his enemy. The ur'droch jerked from side to side as if made of old rags. Bits and pieces of it began to come loose. It made no sound, but things that might have been clawed feet scrabbled at the tile floor and flailed at the air. Still Wraith shook it, braced on all fours, tiger face lifted to hold it aloft.

Then abruptly the ur'droch exploded into black smoke and disintegrated into ash. The small, winged creature that was its withered soul made a futile effort to escape, but Wraith had it in his massive jaws instantly, crushing it to pulp.

With a rush of air and billowing, inky smoke, the ur'droch was gone.

*A*t that same moment, John Ross was struggling to break loose from the giant Twitch. Magic from his staff lanced into the big albino's midsection, burning through him. The massive hands that were fastened about his neck released, but the tree-trunk arms closed about his chest. Ross felt his ribs crack as even the Word's magic was unable to protect him. In desperation, he slammed his forehead into the bridge of the albino's nose. Twitch roared and shook himself, and his arms loosened just enough for Ross to twist free.

Tumbling to the floor, he rolled away from the flailing giant into Penny, who stabbed at him again and again with her knives, her face streaked with blood and her eyes wild. He fended her off with a solid kick, then struck at her with the staff. He caught her across the ankles with a sweeping blow and dropped her to her knees. She dug into the floor with her knives, tearing at the carpet, consumed by madness and blood-lust. Larry Spence staggered past, still pulling the trigger on his empty .45, *click, click, click,* and with a wicked, sideways slash of her blade, Penny cut him open to his backbone.

Larry Spence fell to the floor, dying, as Ross brought the length of his staff across Penny's face, shattering her skull into pieces. Faceless and groping, knives gone, fingers become claws, still she fought to reach him, until his magic burned through the core of her body to her twisted, black soul and turned both to ash.

A fresh gout of fire spurted up the curtains and along the length of the west wall. Leather-bound book clutched to his dark chest, Findo Gask was crouched by the old fireplace, laughing. Ross tried to reach him, but Twitch reappeared in his path, all size and lumbering destruction, tearing at the air and furniture indiscriminately. Ross held his ground, summoning what remained of his strength, calling up the magic one final time. Twitch reached for him, and Ross jammed one end of the staff into the giant's throat and sent the magic skimming along its length. Twitch reared back, body shaking as if he had touched a live wire, voice booming with rage. Ross pushed him back into the closest wall and pinned him there, refusing to let him escape. Fire spurted from the giant's ears and mouth and nose, and his huge body convulsed.

When the demon collapsed finally, Ross found that tiny bat of wickedness that formed its core as it tried to break free of the giant's dead, hollow shell, slammed it to the floor, and burned it away.

With everyone around him dead, Ross sagged to one knee and stared across the room at Findo Gask. The demon stared back. For an instant, neither moved. The room flickered with shadows as the fire sparked by the combatants' magic continued to consume the old house. The fire shone quicksilver and eerie against the darkness beyond, as if something come alive to challenge the night.

'Mr. Ross!' Gask shouted at him.

Ross tried to rise and fell back. He had no strength.

'You're dying, Mr. Ross!' Findo Gask said, and laughed.

His leathery face was streaked with sweat and grime, and his black coat was torn. He began easing his way slowly along the wall toward the back of the house. Again, Ross tried unsuccessfully to climb back to his feet. Nothing seemed to work. He summoned his magic to support him, but he had almost nothing left to call on.

'Demon poison, Mr. Ross!' Gask spit at him. There was venom and rage in his voice. 'Just a scratch would be enough for normal men. But a blade's length plunged inside the stomach wall will put an end even to a Knight of the Word!'

Ross reached down and touched his damaged midsection, willing the wound to heal over and the blood flow to stop. He kept his eyes on Findo Gask the entire time.

'I'll be leaving now, Mr. Ross!' the demon taunted. 'Time to check on Miss Freemark. Down in the basement, isn't she? Don't bother getting up to show me the way. I'll find it on my own. Get on with the business of dying, why don't you?'

He was almost to the darkened hallway when he turned back one last time. 'It was all for nothing, Mr. Ross! All of it! You've lost everything!'

Then he wheeled away and was gone.

*I*n the hushed aftermath of the ur'droch's destruction, Nest knelt before Harper and Little John and touched their faces gently. 'It's all right,' she told them. 'Everything is all right.'

Wraith prowled through the scattered remains of the demon, big head lowered as he sniffed at the ashes. Little John watched him intently. Overhead, the battle continued, violent and unabated.

'Come here, peanut,' Nest urged Harper, and when the little girl did, she took her in her arms and held her, cooing softly. 'It's all right, it's all right.'

Little John looked at them, eyes suspicious and uncertain.

Nest held out her hand to him, but he refused to come. She gestured with her fingers. He stayed where he was.

Gently, she eased Harper away from her, folding the little girl down against her thigh, freeing both arms. 'Little John,' Nest said softly. 'It's all right.'

The boy stared at her with such longing that it was all she could do to keep from bursting into tears. His need was naked and compelling, but he could not seem to free himself from the indecision or doubt or whatever it was that kept him at bay. She held his gaze, her arms outstretched, patiently waiting him out. She noticed for the first time how much the colors of his hair and skin were like her own. She was surprised at how similar their features were. *Odd*, she thought. She had not remembered that his eyes, like hers, were green. They had always seemed so blue ...

In fact, she amended suddenly, they had been blue.

'Oh, my God!' she whispered.

He was changing right in front of her, just a little, barely enough to tell that anything was happening. It was his face that was transforming now, beginning to mirror her own in small, almost negligible ways—just enough that she could not fail to see what he was doing, what he was trying to make happen.

Mama he had called her. *Mama*.

'Do you want me to be your mother, little boy?' she asked him quietly. 'Is that what you want? I want that, too. I want to be your mother more than anything. You and me and Harper. We can be a family, can't we?'

'Luv 'ou, Neth,' Harper murmured without looking up, keeping her face lowered against Nest's thigh.

'Come here, Little John,' Nest urged again. 'Come let me hold you, sweetie.'

The gypsy morph glanced over at Wraith. The big ghost wolf lifted his head immediately and stared back. After a moment, he took a step toward the morph, and Little John instantly reached for Nest, cringing. Nest took him into her arms at once, pulling him against her, stroking his hair.

'It's all right, Little John,' she told him. 'He won't hurt you. He isn't coming over here. He's staying right where he is.'

She glared in warning at Wraith, as if the look alone could convey what she wanted. The ghost wolf merely stared back at her, eyes bright and fierce, revealing nothing of his thoughts. When he turned away again, it was almost as an afterthought.

'Little boy,' she cooed to the gypsy morph. 'Tell me what you want. Please, little boy.'

His head lifted, and he glanced over to make certain that Wraith was not trying to approach.

'He's not coming back to me, not like he was, not inside me. He doesn't belong there. He doesn't even want to be there. It was my fault, Little John. I made him be there. But he won't come back again. I won't let him. It's all right now. It's only you and me.'

It had gone quiet upstairs, but she could smell smoke and feel the heat of flames. The house was on fire, and she was out of time. If she didn't break through to him now, she never would. She had to take him out of there, but she didn't want to interrupt what was happening. She was as close to him as she would ever be. She could feel that he was ready to reveal himself to her. Something crashed overhead, and she wondered suddenly what she would find waiting for her when she finally took the children back up.

'I love you, Little John,' she whispered, a twinge of desperation creeping into her voice.

She felt him stir, worming more tightly into her.

'Tell me what you want, little boy,' she begged.

When he did, it was not at all what she had expected, but ever so much more than she had any right to hope.

CHRISTMAS

CHAPTER 28

Battered and disheveled, his black clothes stained and torn, Findo Gask made his way slowly down the back hallway of the old Victorian in search of Nest Freemark. He had lost his flat-brimmed hat and a good chunk of his composure. He kept his Book of Names clutched tightly to his chest. Behind him, flames climbed the walls and ate through the ceiling, consuming hungrily. His strange, gray eyes burned with the intensity of the fire he turned his back on, reflecting the mix of anger, frustration, and disappointment he was battling.

John Ross and Nest Freemark had been much stronger and more daring than he had anticipated. He could not believe they'd had the temerity to come for him, much less the courage to attack in spite of such formidable odds. It wasn't the loss of Twitch and Penny and most probably the ur'droch that bothered him. They had all been expendable from the beginning. It was his loss of control over the situation. It was the effrontery Ross and Nest Freemark had displayed in attacking him when he had believed them so thoroughly under his thumb. He prided himself on being careful and thorough, on never getting surprised, and the night's events had knocked his smoothly spinning world right out of its orbit.

His seamed face tightened. There was no help for it now. The best he could do was to set things right again. He would have to make certain that Nest Freemark, if she was still alive, did not stay that way. Then he would have to find the gypsy morph and, at the very least, put an end to any possibility that its magic might one day serve the Word.

When he reached the top of the basement stairs, he paused. It was brightly lit below, but devoid of movement and sound. Whatever was down there that was still alive was keeping very quiet. Then he heard someone stirring, heard a child's voice, and knew they had not escaped him. Footsteps approached the stairwell, and he moved swiftly back into the shadows. When he saw Nest Freemark at the bottom of the stairs, he backed into the hall. Where to deal with her? She would attempt to slip out the back, of course, bringing the children with her. It was the children she would think of first, not Ross. It was the children she had come to save, surmising correctly that waiting to make any kind of trade for the morph would get them all killed.

She was intelligent and resourceful. It was too bad she wasn't more her father's daughter. In all the years he had worked in the service of the Void, he had never come across anyone like her.

He sighed wearily. He would wait for her outside, he decided, where he would put an end to her for good.

When she emerged onto the back porch, he was standing

in the shadows by the hedgerow across the way. He could see her clearly in the light of the flames. She carried the little girl in her arms, and the sylvan rode her shoulder. There was no sign of the boy.

When she came down the porch stairs, he stepped out to confront her.

'Miss Freemark!' he called out sharply, bringing her head around. 'Don't be so quick to leave! You still have something that belongs to me!'

She stopped at the bottom of the steps and stared at him wordlessly. She didn't panic. She didn't turn back or try to move away. She just stood there, holding her ground.

'We're finished, you and I, Miss Freemark,' he said, coming forward a few steps, closing the distance between them. 'The game is over. There's no one left but us.' He paused. 'You did destroy the ur'droch, didn't you?'

Her nod of acquiescence was barely discernible. She seemed to be trying to make up her mind about something. 'Congratulations,' he offered. 'I wouldn't have thought it possible. The ur'droch was virtually indestructible. So that accounts for everyone, doesn't it? Mr. Ross disposed of Twitch and Penny, and they disposed of Mr. Ross and the deputy sheriff. That leaves just us.'

To her credit, she didn't react visibly to his words. She just stood there, silent and watchful. He didn't like it that she was so unmoved, so calm. She was made of fire and raw emotion, and she should be responding more strongly than this.

'Think how much simpler it would have been if you'd listened that first day when I asked for your help.' He sighed. 'You were so stubborn, and it has cost you so much. Now here we are, right back where we started. Let's try it again, shall we, one last time? Give me what I want. Give me the gypsy morph so that I can be out of your life forever!'

The faintest of smiles crossed her lips. 'Here's a piece of irony for you, Mr. Gask. You've had what you wanted all night, and you didn't realize it. It's been right under your nose. Little John was the gypsy morph. That boy was what you were looking for. In his last transformation before coming here, that's what he became. How about that, Mr. Gask?'

Findo Gask quit smiling. 'You're lying, Miss Freemark.'

She shook her head. 'You know I'm not. You can tell. Demons recognize lies better than most; it's what they know best. No, Mr. Gask, you had the morph. That was one of the reasons John and I came here tonight—because we didn't have it to trade for the children and had no other way to get them back.'

She shifted the little girl in her arms. The child's head was buried in her shoulder. 'Anyway, he's lost to both of us now. Another piece of irony for you. You notice I don't have him with me? Well, guess what? He ran out of time. His magic broke apart down there in the basement. He disappeared. Poof! So it really is just you and me, after all.'

Findo Gask studied her carefully, searching her face, her eyes, sifting through the echoes of her words in his mind. Was she lying to him? He didn't think so. But if the morph had self-destructed, wouldn't he have sensed it? No, he answered himself, magic was flying everywhere in that house, and he wouldn't have been able to separate the sources or types.

'Look in my eyes, Mr. Gask,' she urged quietly. 'What do you see?'

What he saw was that she was telling the truth. That the morph had been the boy all along, and now the boy was gone. That the magic had broken apart one final time. That it was beyond his reach. That was what he saw.

He felt a burning in his throat. 'You have been a considerable source of irritation to me, Miss Freemark,' he said softly. 'Maybe it is time for you to accept the consequences of your foolish behavior.'

'So now you want to kill me, too,' she said. 'Which was your plan all along anyway, wasn't it?'

'You knew as much. Isn't that another reason why you came here instead of waiting on my call?'

He took a step toward her.

'I wouldn't come any closer if I were you, Mr. Gask,' she said sharply. 'I can protect myself better than most.'

She glanced to her right, and Gask followed her gaze automatically. The big ghost wolf the ur'droch had encountered at her home the night before stood watching him from the shadows, head lowered, muzzle drawn back, body tensed. Gask studied it a moment, surprised that it was still alive, that it hadn't been forced to exchange its own life for that of the ur'droch. He had thought the ur'droch a match for anything. Well, you never knew.

'I don't think your friend is strong enough to stop me,' he said to Nest Freemark, keeping his eyes fixed on the beast.

'I've lost a lot in the past few days, Mr. Gask,' she replied. 'This child in my arms is one of the few things I have left. I promised her mother I would look after her. If you intend to keep that from happening, you're going to have to do it the hard way.'

Gask continued to measure the ghost wolf. He did not care for what he saw. This creature had been created by a very powerful demon magic that had been strengthened at least once since. It was not hampered by the rules that governed the servants of the Word. It would fight him as a demon would fight him. Most likely it had already destroyed the ur'droch. Findo Gask was stronger and smarter than his late companion, but he was not indestructible. He might prevail in a battle with this creature, but at what cost?

In the distance, the wail of fire engines rose out of the silence. Lights had come on in the surrounding homes. On the street, a cluster of people had begun to gather.

He let the tension drain from his body. It was time to let go of this business, time to move on. He could not afford to let personal feelings interfere with his work. There would be other days and more important battles to fight.

A shawl of snowflakes had collected on the shoulders and the lapels of his frock coat. He brushed them away dismissively. 'What is the worth of the life of a single child here or there?' he asked rhetorically. 'Nothing. The end will be the same. Sooner or later, the Void will claim them all.'

'Maybe,' she said.

He backed away slowly, still watching the ghost wolf, still wary. 'You've failed, Miss Freemark. People died for you, and what do you have to show for it? Mr. Ross gave up his life, and what did he gain by doing so? What was the point of any of it? What did you accomplish?'

The yellow eyes in the tiger-striped face glowed like live

coals as they tracked his retreat. Findo Gask backed all the way across the side yard and through the barren-limbed hedge before turning away.

He walked to the street without looking back, fighting to stay calm, to keep his frustration and rage from making him do something foolish. He could go back after her, he knew. He could find a way to get to her, sooner or later. But it was pointless. She had nothing left he wanted. His battle with her was finished. There were other causes to attend to. It made no difference to him that he had failed to secure the morph's magic. It mattered only that it could never be used in the service of the Word. By that measuring stick, he had won. It was enough to satisfy him.

When he reached the street, he saw a pair of fire engines wheeling around the corner and coming for the house. He turned the other way, walking quickly. At the corner, he paused. Standing beneath the streetlight, he opened the Book of Names and looked at the last entry.

The name *John Ross* was faintly legible against the aged parchment. Even as he watched, the name turned a shade darker.

You take away what you can from these battles, he thought. The life of a Knight of the Word was a reasonable trophy.

He closed the book and walked on. In seconds, his tall, dark figure had vanished into the night.

Nest Freemark remained where she was until she could no longer see Findo Gask. Harper nestled against her breast, fast asleep. Pick sat on her shoulder, twiggy fingers wrapped in her parka collar, a silent presence.

Wraith had faded away into the ether, free to go where he wished, but never, she believed, to go too far from her.

'He did a fine job of convincing himself, didn't he?' Pick said finally, gesturing after Findo Gask.

Nest nodded. 'He believed what he saw in my eyes.'

'You didn't lie.'

'I didn't have to.'

'I guess he was looking hard enough that if he was ever going to find out, he would have found out now.'

'I guess.'

The flames from the burning house were growing hotter as the fire spread to the roof. On the front lawn, the firemen were scrambling to contain the blaze, their efforts directed primarily at protecting the surrounding homes. It was clear there was nothing they could do to save the Victorian or anyone in it.

'You think he was telling the truth about John Ross?' Pick asked suddenly.

She watched the activity out front without speaking for a moment, then nodded. 'Yes.'

'I could try to get back inside for a quick look.'

The entire front half of the house was engulfed in flames and the fire was spreading quickly. Any attempt at going back inside would be foolish. Her heart could not accept that John Ross was really dead, but she knew it was so. If he was still alive, he would have come for her by now.

'Let it go, Pick,' she said softly.

Pick went silent, absorbing the impact of her words. In her arms, Harper stirred. The little girl was growing heavy, but Nest refused to put her down. She was reminded of the time she had carried Bennett home from the cliffs of Sinnissippi Park fifteen years earlier after saving her from the feeders. She hadn't put Bennett down either that night, not until she was safely home in bed. She would do the same now with Harper. Maybe this time, it would make a difference.

'You better get going,' Pick said finally.

She nodded. 'You better get going, too.'

He hesitated. 'Don't you be second-guessing yourself later,' he snapped at her suddenly. 'You did everything you could! More than everything, in fact! Criminy, you should be proud of yourself!'

He jumped from her shoulder and disappeared into the tangle of the shrubbery. Moments later, she caught a glimpse of a barn owl winging its way toward the river through the snowfall and the night.

Safe journey, Pick, she wished him.

She turned and walked back toward the street, angling diagonally across the front yards of the old houses, keeping to the shadows of the trees and porches, holding Harper tightly against her. She glanced back once at the burning house, and when she did so, her eyes filled with tears. She began to cry silently, realizing what she was leaving behind, thinking of John Ross. She thought of all they had shared over the past fifteen years. She thought of what he had endured in his twenty-five years as a Knight of the Word. He had given everything in his service to the Lady. In the end, he had even given his life.

She brushed at her eyes with the back of her gloved hand.

John Ross might have died for her and for the children, but he hadn't died for nothing. And neither of them had failed in what they had set out to do.

She fought to compose herself as she crossed down a side street and came in view of her car. She wished he could have lived to see the baby. *John Ross Freemark*, she would name him. He would be born next fall, another of those children Findo Gask was so quick to dismiss as unimportant. But this one could surprise him. Created of wild magic and born to a woman for whom magic was a legacy, he could become anything. She felt him inside her, deep in her womb, transformed into what he had sought to become all along—her baby-to-be, her future child. She did not know his plan, nor perhaps did he know it himself. Even the Word might not know. They must bide their time, all of them; they must wait and see.

She climbed into the car and placed Harper on the seat beside her. The little girl curled into a ball, her head resting on Nest's lap. Nest started the car and let it warm up for a moment. She felt the inevitability of what had happened with the gypsy morph stir in her memories. She looked back and saw clearly all the workings of its transitions and of its journey to reach her. She could feel its final moments outside her body, pressing against her, then into her, then transforming for the last time. She could understand why Wraith had been such an obstacle to its needs. For the gypsy morph to become what it wanted, Wraith could not remain inside her. Her body must belong to her unborn child alone. It had needed to know she wanted this as much as it did. It had needed a sacrifice from her that she herself did not know until tonight she was capable of making.

Why had it chosen to become her child? There was no answer to that question, none that she could discover for a while, if ever. It must be enough that it had made such a choice, that its need matched her own, and that their joining felt good and right.

A child. Any child. It made all the difference in the world. Findo Gask was wrong about what that was worth. One day, he would learn his mistake.

She pulled the car out of the parking lot onto West Third and began driving back through Hopewell. She would take Harper home now and put her to bed. Tomorrow, when she woke, they would open their presents. Then they would go to Robert's to visit Amy and the kids and have dinner.

It would mark the beginning of a new life.

It would be a bright and joyous Christmas Day.

*S*prawled on the living-room floor, flames climbing the walls all around him, John Ross fought the poison that seeped through his system, bringing all that remained of his strength and magic and heart to bear. He got to his feet and staggered down the hall after Findo Gask. It took him a long time. His only thought was to get to the demon before the demon got to Nest. He was too late. By the time he reached the back door, the confrontation between them had already occurred. Gask had disappeared, and Nest was moving away. She did not appear to have been harmed.

He had thought momentarily of going after her and decided he was too weak. It was best just to let her go. He watched her from the doorway, the flames consuming the house around him, working their way down the hall at his back. He watched until she was several houses down, then slipped out the door and into the night.

He would go to Josie instead, he decided. He would make his way to her home, and she would care for him. He would mend eventually, and then they would be together for the rest of their lives.

He did not know where he went after that. His instincts took over, and he did as they directed. He lurched and staggered through backyards, through clusters of trees and along fences and walls, in the shadow of buildings and across snowy stretches, all without seeing or being seen by another living soul. It was after midnight, and apart from those gathered at the scene he had departed, the world was asleep. He leaned on his staff and drew from it the strength he required to go on. He was crushed and broken inside, and his wound from Penny's knife burned and festered beneath his clothing. He was growing colder.

When he reached the banks of the Rock River, close by the dark span of the Avenue G bridge where it crossed to Lawrence Island, he was surprised to find himself so far from where he had intended to go. Josie's house, he knew, was in the other direction. He sagged down against the rough-barked trunk of an old oak and stared out at the night. The river was frozen everywhere but at its center, where the current was strong enough to keep the ice from closing over. He watched the dark water surge, its surface reflecting the lights of the bridge overhead. It would be all right, he knew. It was quiet here. He was at peace.

Soon a fresh brightness appeared on the crest of the flowing water, a light that broadened and spread. The Lady appeared, come out of the darkness in her flowing, gossamer robes, her fine, soft features pale and lovely. She crossed the ice on her tiny feet to where he sat and bent to him.

'Brave Knight, you have done well,' she said softly. 'You have done all that I asked. You have fulfilled your promise and your duty. You have completed your service to the Word. You are released. You are set free.'

A great weariness filled him. He could not speak, but he smiled in acknowledgement. He was satisfied. It was what he had worked so long for. It was what he had wanted so much.

'Brave Knight,' she whispered. 'Come home with me. Come home where you belong.'

She reached out her hand. With great effort, he lifted his own and placed it in hers. The light that surrounded her flowed downward through his body and enfolded him as well.

As he came to his feet, he was renewed and made whole again. The black staff fell away from his hand.

Seconds later, he was gone.

The staff lay where it had fallen. In the deep silence of the night, the snowfall began to cover it over. Little by little, it began to vanish beneath a white blanket.

Then a figure appeared from out of the shadows, a big man with copper skin and long black hair braided down his back, a man who wore army fatigues and combat boots. He walked to where the staff lay and stooped to retrieve it. He brushed the snow from its dark length and held it before him thoughtfully.

A solitary warrior and a seeker of truth, he looked out

across the ice to where the open water flowed, and then beyond, to where the Word's battle against a sleeping world's ignorance and denial still raged.